Praise for *Cowboy Seeks Bride*

"I absolutely adored the outrageously colorful characters… The writing was so expressive that I could almost
hear the country drawl."
        —*Night Owl Reviews* Reviewer Top Pick, 5 Stars

"Carolyn Brown is extremely gifted in creating this cute
and humorous tale of a city girl gone country."
        —*Fresh Fiction*

"Carolyn Brown's books never cease to entertain me…
Filled with moxie and has a hero who is drool-worthy."
        —*Long and Short Reviews*

"Charming, sexy, funny… All the characters just have an
open honesty about them. I was hooked from page one."
        —*My Book Addiction and More*

"I can always count on this author to provide me with
just the right amount of passion mixed with glorious
laugh-out-loud moments that always leave me with a
huge smile and wanting more."
        —*Bitten by Love Reviews*

"Carolyn Brown comes through again with a hot and
steamy Spikes and Spurs story that could have set the
dry grass along the Chisholm Trail on fire."
        —*Romancing the Book*

Praise for *Billion Dollar Cowboy*

"A real page-turner…a compelling cast of characters, the perfect country setting, and a smoking-hot romance that progresses at just the right pace, this is one story where readers won't be able to help getting swept right along for the ride."

—*RT Book Reviews*, 4 Stars

"Sizzling… Brown navigates the pair's rocky journey from friendship to red-hot sex while imbuing her lively story with lots of heart."

—*Publishers Weekly*

"Carolyn Brown delivers yet another steamy cowboy romance…witty dialogue and hilarious banter are here to be enjoyed. Once I started reading, I couldn't put it down…or keep the smile off my face."

—*Night Owl Reviews*

"Sweet and endearing."

—*Tome Tender*

"A must-read series for all lovers of Western romance."

—*Loves to Read for Fun*

"I enjoy a rich hero. I really enjoy a hot cowboy hero. Combined, you can't go wrong."

—*Dirty Girls' Good Books*

Also by Carolyn Brown

Women's Fiction

THE TROUBLE WITH TEXAS COWBOYS

CAROLYN BROWN

sourcebooks
casablanca

Published by Sourcebooks Casablanca, an imprint of Sourcebooks, Inc.
P.O. Box 4410, Naperville, Illinois 60567-4410
(630) 961-3900
Fax: (630) 961-2168
www.sourcebooks.com

Printed and bound in Canada.
MBP 10 9 8 7 6 5 4 3 2 1

This book is dedicated to Blake Shelton and Miranda Lambert.

For the many hours of wonderful country music that inspires me to keep writing about cowboys and their sassy ladies.

Chapter 1

THE SCARIEST SIGHT IN THE WORLD IS A WOMAN'S finger on the trigger of a sawed-off shotgun. Sawyer O'Donnell was not an idiot. When he saw the big hole in the barrel of that gun aimed right at his heart, he dropped the broom and threw up his palms.

"Lady, you might want to put that shotgun down. I'm not havin' no part of this feud business. Let's talk about it," he whispered.

The gun stayed right where it was, and his hands didn't drop an inch.

Gladys hadn't said a damn thing about a crazy woman in Burnt Boot when he was hired on as foreman of Fiddle Creek Ranch. Maybe the redhead with the bloodshot green eyes was a member of one of the feuding families. Hopefully, she wasn't out to shoot first and ask questions later.

"Who in the hell are you, and why are you in my bunkhouse?" she asked bluntly.

"*Your* bunkhouse?" Sawyer raised his voice. "Lady, you made a wrong turn back there at crazy and demented. This is my bunkhouse, and you are damn sure not welcome here. So put that blunderbuss away and take your ass back to wherever you came from."

"Yes, it *is* my bunkhouse. I told Aunt Gladys I'd do my own cleaning when I got here. She said the door would be open and she'd meet me here," she said.

His hands came down. "*Aunt Gladys?* Who are you? She didn't tell me that anyone else would be living here."

Deep-throated laughter preceded Gladys into the bunkhouse. "She'd be my great-niece, Jill Cleary, and I didn't know until last night that she was coming to Burnt Boot. I didn't tell you because I wanted y'all to meet before either one of you went to jumpin' ship." She clamped a hand on the gun and lowered it until the barrel pointed at the ground. "Darlin', you got to load a gun, or it ain't worth a damn. You made good time. I wasn't expectin' you for another hour. Saw you comin' in, but I had one more bale of hay to kick off the back of the truck before I could get here. Now give me a hug and meet my brand-new foreman, Sawyer O'Donnell. He'll be sharin' this bunkhouse with you."

Jill propped the gun against the back of a worn sofa and rolled up on her toes to hug her aunt. "I'm not sharing my living quarters with a stranger. I'd rather pitch a tent by the river."

Gladys pushed her back but held on to her shoulders. "In January?"

"Then I'll stay in the house with you," Jill said. "You said you'd hired a foreman that was living on Salt Draw. Why didn't you tell me he was living in the bunkhouse?"

"Same reason I didn't rush down here and tell him that you'd be living in it too. You'd have bitched. He would have quit. You've lived in bunkhouses before now, and so has he. Looks like only two in this big old place would be a blessing after living with twenty or thirty people. And, darlin', I love you, and someday you'll inherit all I've got and all Polly has got, too, but you are not livin' with me. Not with your temper. And, besides, you said when you called last night that you wanted to live in the bunkhouse, so that's what you are going to do."

Sawyer looked from one woman to the other. Gladys was a tall, lanky woman with a touch of white in her black hair. High cheekbones and dark eyes said she had some Native American blood. She'd said she was past eighty, and that's why she needed help on her small ranch. But she damn sure didn't look it or act it, either. Jill had a mop of wavy shoulder-length red hair, green eyes, a cute little nose, and full lips made for kissing. There was no way in hell they could be related.

Gladys read his mind. "Yes, Sawyer, we really are kinfolk. Jill is mine and Polly's only living relative and she has come to Burnt Boot to work for us. And this bunkhouse is big enough for the two of you."

Sawyer wasn't too sure about that last statement. The bunkhouse had looked huge when he moved in, but a woman living in it would damn sure make it smaller in a hurry.

Travis Tritt's old song "T-R-O-U-B-L-E" played through his mind. The verse that kept running around on a continuous loop said that the men were going to love her and the women were going to hate her, because she reminded them of everything they were never going to be. It said that it could be the beginning of another war, because the world wasn't ready for nothing like her.

With those tight-fittin' jeans attempting to cover up that cute little rounded butt and cinching in a small waist, Jill was sure enough trouble with a capital *T* in Burnt Boot, Texas. The Gallagher and the Brennan men would both love her because she was so damn pretty, but the minute they found out she was in line to inherit Fiddle Creek—well, look out, Burnt Boot.

According to what Verdie had told him already, the feud was already hotter'n a Texas wildfire. Naomi Gallagher, the head she-coon of that clan, was out for Brennan blood. Throwing Jill in that mix would be like throwing a five-gallon bucket of gasoline on the fire. Both families wanted the land separating their properties for the water rights that ran through Gladys's ranch, and even if they didn't, one look at Jill and they'd forget the ranch and want her.

"You two get settled in, and we'll have a long talk in the morning. Welcome home to Burnt Boot, Jill darlin'. Me and Polly are glad that you've finally come home to roost for good." Gladys gave her niece another hug and whistled all the way to her truck.

The engine of the truck had barely died down, and Sawyer was still trying to make sense of the whole scene, when it sounded as if Gladys was coming back. Thank God! She'd been teasing about Jill not living at the house with her and now she was coming back to get her.

A truck door slammed, and Sawyer hurried to throw open the door. Hell, he'd even carry Jill out there, shotgun and all, and put her into the truck.

It wasn't Gladys standing on the other side of the screen door. It was Betsy Gallagher.

"Evenin', Sawyer. I heard you'd gotten moved in. Thought I'd stop by and ask you to Sunday dinner at my granny's place," she said.

Red-haired and cute as a button, Betsy was a member of one of the feuding families in Burnt Boot. He'd been warned about taking sides in any way, form, or shape, but with the mayhem that had just happened, his mind went blank and he couldn't think of a reason why he couldn't go to dinner with her.

"Aren't you going to invite me in?" Betsy asked.

"It's a mess in here." He stepped out on the porch.

"I heard that Jill Cleary was coming back to work for Gladys."

"She is." Sawyer still racked his brain, trying to come up with a plausible excuse not to go to dinner with her.

Betsy ran a hand down his arm and smiled up at him. "I expect you have lots to do, so I should be going. You can take me home from church on Sunday and have dinner with us, right?"

"I suppose," he said.

"Good. I'll see to it you have a good time." She winked slyly.

He went back inside, threw himself on the sofa with a groan, and covered his eyes with his arm.

"What happened?" Jill asked.

A second knock brought Sawyer to a sitting position, but Jill was already on the way to the door. "I'll get it," she threw over her shoulder.

"Hello, Jill," a masculine voice said.

Sawyer fell back and covered his eyes again. At least it wasn't another woman out there asking for him.

"I heard you made it to the ranch this afternoon," he said. "I'm Quaid Brennan. We met years ago when you were a little girl and visited Gladys. I thought I'd come over and invite you to come to the Brennan Sunday dinner after church, and I'd love it if you helped me teach Sunday school and sat with us in church. We'd sure enjoy making you welcome to Burnt Boot."

"Sure, and thank you."

"Good. I'll pick you up at nine for Sunday school, then?"

"That will be great."

She shut the door and melted into a rocking chair beside the sofa. "Shit! Aunt Gladys is going to scalp me. She said I wasn't supposed to get involved with either family, but I couldn't think of a single excuse."

"I know exactly how you feel. But if you sit with them in church, everyone is going to think you've joined up with that side," Sawyer moaned.

"Dammit!"

"Hey, we'll make it through the day and be home in the middle of the afternoon. Let's get back to our cleaning and figure out an excuse if anyone else comes around."

Another knock on the door stopped him before he could finish the sentence.

"Your turn," she said.

He hauled himself up off the sofa, crossed the room, and slung the door open, praying that this time it would be Gladys, but it was Kinsey Brennan. He looked past her to the third truck in the driveway, to see Tyrell Gallagher sitting in the driver's seat. Shit fire! Each side had sent a double team to Fiddle Creek to gang up on them.

"Hey, Sawyer. We haven't been formally introduced, but I met you at your cousin's wedding reception. I came to invite you to Sunday dinner." She smiled.

Tall, willowy, blond, and brown-eyed, she looked like a runway model, but Sawyer had the perfect excuse all ready.

"I'm going to dinner with Betsy Gallagher," he said.

"Oh, well then, you must give us equal time, darlin'." She opened the screen door and stepped inside. Before he could take a single step back, her breasts were brushing against his chest. "You have to come to supper at the Brennan household. It'll be more private anyway without the whole family there." She picked up his hand and wrote a number in the palm. "This is my cell phone number. Call me at a quarter to six, and I'll talk to you the whole way and give you instructions on how to get to River Bend. See you then." She blew a kiss off the tips of her fingers and then touched his lips with her forefinger.

"Holy shit!" Jill said. "What's going on?"

"News travels fast in a small town. They know you have arrived, and they're going to swamp you with dates," he said.

"But why?"

"Fiddle Creek, and you're a damn fine-lookin' woman."

"But why you?"

"They just want to get rid of the threat. If one of those women can snag me, then that's one cowboy out of their way," he said.

"You sure about that?"

A heavy knock landed on the door.

"I bet you dollars to cow patties that's a Gallagher wanting to take you to Sunday dinner," he said.

She grimaced. "Maybe it's for you."

"If it is, tell the woman I've got the plague."

Jill answered the door, and there stood a tall, dark cowboy with pretty brown eyes. *Lord, please let this be a Bible seller who's lost his way and is looking for directions*, she prayed.

Her prayer fell on deaf ears.

"Miss Jill Cleary, I swear you have grown up to be a gorgeous woman. The last time I saw you, you were in pigtails. You won't remember me, probably. I'm Tyrell Gallagher. I heard you'd made it to town and I wanted to ask you to Sunday dinner." His Texas drawl was sexy as hell, and he was easy on the eyes.

"Thank you for coming by and for the invitation, but I've already got dinner plans for Sunday," she said.

"Well, then, darlin', you could invite me inside," Tyrell said.

"It's a mess in here." She used Sawyer's line and stepped out on the porch like he'd done.

He pinned her against the rough wood wall of the bunkhouse with a hand on either side of her. "I can't change your mind about dinner?"

"Sorry, but the plans are made." She felt like a caged cat and fought the urge to holler for Sawyer to come save her.

"Then supper? We have two meals at Wild Horse on Sunday. Supper is buffet instead of a sit-down dinner, but you can still meet the family," he whispered close enough that she caught the faint scent of peppermint gum over the top of whiskey.

"Okay," she said. "What time?"

"I'll pick you up at six. What's your favorite color of roses?"

"I don't have a favorite," she said.

He took a step back and grinned. "Then red it is. I'll see you Sunday."

She hurried into the house, and Sawyer was gone from the sofa. Surely he hadn't slipped out the back door and left her alone. *I take back everything I thought about him when I first got here, Lord. Please don't let him be gone. I'm going to need a friend and lots of support*, she prayed again.

She had a moment of panic until he came from the kitchen with two opened bottles of beer in his hands. He handed one to her and downed a third of the other one before he went back to the sofa and sat down on one end.

"I thought you'd left me to the wolves all by myself. It was a scary moment. I don't even know you, Sawyer O'Donnell, but please promise you'll stick around."

"I gave Gladys my word I'd stay for a year," he said.

She exhaled loudly. "We got off on the wrong foot. I'm tired and weary from driving and worried that I made the wrong decision in coming here, so I'm sorry for aiming my gun at you."

"Same here. I'm not a bit sorry that I took this job, but I wish to hell Fiddle Creek wasn't right in the middle of two feuding families," he said.

"I'm going to supper at the Gallaghers' ranch and dinner at the Brennans'. At least no one can say I'm choosing sides," she said with a long sigh as she plopped down on the other end of the sofa and kicked off her boots. "I shouldn't sit down, or I'll never get up and get this cleaning done. My feet hurt. My head is aching, and damn, Sawyer, why did I just agree to do two things I don't want to do?"

He picked up her feet and put them in his lap, massaging the soles through her socks. "I'm going to Wild Horse for dinner and River Bend for supper, but believe me, it's not happening but this one time," he said. "I'll be ready for them next time around."

She dramatically threw a hand over her eyes. "Next time? Shit! We're going to have to outrun them again? That feels so good. Did you ever think of leaving ranchin' and going into massage work?"

"No, ma'am. My heart is in ranchin', but it makes a person plumb cranky to have achin' feet." He cocked his head to one side, drew his eyes down, and asked, "What is that noise?"

"Sounds like thunder. Maybe if it rains, they'll all stay on their asses at home and leave us alone so we can get this place cleaned up before dark. Thanks for the foot rub. It really did help."

He cocked his ear to one side. "It's not thunder. That's cattle and four-wheelers."

She set her beer down and ran to the back door. Sure enough, there were four-wheelers out in the distance. She couldn't make out who was driving them, but she distinctly counted six.

Sawyer went the other way—to the front door. "I see three four-wheelers out on the far side, going toward the store. What the hell are they doing on Fiddle Creek?"

That's when they saw the cattle stampeding toward the bunkhouse. She jumped back and slammed the door shut. "Shit fire, Sawyer! What is going on?"

"It's a full-out stampede, but when they reach the bunkhouse, it'll break their momentum and slow 'em down. Gladys is going to have a hissy. I see River Bend brands all mixed up with ours, and I was right, there's Wild Horse brands in there too. Both sides must've had the same idea."

"To cut fences and create havoc?" she asked.

"That's the general definition of a feud," he answered.

Gladys, Quaid Brennan, and Tyrell Gallagher all arrived at the same time, braking so hard that gravel spewed all over the front of the bunkhouse.

"You son of a bitch." Tyrell jumped out of his truck and bowed up to Quaid, who had barely gotten his boots on the ground. "Why did you cut our fence and cause this mess?"

Gladys stepped between them.

Jill grabbed her boots and headed outside, yelling at Sawyer the whole way. "Go help her. I swear, if one of them throws a punch and hits her, I'll shoot him dead."

Sawyer didn't hesitate. He and Jill might have gotten off to a bad start, but she was right. If one of those fools hurt Gladys, she could shoot him, and Sawyer would carry the body down to the Red River and toss it into the water.

Sawyer joined Gladys. "Looks like you two need to use your energy to sort out your cattle rather than fightin'."

"That's right," Gladys said. "I'm damn sure not sortin' them out, but I will be doin' a count tomorrow, and if a single one of Fiddle Creek cows is missin', you'll both answer to me. Now get busy roundin' up your herds, and then get the hell off Fiddle Creek."

"Don't worry, Miz Gladys. I'm going out there to make sure that anything with our brand stays right here," Sawyer said.

"And I'm going with him," Jill said from the porch.

Gladys nodded. "And you had best fix your own fences too."

Without a word to her or to each other, both cowboys headed toward their trucks. They had phones to their ears as they backed away from the bunkhouse.

"Welcome to Burnt Boot." Gladys laughed. "I'm glad I hired y'all, because I'm going back to the store and leaving you to take care of it."

"My truck or yours?" Jill asked.

"I'll drive if you'll bring that shotgun with you."

"You got it. And, Sawyer, it's beginning to look like we'd best stick together if we're going to survive living here."

He held out his hand. "Deal."

She shook it and then went back inside to get her gun.

The truck engine was running when she got back. Sawyer put it in gear and drove toward the herd of cattle right smack in the middle of the Fiddle Creek pasture behind the bunkhouse.

"We need to be cleanin', not settling feud wars," she said.

"I know, but here we are. Speaking of cleanin', I didn't know that you were moving into the bunkhouse. Thought I had it all to myself, so I unloaded my things in the fore-man's bedroom. That comes with a private bathroom. I can move them to the other side if you want," he said.

"I remember the bunkhouse very well, and there are two bedrooms on the other side. One will serve as my office. Let's get a few things clear though, Sawyer. I don't cook, but I will take my turn at cleaning."

He nodded. "You don't cook or you don't like to cook?"

"I never learned."

"Well, I did, so we're in pretty good shape there."

~~~

His dark brown eyes met hers over the top of the console separating the two seats. He'd never been attracted to redheads or green-eyed women. He'd always gone for willowy blonds with pretty blue eyes, but something vulnerable in her eyes said that she needed a friend. And that light sprinkling of freckles across her nose was downright adorable.

"This has been a hell of a day. I expected to have the whole place cleaned and maybe go grab a beer tonight down at Polly's," he said.

"I had the same idea." She smiled. "But don't plans get turned around quick? Here they come."

"Where?"

She pointed. "Four-wheelers from both sides."

Sawyer got out of the truck and stood at the front, arms crossed over his chest until they arrived. They cut the engines—Brennans on one side of his truck, Gallaghers on the other. He saw Betsy and Kinsey and Quaid and Tyrell. The only sounds in the pasture were a bunch of heaving cows still trying to catch their breath from running and the occasional disgruntled snort from a bull or two. But the tension was so thick that a good sharp machete couldn't have split it.

"Okay, this is the way it is," he said. "I'm the foreman here, and to avoid any more trouble, the Brennans are going to gather up their cows first and head them back to River Bend. Then you Gallaghers can get yours out from the Fiddle Creek cattle and take them to Wild Horse."

"Why do the Brennans go first?" Betsy asked.

"Because *B* comes before *G* in the alphabet."

He heard Jill chuckle as she crawled out of the truck, the shotgun in her hands.

"And why has she got a gun?" Kinsey asked.

"To keep things nice and friendly," Sawyer said.

"We didn't do any of this," Quaid said.

"Yeah, right," Kinsey shot across the twelve feet separating them.

"Don't you think it's strange that both fences were cut and cattle from both ranches stampeded?" Kinsey stared right at Sawyer.

"I don't give a shit," Jill said. "Your cows are mixed up with ours, and we're being kind enough to let you take them home. Now quit your bitchin' and get on with it. Sawyer and I haven't even unpacked yet, and we've got things to do other than babysit you people."

The Brennans started the tedious job of rounding up fifty head of cattle. Tyrell Gallagher started toward Jill, but she shook her head. "Not today, cowboy. Today it's all business."

He turned and said something to Betsy that made her laugh loudly before the two of them sat down on the cold ground behind a four-wheeler. Their tone said they were brewing up some kind of trouble, but Jill didn't care. Her feet were hurting again, and she and Sawyer had too much to do for her to get another foot massage tonight.

"When we get back to the bunkhouse, if anyone else knocks on our door, one of us is going to shoot them," Jill said just loud enough for Sawyer's ears.

"My gun isn't loaded. You shoot, and I'll get out the shovel to dig the hole to bury them."

"It's a deal," she said. "I'm too tired to dig, but I think I can still shoot pretty straight. Man, who would have thought the day would be like this when it dawned?"

"Ain't it the truth?" He nodded. "How long did you drive?"

"I left at four o'clock this morning from the south-west corner of Texas and drove until, what time is it?"

He took a phone from his shirt pocket and checked. "Four thirty. Be dark in an hour."

She laid the shotgun on the hood of the truck and pulled gloves out of her pocket. "There's a nip to the wind. Feels like snow."

"Yep," he said. He waited until the Brennans were halfway across the pasture with their herd before he gave the Gallaghers permission to start getting their cattle together.

"They don't like taking orders," she said.

"Maybe it will make them mad enough to leave me alone the rest of the time I'm here."

"We've eaten our bullfrog," she said.

"What's that?" he asked.

She smiled. "It's an old adage. Wake up every morning and eat a bullfrog first thing, and the rest of the day will go just fine."

"Honey, I'm afraid we've just eaten his scrawny old toes."

"Then I'm going to need a lot of help."

"Me too, Jill Cleary. Me too," he said.

Chapter 2

JILL CARRIED HER GUN AND HER SUITCASE TO THE larger of the two bedrooms on the other side of the room. Dust flew when she dropped them on the bed, and she groaned when she flipped the light switch.

She might not be a neat freak, but nothing more was coming in from the truck until she'd done some massive cleaning. Rather than a broom, she might need a scoop shovel to clear out the layers and layers of dust.

"I'll help you unload your stuff soon as you get things ready," Sawyer said from the doorway. She glanced up, seeing him in a new light. She'd lived in bunkhouses before with lots of men around. His face would make a good study for artists, with all the acute angles from cheekbones to the cleft in his chin. He had skin the color of coffee with lots of pure cream in it and at first glance she'd thought it was the result of working outside in the sun. But it went deeper than that. There was a Latino in the woodpile somewhere in Sawyer's background, in spite of an Irish surname.

"Thank you. Are all of your things unloaded?"

"No, ma'am. I'm not bringing out my stuff until things are cleaned up. No sense in dragging them through all this dust and having to move them around to clean. I was finishing up the living room when you arrived. The kitchen is fairly good, but I did see a few mouse tracks in the dust on the cabinet before I cleaned it."

Speak of the devil, and he shall appear. A mouse shot across the tip of her boots and started up the bedpost. Instinctively she slapped at it with the butt of the shotgun, and it fell onto the floor. She hated mice almost as bad as rattlesnakes, but she wasn't afraid of them. Now spiders? That was a whole different story.

She picked up the dead mouse by the tail and carried it across the living room floor to the front door, where she pitched him out into the yard. "I'll get a cat tomorrow."

He raked his fingers through his jet-black hair and then down over a day's worth of heavy black stubble. "I like cats, especially if they take care of mice and rats."

"Good, maybe we'll get a couple," she said.

"That's pretty bold of you, Jill Cleary." His eyes sparkled when he teased. "We've only known each other a few hours, and you're already talking about us getting pets together. A foot massage doesn't mean that we are in a relationship."

"Honey, we've been through more in those few hours than most folks go through in a month, and the cats are not going to be pets," she said. "They're going to be mousers. And believe me, I'm not ready for a relationship with anyone, so you don't have to worry about that, and, yes, I will take a foot massage any time you want to give one."

"Just so we're clear," he said. "Now, I'm going to clean my quarters. One more time before I get things all spick-and-span, do you want that side of the bunkhouse?"

She shook her head, red hair flying. "I do not. I can be very happy right here with my two rooms."

Faded jeans hugged his muscular thighs and butt. His dark brown eyes were kind, mischievous, and full of excitement. Tiny little crow's-feet at the sides of his eyes said that he wasn't a teenager and that he had a sense of humor. His biceps stretched at the seams of the blue chambray work shirt. Two buttons were undone, showing a bed of soft black hair peeking out. She wished he'd left all the buttons undone and she could run her fingers across the hard muscles under the shirt.

Lord, she needed to get a grip! The last thing she really wanted was a relationship, and there was a very good possibility that Sawyer had a girlfriend, or maybe even a wife. Friendship would be easy and okay, but not a thing past that. She quickly glanced at his hands. No ring! At least she hadn't been lusting after a married man.

"Why are you here?" she asked.

"I needed a job."

"Ranchin' jobs can be found anywhere in the state of Texas. Why did you come to Burnt Boot?"

"For a brand-new fresh start."

But his eyes said more. Disappointment was written there. Someday, when they knew each other better, she intended to play poker with him. He was one of those open-book men who couldn't hide anything. Whatever he felt was written plain and clear in those mesmerizing dark eyes, and there was a story in there. If they were playing for clothes instead of dollars, she could win everything from that shirt to his pretty belt buckle to his scuffed-up boots. Did he wear boxers or briefs? Hopefully, he went cowboy, which meant neither one, and she would have it all when he peeled those jeans down.

Crap! She really did need to get a hold on her thoughts.

It had to be because she was so tired and he'd been so nice after she'd started things off like a first-rate bitch.

"Well, it looks like we've both got a job," she said. "I haven't been here since I was a little girl. Is that the other bathroom?" She pointed to one of two closed doors.

"No, that's a tack room. That one"—his finger went to a door right beside what would be her office—"is yours. It's got a tub. If you are nice, I'll loan you my shower when you don't have time to run a bath."

"Thank you, and when you'd like to soak away the aches and pains, you are welcome to use my tub," she said.

She grabbed a broom and headed back to her room, but she could feel his eyes on her, creating a faint flutter in her heart. Oh, yes, she definitely had to get control of herself!

It was late when things were clean enough that she could take a quick bath and fall into bed, but Aunt Gladys was a night owl and she would still be awake. If a person looked up "night owl" in the phone book, Gladys Cleary's picture would be there. It would show an eighty-year-old woman with a strong chin and lots of jet-black hair with just a hint of gray in it. Jill propped two pillows against the iron headboard and reached for her phone. The old metal springs squeaked under the mattress every time she moved. She hit the speed-dial button and leaned back.

"You got them cows sorted out?" Gladys asked.

"And my bedroom and bathroom at least livable," she said.

"And Sawyer, is he alive?"

"We buried the hatchet and made a treaty."

"Well, hot damn! I knew you'd see that he is a good man. What's the treaty say?"

"That we'll have each other's backs after Sunday," Jill said.

"Sunday?"

Jill told Gladys about how both Brennans and Gallaghers had blindsided her and Sawyer and now they had to go to dinner and then supper with them. "But you can't accuse me of taking sides," she said.

"Sounds like you've both done stepped in a fresh shit pile." Gladys laughed. "But it will be good for you."

"One of those things that makes you stronger if it don't kill you?" Jill asked.

"Something like that. Now get some sleep. Y'all meet me at the barn at eight tomorrow, and I'll show you how I want the feeding chores done."

"Yes, ma'am. Good night, Aunt Gladys. And thanks for the job."

"Honey, it's only a job until I'm dead, then Fiddle Creek is yours. Good night and good-bye. See you kids in the morning."

Jill said good-bye and poked the "end" button, but it was a while before she went to sleep.

Sawyer awoke with a start, sun warming his face through a dingy window and the smell of coffee filling the bunkhouse. He sat straight up and inhaled deeply. It took a few seconds to get his bearings. He hadn't slept past daybreak in years, much less until seven o'clock, but then he hadn't gone to bed until three that morning. He fell back onto the pillows, pulled the clean flannel sheets and down comforter up to his neck, and listened to the sounds of a lonesome old coyote howling somewhere outside.

The aroma of coffee drifted under the door. Evidently, Jill was already up and around, which meant she'd gotten into his stash, since that was the only thing in the kitchen. There wasn't even a stray ice cube in the refrigerator freezer, much less a quart of milk and stale doughnuts. That also meant she'd used his coffeepot.

He sat up, slung his legs over the side of the bed, and his feet hit the cold tile floor all in one motion. He might tolerate someone dipping into his stash of dark-roast coffee, but nobody messed with his pot. Not even if she was cuter than a bug's ear, with that faint sprinkling of freckles across her nose.

He made a mad dash for the top drawer of the dresser and yanked out a pair of warm socks first and pulled them on as he tried to keep from putting his entire foot on the floor. The room was so cold that ice had formed on the inside of the window. He glanced up at the ceiling to make sure the vents were on, but there were no vents. Evidently, the only heat in the place came from that wood-burning stove in the living area, and the fire he'd built when he arrived the evening before had gone cold. He'd have to remember to leave his door cracked from now on, which meant no more nights of sleeping in the raw.

He jerked on a pair of jeans and a long-sleeved, oatmeal-colored thermal shirt, and stomped his feet down into boots. He shivered as he shaved, brushed his teeth, and ran a comb through his thick black hair. He needed a haircut, but it could wait another week.

Warm air rushed into the cold room when he opened

the door. A burning fire crackled in the cast-iron stove. On top, a chipped blue granite pot gurgling away as it boiled coffee. Sawyer hadn't had a cup of campfire coffee in ages, and it sure smelled good.

He rounded a corner into the kitchen area, and there was Jill coming right at him, head down, with an empty coffee mug in her hand. He checked the cup out carefully. It wasn't dark brown with writing on it, so she hadn't stolen his cup as well as his coffee.

She looked up a split second before stopping so quick that her boots made a high-pitched squeak on the tile floor. "Don't sneak up on me like that," she said breathlessly.

"I didn't, and who gave you permission to use my coffee?" he asked.

"Hey, you woke up to a warm living room and coffee. Quit your bitchin', and I might share. I woke up to a cold house because a tall, dark—" She stopped shy of saying *handsome*. She faked a cough and went on. "A cowboy didn't bank the fire, and there's not a single thing to eat. I'm grouchy when I'm hungry, and I bite before I have my morning coffee. So stand aside and let me pour a cup. And from this standpoint, Sawyer O'Donnell, you don't look like you wake up in a good mood either, so pour a cup and let's talk."

"It's my coffee, so you don't have any say-so about sharing it," he said.

"It's my pot, so don't argue with me. Didn't you hear that part about biting? I haven't had rabies shots, either," she shot back over her shoulder, her green eyes dancing with mischievousness. "Much more of your whining, and you can brew a cup in your sissy pot and leave my real stuff alone."

Sawyer poured a cup, tasted it, and nodded. "Delicious, madam barista."

"Don't give me a fancy name. I can't even run that prissy pot you've got sitting on the cabinet. If it's more complicated than putting coffee in one place and water in another, I'm lost," she admitted.

She bent over to set her blue granite cup on the stove, and the way she filled out the butt of those jeans made his mouth drier than the damn Mojave Desert. She straightened up and dragged the second wooden rocker across the floor to the other side of the stove, sat down, and reached for the metal cup.

"Ouch!" she said, quickly wrapping the handle in her shirttail.

"Got a little warm, did it?"

"Oh, yeah!" Her smile was bright and honest. "Aunt Gladys left me a voice message. She's got the feeding chores done, and we're supposed to meet her at the bar. I vote that we go to the bar early and have breakfast there. There's always bacon and eggs in the refrigerator and bread for toast on the shelf. Then we'll stop by the store and get a week's worth of supplies after we talk to the aunts," she said.

"Sounds like a plan to me, but I thought Polly only fired the grill up for dinner and supper," Sawyer said.

"You said you could cook, cowboy. If I'm stealing the food, surely to God you can make breakfast for both of us." That sparkle was back in her eye that said she liked to banter.

The mug cooled enough that she could handle it, and the hot liquid warmed her insides while the old woodstove took care of the outside. She stole glances at Sawyer with his long legs stretched out, black hair falling down on his forehead, and sleep leaving his big brown eyes. It should be a sin for a man to have lashes that long and a smile so damn bright that it could put the summer sun to shame.

Never before had she been attracted to the tall, dark, handsome man. She'd always gone for the blond-haired, blue-eyed guys. Being a cowboy had always been a plus, but it had never been a necessity. But it would be just downright wrong to start up anything with Sawyer. They had to live in the same house and work together. Friends might work…but that was as far as it could go.

"Aunt Gladys will fire your lazy ass if you sleep until seven every morning," she said.

Sawyer drew down his eyebrows and tucked his chin to his chest. "For your information, come Monday morning I'll be out there with the cows at five o'clock. That means I'll be up at four to make my breakfast."

"I know ranchin', Sawyer. I've been doin' it my whole life. One set of my grandparents had a little spread down near Brownsville. That would be my mama's folks, but Daddy's lived close by on the outskirts of town. Mama remarried after Daddy died, and we moved to Kentucky, but I got to spend summers and holidays in the area until they passed on a couple of years ago."

"Your dad's folks been gone long?"

"They both died within a year of each other when I was in high school."

"And then?" he asked.

"I completed a bachelor's degree in business agri-culture, and I went to work full-time on a ranch. Now I'm here."

"You ready to go raid the bar's refrigerator?" Sawyer asked.

"Oh, yeah, I am."

"Are we going to have to add breaking and entering to a felony conviction of stealing bacon and eggs?"

She frowned. "Well, dammit! I hadn't thought of getting inside. Aunt Polly has always been there. We may have to eat peanut butter sandwiches after all. The store should be open now, though, so we can get some food there, I guess."

"I don't like peanut butter."

"Next thing you'll be tellin' me is you don't like pinto beans and fried potatoes," Jill said.

Sawyer threw a hand over his heart and rolled his eyes toward the ceiling. "That would be sacrilege. I'm not sure you can get into heaven if you don't like pinto beans and fried potatoes. Saint Peter would send you straight on down to the blazing fires of hell, so don't even whisper such blasphemy."

"It would be almost as bad as not liking a good thick steak," she agreed with a nod as she pulled her cell phone from her shirt pocket.

"Callin' the boyfriend?" he asked.

"I'm calling Aunt Polly, and if you are askin' if I have a boyfriend, I don't, and I don't want one, especially not a Brennan or a Gallagher. What time of morning do you call your girlfriend or your wife?"

A grin showed perfect white teeth. No tobacco stain and no cigarettes in his shirt pocket. That was definitely a plus if she had to live with the man. She hated a spit can and smoke.

"No wife or girlfriend. Both are too much trouble," he said.

"That applies to boyfriends too," she told him. "I'll set the pot on the cabinet so it doesn't boil dry. We can reheat the coffee in the microwave this evening. Do we take one truck or two?"

"Might as well take one. I'll drive," he said.

She held up a finger. "Hello, Aunt Polly. We thought we'd make breakfast at the bar this morning, since there's nothing in the bunkhouse until we do some shopping. You're kiddin' me! That's not safe. Everyone knows that's where people put spare keys." She nodded. "Yes, we're going to make bacon and eggs. Pancakes? Do you have the stuff for that at the bar?" Another pause. "That's fine with me. I love pancakes. Right now I could eat cow patties, I'm so hungry."

Sawyer was staring at her when she ended the call.

"The spare key is in the flowerpot outside the bar. Aunt Gladys is bringing a box of that mix where you only add water to make pancakes, and some maple syrup. I guess we're having a party. I promised you'd cook and clean up the grill and wash the dishes."

When she looked up, Sawyer was standing above her. "I'll cook because I'm hungry, but if I cook, I don't wash dishes."

"Looks like we're lucky that the bar always uses disposable plates. Aunt Polly doesn't like to wash dishes either, and she's too tight to hire a full-time dishwasher."

<hr />

Polly and Gladys were sitting on the bar stools. Gladys wore jeans, a red sweatshirt, and a big smile. Both of them had smiles that said they were up to no good. They weren't any better than Sawyer at hiding what they were thinking, and Jill didn't like it. But then again, maybe they'd only been talking about everything that had happened the afternoon before.

They'd married brothers, so they weren't blood kin, but folks tended to think they were, since their last names were Cleary. Polly was dressed in her usual bar garb, which was bibbed overalls, a long-sleeved knit shirt of some description, and tennis shoes. That day her shirt was the color of a summer sky, which matched her eyes perfectly. Her short gray hair was still wet with whatever mousse she'd run through it and reminded Jill of the spiked hairdos that rockers liked.

Gladys was a tall, lanky, part–Native American woman with a touch of white in her chin-length hair, a gravelly voice that said she probably smoked on the sly, and brown eyes. Her skin wasn't nearly as wrinkled as Polly's, but then folks with her DNA usually leathered rather than wrinkled.

They both cussed like sailors, even if Polly did play the piano for the church, and they couldn't have been a bit closer if they'd been blood sisters.

"We're hungry. Bacon, eggs, and bread is over there beside the grill. Gladys already stirred up the pancake batter," Polly said.

"Who's minding the store?" Jill asked.

"Verdie came in and agreed to watch it for a couple of hours if I brought back a bacon, lettuce, and tomato sandwich, so cook the whole pound, Sawyer," Gladys answered.

"Give me a hug, girl," Polly said.

Jill hiked a hip on the bar stool next to her aunt and leaned in for a hug. "I've missed you."

"I ain't moved since you was here last."

"Or got any sweeter either," Jill said.

Polly laughed. "Ah, Gladys, she still loves us."

Sawyer fired up the grill. While it heated, he removed the white butcher paper from around the fresh-cut bacon. "Did you smoke this yourself?" he asked Gladys.

"No, but the man I get my pork from down in Salt Holler did," she said.

"Is that legal? Buying meat from an individual?"

She shrugged. "It's don't ask, don't tell. I don't ask the gover'ment if I can buy my bacon and pork from him. He don't tell the gover'ment that I do."

"Well, it smells like what my grandpa used to make out in his smokehouse," Sawyer said.

"Don't you dare burn it," Polly said. "She don't offer it up free very often."

"And the eggs came from the same man, as well as half my fresh produce in the summertime," Gladys said.

He opened two cartons to find big brown-speckled eggs. Sawyer pulled slice after slice of bacon from the thick stack and lined them up on the grill. The sizzle and the smell filled the bar, and Jill's hungry stomach grumbled.

Polly patted her on the shoulder. She and Gladys had been sisters-in-law for more than fifty years, and Jill loved both of them.

She hugged Polly tightly. "I'm glad to be here. Did you hear about what happened at the bunkhouse?"

"Get up here on this stool beside me." Polly motioned to her. "Gladys already told me about it. You be careful, girl. I swear them Brennans and Gallaghers are sneaky."

"Yes, they are," Sawyer agreed.

A granddaddy long-legged spider jumped from the bucket of peanuts on the bar in front of Polly and landed right on her nose. She squealed, swatted at it, and leaned backward. Everything happened in slow motion and yet too fast for Jill to do a blessed thing to help. She reached out to grab Polly, but all she got was a fistful of air.

"Well, Polly!" Gladys said.

Then there was a crack, and Jill thought the leg of the stool had broken when it hit the hard floor. But when she saw Polly's ankle, she knew it was far worse.

"God, that hurts," Polly said.

"It's broken. Aunt Gladys, call 911 and get an ambulance," Jill said.

"What can I do?" Sawyer was suddenly beside her, supporting Polly's head with his big arms.

"Just hold her right there while I make a call. Don't move, Polly. The bone isn't out of the skin just yet, but it looks bad." Gladys fished in her purse for her cell phone.

Sawyer jerked his out of his shirt pocket, hit 911, and handed it to Gladys. She talked to someone who assured her that an ambulance would be there in twenty minutes.

"I'm supposed to keep you right here, and you ain't supposed to move a muscle," Gladys said.

"Y'all could pick me up easy-like and load me in the backseat of my truck and take me to the hospital. Damned ambulance comin' this far is going to cost a fortune."

Gladys narrowed her eyes and said, "And if we dropped you and you got a worse break and gangrene set in and rotted your foot off?"

"Who's going to take care of the bar?" Polly groaned.

"We've got two kids right here who can do that until you can walk again," Gladys said.

"I can't cook," Jill said.

"I can cook." Sawyer patted Polly's hand. "Don't you

worry. We'll hold down the fort until you are all better. I've done a little bartending in my day. It wasn't an operation like this, but I know how to fill beer pitchers and make a few fancy drinks."

"And I'll take care of you. When you get released from the hospital, you can come to my house, and we'll do just fine," Gladys said.

"The store?" Jill whispered.

"I'll take care of it in the morning while you do the ranch work, and then in the afternoons you can relieve me, just until Polly gets better. Can't leave her all day by herself," Gladys said.

"That's doable," Jill said.

They could hear the ambulance long before two big strapping men brought in a stretcher. They loaded her up, and Gladys glanced at Jill.

"Go with her," Jill said. "Call us when you need a ride home or want us to bring anything to you. Keep us posted and, Aunt Gladys, don't worry. Sawyer's got the bar, and I've got the store. The ranchin' part we might not do just like you do, but we'll get it done."

Gladys started out the door and turned around to say, "My cows are used to breakfast at eight. Don't go spoiling them by giving it to them at six. You treat Fiddle Creek like it was your ranch and do whatever you see that needs done."

"Yes, ma'am," Sawyer said.

Chapter 3

A COLD NORTH WIND WHIPPED DOWN THE ROLLING hills of North Texas, creating music in the bare tree limbs as it rattled through them. After living right next to the Gulf of Mexico the past two years, in the balmy salt air and year-round pleasant weather, Jill could scarcely believe she was in the same state.

"It's as different as the tropics and the North Pole," she mumbled on her way from Gladys's truck to the general store. According to the old wooden sign swinging between the two porch posts, the official name was The Burnt Boot General Store. But local folks referred to it as *the store*, just like they called The Burnt Boot Bar and Grill, *the bar* or else *Polly's place*.

Jill hung her coat on the rack behind the counter and wandered through the store. It was good to see that some things never changed. The shelves were full and free of dust. The meat counter looked like something out of an old black-and-white movie, but the glass was sparkling clean, showing a display of pork chops, bacon, hamburger, steaks, and big thick roasts.

Her phone rang, and she grabbed for it. Gladys said they'd done preliminary work and decided that Polly would need surgery. They were taking her in right then, and with any luck, they would release her in a couple of days. Verdie, their other lifelong friend, had already come to the hospital and would bring Gladys home when the surgery was done, and Polly was settled into a private room.

Gladys sighed. "I'm sorry to unload all this on you, kiddo. Did Sawyer stay with you?"

"You just worry about making Aunt Polly happy," she said. "And Sawyer isn't here. It's so boring, we sure don't need two of us to take care of the place. He's out making sure the fences are mended from yesterday and that things are quiet on the ranch. I'll be fine. It's just a little store, Aunt Gladys, but I promise if there's a problem, I'll call you."

"Just ring up sales and take their money or put their charge tickets in the little box under the counter. They're listed alphabetically. Best way to learn to swim is to jump headfirst in the water," Gladys said.

"I'm not so sure I know about the meat sales, though," Jill said.

"There's a scale and a calculator back there. Prices are on the front of the glass as well as taped to the wall by the scale. I made up enough last evening to last all day, and the shelves are stocked and dusted. If you get hungry, make yourself a sandwich. There's an open loaf of bread beside the scales, and you can get ham or bologna and cheese from the refrigerator. Help yourself. Quittin' time is five o'clock."

"Don't worry, Aunt Gladys. I can take care of this."

"I'm glad you arrived when you did," Gladys said.

Jill wasn't used to being still. From before daylight to dark she'd had something to do, none of which required sitting in a chair behind a counter. She turned the chair so she could see out the window. A squirrel with a fluffy red tail scampered across the road, scaled the single gas pump like it was a tree, and perched on the top.

"King of the mountain." Jill smiled.

A truck went by and spooked her entertainment. He made a flying leap and hit a drooping branch on the pecan tree at the corner of the store. In seconds he'd disappeared into the limbs, probably to scramble on to another tree and another, until he felt safe enough to come down to the ground again.

Then there was nothing but a small store with three aisles, a refrigerated section on one side, and a freezer on the other. Meat counter at the back, checkout counter with an old cash register at the front, and a few newspapers left over from the week before.

She read though one in less than ten minutes, then riffled through the magazines under the counter. The newest one was dated two years before and had nothing on the front to entice her to go further. On Monday she'd bring a big thick romance book with a bare-chested cowboy on the front.

An hour passed before a truck pulled up to the front of the store. She glanced at the clock: it was well past noon, so he was late. Sawyer got out, shook the legs of his jeans down over the top of his boots, tucked his gloved hands into the pockets of his mustard-colored work coat, and jogged to the porch. She jumped up so fast, the chair fell over backward. By the time she'd righted it, he was in the store.

"Hey, it's damn cold out there," he said.

"I'd rather be out there than sitting in here bored to death," she told him.

"You'd change your mind pretty quick. I drove all

around the ranch. Got out and walked a few times so I could get a feel for the land. Fences look good for now. There's a couple of old wood posts that need to be replaced with metal ones, but that can wait until spring."

He paused and looked around the store. "Looks slow in here."

"Boring." She drug out the word into half a dozen syllables.

He removed his coat and hung it on the rack beside hers. "Let's do our shopping then. Gladys said I could put whatever I buy here on a ticket, and she'd take it out of my monthly paycheck."

She motioned toward the line of five carts. "Help yourself. How many head of cattle is Aunt Gladys running now?"

"Looks to be about a hundred and fifty, but the ranch has good fertile ground. It would support twice that many, especially if we cleared the mesquite off the west side and put it into hay this spring. Figured I'd get out the chain saw and go to work on it next week. The wood will keep us warm, and we can stack up what we don't use for next winter."

She pulled the next cart out and followed him. "You can take my food back to the bunkhouse with you."

He stopped and turned around to face her, the empty cart between them. "Is that an order or a request?"

She batted her eyelashes at him. "Please, kind sir, would you take my groceries home for me? I'll keep the perishables in one bag, and you can set the whole thing in the refrigerator, and I'll put everything away when I get there."

"You aren't very good at that," he said.

"What? Asking or flirting?"

He cocked his head off to the side in that sexy little gesture that tightened up her gut. "Fake flirting. But yes, ma'am, I'll…hey, how are you going to get home anyway? You don't have a vehicle here."

She shrugged. "I'll walk. Believe me, after all afternoon in this boredom, I'll be ready to walk all the way to the river, not just to the bunkhouse."

He put two cans of green beans into his cart and added a couple of cans of corn. "I need both. I'm making a pot of soup and one of chili this afternoon. That will last several days and taste good in cold weather."

She picked up a container of cocoa, a bag of flour, and one of sugar, and put them into her cart.

"I thought you didn't cook," he said.

"Cooking is one thing. Baking is another. I have a terrible sweet tooth, and I don't like store-bought cakes, pies, or cookies."

Sawyer looked over his shoulder at her. "How are you at apple pie?"

"One of my specialties. Granny Cleary taught me to make the crust when I was a little girl."

"I'll make a deal with you," he said. "I'll keep the real food on the table if you keep sweet stuff in the bunkhouse, and we'll share. I'll buy staples. You buy baking goods each week."

"Sounds fair enough to me. Move aside so I can pick out six good cooking apples. I'll start this afternoon with an apple pie and a chocolate cake."

"But you have to work here until five o'clock."

"There's an old cookstove with a perfectly good oven in the storeroom. Aunt Gladys often heats up soup for her lunch on it," she said. "And truth is, I'll be thankful for something to do."

"Then I'll be here at five to take you home," he said. "Even if the pie is mediocre, I don't want to have to eat it off the ground with a spoon because you stumbled and fell with it on the way home."

"Cowboy"—she smiled brightly—"my pies are not mediocre."

"I'll save my opinion until I've tasted it," he declared. "But believe me, darlin', I will be here at five to protect that pie."

Neither of them heard the truck park outside. Not until the bell above the door jingled did they turn away from the meat counter where they were discussing whether he should buy two or three pounds of hamburger for his chili and soup.

"Hello. Where is Gladys?" Quaid Brennan said.

Jill left her cart sitting beside Sawyer's and started forward. "Aunt Polly broke her ankle this morning, and Aunt Gladys is at the hospital with her. I'll be taking care of the store for her for a while."

"Hello, Quaid." Sawyer waved.

He gave a brief nod toward Sawyer. "Gladys is lucky she'd already hired him before I knew he was lookin' for a job. I'd have given him a job in a second."

His big beautiful blue eyes never left hers. His shoulders were broad. His jeans fit right. His boots were scuffed and worn, showing that he was a real cowboy. His blue-and-black-plaid flannel shirt peeked out from under a work coat and hugged his body like a glove. With his blond hair and blue eyes, light skin and square face, Quaid was the exact opposite of Sawyer, but he was a damn fine-looking specimen all the same. He picked up her hand, brought it up to his lips, and kissed the palm. "I'm looking forward to seeing you tomorrow."

She pulled her hand back and tucked her thumbs in her hip pockets.

"So did we decide on two or three pounds?" Sawyer asked.

Quaid raised an eyebrow.

Jill spoke up before Sawyer could catch his breath. "He's going to do the cooking, and I'll do the baking. You know that we are sharing the bunkhouse, don't you?"

"Of course I did know that." Quaid smiled.

"What can I help you with today?" Jill asked.

"I need"—Quaid looked around the store—"ten apples."

"Making a pie?" Sawyer asked.

"No, eating them," Quaid said.

Jill picked up a paper bag and set it on the produce scale. "You must love apples."

"Not for me. I'm taking them to my Sunday school class in the morning, so pick out good eating apples, not cooking ones."

"You'll want these pretty red ones. They're firm but still sweet. I wouldn't buy them for a pie, but they are wonderful for eating," she said as she loaded up the bag.

"So you know how to make a decent apple pie?" Quaid asked. "Since you like to bake, maybe when you get settled in I'll talk you into bringing cookies to the class some Sunday?"

"We'll see." She smiled.

Sawyer cleared his throat to get her attention and pointed at the hamburger.

"Be there in a minute," she said.

She handed the bag to Quaid and followed him to the front of the store.

Quaid settled his black felt hat back on his blond hair. "Put it on the River Bend Ranch bill."

Truck tires crunched on the gravel outside, a door slammed, and Tyrell Gallagher pushed the door open, bringing a blast of cold air with him. "Hello, Miz… What are you doing here?" He glared at Quaid.

"Buying apples and talking to Jill," Quaid said.

"Where is Gladys?"

Jill stepped out around the counter. "Aunt Polly broke her ankle this morning. Aunt Gladys is with her, and I'll be takin' care of the store for a few days."

"You are still coming to Wild Horse tomorrow, aren't you?" Tyrell asked.

"For supper, yes, I am," she answered.

Quaid picked up his bag of apples and started out the door, stumbled over the cart he hadn't put back in the corner, and blamed it on Tyrell. "You tripped me, you son of a bitch."

He threw the apples across the store and swung at Tyrell, who wasn't about to back down or talk sense to a Brennan. The first punch landed on Tyrell's cheek. He spit blood and hit Quaid right between the eyes with a heavy fist. Then they were on the floor, rolling around like a couple of schoolboys. One long leg kicked over a display of corn, and cans fell like snow, landing and rolling everywhere. Tyrell tried to get away from the cans and fists peppering down on him, but he stepped on a can rolling across the floor and landed smack in the middle of Quaid's back. He got a couple of punches in before Quaid picked up a can of corn and hurled it over his shoulder, hitting Tyrell in the left ear.

It was like Polly's fall, happening in slow motion as Jill picked her way through the cans to grab Tyrell by the hair and give it a yank. He drew back his fist, thinking it was Quaid, and she would have felt the brunt of it if Sawyer hadn't clamped his big hand over it in midair.

"You lay a hand on her, cowboy, and you won't live to see the light of day." Sawyer pulled them apart and shoved Quaid toward the door. "Get out of here. This is neutral territory, and you know it. If either of you ever start anything in here again, you won't get a warning, you'll get a royal ass whuppin'."

"Why aren't you runnin' *him* off?" Quaid growled.

"I am, soon as you clear the parking lot. I don't give a shit if you two drive out in the middle of the road and kill each other. At least that way Jill wouldn't have to go out with either of you tomorrow, so have at it. But you're not fighting in this store."

Tyrell bowed up to Sawyer. "You can't tell me what to do."

Quaid spun out of the driveway, throwing gravel everywhere at the same time that Betsy parked her truck in front of the store. She hurried in out of the cold and looked around wide-eyed at the mess.

"Was that… Holy shit, Tyrell, what happened in here?"

"He can tell you later. He's leaving," Sawyer said.

"This store will fold up without Wild Horse's business, so you'd better watch your smart-ass mouth," Tyrell said.

Betsy reached out to touch his shoulder. "Come on.

Let me help you to your truck. Hell, you look like you got slammed by a semi."

He shook off her hand. "I don't need your help. This isn't over, Sawyer. I'll see you tomorrow evening, Jill." He marched out to his truck and drove away.

"One of y'all want to tell me what happened? Who are you and where is Gladys?" Betsy asked.

"Jill, meet Betsy Gallagher. Betsy, this is Jill Cleary, Gladys's niece who's come to live on Fiddle Creek and learn the business."

Jill wiped her hands and came out from the back of the meat counter. "Pleased to meet you."

"Likewise." Betsy nodded. "I heard you were coming to our place tomorrow and that you were here to help Gladys with Fiddle Creek. And I heard Polly broke her ankle. That mean you'll be takin' care of the bar, instead of the ranch?" She turned to look at Sawyer as if she could start a make-out session right there in the store. "I bet a big strong cowboy like Sawyer can take care of this little bitty spread all by himself."

Sawyer picked up an armload of cans and put them in a cart. "I'll be taking care of the bar. Jill is going to run the store so Gladys can help with Polly. And you can tell your kinfolk that there better not be any more altercations around here. Gladys didn't abide it, and we won't either."

"Boys will be boys." She laughed, and with a wave over her shoulder, she was gone.

"Good grief, Sawyer. What have we gotten ourselves into? I thought I was going to be helping run a ranch, not having to deal with these people on an everyday basis. I'm glad you were here. I would have never gotten those two apart without you, and I have no doubt they would have torn the place apart. Thanks for helping to get this corn all gathered up."

Sawyer continued picking up the cans that had rolled every which way. "We have to deal with them, but we'll keep it professional. Just put all the corn into a basket, and we'll push it into the back room. We'll restock the shelves as we need it, and we'll forget about a pyramid display."

"Sounds good to me, but tomorrow won't be professional. Dinner and supper with families, that's personal."

Sawyer put four more cans into the cart. "We'll get through it, and we won't ever let them corner us again. We need two pounds of bacon and honey. If I'm cooking breakfast, then you are making some kind of muffins for breakfast dessert. I'm real partial to blueberry, but I won't fuss about banana nut."

"I like western omelets with peppers, onions, and tomatoes," she said.

"For blueberry muffins, I can make an omelet that will melt in your mouth."

"They'll have to be from frozen berries. There's no fresh at this time of year."

"I'm not that particular. It can even be out of one of those boxed mixes." Sawyer picked up a piece of paper and wrote a number on it. "This is my cell phone. It's in my pocket all the time. If you need me, call and I'll be here in less than five minutes."

"Thanks, Sawyer. Seems like I've said that more in the past twenty-four hours than I have my whole life."

Sawyer left with the groceries, and not another soul came into the store. Gladys called twice to give Jill updates on Polly. They had to put pins in the ankle, and it would be at least two months before she could put weight on it.

Jill sighed and looked at the clock. It was only two hours until she could leave, and she had a pie and a cake to make, but her heart wasn't it in. Not even to prove to Sawyer that she could make a damn fine apple pie. Just thinking about sitting in that store, day in and day out for two whole months, maybe even longer, put her in a Jesus mood…that's the worst kind of mood, one where even Jesus couldn't live with her.

Chapter 4

NOT MANY FOLKS WERE INTERESTED IN FOOD THAT Saturday night. They wanted cold beers, either by the pitchers or red plastic cups, and dollar bills or quarters to plug into the jukebox so they could dance. Other than a couple of burger baskets, Sawyer was pulling beer or else pouring whiskey all evening. Jill called early in the evening to tell him that the surgery was over and they expected Polly to be fine, but to heal slowly at her age.

It was after nine when Betsy Gallagher claimed the only empty bar stool in the place, right beside her cousin, Tyrell.

"Hey, good-lookin'," Betsy yelled over the top of the loud jukebox.

"You talkin' to me?" Sawyer asked.

"Ain't nobody else back there, is there?" Betsy said. "Take a break and dance with me."

"Rule Number One, according to Aunt Polly, is that work and pleasure do not mix. What can I get you to drink, Betsy?"

"You aren't a nice cowboy. Are you going to break my heart so bad that I have to write a country song about it?"

Sawyer smiled. "Sounds like a plan to me. Call me when it hits the charts, and I'll have Polly put it on the jukebox. Beer?"

"Double shot of whiskey. I'm a whiskey girl, and

when I have had about three shots, I get very, very horny," Betsy said.

"Then I'd advise you to stay away from Quaid Brennan. That could cause a whole new phase to the war."

"Quaid is a pansy. He wouldn't know what to do with a real woman."

One second she was grinning at Sawyer. The next, Kinsey Brennan had jerked her off the stool and was screaming something about not calling her cousin names. Fists were flying, right along with hunks of hair, by the time Sawyer made his way around the end of the bar. His first thought was that women fought dirtier than men, because they were going at each other's eyeballs, scratching at whatever skin was bare and landing wild punches everywhere. It put a whole new meaning to catfight, and not a single soul was doing a thing to stop it.

He tried to get ahold of either one of them, but it was like holding onto a greased hog. One minute he had an arm or his hands around a waist, the next it was gone, and there was more screaming and hair pulling. Then out of the blue, Jill Cleary was there beside him.

For a full thirty seconds she watched the fight, and then she went behind the bar, drew up a pitcher of beer, and carried it back around to the floor where a circle of people had gathered. Dollars exchanged hands as to who would come out the winner. The Brennans cheered for Kinsey; the Gallaghers for Betsy. The neutral folks cheered for whoever was on top.

Jill pushed through the people until she was right above the rolling mass of red and blond hair and dumped an entire pitcher of beer right on their heads.

They came up spitting and sputtering, and the fight ended. People headed back to their tables or claimed a bar stool. Betsy's red hair hung in limp strands around her face. Her lacy shirt hung like a dishrag on her body, and pure old unadulterated anger flashed from her eyes.

Kinsey started toward Jill, but Sawyer stepped between them. "It's over. You two get on out of here for tonight. I'll tell you the same thing I told your two cousins. Take it out in the road and kill each other. That way I don't have to go to dinner or supper with either of you tomorrow."

"Well, that's real sweet"—Betsy pointed at Kinsey— "but believe me, darlin', you won't want to touch that once you've seen what I've got to offer."

"You bitch," Kinsey said.

Jill pointed. "Outside, or I'll fill up another pitcher of beer. Sawyer, if you'll go on back to the bar business, I'll take care of the mess."

She took a mop from a closet, filled it with water from the bathroom, and cleaned up the beer, then joined Sawyer behind the bar.

"This is horrible. I can't imagine grown people acting like this for anything or anyone," Jill said.

"I told you earlier. First and foremost it's Fiddle Creek," Sawyer said. "You will inherit, and they both want it, plus you are a prize even without Fiddle Creek. Either one would crow that they'd won you away from the other side. And right now, the feud is in full-blast hot fire. Take your choice. Either one can make your wildest dreams come true. But I've got to tell you, Jill, that pitcher of beer was sheer genius."

She shrugged. "Thank you, but it's not my idea. I saw Aunt Gladys do that with a pitcher of water one time when two dogs were hung up."

Sawyer threw back his head and roared.

"Why is that so funny?"

"Tonight it was two bitches all right, and they were stuck together."

She smiled. "Probably so, but you're going to have to deal with both of them tomorrow. I'd rather deal with struttin' roosters as those two. Sawyer, we are going to have to rethink the bar and store business."

One of his dark eyebrows shot up. "Oh, yeah?"

"I think we'd best stay together in the store and in the bar. It'll take both of us in both places," she said.

"That means very little sleep, except on Sunday."

"It won't be forever. Just until Aunt Polly is on her feet again. And we could take catnaps at the store when it's slow."

"Got a bed in the back room with that stove you mentioned?"

"No, but I know where there's a cot we could set up and take turns taking hour-long naps." She smiled.

"Starting right now?"

She grabbed a bar rag and threw it over her shoulder. "You take care of the grill, and I'll fill beer pitchers and take money."

Tyrell slid onto a stool and crooked his finger at Jill. "A double shot of whiskey, darlin'. You are a feisty one. You really don't want Betsy for an enemy."

"Frankly, I don't give a damn if she's my friend or my enemy. She's not tearing up the bar. It's neutral, just like the store," Jill said.

Sawyer poured up a shot of whiskey and set it on a paper coaster in front of Tyrell.

"Thank you," Tyrell said, but his dark eyes were on Jill, not Sawyer or the whiskey. "Jill, darlin', did I tell you that I'm named after the best-lookin' Sackett brother that Louis L'Amour wrote about? Only my mama put two L's in my name so I'd be twice the lover, but I ain't nothing but a rough old cowboy. I do like my whiskey neat and my women beautiful, and you, darlin', are the prettiest thing I've laid eyes on in years. Please don't be mad at me for fighting in the store or at my cousin for fighting in the bar tonight. I'm sure they'll have to call the undertaker to come haul me out of this bar feetfirst if you break our date."

"I'd hate to see someone as full of shit as you die in Aunt Polly's bar, so I will go to supper with you tomorrow night."

"I will knock on your door promptly at five with roses in my hand."

"And now, Mr. Tyrell Gallagher, named after the famous Tyrel Sackett, only with two L's in his name, I must get back to work. I'll see you tomorrow."

She looked back at Sawyer. Both dark-haired. Both with brown eyes. Both cowboys. What made the difference in the way they affected her? Could it be that one was full of bullshit and the other was honest?

Tyrell picked up the whiskey and downed it in one gulp. "I believe I'll live to dance another day with that shot and the promise of spending time with the gorgeous Jill Cleary tomorrow night."

"Be sure to get her home before midnight. She turns into a rabid coyote when the clock strikes twelve." Sawyer moved on down the bar to fill a pitcher with beer.

"That true, darlin'?" Tyrell asked.

"Got to take the bad with the good," Jill answered.

The jukebox played its last song a few minutes before eleven. The grill was cooling. Beer and margarita pitchers were in the dishwasher.

"I'll sweep if you'll wipe down the tables, and then we'll be done," Sawyer said.

Jill picked up the spray bottle filled with cleaner, and a couple of bar rags, and went to work. Sawyer grabbed a broom.

He'd known her for twenty-four hours. They'd started off arguing, but had quickly worked things out until they were like old friends now. He leaned on the broom handle and stared at her, careful to go back to his job when she straightened up to go on to the next table.

She turned the chairs upside down on the table after she'd wiped them all down, so he could have easy access for sweeping. "Better hurry up and stop taking breaks if you want to get me home by midnight, so I don't turn into a rabid coyote."

"I was trying to help you out there, woman."

"I know that. I wish we could both go back to yesterday and undo tomorrow. I dread it."

"Then be a rabid coyote so neither one of them will like you," he said.

"Might be an idea. If you work faster, you'll get home to that apple pie quicker. It's cool by now, and there's ice cream in the freezer to go with it." She straightened up and rolled her neck to get the kinks out.

He made a big show of sweeping faster. "Work, good

woman. Work fast and hard. I'd forgotten that pie and chocolate cake await us at home. You might have to bake something more on Monday morning."

She flipped two of the three chairs upside down on the last table and sank into one of the remaining ones with a long sigh. "I can't wait until Monday gets here, because then all this Sunday shit will be done with. Hell, I can't even remember their names most of the time. What if I call a Brennan by a Gallagher's name, or vice versa?"

"Say the name three times and picture an animal to go with the name, so you don't call him by the wrong feuding family name. Quaid looks like big old Angus steer to me, so picture a bull. Now the other one, Tyrell, is a wolf for sure, so picture him as that, and you'll never forget his name." Sawyer leaned the broom against the jukebox, sat down in the remaining chair, and propped his feet on the table.

"Quaid the bullshit cowboy. Tyrell the hungry wolf cowboy. You're getting my table all dirty," she said.

"I'll wash it. My feet are tired. At least you are getting red roses. I'm not taking roses or any other kind of flower to Betsy or to Kinsey. Maybe they'll take that as a slight and leave me alone."

She tucked a few strands of flaming red hair behind her ear. "I don't even like roses. I said that so he wouldn't know my favorite flower and bring them. I have a problem relating flowers to people or events, and I damn sure don't want my favorite ones ruined by a one-date cowboy."

"And the favorite ones are?" Sawyer asked.

"Daisies. They outlast roses, and they're tough little flowers. If you tell him…"

Sawyer held up a palm defensively. "I understand. Say no more. Want my advice?"

"Hell, no! But I expect you are going to give it to me anyway."

"Maybe you've gotten off on the wrong foot with them, like I did," he said. "It could be that one or both of them are really decent cowboys. Go with an open mind. Don't think about their last name or where they live or how much money they have or how big their ranch is or even the damned feud. Just spend a little time getting to know them as the men they are, and then make up your mind which one or both or neither that you might like to see again."

She pinched her nose with her thumb and forefinger. "It's going to be a long Sunday."

"Be nice if it was only one day."

"What's that supposed to mean?"

"Darlin', you are the princess of the Fiddle Creek kingdom. Both of the kingdoms beside yours would benefit greatly from the water rights on your land, so they're going to do their damnedest to get one of their knights in shining armor, or maybe its knight in shining pickup truck, to win your favor."

"Aunt Gladys has always said that neither one of those families will ever get Fiddle Creek. Maybe that's all I need to put out on the rumor vine, and they'll leave me alone."

Sawyer chuckled.

She sat up with a start and frowned at him. "What's so funny?"

"You looked in the mirror lately?"

"Of course."

"Enough said, then."

"You best start explaining, or I'm throwing that pie out in the yard," she said.

"I'm repeating myself, and I won't do it again, so listen to me, Jill Cleary. Fiddle Creek would be a nice trophy. Whoever wins gets a woman with ranching experience that looks like a trophy wife. Quaid is going to try to woo you with his good deeds. Tyrell is going to smother you with fun and flowers. The feud is officially blown wide open right now, so everything is fair. Each side wants to win, and you are the prize. It won't be so bad, darlin'. You'll have a big ranch, a cowboy, and a hell of a big diamond engagement ring whichever way you go."

"I'll say no after tomorrow. And what about you? You've also got two after you," she said.

"Quaid and Tyrell are the knights, but the whole castle on both sides, including women, kids, and even the grandmothers are probably already plotting. I've got a feeling I'm part of that plot. If they can put me out of the picture, that's one less cowboy in your world. I think I already said that, didn't I?" Sawyer said.

"How do you know so much about it?"

"You can't be in Burnt Boot two hours without hearing feud stories."

"Dammit!" She slapped the table hard enough that it reverberated right though his boots.

"Now you are beginning to understand. You ready to go home now?"

"I'm ready to go back to Brownsville and get a job making tacos in a fast food joint," she said.

"Ain't neither one of us the kind to run from

problems." He stood up, wiped the table one more time, and set his chair on it. "Polly didn't mention mopping, did she?"

"Just a quick damp mop if there's spills, but I don't see any tonight. She's got a cleaning lady that does that on Sunday when the place is closed. She takes care of the deep cleaning. All we have to do is sweep up every night."

"I'll put the broom up and get our coats," Sawyer said.

It was almost midnight when they reached the bunkhouse, and Jill melted into the corner of the sofa. "Just ten minutes, and then I'm going to take you up on borrowing your shower before I go to bed."

Sawyer went straight to the kitchen. There was only enough leftover coffee for one cup, so he popped it into the microwave. Then he cut a piece of pie big enough for two people and put it on one plate, along with two small pieces of chocolate cake. When the microwave dinged, he picked up the plate with one hand and the coffee with the other.

"We're sharing. I couldn't carry three things." He sat down right next to her and handed her the coffee.

She put it on the end table and picked up one of the forks, ate two bites of pie, and shook her head. "I'm too tired to eat."

"I could feed it to you."

"I'm too tired to chew."

"Then you are on your own. I'm not doing that for you," he said.

She laid her head over on his shoulder and stretched

out her legs until her feet were resting on the well-used coffee table. "Looks like lots of boots have been propped up on that table."

You are getting mighty friendly there, her inner voice chided. *You never snuggled up to a man this quick before. Better watch out, or you'll be making another mistake.*

Hush, she argued. *We're just friends, and he already gave me a foot massage. This is resting, not flirting.*

"Yep, it does look like lots of cowboys have come through this bunkhouse and done just what you're doing. This pie is amazing. I'll just eat all of it, since you are too tired to eat," he said.

"Enjoy. I could sleep right here all night."

"After our last twenty-four hours, it is pretty nice to be in a peaceful place where Gallaghers and Brennans aren't welcome."

"Let's make a pact." She yawned. "Even if you like one of those brazen hussies who got a beer bath tonight, don't bring them into the bunkhouse."

He kissed her on the forehead. "And if you fall for one of those sumbitches, you don't bring them here either."

She snuggled down tighter. "I'm not going to fall for one of them, but I promise I won't bring anyone into our sanctuary."

"Me, either," he said.

Chapter 5

J ILL FOUND IT IMPOSSIBLE TO KEEP A FEW INCHES OF space between her and Quaid. That side of the church was packed with Brennan families, settled into the pews so tight that daylight couldn't get between them. If church services lasted past the customary hour, she feared she'd smother plumb to death right there on the fourth pew between Quaid and Kinsey.

"We're so glad you are coming to Sunday dinner," Kinsey whispered. "It's been a long time since my cousin was interested in someone. We'll have to talk about him later, and I'll tell you how sweet and kind and wonderful he is."

Quaid leaned over and spoke softly in her other ear. "You were such a big help in the Sunday school class. I sure wish you would consent to help me out every Sunday. The girls in there really took to you."

"I need to get settled in before I make any commitments, but thank you for making me feel so welcome," she said.

The section on the other side of the church was filled to capacity too. She was thinking about Sawyer and how lucky he was that he hadn't gotten roped into Sunday school, church, and dinner when she looked past him sitting in the center section. She was actually looking for red hair to see if Betsy came to church that morning, when Tyrell caught her eye. His bright smile and sly wink reminded her that the day was still young.

The Sunday school secretary took his place behind the podium, held up a hand, and all conversation stopped. "We broke our Sunday school attendance record this morning. We haven't had this many people in church since the Christmas programs more than a decade ago. I'm hoping you all made it your New Year's resolution to attend church every Sunday this year." He went on to tell about the Sunday school offering that morning and to make the announcements for the past week concerning births and deaths. Then he covered the events for the coming week: visits to the nursing home in Gainesville, a youth rally in the middle of the week that included supper in the fellowship hall, a baby shower, and a wedding shower.

Jill caught Sawyer's gaze when the man mentioned the youth rally. The unspoken message couldn't be clearer. Thank God she had agreed to help man the bar all week. That would give her a damn fine excuse for not going to the rally. As if on cue, Kinsey cupped her hand over Jill's ear and said, "I'm one of the supervisors of the youth group. I'd love to have your help at the rally. Quaid and I get pretty rushed at these things."

Jill mouthed, "I have to work."

"We could find someone else to help Sawyer at the bar for one night," Kinsey pressed.

Jill shook her head. "Sorry, but I can't do that."

Kinsey pouted. "But I thought you could bring one of your apple pies."

Jill stuck to her guns. "Can't."

Two days and the whole town already knew about her

baking skills. Holy hell, by the end of the week would they know what color underbritches she wore and where she ordered them from?

It was the music director's turn next. A tall, willowy blond, with big brown doe eyes and a red knit dress that left little room for underwear and even less to the imagination, took her place behind the podium. "Some of you might not have heard the news, but Polly Cleary broke her ankle yesterday. She'll be in the hospital a couple of more days, and then she'll be staying with Gladys for a while. Keep her in your prayers. Now let's sing 'Victory Ahead' before the sermon is delivered."

Jill's eyes settled on Sawyer while she sang that by faith she saw victory ahead. Would he stand his ground with those two women, or would they wear him down? Just how strong was he when it came to determined women? She felt sympathy for him, almost as much as for herself. By summer, he might be wishing she had shot him when they first met.

She was glad there wouldn't be test questions on the sermon that morning, because she hadn't heard half a dozen words. She thought he mentioned something about starting over, and she did hear the name Ruth a few times, so possibly she could fake her way through part of the test if it meant going to heaven or being sent straight to hell. She spent most of the time stealing glances over toward Sawyer. Eight times he'd been looking at her at the same time. Three of those he grinned; two of them he winked. It gave her confidence that she could get through the day and that tomorrow would start a brand-new week. Hopefully with no Gallaghers or Brennans to plague them.

—⁓—

"Back the truck in slow like, right up to the chute. Me and Hart will herd them into the truck. Won't take thirty minutes," Eli Gallagher said.

Randy nodded. "This is the first job Granny has trusted us with. Y'all better not mess it up. She said every single one of them hogs, babies and all, was to go in this truck. I'll get parked right up next to the chute and come help y'all herd them, but I'm tellin' you, if there's a single problem, I'll whip both y'all's asses."

"Hey, you're the youngest one of us, so don't try to be the big boss man. We're in this together, and we ain't makin' no mistakes. Granny said that we got to be in Salt Holler by the time the benediction is done at church this mornin', and on our way to Mingus by the time the Brennans realize their hogs are gone," Hart said. "Now back her up easy-like, and we'll make Granny proud."

Randy clicked off the instructions in his head: Load 'em up. Make sure to cover any tracks by runnin' some cattle across the ground after they'd loaded the hogs. Unload them at Wallace's place, and then take the cattle truck to Mingus, Texas, where there was a bull and two heifers waiting to come to Wild Horse Ranch. Job done and alibi in place.

It was the wrong time of year for piglets, so the job wasn't as difficult as it could have been. Lord, rounding up squealing piglets was tougher than herding cats. Eli did have a problem with one old sow that set her heels and lowered her head. Damn near set him on his ass in the mud before he got his balance and was able to turn the pig into the chute. Other than that, it was an easy job.

They were in the hog house and out within the allotted thirty minutes, hogs grunting and squealing in the cattle truck as it made its way back to the main road. Randy and Hart stayed behind to chase about fifty head of cattle across the ground to cover the truck tires, and then jogged to the truck.

"Next stop—Salt Holler and turnin' these over to Wallace," Eli said.

To get to Salt Holler, they had to cross a bridge that should have fallen down years ago and would in no way support a cattle truck. Besides, there was a gate with a padlock closing off the bridge. Eli parked on the far end and grew impatient with the wait after ten minutes.

"Where is he?" Randy asked.

"It's only eleven fifteen," Hart said. "Don't go pissin' your pants yet. Benediction ain't over until smack up twelve o'clock. And if the preacher calls on Quaid Brennan to give it, it might last another ten minutes past that. He does love the sound of his own voice."

Five minutes later, Wallace appeared at the other end of the bridge in an old beat-up pickup with a cage on the back. He was a big man with a bald head and wire-rimmed glasses. He came to the end of the bridge, unlocked the gate and threw it up, and then he held up one finger.

Fog settled around the bridge, giving it an eerie feeling. A freezing mist had started falling that morning. It reminded Hart of an old black-and-white movie about villains appearing in a fog. Wallace didn't look like a machine-gun-toting gangster as he crossed arms as big as hams over his wide chest and waited. But something about his stance made him every bit as scary.

"What does that mean?" Eli asked.

"I reckon he wants one of us to meet him there. I'll go," Hart said.

He bailed out of the truck and stuck out his hand as he drew close to Wallace. "Hello, I'm…"

"That'll be far enough, son, and I don't need to know your name," Wallace said in a deep voice. "Y'all boys get that truck turned around, and then set them pigs loose on this bridge. I'll let my hog dogs out of the truck, and between them and my family, we'll herd them hogs to where we want them. Y'all best keep quiet about this sale, because if the law comes snoopin' around Salt Holler, it's your face that I'm keepin' in my head."

One of Wallace's front teeth was slightly longer than the other one. He didn't blink, and his expression didn't change a whit. Hart felt like he was standing before the devil on judgment day.

"That's a narrow dirt road out there, sir. I'm not so sure we can turn the truck around," Hart said.

"Little place a hun'erd yards backwards that you can nose into, and then back it up to the edge of the bridge. Time you get that done, my family and friends will be here to herd hogs. Once you open the truck gate, your job is done. Now you can get on back in your seats, and I'll slap the side right hard when we get the last one out. That's your signal to get the hell away from Salt Holler."

Hart nodded.

"You be rememberin' what I said, boy," Wallace said. "And tell your granny that it was a pleasure doin' business with her."

"Yes, sir," Hart said and jogged back to the truck,

his cowboy boots sounding like they were beating on a snare drum with every step.

"What did he say?" Eli asked.

A cold shiver ran down Hart's back when he relayed what Wallace had said. "I don't think it's only our cattle truck that isn't allowed to cross that bridge. It's anyone that doesn't live in Salt Holler."

"How do you reckon they intend to get all those hogs across that bridge?" Randy asked. "There's got to be fifty or sixty back there."

"It's need to know, and we don't," Hart said.

Eli put the truck in reverse and watched his side mirrors until he saw the dirt pathway cutting off to the south. He carefully backed into it and then pulled out as if going back the way he came from. When he looked in his mirror again, people lined both sides of the bridge and Wallace waited at the end with a hand up in the air. When the hand went down, Eli applied the brakes.

Hart opened the door, and Wallace yelled, "Y'all boys stay on in the truck. Gates ain't locked. We'll take care of the rest."

Hart slammed the door shut and waited. "This feels crazy, like a scary movie."

"Granny knows what she's doin'," Randy said. "Them Brennans embarrassed us and caused a hell of a lot of damage to the ranch house at the Christmas party when they pulled that plate glass window right out of the wall. Had to replace the carpet and redo the whole damn room, and like to have never got them cows out of the house. We can put up with a scary movie long enough to get these hogs out of the truck."

"Then we drive out to Mingus and get to eat at the Smokestack for supper. Lord, I love that food," Eli said.

"But we will miss getting to meet Tyrell's new woman when he brings her to supper. I'd love to see Quaid's face when he loses his hogs and his woman both." Randy laughed.

"We'll go to Polly's tomorrow night and see her. I hear she's the barmaid there at night, and that Gladys's new foreman is the grill cook."

Wallace slammed the gates shut and rattled the side of the trailer. Eli shifted gears and pulled out.

"We did it," Randy said. "We got our first assignment from Granny, and we did it."

"Y'all know what we have done is felony larceny, don't you?" Hart asked.

Randy slapped him on the shoulder. "Don't be studyin' law right now, Cousin. Just be a Gallagher."

They were heading south on Interstate 35 when the church doors opened and kids poured out like puppies let out of a kennel to romp and play in the pasture.

After the last amen had been said, the Brennan family surrounded Jill, throwing out so many names that they all mixed together. No way would she remember any of them, except Kinsey, with the extra makeup on one cheek, and Quaid with a black eye and a cut across his nose. It was amazing that corn could do that to a big, strong man when it fell from a distance of six feet.

She spotted Sawyer's black truck pulling out of the parking lot as she and Quaid made their way to his big white double-cab vehicle with an extra-long bed. She was in the process of snapping her seat belt when a bright red truck skidded to a stop right in front of her eyes. Tyrell blew her a kiss, held up five fingers, and then sped off toward the only paved road in Burnt Boot. She hadn't seen a single sign to point her toward anything but a one-Sunday-stand for both of the feuding families.

"Hungry?" Quaid's felt hat preceded him into the truck and found its place in the backseat. He strapped the seat belt in place and started up the engine.

"Starving," she said.

"It's a potluck, so there will be plenty."

"You should have told me. I would have brought something. Your family will think I'm horrible, showing up empty-handed," she said.

"My family will think that you are adorable. And guests aren't expected to bring food. A heads-up though. Kinsey's potato salad is fantastic, but Granny's beet salad tastes like shit." He laughed.

His laughter was as deep as his voice and downright sexy. His jeans were creased perfectly, his white shirt spotless, and his leather sports jacket fit his wide shoulders like a glove. Three years ago she would have stumbled over her own two feet to get him to ask her out.

Sawyer had told her to forget about the feud, the size of the ranches and bank accounts, and to focus on the man. There was not one thing wrong with Quaid so far. If he kissed as good as he looked, he'd be quite the catch, but there wasn't a bit of zing, not a single spark or bit of fizzle between them.

"Penny for your thoughts." He pulled out onto the road and turned right.

"Hundred dollar bills couldn't buy them." She smiled. "How far is it to River Bend?"

"River Bend is to your right, but it's about three miles to the lane back to the main house. River Bend is a con-glomerate of several ranches. We've already passed the road back to my land. Anytime you want a tour, I'll be glad to give you one. I've got about a thousand acres."

"How does that work?"

"The land from Fiddle Creek west for more than twenty miles belongs to the Gallagher families, and the whole thing makes up River Bend. Granny still lives in the main house with her youngest son, my uncle, and his family. That's where we're going for dinner today. Kinsey is my sister and has a part-time job as a paralegal in Gainesville, but she helps me out on my ranch too. I hate paperwork, so she takes care of that, and she's good at it," Quaid explained.

"And the whole family is going to be there today?" she asked.

"Everyone that took up our side of the church." He smiled. "Just lookin' over at you makes my heart jump around in my chest. You are gorgeous this morning, Jill. Your sweater is the same color as your mesmerizing eyes."

It might not be the best pickup line she'd ever heard, but it wasn't too bad, and he did seem sincere.

"And here we are." He pulled the truck under a cov-ered circular drive, handed the keys off to a short fellow in a heavy coat and a cowboy hat, and hurried around the front of the truck to open the door for her. The guy didn't look like a butler or a valet, but evidently he was serving as both, because he opened the double front doors for them when they crossed the wide veranda.

"I'll put it close by, Mr. Quaid," he said before he trotted back to the truck. A glance over her shoulder showed that the pasture beside the house was filled with vehicles of one kind or other, with the majority going toward trucks.

Quaid ushered her inside with a hand on her lower back, helped her remove her coat before he took his off, and handed both to an older woman who said, "Welcome to River Bend, Miz Jill. We're glad to have you here. I'm Rita, one of the housekeepers."

Double doors were opened into a massive room to the right where people had already gathered. The aroma of food mingled with scented candles in the middle of at least a dozen round tables with snowy white cloths. A potluck, her ass, this was a full-fledged party, even if there was every kind of food imaginable lined up on tables over there against the wall.

A tall woman with black hair and eyes almost that dark crossed the room and held out her hand to Jill. "I'm Mavis Brennan. Welcome to our little place. You should have brought Gladys with you. She and I go way back."

"Thank you. Aunt Gladys is going back to the hospital to stay with Aunt Polly. I'll tell her that you asked about her," Jill said. "You have a lovely home. Everything looks and smells wonderful."

Mavis nodded. "I love it when I can gather them all home, even if it's only for dinner. Declan, darlin', come meet Jill. This is Declan, my grandson. He and Leah live here with me. And please give my best to Polly. We'll be praying that she gets along all right with this ankle. At our age, we don't heal like you young folks do."

Declan nodded and said something about being pleased to meet her, and then he was gone.

Quaid's arm slipped possessively around Jill's shoulders. "I think it's almost time to eat. We have a place at the head table with Granny."

"Yes, you do. I want you to sit right beside me. You tell Polly to do what they say, because if you ever sit down at our age, you wind up moldin' and dyin'. We'll hope to see you often here at River Bend." Mavis smiled. "I hear you are working at the bar and the store while she's out of commission. I'm sure you'll see lots of Quaid at Polly's. My husband's old granddaddy would have had a fit if he'd known one of his kin was in a bar, but times are changing."

Quaid tapped a water glass with a knife, and the whole room went silent. "Granny, will you say grace?"

"I'm going to ask Declan to do that for us today," she said.

Declan bowed his head, but Jill caught the look on his face and the way he rolled his eyes before he closed them. So the Brennan family had a black sheep, and its name was Declan.

With his hand on her lower back, Quaid steered her toward the table with Mavis and half a dozen other family members. Seated between Quaid and Mavis, she felt like a heifer at the county fair. All eyes were on her, and she was expected to perform well so she'd win the big trophy and a bunch of blue ribbons.

"Jill, this is my uncle Russell. He's Leah and Declan's father, and they live here in the big house with Granny," Quaid said.

Jill smiled and nodded at them. "Pleased to meet you all."

Like Sawyer told her, she assigned animals to each face. She couldn't think of a single animal that Mavis would resemble, with her height, her round face and thick neck, blue eyes, and black hair right out of a beauty shop bottle. She didn't need to, because Mavis wore confidence as well as she did that tailor-made royal-blue suit and that sparkly set of wedding rings that would rival the crown jewels. She'd never forget her name.

A tall, lanky kid that hadn't grown into his height made his way from the back of the room to their table and whispered in Mavis's ear. She turned scarlet and slapped the table with such force that the water glasses shook.

"She's gone too damned far," she said through gritted teeth.

"Grandma?" Quaid said softly.

"My hogs are gone. They vanished in the damned air while we were in church this morning. Every single one of them." Every word got louder, until she was yelling at the end and the whole room went silent.

"Maybe they got out and they're runnin' around on the ranch," Quaid said.

The kid shook his head. "Daddy said to tell Miz Mavis that we checked the whole place. There isn't a single gate open or break in the fence. There's not even any hog footprints around the place showin' where they got out. All we got is cattle prints. It's like they grew wings and flew."

Mavis was on her feet. "Russell?"

He was already pushing back his chair when he said, "You going with me, Mama?"

"Yes, I am. You will all excuse us. Please finish your food and enjoy the afternoon." Mavis didn't even try to lower her voice as she and Russell stormed out of the room. "That damned Naomi Gallagher will pay for this. She did it while we were all in church and the ranch was unprotected. Dammit all to hell! Well, as of right now, we'll be standin' guard, and she'd better watch out, because I'm not takin' this layin' down."

"Is she going to be all right?" Jill asked.

"She will be," Quaid said. "The Gallaghers shouldn't have messed with her pigs. She doesn't trust anyone to take care of them but Adam and his daddy. They know pigs better than anyone in these parts, except for those folks who live down in Salt Holler. Granny hates store-bought meat with a passion."

"This is personal, and Naomi is in deep shit," Kinsey said from the far end of the table. "Grandma is liable to jerk every hair out of Naomi's head when she confronts her."

"Dear God," Quaid groaned. "I'd best go make sure Uncle Russell can handle them both. I hate to do this, Jill, but…"

"I'm going with you," she said.

"This is not the way I expected our first date to go. I'll make it up to you, I promise," he said.

She laid her napkin on the table and stood up. "No problem."

Quaid made a phone call on his way to collect their jackets, and the truck was waiting in front of the door when they arrived.

Mavis shook her head and her finger at the same time. "What in the hell are you doin' here? You've got a date."

"Where are you going?" Quaid asked.

"I'm going to shoot Naomi Gallagher," Mavis said.

"Then I'm going to keep you out of jail."

"How can you do that? You aren't a lawyer. I'd do better with Kinsey." Mavis buckled the seat belt and crossed her arms over her ample bosom.

"Well, you've got me," Quaid said.

Russell turned to his nephew. "One of the others can go. You've got plans."

"I'm the one who's here. We need any more help, someone will be there in ten minutes," Quaid said.

Russell nodded. "Sorry about this, Jill. You'll have to come back another time. Let's go see if we can straighten this out. She's liable to have a stroke and really shoot Naomi if she finds out for sure that she's behind this."

"Why would your grandma think the Gallaghers stole her hogs?" Jill asked as she settled into the passenger's seat and Quaid started the engine.

"It's a long story. Our families have feuded for more than a hundred years."

She pretended to not know anything. "Like the Hatfields and McCoys?"

He nodded. "Modern day. So far none of us have murdered each other, but it might be comin' if Naomi stole Grandma's pigs."

"Why would she do that, anyway, if she does turn out to be the thief? And, besides, wasn't she in church this morning? How could a little old lady do that?"

Quaid's jaw worked like he was chewing bubble gum. "She wouldn't, but her family would. This is horrible. We shouldn't be following Grandma out to Wild Horse Ranch to confront Naomi on our first date."

First date, hell. It was their last date. She didn't want

to be mixed up in any of this shit. To top it all off, she'd be there with Quaid, with all appearances saying she was supporting the Brennans, and she had a supper date with Tyrell Gallagher. She couldn't wait to get home and tell Sawyer all about it. Come to think of it, he was at the Gallaghers right now, having dinner with them. Did that mean they were on opposing teams?

They reached the stone entrance into Wild Horse, and a man held up a hand to stop them from crossing the cattle guard. Russell and Quaid both rolled down their driver's side windows and leaned out.

"Mama has come to talk to Naomi," Russell shouted.

"Brennans don't come no closer, and they do not cross onto Wild Horse. Read the sign." He pointed.

"Trespassers will be prosecuted. Brennans will be shot," Jill read aloud. "Do they mean it?"

"We've got one on our fences, only it says that Gallaghers will be shot," Quaid said. "We mean it. We assume they do."

"We just want Naomi to tell Mama that she had nothing to do with her hogs going missing this mornin'," Russell said.

"Granny is entertaining dinner guests. Y'all go on back home."

"Did the Gallaghers steal our hogs?" Russell asked.

"You call the sheriff. He can come onto Wild Horse and check every square inch of our property. You won't find a single hog here. We don't raise those filthy things, and we damn sure don't want them on our place. They stink worse than Brennans."

The passenger side door opened, and Mavis crawled out. She marched right up to the stone entryway, but she didn't put a foot on the cattle guard. "I know Naomi is behind this, and those hogs were worth enough that this will draw someone some jail time when I find them. You tell her that she's going to wish she'd never been born."

"Get on out of here, you crazy old woman," the man said.

Russell pushed out of the truck and marched right up to the man. "You don't talk to my mama like that."

"Well, you don't accuse my granny of thievery," the man yelled back in his face.

"You better hope she didn't instigate this, or she'll spend the rest of her years behind bars. I don't give a shit if she's an old dingbat who steals pigs," Russell yelled.

The man threw the first punch.

Jill sat there in stunned silence.

Quaid groaned and slung open his door, left it hanging in the cold wind, and ran onto Wild Horse property to separate the two men rolling around on the ground in their Sunday best. The first person he had to get control of was Mavis. She was kicking, hitting, and slapping the Gallagher grandson like a madwoman.

Since she was his date, Jill thought that she really should go help Quaid, but she didn't want to be accused of fighting for either side. She heard him yell her name, and she bailed out of the truck.

"Sit with Granny in the truck while I get a handle on Daddy. I swear he will be in the hospital with chest pains over this," Quaid said.

"Damn rotten Gallaghers. Lower than chicken shit. I swear they should be wiped off the face of the earth," Mavis cussed as she strapped her seat belt. "Dammit to hell!" Mavis hit the dashboard hard enough to wince.

"Now I'll have a bruise on my hand, and that's her fault too. Next time I see her outside of church, I'm going to scratch her old eyes out and feed them to the coyotes."

Russell was huffing and puffing when Quaid finally pulled the two men apart and guided his father back to the truck. The grandson had taken his phone from his pocket and was making a call as they drove away.

Jill checked the clock on the dashboard. The whole thing hadn't lasted fifteen minutes, but when it was going on, it seemed like a month. Maybe she should have kept right on driving to Wyoming or Montana instead of coming to Burnt Boot. There were ranches there that could always use help.

Betsy sat on one side of Sawyer with one of the Gallagher cousins, Eli, on Sawyer's other side. Naomi Gallagher, the queen of the Gallagher clan, was on the other side of Betsy. It was easy to see where Betsy got her red hair and her spiciness. When she was seventy years old, she'd probably look and act just like Naomi. It wouldn't surprise Sawyer if Betsy didn't grow up to be the next Gallagher matriarch who carried the feud flag for the family.

The salad was crisp. The potato soup scrumptious. The steaks out-of-this-world tender. Then there was dessert, which was turtle cheesecake served with good dark coffee. He'd barely gotten the first bite into his mouth when Betsy's hand slipped under the floor-length tablecloth and started at his knee and made a slow journey to his thigh.

He cut his eyes over at her to see that she had turned

to say something to her grandmother. Evidently she caught him looking at her from her peripheral vision, because she gave his thigh a gentle squeeze and moved on up to start massaging what lay beneath his zipper.

He inhaled deeply, and she patted his thigh before she turned with a smile and whispered, "Just a taste of what is to come later when we take a tour of the ranch."

The steak didn't taste nearly as good after that as he tried desperately to think of an excuse to go home early. "Pardon me," he said. "My phone is buzzing. I'm so sorry. I have the sound turned off, but…"

He removed the phone from his pocket and took a look at it. "I'm sorry, Betsy, but I have to take this. I'll step outside. Y'all excuse me."

Putting the phone to his ear, he laid the white linen napkin on the table and nodded a couple of times on his way through the door out onto the patio. "Yes, I'll be right there," he said in case anyone was watching and could read lips.

"What is it?" Betsy said so close behind him that he jumped.

"It's Gladys. She's gone to the hospital to be with Polly, and there's a cow down having trouble. I need to go pull a calf. Sorry to cut this short," he said.

"How'd she know that if she's at the hospital?" Betsy asked.

"A kid on a four-wheeler called her. Don't know who it was."

"Well, darlin', good things come to those who wait, and you are worth waiting for. Next weekend, we'll give it another whirl." Betsy plastered herself to his body, tangled her fist into his hair, and rolled up on her toes to kiss him. He'd never felt less passion, heat, or feeling in a kiss before in his entire life. It was more like his mouth had been attacked than kissed.

"I'm not making promises for anything," he said when he could break away. "What with Gladys and Polly both busy, Jill and I are going to have our hands full. Give my apologies to your grandmother for leaving early, and I'll see you around," he said as he made a hasty retreat to his truck.

A couple of men waved him through the cattle guard, and he could have sworn he saw a redhead in the back of a truck barreling down the highway at breakneck speed on his way back to the main road. But Betsy was in the house with her family, and there was no way Jill Cleary would be headed for Wild Horse.

Quaid drove right up in front of the bunkhouse, held the truck door open for her, and walked her up to the porch.

"Again, I'm sorry for all this," he said.

"Not a problem. Stuff happens in all families," she said.

She had two hours to change clothes and get ready for supper on the Gallagher side of Fiddle Creek. What she really wanted was a long, long nap and a big thick book to read until she fell asleep, but a promise was a promise. And once she'd done her duty at Wild Horse, then she'd never set foot on either ranch again.

He removed his hat and held it in one hand while he ran the back of his other one down her cheek from temple to chin. "I want to spend more time with you, Jill. Next time we'll take a drive around all of River

Bend, and I'll show you where Kinsey and I call home. We'll steer clear of the feuding business."

His green eyes went all soft and dreamy. She moistened her lips with the tip of her tongue a moment before the kiss. It was a good kiss, a man's kiss who'd honed his craft to an art; one that left no doubt that Declan wasn't the only black sheep on River Bend. One hand had tangled itself into her hair for leverage. The other had slid down below belt level on her slim-cut denim skirt to cup her butt. Her hormones should have been humming, but there wasn't a peep out of them.

"Until next time. I'll be by the store tomorrow," he whispered seductively.

"Then I'll see you tomorrow." She took a step back and opened the door.

He brushed a sweet kiss across her lips and settled his hat back on his blond hair.

The second one didn't stir up anything more than the first one did. Not even one little hitch in her heartbeat. Maybe there was something drastically wrong with her.

Chapter 6

"CINDERELLA MADE IT HOME, DID SHE?" SAWYER peeked over the back of the sofa. His dark eyes still had sleep in them, and his face showed slight amusement. "Did poor old Quaid get a good-bye kiss, or was the afternoon so good that it was a see-you-later kiss? I heard that you had to cut your dinner short, since there was a pig incident."

She pushed his legs off the sofa and melted into the corner. "You should have been there, Sawyer, instead of up there in the big house, eating dinner with the Gallaghers. The Brennans figured out that the pigs had been stolen, and Mavis tried to kick the shit out of one of Naomi Gallagher's grandsons."

Sawyer's skin turned scarlet. "You're shittin' me, and I missed it all for a damn steak that wasn't even good."

"How'd you get home before me, anyway?"

"I made the excuse that I needed to do the evening chores early. Hey, did I see you in a truck headed toward the Gallagher place?"

She pushed him on the shoulder. "You probably did, because I was."

He grabbed his shoulder and faked injury. "Don't be mean to me."

"I wouldn't do that to a man I'm livin' with," she said. "If you can get me out of this next date, I'll clean the whole bunkhouse next week."

"Sorry, sweetheart. You gave your word. Tyrell will be here with roses in his hand in fifty-five minutes, but I do make this promise. I'll do my damnedest to run interference, so you won't have to go out with them again, if you'll do the same for me. Looks like we are going to have to watch each other's backs, or we'll both go down as collateral damage in this war. Now tell me more about this pig thing."

"I'm tired. I don't want to go. I don't want roses. I'd rather stay here and tell you what happened when they fired the first shot of the pig war," she whined.

"You've got enough time to do both." He grinned. "So start talking. Gladys laughed when she called me and said the same thing, that it would be known as the pig war."

Jill told the story from start to finish, omitting the kiss at the end. "Now tell me how it looked from the other end."

"I wouldn't know. I must've left just before the fireworks. Betsy felt me up under the tablecloth, so I faked a phone call. I'm supposed to be pulling a calf right now, but I don't think God will lay the sin of lying to my charge when it comes to Betsy. Lord, that woman is brazen."

Jill gasped. "You are kiddin' me. She actually did that?"

"Yes, she did. Right up my knee to…"

She slapped her hands over her ears. "Hush! That goes beyond brazen. Did she kiss you too?"

"If you call that grinding of two lips against mine, then I guess she did. You didn't answer me about Quaid. Kiss or no kiss?"

"Kiss. Not bad. Not good. Generic, I guess. Rub my

feet, and tell me that you'll call the Gallaghers and tell them I have an intestinal flu and can't go to their place."

"Nope. I have to go listen to the Brennans bitch because their hogs have been stolen, so you have to go to the Gallaghers. Take off your high heels and throw those feet up here. Poor little things. The way you women punish them with those kinds of shoes should be a sin."

Chapter 7

SAWYER RUBBED HER FEET UNTIL HER EYES GREW heavy, and she was almost asleep before he set them on the cold floor. "Get your cute little ass up off this sofa and go do whatever it is you women do to be gorgeous for a date. Next Sunday, I'm figuring that we need to go to Gainesville right after church to pick up supplies. We could get them at the store, and we will, but we will forget milk or eggs or even sugar, and Lord knows we can't live without whatever the hell we forgot until Monday morning."

"That won't take all afternoon," she groaned.

"They've got motels. We'll split the price of a room with two beds. You can read, and I'll take my earphones and watch television all afternoon."

"Isn't that running from our problems?" she asked.

"Hell, no! It's well-spent money on hours of peace and quiet. You bring the cookies, and I'll bring a case of beer. We'd spend that much on dinner and a movie if we were dating, which we sure as hell aren't," he said.

She sat up slowly. "Aunt Gladys says that you can endure anything as long as there's an end in sight. I'm tough. I can do this. But why the hell aren't we dating?"

"You're not my type. I don't date women who point shotguns at me. I don't date women who can't cook, even though you make a hell of an apple pie. There's only one little bitty piece left in there."

She flipped around to face him. "You ate half a pie after a dinner at the Gallaghers?"

"Nope, I ate half a pie after I didn't finish my dinner at the Gallaghers." He grinned. "Shoo!" He flipped his hands out to motion her away. "Go change clothes six times and stand in front of the mirror. I'll tell you if your jeans make your butt look fat." He flopped back down on the sofa, shut his eyes, and stretched out his long legs until his feet rested in her lap.

She shoved them off and stood up. "You are horrible."

"I'm your roommate, darlin', not your relationship. Roommates are honest with each other."

"In that case, darlin'," she said, "your soup needs a little more picante sauce to make it good."

"Ouch!" He opened one eye. "You don't have to talk mean about my soup because your butt looks fat in them low-ridin' jeans."

She flounced off to her room. He made her mad, but at the same time he kept her from thinking about another long evening, trying to remember people's names that she had no intention of ever seeing again outside of the store and the bar.

She changed four times, not six, and she looked at her rear end every time. He was right—the low-riding jeans did make her butt look bigger than the ones that sat a little higher.

At five o'clock on the button, a loud, demanding knock sent her out of her room and across the floor. "Why didn't you let him in? It's cold out there," she fussed at Sawyer.

"Ain't my boyfriend or my roses. I don't give a shit if he freezes and the roses have ice on them,"

Sawyer mumbled as he flipped over so his back was to the room.

She slapped him on the shoulder when she passed by. "You are horrible."

"Maybe so, but my soup is fine the way it is, and your butt looks almighty fantastic in them jeans. If you shoot a game of pool, at least the top of your thong underbritches won't show. Have a good time. I'll wait up for you."

"Don't bother. I know how to get inside. And right back at you on the good-time shit. We'll compare notes when I get home."

"Alone? Remember our pact."

"Hush," she hissed and then put on her best fake smile as she opened the door. "Hello, Tyrell. You are right on time."

"One perfect red rose for one perfect red-haired beauty." He held out a long-stemmed rose wrapped in cellophane. "Each time we go out, I will add a rose to the ones I bring you, but none will ever be as important as this one."

"Why is that?"

"Because today is the first day of a perfect relationship that will last forever," he said as he put the rose in her hands.

"Sawyer, I'm putting my rose on the table right inside the door. Will you please put it in water?"

One thumb shot up over the back of the sofa.

"Thank you, Sawyer. And thank you, Tyrell. It's truly beautiful."

"I see you already have your coat on and, darlin', that rose can't compare to your beauty. I'm going to be the envy of all the Gallaghers at the party tonight." He crooked his arm, and she slipped hers through it.

Wild Horse Ranch's setup was a lot like the one for River Bend. Different families had their own acreage, but the whole thing combined to make Wild Horse. It all bordered on Fiddle Creek. He drove down his lane and showed her where his long, low ranch house, with a sweeping porch around three sides, sat in a pecan copse before he took her to the main house.

There wasn't a valet at the Gallagher place, and they were one of the last ones to arrive, so they had to walk from the truck to the house. He laced his fingers in hers and didn't let go until they were inside the warm house. He helped her remove her coat and whistled under his breath, "Whew! Darlin', you really are a knockout in that getup. You look like you should be modeling for a Western-wear company."

She wore a black shirt with long, billowy sleeves caught up at the wrists with white pearl snaps on the cuffs. A gold scarf pendant with crossed six-guns over angel wings hung from the center of a black lace scarf, and a matching belt buckle cinched in a pair of black jeans.

"Well, thank you. I hope I'm not overdressed."

"Honey, you could have worn a burlap bag with a rope around your waist, and I would have thought I'd brought the princess to the ball, but, wow," he said.

"Well, look at you!" Betsy met them at the door into the oversized great room. "Tyrell, you lucky dog. I believe she's gotten all dolled up for you. You did leave the pitcher of beer at home, I hope. I'm here to steal you away and introduce you to my grandmother, Naomi. Sorry, Tyrell."

"I'll be around to collect her in a few minutes, so don't let Granny get started on her long stories," Tyrell said.

Naomi Gallagher spun around on a bar stool and motioned toward Betsy. She was a short woman with delicate features, few wrinkles, and dark green eyes.

"I see where you get your red hair," Jill said.

"Oh, yes, and my temper and my controlling nature. And my hang-on-like-a-bulldog-until-I-get-what-I-want attitude. It all comes from her. I bet you've got one like her in your woodpile."

Jill nodded. "Yes, I do."

"Well, would you look at this? You grew up to be a beautiful woman, Jillian. I'm glad you've had the good sense not to dye your red hair. That speaks volumes to me," Naomi said.

"Have we met?" Jill asked.

"When you were a little girl, Gladys brought you over here to Tyrell's birthday party. Don't you remember it? I believe you were about seven, and folks thought you and Betsy were sisters."

"I'm sorry. I don't. I remember visiting Aunt Gladys a few times before my dad died, but I don't remember being here."

"Oh, it wasn't here. We had the party in the barn, and we had pony rides."

"I remember that," Betsy said. "You and Tyrell had an argument about the spotted pony."

Jill gasped. "That was Tyrell?"

"Yes, it was. We'll have to tell him that story later, but now you must sit down here. Bartender, darlin', bring us two whiskeys. Jameson. Double shots and neat. Good Irish lasses don't water down their whiskey," Naomi said.

Jill hopped up on a bar stool. It had been a long time since she'd had a shot of Jameson, and she intended to savor every single drop of it.

"How's Gladys? I don't get over to the store much anymore. I only see her in church, and she's lookin' good. She's not sick, is she?" Naomi asked. "That's not why you came back to learn the business, I hope."

"Aunt Gladys is fine, but I suppose you heard about Aunt Polly breaking her ankle."

"I did. I'll send over some flowers when she comes home," Naomi said. "You girls excuse me. One of my grandsons is over there, motioning for me. I'll have to see what he needs."

"How's the new calf?" Betsy asked.

It was on the tip of Jill's tongue to ask what calf she was talking about, but then she remembered how Sawyer had gotten free from her clutches.

"I haven't seen it yet, but I bet it's a beauty. Don't you just love them when they're little guys and they like to romp and play?" Jill said.

The bartender set a whiskey in front of her, and a frosted mug of beer before Betsy. Jill raised one eyebrow, and Betsy shrugged. "I like Jack Daniel's, but today is a beer day."

Jill took the first sip, and Tyrell propped a hip on the stool right beside her. He pointed at the Coors handle, and the bartender nodded. His arm went around Jill's shoulders, and he leaned in to whisper, "Thank you for drinking that. Granny's going to love you for it. The rest of us hate Irish whiskey."

"It's the best," she said softly.

"I heard that you were out at the gate when the fracas went down this afternoon," Betsy whispered. "I don't expect, after a first date like that with Quaid, you'll be going back for more, will you?"

Jill raised one shoulder. "Never say never."

Betsy smiled. "Mavis is really bad, isn't she? My cousin, Eli, said she tied into him like a banshee over those hogs, blaming us for their disappearance."

Jill changed the subject. "How long has this feud been goin' on?"

"You'd have to ask someone older than me," Betsy said.

"Well, if y'all are done with the girl talk, supper is about ready. I promise, darlin', that we'll act more civilized than your dinner date turned out," Tyrell said.

People were everywhere. Names blending one with the other, but not matching the faces. When it was time to leave, she could remember Tyrell, Betsy, and Naomi.

She was supposed to be giving points to each family, but mostly she wished she was home on her sofa in the bunkhouse with Sawyer on the other end. A foot massage would be nice, but leaning her head on his shoulder would be better. Maybe with an ounce of luck, she could hurry into the house without a kiss when the evening ended.

There was no luck.

Tyrell walked her to the door and caged her against the house by putting a hand on either side of her shoulders. He'd left his hat in the truck, so it didn't even get in the way when he closed the space, fluttered his eyes shut, and kissed her hard right there in the moonlight with the north wind howling through the trees. He was every bit as good as Quaid, showing he'd had some very fine experience in the kissing business.

But again, there were no bells and whistles, no weak knees or even a desire to snake her arms up around his neck and press her body close to his. It was a good kiss, but it did nothing for Jill.

"I'll see you at the bar tomorrow night, darlin'," he said softly. "I'll be the one on the bar stool, drooling on my shirt at your beauty."

"Good night, Tyrell. Thank you for the evening and the rose." She ducked under his arm and opened the door.

"Invite me in for a cup of coffee," he said.

"Not tonight. I have to get up early to run the store." She waved and eased the door shut before he could say another word.

Sawyer looked up over the back of the sofa the same way he'd done earlier. "So was this one any better?" he asked.

She removed her coat and hung it on one of the huge nails on the wall inside the entryway. "The whiskey was better. I had a double shot of Jameson."

"Don't go teasing me about good Irish whiskey. That happens to be my favorite." He sat up and motioned her to the sofa.

"Where's my rose? Did you put it in water?"

He pointed to the kitchen table. "Yes, ma'am. I aim to please."

She gasped. "Sawyer O'Donnell!"

"You said to put it in water. I did that, didn't I?"

There it sat, crammed down into a Mason jar, blossom on the bottom, the stem sticking up in the air with the paper still around it. "You got to admit, it looks fine for a rose. If it had been a daisy, it would be right-side up. Now it will be drowned by morning, and you can toss it over the pasture fence without feeling guilty."

"Tell me about the Brennan date," she said. "Did Kinsey come on to you?"

"She was worse than Betsy. She walked me to the truck and tried to climb my frame. Had my belt buckle undone and was working on my zipper before I could…"

"No more," she cut him off. "Don't tell me any more. Why? I mean you are a damn fine-looking cowboy, but that's acting like a hussy."

"I imagine that they expect me to have sex with them one time, then they'll shout that they are pregnant. The family of whichever one gets the sex first will make me marry her, and that will get me off Fiddle Creek. It's all a game, and I'm not playin' with either of them or getting myself shoved into a corner with them either. You are going to protect me."

"Only if you make good on your word and do the same for me." She plopped down on the sofa and stretched her legs out.

He picked up her feet and put them in his lap, removed her boots, and massaged her feet. "Poor little doggies have had too much party put on them today."

"That is wonderful," she moaned.

He removed her socks and dug his fingers into all the pressure points. His touch made every nerve tingle, from the top of her head all the way down to her little toes. If either one of those cowboys she'd seen that day had caused a reaction like that, she might have consented to go out with them again.

"Now, princess, it is eleven o'clock, and you need a long, hot bath to get all that feudin' stink off you. How was the last cowboy's kisses? Any better? As good?"

She shrugged.

"That bad, huh." He shoved her feet down to the floor, slid down the sofa, and cupped her face in his hands.

She barely had time to moisten her lips and shut her eyes before his mouth closed in to claim hers in a fiery-hot kiss. She felt as if her whole body was floating off the sofa toward the ceiling. His hands on her cheeks were the only thing that kept her grounded. Her arms went around his neck. Both hands twisted into his hair for better leverage as his tongue found its way past her lips to do a beautiful two-step with hers.

Sweet Jesus! A kiss had never done that to her before. She wanted more, to see if it would be the same the next time, but he pulled away and stood up.

"They say the third is the charm, darlin'. When you decide to kiss and tell, you let me know if they're right."

He swaggered off to his room, shut the door almost all the way, and left her sitting on the sofa with weak knees, a racing pulse, and a jittery feeling down deep in her gut.

She made it to her bedroom, but her head was still reeling when she flopped down on top of the covers and touched her lips to see if they were as hot as they still felt.

Chapter 8

"Hey, Aunt Gladys, where are you?" Jill yelled from the front of the store.

There was no answer, but she could hear the meat grinder going, so she hung her coat and hat on the rack and went to work. Most of the suppliers arrived on Monday morning, so the bread shelves had been restocked. But the aisles were full of boxes to be unpacked onto the shelves.

"Thank goodness," she said.

The noise stopped. "That you, Jill?"

"Yes, ma'am."

"Give me a minute to take off this apron and wash my hands, and I'll tell you about Polly. She gets to come home tomorrow morning, as long as she has help, so I'm putting her in my spare bedroom." She raised her voice a notch over the sound of running water. "I've got the meat counter filled all the way up to capacity, and I'm going to Salt Holler for a whole hog this afternoon so we'll be well stocked. I might need you to come in for a few days earlier than we'd planned, since she'll require more help here at first. I was goin' anyway, but Wallace called and said they'd had a big butcherin' day yesterday. His whole family came for it, and he's got a lot of meat on hand. I'm getting a whole hog and half of another one. Since Mavis ain't got her own hogs to butcher, she'll be needin' some decent meat. At least these hogs haven't been raised in a factory. Wallace has good pigs."

"Will we sell that much pork in a week?" Jill asked.

Rubbing sweet-smelling lotion into her hands, Gladys came out into the store and smiled. "Honey, feudin' brings in the business. It's going to be wild around here, and then you toss in the fact that both parties are out after your undying love, why, people will be comin' here in droves."

"But I'm not going out with either one of them again," she said.

"You think either one of them is going to lay down and roll over like a defeated puppy? By saying no, you'll fire the whole thing up hotter and hotter, so the job description has changed. Besides, if I dropped dead tomorrow, you'd have to run the whole place by yourself with no one but Sawyer to help you."

"I can come in whenever you need me, but once Aunt Polly is settled, I want to drop by and see her once a day too," she said.

"Don't go feelin' guilty because you didn't get down to the hospital. She's been sleepin' a lot anyway, and she told me to tell you that you were needed here more than there."

"Good mornin'." Sawyer's deep voice filled the whole store. "I'm only five minutes late. Hope I didn't miss anything, but I got the alfalfa field disked this morning after feeding chores. And then I started workin' out in the tack room, organizing it, and time got away from me."

He hung his coat and hat on the rack beside hers. They looked so personal hanging there beside each other, as if they belonged together. She touched her lips as a vision came to mind of him walking away from her the night before. He'd worn flannel lounging pants and a chocolate-brown T-shirt then. Now he had on jeans, a blue-and-brown-plaid shirt, and his work boots, but the swagger was still the same. The jittery feeling from simply remembering the kiss told her that yes, sir, the third was the charm.

You're not a teenager with raging hormones. You are a grown woman. You can work with this cowboy from noon until eleven o'clock every night, she reminded herself sternly.

Gladys picked up her coat off the back of a chair behind the meat counter and shoved her arms into it. "I'm glad you are going to be here with Jill, Sawyer. This is the hottest I've seen the feud in my lifetime. They've done some crazy things, but they've never done something so stupid as to steal hogs. We'll be hiring some extra help in the spring, and then hire some more in the summer for the store, so this won't be forever."

Sawyer popped open one of the three metal folding chairs and sat down. "Tell Polly hello for me, and I'll drop by when she gets home."

Gladys patted him on the shoulder. "I will do that, but right now, I'm going to the holler to buy a hog and a half."

Jill wanted to tell her aunt Gladys that she didn't want any part of this crazy life, to throw her things in the back of her little dark-green truck and head north. She could be in Montana by Wednesday if she didn't stop for anything but bathroom breaks and to grab a hamburger.

A Cleary does not run, she reminded herself sternly.

"How many customers have you had this morning?" Jill asked.

"Not a single solitary one. That means the storm is gathering strength. It will hit with enough power to blow my poor little general store off the map this afternoon. Oh, and, Jill, since y'all are having to work such long hours, I'm doubling your salaries until we hire in some help."

"You don't have to do that," Jill said.

"You said you wanted to work all you could to get your mind cleared, and I don't expect you to work for pennies. Y'all hold it down now, and I'll call you later." Gladys picked her coat from the rack. Sawyer stood up and helped her put it on, and then wrapped her scarf loosely around her neck. "Thank you. See y'all after a while. Verdie is going to sit with Polly until I get back from Salt Holler. Y'all need anything special from Salt Holler?"

"Like special what?" Jill asked.

"Oh, like a pint of special brewed blueberry wine, or maybe a jar of moonshine?"

"One of each," Sawyer answered.

"Consider it done. Hold down the fort and keep the shelves stocked. There's extra supplies in the storeroom." Gladys talked as she made her way to the front. "I've got my cell phone in my purse, so call me if you run into trouble and can't find anything. Looks like Hurricane Kinsey has arrived. Duck and dodge, Sawyer. And don't laugh, Jill. I see Quaid parking right beside her."

"I'll flip you for which one of us gets to hide in the storeroom," Sawyer whispered.

"Strength in numbers," she answered. "Hello, Kinsey. Can I help you with something?"

"I'm meeting Quaid here to do some shopping for the week." She unbuttoned a long black coat to reveal a black-and-white sweater hugging every single curve, and an equally snug, short black skirt that showed lots of leg in dark panty hose. She was tall and willowy, and in those spike-heeled boots, she and Sawyer were almost the same height.

Jill felt dowdy in her jeans, work boots, and a Western-cut shirt she hadn't even bothered to tuck in. She should have taken time to put on makeup and done something with her hair other than pull it up in a ponytail.

"I'm not one to beat around the bush," Kinsey said. "I like what I'm lookin' at"—she took a step back and slowly went from Sawyer's toes all the way up to his dark hair, hesitating a few extra seconds at his belt buckle—"and I'm asking you out, not to a family dinner, Sawyer, but on a date. I understand you work every night at Polly's, so next Sunday we'll leave right after church. I know a cute little place in Dallas, and then we'll see a movie or do something to while away the rest of the evening. Now, Quaid, honey, how much of that sliced ham do we need for the week? And you might call Granny and ask her if she wants us to bring anything for her from the meat counter. We've got our own beef, but our pork freezer is empty. We'd planned on butcherin' next week."

"A pound should do for us, and I'm not callin' Granny, because she's still cussin' mad," Quaid said.

He'd closed the space between him and Jill so quietly, she wasn't aware he was that close until his warm breath brushed her bare neck. She jumped and whirled around to find that he had four eyes and two noses. She blinked and took a step back so she could focus.

He put a hand on her shoulder and smiled brightly. "Sorry. I didn't mean to sneak up on your blind side. I wanted to tell you again how much fun I had yesterday, and to apologize once more for the way it turned out. The whole family fell in love with you. Granny Mavis has invited the two of us to dinner next Sunday so she can get to know you better and make it up to you. Then, I thought I'd show you my place in our horse-drawn carriage."

She glanced over her shoulder at Sawyer. Bless his heart. His face told the story, and it wasn't pretty.

"Thank you for the invitation." Jill raised her voice enough that Kinsey could hear what she had to say to Quaid. "But Sawyer and I have made plans for that afternoon."

Kinsey whipped around so fast that the tail of her coat slapped Sawyer on the leg. "Are you two more than roommates?"

"That's a very personal question, ma'am," Sawyer drawled.

"Which requires a personal answer," she said.

"I'd say that's our business. Now how much ham did you want, again?" Jill asked.

"A pound of ham and the same amount of white American cheese, and half a pound of bologna. Quaid, honey, you get two loaves of bread and a gallon of milk," Kinsey said. "And, Sawyer, you might do well to remember I get what I want, and I can make you a very happy man. And I never, ever give up until I have what I want. I will wear you down. Now I'm going to do some shopping, and since I understand you have a sweet tooth, I'll bring something to the bar tonight that's especially for you."

"Hello, Sawyer!" Betsy pushed her way into the store.

Thank God she was dressed in boots, jeans, and a denim duster, and had a dusty felt hat pulled over her red hair. The general store wasn't big enough for two fancy-smancy divas. Jill would have had to shoot one of them or shove them out the door and hope they killed each other.

"Hey, Kinsey, what are you doing in Burnt Boot on a Monday morning? Aren't you supposed to be doing important lawyer shit?" Betsy asked.

"I'm asking Sawyer out on a date. What are you doing in the store on Monday? Aren't you supposed to be shoveling shit?" Kinsey fired right back.

"Did he accept?" Betsy asked coldly.

"Not this time," Kinsey answered.

"Maybe you ought to shovel some shit. He's a rancher, not a lawyer who wears three-piece suits and likes to go to Dallas for supper. Oh, excuse me, that would be dinner in your world, wouldn't it?"

"Ladies, I'm not a piece of beef for sale in the meat counter," Sawyer said. "I'm not going out with either of you, and that's final. Now can I help you with something other than dating or catfighting? Remember, this store and the bar are neutral territory."

Evidently he'd gotten his bearings, and they weren't going to talk him into anything again. But there wasn't a man on the face of the earth who wouldn't be flattered to have two women fighting over him, no matter what the reason.

"Looks like a party going on in here." Tyrell poked his head in the door. "Betsy, Granny is making dumplings for supper, and she said we'd better be there. Hey,

Jill." He blew a kiss her way. "I'll see you tonight at Polly's. I'll be the one hogging the jukebox, and every song will be for you."

"I'll be right back. I've got a cake in the oven." Jill disappeared into the storeroom. She did turn on the oven to preheat, and she did plan to put a cake in the oven, so it wasn't too much of a lie. Then suddenly she realized that the store was too quiet. Lord, what if they'd kidnapped Sawyer and carried him off to some remote area? She peeked out the door and exhaled loudly. He was over there stocking shelves like he'd been born to do that rather than run a ranch single-handedly.

"Is the coast clear?" she hollered.

"For now. They've all gone home. But I see two more vehicles pulling in, so you'd better get on out here and stop hiding in the storeroom. That cake idea was pretty slick," he said.

"It was the best I could do. If I'd had to put up with those two men another minute, I would have bonked them both on the head with cans of peaches."

"Why peaches?"

"The cans are bigger than corn. It was so quiet, I thought those two women had kidnapped you."

"Did that make you sad?" His eyes twinkled, and a smile tickled the corners of his mouth.

Dammit! Why did she have to look at his mouth? That made her think of that amazing kiss, and that put a little extra giddy-up in her pulse. "It sure did. I didn't want to stock shelves and slice bologna and still keep everyone from killing each other." She smiled sweetly.

"I saved you from a carriage ride with Quaid, and you treat me like that. You could have said that you liked me enough to worry about me if they'd kidnapped me," Sawyer teased.

She bit the inside of her lip, and her brow wrinkled in a frown. "I understand that they both want Fiddle Creek, but isn't there supposed to be something like friendship and love involved in a relationship?"

Sawyer's fist shot up toward the ceiling. "Testify, sister!"

Jill had never giggled. Even as a child, when something struck her as funny, she laughed from the belly, and it sounded like it had erupted from a three-hundred-pound truck driver. That day it rattled around in the store like a rock band practicing in a bathroom.

"It wasn't that funny," Sawyer said.

"Yes, it was. I needed to laugh like that, so thank you. Here comes the next round, but I don't recognize them as Gallaghers or as Brennans, do you?"

He shook his head. "No, but there's so many uncles, aunts, and cousins on both sides that I wouldn't swear to anything. Just duck and dodge if the bullets start flying."

The door swung open and started a steady flow of traffic for the next two hours. By the end of the day, they'd worked out a system. Sawyer worked the meat market and stocked when he had time. Jill worked the counter, checking folks out and sacking groceries.

When it finally slowed down, Jill went straight to the storage room, drug out two lawn chairs, and popped them open behind the meat counter. "I'm hiding for a ten-minute break." She slumped into one and propped her boots up on the rungs of the table holding the meat slicer. "Lord have mercy! This is tougher than hay hauling."

"And to think come summer, we'll be doing this *and*

hauling hay." He sat down beside her, his boots only a few inches from hers when he stretched out his legs.

"But we will have help. At least two high school kids who are willing to work hard, especially if we're putting in more alfalfa acreage, and a kid to work the store in the afternoons to free us up from this job," she said.

"Hungry?" he asked.

"Starving, but I can wait until we get to the bar. What I want is a big old greasy cheeseburger and French fries, even if I have to eat it on the run between customers. What about you?"

"Sounds good to me. Right now I want to sit here and let my feet rest."

"This is going to sound crazy after only three days. But even with the feud and all the work, I feel like this is where I belong," she said.

"It's not crazy at all. I've been lookin' for a place to light for almost two years now, and when I came up here to visit my cousin, it was like my soul came home to roost. Then when Gladys offered me the job, it was like I belonged on Fiddle Creek. Sometimes the time, past experiences, and future hopes all work together to make the whole picture."

"Well, butter my butt and call me a biscuit, I'm livin' with a prophet." She smiled.

"Pass the butter. I'll be glad to take on that job."

"How do you do that?" she asked.

"Butter your butt? Well, first you drop your jeans and those fancy, red-lace underbritches," he answered.

"I'm not wearing red-lace panties," she snapped.

"In my mind you are. Then I melt some butter until…"

"Hush!" She held up her palm. "How do you go

from making profound statements to joking without even thinking?"

He pushed up out of the chair and said, "My name is Sawyer O'Donnell. I come from a long line of Irish folks who have kissed the Blarney Stone, but there's also a few serious folks in me lineage too. I like Irish whiskey and I like to dance, and it's been said, like me Irish ancestors, that I talk too much, but it all goes together to make up Sawyer O'Donnell. Whether you like me or not is your privilege, m'lady, but as old Rhett said at the close of the movie, 'Frankly, I don't give a damn.'" His fake Irish accent left a lot to be desired, but he was funny as hell.

Laughter filled the store again as he sat back down.

"You can leave a tip beside the cash register if that entertained you, darlin'."

"And you can stop the Irish talk. Lord, I'd shoot Kinsey Brennan for a double shot of Jameson right now," she moaned.

"I'd give you a whole bottle if you'd go on and take out Betsy Gallagher at the same time. There's one hiding back behind the Jack Daniel's at the bar, but nobody asked for it Saturday night."

"It's probably there for Naomi Gallagher when she comes to town."

"Will we have to pour beer on her and Mavis if they show up at the same time?"

"Probably, but I bet she could snap her fingers and transport herself back to Wild Horse in a split second. She steals pigs and makes them disappear into thin air. I met them both yesterday, and I liked them both better than I liked their grandsons. Maybe it would be different if I didn't feel like a prize Angus heifer at an auction. How about you? Did you like the grannies better than the granddaughters?"

"I didn't like any of them, period. And, darlin' girl, you could never be a prize Angus heifer. They've got black hair, and yours is red. You'd have to be a Guernsey or a Jersey heifer," he teased.

She slapped at his arm, missing by six inches. "You know what I mean."

He nodded. "Yes, I do, but they really want you. They just want this poor old rough cowboy without two nickels in his pockets to go away any way they can make it happen."

She reached over and pinched his cheek. "You're so cute, they can't help themselves. And then there is the feud. Whichever side gets you gets a fine rancher, and the other side loses."

A grin twitched the corners of his mouth and kept getting bigger until he chuckled. "And of course I am a stud bull."

"Sawyer!"

"If you can be a heifer, why can't I be a bull?"

"What about a bull?" Gladys asked as she came through the back door.

"Jill says she feels like a prize heifer at the auction. Like the two feuding families are trying to outbid each other for her," Sawyer said.

"And you're the bull that the women are fighting over?"

Sawyer blushed.

Gladys didn't wait for an answer. "I heard about the catfight and the carriage ride and that Tyrell is going to hog the jukebox tonight. There's a meeting going on at each ranch right now. They are talking strategy about you and this war that's come down because of Mavis's hogs. I haven't seen the feud heat up like this in more than twenty years. You two best dig in for the fight, because it's comin' from both sides."

"Shit!" Jill groaned.

Gladys pointed her finger at Jill. "I've told you before. Fiddle Creek isn't going to either one of those families, so if you liked the way either one of those cowboys kissed you last night, you'll do well to remember that I'd give it to a wildlife preservation group to raise wild hogs on before I'd let them have it. Do you understand?"

"Yes, ma'am, and for the record, I wasn't too impressed with either of them," she said.

Chapter 9

JILL TOSSED A SMALL BALE OF HAY OVER THE SIDE OF the truck bed, put one hand on the edge, and hopped out to the ground. The cows were so tame that they didn't even hesitate to start feeding on it the minute she cut the baling wire and scattered it for them.

"Aunt Gladys called this morning."

"And?" Sawyer asked.

"And she said that Wallace Redding down in Salt Holler called her with a good deal on hogs, so she needs us to come to the store as early as we can. I thought we'd go see Aunt Polly on the way."

"Didn't she buy a hog on Monday?" Sawyer kicked the hay to scatter it a bit for the cows and got back in the truck to move on to the next pasture.

She settled into the passenger's seat. "Yes, but it's warmed up, and Wallace says he's got to sell a couple cheap because his freezers are all full and his smoke-houses are going full-time. Long as it was cold, he could hang a few in a cooling shed, but not when it's getting up close to sixty degrees. He'll probably talk her into buying two, and our big storeroom cooler will be full."

He put the truck into gear and eased on to the next feeding place. "Think any of it will ruin?"

"No, Aunt Gladys said that it's selling fast as she can cut it up. And since Mavis Brennan hasn't got any pork, she called her and made her a deal on buying a couple extra to sell her for her freezer on River Bend. That will just be a matter of delivery, but I bet Aunt Gladys makes a profit on that job."

Jill got out of the truck and jogged to the gates into the next pasture, opening and closing them once Sawyer had driven through. Cattle moved along slowly in a single file against the fence row. An old black bull threw back his head and bawled when the cows behind him didn't keep up, as if telling them the breakfast buffet was about to be spread, and he wasn't waiting for grace.

She hurried from the gate to the truck and had tossed two bales out before Sawyer got out. "Slow movin' today, are you?" Jill commented.

"Had a call from Gladys right then. She wants us there soon as we get done here. Verdie is going to stay with Polly. We'll have to go see her again tomorrow. She sure looked better yesterday than I thought she would."

"She's a tough old broad. I'm going to grow up and be just like her," Jill said.

"I guess Mavis wants three hogs if Wallace is willin' to share them, and Gladys needs the ranch truck to go get it all. She said she's making a fifty-dollar profit to deliver them to River Bend," Sawyer told her.

"Aunt Gladys could make money selling cow patties for chocolate." Jill laughed.

"Why doesn't Mavis go to Salt Holler or send one of her hired hands to get the pork for her?" Sawyer asked.

"Because Aunt Gladys knows Wallace. I think they went to school together, but even she can't cross that bridge until he gives permission. Wallace comes out of the holler on occasion, but folks don't go into it. They're real superstitious down there."

"Cross the bridge?"

"The way Aunt Gladys explained it to me is that about five miles from Burnt Boot there's a bridge that Wallace and his family built, so they own it. State, county, or city doesn't have any say-so over it. It's the only way into the holler for cars or trucks, and there's a gate at the end that's padlocked. So if you got business in Salt Holler, you'd have to get in touch with Wallace beforehand, and few people even have his phone number."

"Their kids go to school?"

"Oh, yeah, they bring them to the bridge, and the bus picks them up, but it doesn't get on the bridge," Jill answered.

"Why?"

"When I was a little girl, Aunt Gladys took me down there one time to see where it was, but we didn't cross the bridge, thank God. The people who live down there in the holler get across in pickups and cars, but believe me, I wouldn't cross it on a skateboard."

"Does it cross a river by that name, or what?" Sawyer kicked the bales when she clipped the wires.

"A big gully that gets marshy in the springtime. Aunt Gladys said before they built the bridge, it would get so muddy that the bus couldn't get the kids for school, and the Reddings couldn't get out for supplies. It must have been a long time ago, because that bridge looks like it was built from scraps of the Ark, and I'm talking about the one that Noah built," she said.

Sawyer laughed out loud. "You'll have to show me where that bridge is someday. Anything that scares you has to be pretty damn bad."

Jill smiled. "Well, thank you! That's the best compliment I've had since I got here."

"Aww, shucks! You mean you wasn't impressed when I told you those jeans looked better than the low-rise ones you had on that showed the strings of your thong when you bent over?"

She slapped at him, but he grabbed her arm and pulled her forward over the loose hay to hug her tightly. Her hands landed on his chest with a snap. She looked up, and before she even had time to shut her eyes, his lips were on hers. Warmth—that's what she felt at first. As the kiss deepened, it grew hotter, and when his tongue traced the outside of her mouth, it turned downright scorching.

Her knees had no bones in them when he broke the kiss, and she was glad he kept his arms on her shoulders when he took a step back.

"Well?" he said.

"Well, what?" she gasped.

"Judgment day. Did that do more for you than either one of the rich cowboys' kisses?" He grinned.

"To be fair, I might have to kiss them again." She tried to control the breathlessness in her tone, but it still sounded hollow. "What about you? Did it do more for you than when you kissed Kinsey and Betsy?"

"I didn't kiss them. They kissed me. And it wasn't nothing like what we just shared. That flat-out made my knees go weak. I saw stars and sparkles, and even this old hay looks brighter. Hell, Jill, my mouth is going to feel warm all day after that kiss," Sawyer said.

"You are full of shit, Sawyer O'Donnell. I believe that you invented the Blarney Stone instead of kissed it."

—~~—

Gladys was putting on her jacket when Sawyer and Jill reached the store. She grabbed her pickup keys and waved over her shoulder. "When Wallace gives a time for me to meet him, he doesn't wait one minute past that, even when he's selling a truckload of butchered hogs. He sets the time, and I always get there early and wait for him to unlock the gate. If I'm not there, he doesn't wait around. I heard that Mavis is still steaming, and that Naomi has twenty-four-hour guards posted around her place."

"You really think that Naomi did something with those hogs?" Sawyer asked.

"Yes, I do. She probably turned them loose in the backwoods, and we'll have a whole raft of wild hogs sproutin' up in another year," Gladys answered.

"If you get stuck in the mud, holler at us, and we'll come drag you back to civilization," Jill yelled as the door closed.

Sawyer hung his jacket on the rack. "Is there a possibility that Gladys is buying stolen pork?"

Jill's eyes got wider and wider, then they went back to normal size, and she shook her head. "Folks down in Salt Holler grow hogs. They don't have cattle down in that place, and Aunt Gladys would have already thought of that. Besides, Wallace wouldn't take a chance on the law coming to investigate."

"Why do they call it Salt Holler, anyway? These are just little rolling hills. The valleys aren't big enough to call them a holler by any means," Sawyer wondered aloud.

"Aunt Gladys told me that the 'salt' part of it is because those folks salt-cure the pork, and the 'holler' has little to do with the land but the fact that it's not really very big. You can holler on one end, and they can hear it on the other."

"How long has it been there?"

"Have to ask Aunt Gladys about that, unless you want to sneak past the guards and ask Naomi Gallagher. I hear she's got distant relatives down there even yet, so she might know."

"I think I'll stay on this side of the fence and kiss you rather than talk to one side of the feuding family about pigs."

She couldn't think of a single smart-ass remark, and the blush was still faint two minutes later when a dark-haired lady that looked vaguely familiar pushed her way into the store.

"Hi, Sawyer. How's the foreman business goin'? I heard it extended out to store-keepin' and bartendin'," she said.

"Looks like it." Sawyer made introductions. "Jill, meet my cousin-in-law Callie. She and my cousin Finn live over on Salt Draw. You might have seen them in church last Sunday."

Callie smiled. "We're the ones with the line of kids on the pew with Verdie."

"Cute bunch of kids. How long have you been in Burnt Boot?" Jill asked.

Callie started putting items into a cart. "Only since the first of December. I understand you aren't really new to the area, just returning to it. When you have time, give me a call, and we'll sneak away for a girls' afternoon.

Maybe a pedicure and coffee if we can't squeeze anything else in."

"That sounds like fun. I've visited, but never lived here until now, and I got to admit, walking into a feud isn't what I had in mind."

"I know. We had a taste of it over on Salt Draw, but it seems to have blown over us now that we are married. I heard there's two ladies after Sawyer, though, and a couple of cowboys fightin' for your hand." Callie smiled.

"It's not me they're after, it's Fiddle Creek," Jill said and then changed the subject. "So where did you meet Finn?"

"He was a sniper and I was his spotter when we were in the military. It's a long story that I'll share sometime when we have more time." Callie's green eyes glimmered. "Maybe that's why those feudin' fillies left us alone. Once they found out I could shoot and wasn't afraid to use a gun, things died down a little bit."

"Well, shit, Sawyer. I just need to wing one of them, and they'll leave us alone," Jill said.

"Sounds like you've got the right idea."

Jill pointed to the truck pulling up outside the store. "Speak of the devil, and me without my shotgun. Some days it don't pay to get out of bed."

Callie leaned over and whispered, "I've got a twenty-two pistol in the glove compartment of my truck. If it gets too heated, I'll sneak out there and get it for you."

"I do believe we are going to be more than spa buddies," Jill whispered back.

Betsy breezed into the store, didn't even look sideways at the two women, but went straight to Sawyer. "Hello, handsome," she said.

"Betsy." He nodded. "What can I do for you today?"

"Granny needs five pounds of sugar, but while we're talkin' about sugar, I can think of a few things you could do for me today." She smiled up at him.

Jill peeked around the end of the aisle where she and Callie had been conspiring. "Need some chickens? Aunt Gladys has a sale on whole fryers today and tomorrow."

"Good Lord, no! Grandma raises her own chickens. She's pretty picky about the henhouse. It won't be long until she has baby chicks everywhere, and then in the spring, she'll get them ready for butcherin' day. She's real prone to chicken and dumplin's, and believe me, she wouldn't think of makin' it with anything but her own range chickens. All I want is five pounds of sugar and a sexy cowboy to take home with me for the weekend. I'll be gentle, Sawyer," she flirted.

Jill picked up a bag of sugar and handed it to Betsy. Maybe if she had something to hold, she wouldn't find an excuse to put her hands on Sawyer. After the way his kiss affected her that morning, she damn sure didn't want another woman—Brennan, Gallagher, or even a Redding—to be getting too close to Sawyer.

Betsy told Jill to put the sugar on the River Bend account, and was reaching for the doorknob when Kinsey pushed her way inside. They reminded Jill of two stray bitch dogs circling and measuring each other up before the big fight.

"Too late, Kinsey. I've already branded him. He's mine," Betsy said.

"The war isn't over until there's a gold band on his finger," Kinsey growled.

Yep, a couple of mongrel bitches. Not even purebreds, Jill thought.

"Speakin' of war"—Betsy's tone turned threatening—"we know you took Granny's pigs, and you will pay for it."

"Prove it. We didn't start this pig war, and we won't take the blame for it," Kinsey said with a flip of her long hair. "Sawyer, darlin', my grandmother sent me to buy a dozen of Gladys's premade shish kebabs for supper tonight. Tyrell is grilling for a few of us. Oh, and a bag of sugar. She's run out, and we're havin' sweet tea with lunch today."

"Yes, ma'am," Sawyer said.

"I'll be glad to take fourteen if you'll come to supper with me. Big old rough cowboy like you wouldn't be satisfied with one little shish kebab, would he? I bet he likes seconds on everything."

Jill had never heard talk of shish kebabs sound so seductive. She rolled her eyes toward Callie and made a gun with her forefinger and thumb.

Callie took a step forward and whispered, "Sawyer best put his boots in the closet and get out some runnin' shoes. We can always hide him out on our ranch if it gets too tough. I thought Finn was the only one who drew women and trouble to him like a magnet, but it must be all the O'Donnell cowboys."

"You got that right, and it gets worse some times," Jill said. "There are times when he infuriates me so much, I'd like to throw him out there for them to fight over like two old hound dogs with one ham bone between them. Then there are times when he's so damn sweet, I'd pen them up like hound dogs and starve them to death before I let either one of them even get close to him."

Callie laughed. "Been where you are, and don't want to go back. Pull out your phone, woman. You need to program in my number in case the fire gets too hot and you need a place to go or someone to talk to."

Jill nodded. "You read my mind."

—∿∿—

Gladys returned right after noon with a pickup load of meat to be unloaded and put away. "You mind the store, Jill. Get a cart, Sawyer. While I put one basketful away, you can fill another. We'll get done faster that way. And then I'll take care of the store. I want you two to go into town and go to the tag agency for me. Wallace pointed out that my pickup tag was a month overdue. I could go, but I'm plumb tuckered out, and I want to prop up my feet for a while."

"Aunt Polly?" Jill asked.

"Verdie is still with her. They're watching all four *Lethal Weapon* movies and said they wouldn't be done until after eight. I'm supposed to bring them ice cream, popcorn, and two thick steaks at five o'clock. I guess I'm cooking. Oh, and yesterday morning a lot of folks paid their bills, so I need you go take a deposit to the bank. You can hand it to them at the drive-through, and they will give you an empty bank bag so I can start all over."

"It won't take both of us to do that chore," Jill said.

"Probably not, but I need to catch up on book work, so you might as well go together and go on and get some supper before you come back. I'll get you the papers for the truck and a check for the tag. I shouldn't have put them in the glove compartment when they came. If they'd been layin' out where I could see them, I wouldn't have let it go so long. Sawyer, there's a cute little doughnut and ice cream shop on California Street, not far from the tag agency, that makes the best tortilla soup. Y'all should go there."

"We will, and don't worry, we'll be back in time for chores and to take care of the bar," he said.

Gladys handed the papers off to Jill, who took them and headed out the door. "If you are going with me, you'd best slap that cowboy hat on and grab your coat, Sawyer."

"This is such a treat," Jill said as she tossed the keys to her truck to Sawyer and buckled her seat belt. "I am so excited that we get some time out of Burnt Boot."

"You could have called Callie and had a manicure," Sawyer said.

"I'd rather have tortilla soup and ice cream afterwards." She smiled.

They were halfway there when she slapped the dash and said, "Dammit!"

"What did you forget? Your purse? Not to worry, I have money in my pocket, and I don't think two bowls of soup and a couple of dips of ice cream is going to break me," he said.

"No," she groaned.

"Are you afraid it's a date?" he asked.

"You are getting warm."

"What, then? Just spit it out."

"Aunt Gladys and Aunt Polly are matchmaking, and we are the subjects. We are getting along, so they are hearing wedding bells and seeing grandchildren."

He chuckled. "You are kiddin' me."

"Nope, I'm not kiddin'. There was no reason to send us both to do this errand, and absolutely none to tell us to go out to supper. They're afraid I just might fall for a Brennan or a Gallagher. And with them getting up over eighty, and dammit, I forgot about Verdie."

"What about Verdie?"

"She's got all those adopted grandkids, and she brags about them all the time. Aunt Polly and Aunt Gladys will be feeling the pinch and wanting some of their own," Jill said.

"Well, I got to admit"—Sawyer's smile brightened the whole cab of the truck—"an O'Donnell is better than either one of those, even if we are paupers by their standards. And, Jill, any children you produce won't be their grandchildren."

"Don't tell either of them that, or Aunt Gladys will fire you." She crossed her arms over her chest and looked out the side window.

"Well, darlin', don't let knowing what they are up to spoil our afternoon out of town. We shall eat soup and ice cream and enjoy our time without having to think about feuds or red roses or women with wandering hands," he said.

"Make it backfire? I like that," she said. "Since I can't cook this afternoon, I'll buy a dozen doughnuts to take home for our midnight snack."

"Just a dozen? I can eat that many on the way home and still need a bedtime snack. O'Donnell men are all blessed with a sweet tooth. We'll each buy a dozen. If they don't stay fresh, we'll microwave them and dip 'em in hot coffee."

Jill nodded in agreement. "I wonder if they freeze well."

Sawyer nodded and swung out onto I-35 heading south. "Bank first, and from what Gladys said, we can park there and walk to the tag agency and to the café. If you see a store in between, we'll have plenty of time for you to browse."

"And if there's a nail shop, I can go in and get my toenails done?" she teased.

"Of course you can. I'll get mine done too," he shot right back.

"Be careful, Mr. O'Donnell, I might make you do just that."

The bank didn't have a waiting line, so they were through in less than ten minutes. It would have been quicker if they hadn't had to count the money twice to make it agree with the deposit slip Gladys had made out. The lady in the tag agency didn't have a single customer, so Jill was in and out in five minutes, tag in hand as she left.

They were on their way to the pastry shop when Jill got a case of guilt fever. She checked her watch and dug in her purse for her phone. "I'm going to call Aunt Gladys. What if there's been another fight in the store and she needs us?"

Sawyer pushed a lock of dark hair back off his forehead. "If I was either one of those feuding guys, I damn sure wouldn't mess with Gladys."

"How are things?" she asked when Gladys answered.

"Haven't had a customer since you left, so I've gotten caught up on paperwork. It's like the eye of a tornado, but why are you calling me? You are supposed to be having some fun," she said.

"Why did you say that about a tornado? Are there clouds coming in? Do we need to come back right now?"

"Polly called and said there is a meeting at River Bend. Something is coming. There's a change in the air. But it won't happen today, so go enjoy yourself. Be young and free and forget all about what's going on here. Good-bye," Gladys said.

"Oh, yeah!" Jill pushed the "end" button. "They are definitely matchmaking."

He draped an arm around her shoulders. "What do you want to do about it?"

"Nothing. Let them have their fun," she said.

"I vote that we take doughnuts home to them. I bet Polly would love some, and maybe if we get there in time, we could even take some to Verdie for staying with Polly," Sawyer said.

Jill stopped so quick that Sawyer took two steps before he realized she'd slipped out from under his arm. He dropped it to his side and looked back with a question in his expression.

"Damnation!" She pointed.

Kinsey Brennan was sitting in a booth in the little café, with a huge banana split in front of her.

Sawyer grinned. "They're everywhere. They're everywhere. Name that song."

"It's 'he's everywhere, he's everywhere,' and it's a Ray Stevens song."

"You got it. You win one maple-iced doughnut with sprinkles. Now, sugarplum, honey bunch, cutie pie, you know we got to act like lovers should, because Santa Claus"—he wiggled his dark eyebrows—"is watchin' you. And he's everywhere, he's everywhere."

She giggled. "I don't think that's what the lyrics say."

"It's pretty damn close." He laced his fingers with hers. "If Aunt Gladys wants to play at matchmaking, then we'll act like lovers should. I damn sure don't want to be on Santa's shit list come next Christmas."

"And what better way to get news back to Burnt Boot than through a bitchy Brennan, right?" Jill squeezed his hand.

Sawyer touched her cheek with his palm. "Are you blushing? The wielder of the shotgun? The beer-slingin' bartender with a blush on her face?"

"Oh, hush, or I won't protect you when she tries to undress you in public. And you know what, this might be the answer to any more badgering for dates. We can pretend that we are dating."

Kinsey looked up, smiled, and waved when they were inside the shop. The grin quickly faded, though, when she saw that Sawyer was holding Jill's hand.

"Hey, Kinsey," Jill called out. "What's that you've got there? It looks pretty good."

"Brownie fudge banana split. They just started making them this week. I'm addicted already," Kinsey said. "Sawyer, get a spoon from the clerk and come share it with me, or better yet, come sit with me, and I'll feed it to you one bite at a time off my fingertips."

"They don't give up, no matter what," Sawyer said out of the corner of his mouth. "Jill and I have our hearts set on a bowl of soup before we have dessert. You go on and enjoy every bite of it all by yourself," Sawyer said.

Kinsey shrugged and went back to eating, but her eyes never left Sawyer. Jill picked up a plastic spoon from the counter while Sawyer ordered, marched over to the booth, and sat down across from Kinsey.

"Since you are offering, I'll have a couple of bites just to see if we want to share one when we finish our soup." She dug into the ice cream without waiting for Kinsey to give her permission, put the bite into her mouth, and rolled her eyes. "Wonderful. One more little bite, and then I'll leave the rest for you." She dipped into it again with the spoon that had been in her mouth, and Kinsey flinched. "Oh, yes. Thanks for the offer."

She slid out of the booth and joined Sawyer at a little round table for two. Kinsey picked up the ice cream and made a big show of throwing it into the trash can beside the door as she left.

Bending low, she whispered in Jill's ear, "Never cross a Brennan, Jill Cleary, or you will live to regret it."

"Darlin', that road goes two ways. Leave me and Sawyer alone, or you'll see just how mean a Cleary woman can be when she is crossed."

Kinsey raised up, shot her a dirty look, and flipped her off as she marched out the door.

Sawyer chuckled. "You fight dirty."

"Yep, I do, but it was good ice cream, and now she's gone and I don't have to look at her while I eat. I noticed that you took the chair so your back would be to her."

"Yep, I did." His grin widened.

—∾∾—

They were on the way home when Gladys called to tell them that she was going to go ahead and feed the cattle that evening. "Polly is in a pout to see you two, so go on to the house, and I'll be there soon as I dump a load of feed out for the cows."

"We are bringing doughnuts," Jill said.

"Don't you let her eat them all. Hide a few for me."

"I don't reckon she can eat two dozen."

"You don't know Polly. She's got a sweet tooth that is unreal. See you later," Gladys said.

"Aunt Gladys is taking care of feeding. We're supposed to go see Polly, which we planned to do anyway, but now we can spend a little more time with her," Jill explained.

"No mention of Kinsey burning down the bunkhouse?"

Jill shook her head. "Not yet, but it's only been an hour."

"I'll bet you that's the first thing Polly mentions. Rumors travel fast, but anything that has to do with the Gallaghers or the Brennans can break the sound barrier, and I heard something that resembled a jet airplane a couple of minutes ago," Sawyer said.

"You've got a bet. She or Aunt Gladys will call me at the bar, but if the rumor was already spreading, Aunt Gladys would have said something about it right then. What's the stakes?"

"A kiss."

She slowly turned. "You sure about that?"

"I am."

"Lips or cheek?"

"You can decide where, if you win. I already know where mine is landing if I win," he teased.

"And you're not telling?"

"It's classified." His eyes sparkled.

She loved it, and, hey, after that last kiss, she wouldn't mind testing the waters just to see if more would turn her toes up and make her insides melt like ice cream on a hot Texas afternoon.

The corners of her mouth twitched. "Do we need to shake on it?"

"I reckon your word is fine. I trust you, Jill." He parked in front of Gladys's white frame house, a low-slung ranch house with a wide porch facing the east, and open on both ends to catch the evening breeze, whether it came from the north or south.

She reached over her shoulder and picked up one flat box of doughnuts. "I'll take one box. You take the other. Then we'll both be the fair-haired glory child."

"I don't think anyone would ever call me fair-haired," he said. "And there's no way I'll ever be on a level with you in their eyes, but I'll gladly carry one in and rack up however many points I can get."

The door flew open before Sawyer had time to knock, and Verdie motioned them inside. She was shorter than Polly, had jet-black hair that enhanced every wrinkle in her face, and there were plenty there to work on, but when she smiled, her brown eyes sparkled, and that's all Jill could see.

"You take that box out of her hands so she can hug me." Verdie talked the whole time she hugged Jill. "I swear, girl, it's been years since I've laid eyes on you. I'm so glad you've come home to roost, and at just the right time. Don't know what these two old buzzards would do without you and Sawyer."

"It's about time y'all got here," Polly hollered from one of two recliners in the living room. "Gladys called and said you were bringing doughnuts, and my mouth has been watering ever since. Bring 'em in here and have one with us. Verdie already made coffee, but she could make a cup of hot chocolate if you want one."

Sawyer set one box on the table beside Polly and carried the other through an archway into the kitchen. "I'd take a cup of coffee, but nothing more. Jill and I had tortilla soup and ice cream. We've got a box of doughnuts in the truck to take to the bunkhouse for a midnight snack."

Jill sat down on the sofa and turned to face Polly. "You're lookin' good today."

Polly patted her hair. "Verdie fixed it for me and painted my fingernails too. It makes a difference to have on some clothes and not nightgowns, and to get fixed up a little. I feel human again."

Verdie set a cup of coffee beside the doughnuts and picked up a chocolate-iced one with multicolored sprinkles. "I was going to go on a diet this week, but I can't resist doughnuts."

"Diet, hell!" Polly fussed. "We're past eighty, woman. None of us need to diet. We should be eating what we want, and dying when we're supposed to."

"Just for the record, she made me cut the leg down the side of that pair of overalls." Verdie sat down on the other recliner.

"They're my overalls. I was lost without my bib pockets. You can all be thankful I made her cut them at the seam and not off right above the knee. An old woman's varicose veins are not a pretty sight to see. Might ruin your appetite for doughnuts." She reached for a second one.

"So tell me"—Verdie smiled, and part of the wrinkles disappeared—"how was your tortilla soup?"

Sawyer brought two cups of coffee from the kitchen and handed one to Jill. "It was great. I understand in a few weeks they are having some kind of Valentine's Day special thing in Gainesville. We should put Polly in a wheelchair and go check it out."

"Hell, no! By Valentine's, I'll have this cast off, and I can maneuver with a pair of crutches. I'm not letting this get me down, Sawyer."

"Yes, ma'am." He grinned. "I see where Jill gets her stubborn streak."

"That ain't from me. She got that from Gladys," Polly protested.

"Got what from me?" Gladys came through the back door.

"Your stubborn streak," Verdie hollered.

"Bullshit. That came from her grandpa. All three of them Cleary boys could put a Missouri mule to shame. What did you do to that perfectly good pair of overalls?"

Verdie pointed. "She made me do it."

"I missed my pockets," Polly said.

Jill glanced from one to the other. All different in looks. Best friends since they were little girls. The solid foundation of Burnt Boot that kept some kind of sanity amongst a feud. And she was so glad she could claim kin to two of them, and shirttail kin to the other one.

Chapter 10

"I CAN'T BELIEVE THEY HADN'T HEARD ABOUT KINSEY. The whole town knew when I arrived and when you moved into the bunkhouse," Jill said.

"I didn't know, and you didn't know I was living in the bunkhouse. Maybe rumor-spreading is selective." He grinned. "Which reminds me, you owe me a kiss."

She picked up a bar rag and cleaned the area around the beer machine. "Want to collect it now?"

"No, ma'am. I want it later."

"But what if I decide to give you a peck on the cheek instead of a wild, passionate kiss? What difference would it make if it was now or later?"

"I want to have a while to enjoy the anticipation, no matter where I get the kiss," he said.

The words were barely out of his mouth when her phone rang.

She answered it. "Hello, Aunt Polly." And then there was a long pause before she said, "The doors are open, but nobody is here."

Sawyer walked up behind her and slipped his arms around her waist. When she tried to wiggle free, he said, "Don't get all hyper. I want to hear what Polly is saying. I caught something about Kinsey Brennan."

"Aunt Polly, I'm putting it on speakerphone until and unless someone comes in." Jill laid the phone on the counter, but Sawyer did not remove his arms.

"Y'all are in deep shit. Kinsey is telling everyone that Gladys is going to fire Sawyer," Polly said.

"Why?" Jill asked.

"For sleeping with you. She says that y'all were totally inappropriate in public, carryin' on like a couple of teenagers all gaga over each other on the street and in the little café. And she says that you slobbered in her ice cream, and that you threatened her. They tried to get a restraining order on you, but Quaid pitched a fit and said that he was going to marry you and how could he even date you if there was a restraining order and besides all that, the sheriff said they didn't have enough evidence for one. It would just be her word against yours."

"Well, dammit! I wish the sheriff would let the whole family have their restraining order. You reckon they'll bring the feud to the bar?"

"Think, Jill!" Sawyer said.

"What?" She whipped around to face him.

"If they did, it would halve the business in the bar. It's all hot air, Polly, because she made the first threat, and Jill stood up to her. Evidently the Brennans don't take rejection too well."

"There's a sawed-off shotgun under the beer machine. Just open up the doors, and you'll see it, along with a box of shells. Get it out if it starts to look rowdy," Polly said. "Friday nights are usually hopping, and that's before Kinsey got her damned feelin's hurt. Everyone loves a good fight, gossip, and cold beer. You know what old Billy Currington says: 'Beer is good. God is great, and people are crazy,' or something like that."

"Give me that phone," Gladys said.

"Aunt Gladys, are you two fighting over the phone?"

"Damn straight, we are. She gets testy when it's almost time for a pain pill. If things get too rowdy down there, you call me. Don't call the sheriff. He's afraid of the Brennans and the Gallaghers. Okay, okay, I'll get your pill, Polly."

"Bye, Aunt Gladys," Jill said.

"I'll call you later when she falls asleep."

"I want a swallow of whiskey to take that pill," Polly yelled. "Damn things get stuck when you make me take them with water."

"Bye, Jill." Gladys sighed.

The phone went silent, and Jill pressed the "end" button. She turned around slowly and put her arms around Sawyer's neck, lacing her fingers together. "Looks like it's me and you against the world, partner."

He grinned. "I'm glad that we banded together. They would have dragged us into this kickin' and screamin', whether we wanted to join the pig war or not."

His eyes fluttered shut, leaving thick lashes fanned out on his cheekbones, just before his lips found hers. It was every bit as hot as the first kiss and twice as passionate. No, sir, that first one was not a fluke and had nothing to do with her frustration at having to spend time with the Gallaghers and the Brennans.

She swayed slightly when she opened her eyes.

He drew her close to his chest and held her tightly. "Whoa, get your balance there, sweetheart. Your kisses make my knees go all rubbery, but tough as you are, I didn't think mine had the same effect on you."

"It's the lighting in here. Trying to focus when I opened my eyes made me dizzy," she said.

He scooped her up, settled her on a bar stool, and sat

down beside her. "I kissed you, Jill Cleary. You kissed me back, but you didn't instigate the kiss, so you still owe me one later."

Tyrell Gallagher slung open the door and waited a second for his eyes to adjust to the dim light before he removed his hat and hung it on the row of nails along the wall. He pulled up a stool right beside her, propped his elbows on the bar, and put his chin in his hands. "Jill Cleary, darlin', let me look at your beautiful face so I can get out of this foul mood."

Quaid Brennan pushed his way into the bar, with Kinsey right behind him. He passed behind Tyrell on his way to the other end of the bar, and muttered, "Oink, oink," on the way.

Jill heard him, rounded the end of the bar, jerked the sawed-off shotgun out from under the counter, jacked a round into it, and said, "Okay, boys, it's like this. Polly's is neutral. If you two want to play big bad cowboys in your pig-shit war that's going on between your families, you'll do it outside this place. Understood?"

"Anything you say, princess." Tyrell grinned.

"Quaid?" she asked.

"I hear you, gorgeous," he said. "Now put that gun away."

Tyrell pointed toward the whiskey on the counter behind Jill. "I think you are sexy, holding it like that. Want to do some target practice with me tomorrow afternoon? We've got a real nice shootin' range on Wild Horse. I'll start off with a double shot of Jack Daniel's tonight, and then it'll be beer for the rest of the evening."

"I'm not going out with either of you ever again. I don't like this feud crap, and I don't intend to be a part of it," she said.

"Little late there, not after what you said to me today," Kinsey stated. "You're in this whether you want to be or not. You should have kept your mouth shut. Now, to you, Sawyer, darlin'. I'm going to knock on your door Sunday morning, and you are going to church with me if I have to handcuff your hand to mine."

"Jill and I have plans on Sunday, folks, so that's the end of our part in your feud. What can I get you, Quaid?" Sawyer asked.

"Beer for both of us," Quaid said. "In the bottle instead of the mug. We'll take them to a table and wait for the rest of our party."

"That was too easy," Sawyer said. "Something is going on."

Jill shivered from head to toe. "I can feel it too. It's a good thing we're together, or they'd tear us to pieces."

People kept arriving until the bar was too full for another person to get inside. Gallaghers took up one end; Brennans the other. The stools were full, the music loud, and the dance floor crowded. Jill patted the shotgun under the counter and smiled up at Sawyer. "I had no idea Aunt Polly had this thing in here, but I'm damn glad that she does."

~~~~~

Sawyer sprawled out on the sofa, long legs out in front of him and his head thrown back so far that he was looking at the ceiling. "Lord, it's been a day and a half. Thank goodness tomorrow is Sunday. Chores and then church and then we're going to nap all afternoon."

"In a motel?" she asked.

"We'll let everyone think we're going into town, but

I vote we slip back here, have some canned chili and doughnuts for dessert, and lock the doors. We can turn off our phones and sleep until Monday morning."

She flopped down on the other end of the sofa and stretched out until her feet were in his lap. Without sitting up, he picked up one and started massaging it. "It's tiring, but we're not doin' too bad keepin' up with three jobs."

"Wouldn't be any big deal if it wasn't for the feud shit in the middle of it. What do you think they're plannin' next?"

"I think the Gallaghers done stepped in the deep water over them pigs. But forget the feud, I'd rather talk about the woman that these feet belong to and when she's going to pay up with a kiss."

"Right now that woman is so tired that she's about to fall asleep, and she still needs to take a quick shower. Reckon she could use your bathroom if she hurries?"

He sat up straight. "She can even fall backwards and sleep in my bed if she wants to. This old cowboy would be too tired to even kiss her good night. And he's glad that she's saving that kiss for later, when he has the energy to kiss her back."

She stood up and stretched, then leaned down and brushed a quick kiss across his forehead. "That's not the bettin' kiss, but a thank-you kiss for having my back."

He grabbed her around the neck and pulled her into his lap. "Well, then this one is my thank-you for the same." The kiss was lightning and fire mixed together.

She pushed herself up out of his lap. "That, Sawyer, was a mind-boggling kiss. Now good night. I'm going to take a shower and go to bed. I'll see you at breakfast."

He sat there for a long time after she'd gone to her

own side of the bunkhouse. Ten days ago he was content in his peaceful little world. Now everything was upside down, and yet he hadn't felt so alive in ages.

Chapter 11

IT WASN'T A LITTLE SNORE BUT ONE THAT RATTLED THE windows in the church. Thank goodness the preacher had said something everyone agreed with, and more than a dozen deep drawls around them had hollered, "Amen!"

Jill poked Sawyer on the shoulder.

His head popped up. "What? Is it over?"

"You were snoring," she said softly.

For the rest of the service she kept a watch on him. If his eyes shut, she touched his thigh. If his chin started toward his chest, she squeezed his thigh.

The church was packed in the middle, but the two sides were sparse. The Brennan side was represented fairly well, but Mavis wasn't there. Too bad she'd stayed home and sent Kinsey and Quaid, but then they were Sunday school teachers.

There they sat—the Brennan bitch on one side, and Betsy, the Gallagher bitch, on the other side of the church. Rather than listening to the preacher, Jill entertained herself by imagining Betsy in full camouflage gear, rifle over her shoulder, as she paraded up and down a fencerow. Jill was imagining dozens of pigs rushing through the fence, breaking it down, and running right at Betsy, when Sawyer's hand on her shoulder jerked her back into reality.

"What?" she whispered.

"You were snoring." He grinned.

She cautiously looked around to see if anyone was staring at her. "I don't snore, and I wasn't asleep."

"It was more like a purr, but in another minute you'd have been sawin' logs for sure," he whispered. "It's only five more minutes, and he'll wind it down."

"Thank God!"

"Church is definitely the place to do that," Sawyer whispered.

As soon as the benediction had been delivered, Jill and Sawyer were both on their feet, headed for the door. Sunday dinner didn't matter, not when they needed a nap.

"Hey, y'all should come home with us. Verdie has a pot roast in the oven that will melt in your mouth," Finn said.

He was as tall as Sawyer and had the bluest eyes Jill had ever seen on a man. Callie nodded at his side as she corralled four kids, and Verdie poked her head out around Finn's shoulder to say, "Yes, we'd love to have you. Got plenty of food and plenty of these wild urchins to entertain you. If that don't keep you laughing, then there's a parrot that never shuts up and a bunch of dogs."

"And a cat," a little girl said shyly.

"Y'all could play Monopoly with us this afternoon," one of the boys offered.

"The children: Martin, Adam, Richie, and Olivia." Callie laid a hand on each kid's head as she introduced them.

"Pleased to meet you all. But I need a nap more than fun today. Can I take a rain check? I'd fall asleep in the middle of a board game, even if I drank six cups of coffee. I'm afraid that sleet, snow, or even"—she hesitated before she said anything about the promise of an afternoon of glorious hot kisses, and then chose her words carefully—"chocolate could keep me away from a Sunday nap. It's been a long, busy week."

"Jill snored in church," Sawyer said.

She poked him in the chest with her forefinger. "So did you and a lot louder."

"I thought I heard a bullfrog right behind me." Verdie laughed. "Another Sunday then or maybe a lunch in the middle of the week?"

"That sounds wonderful." Jill smiled.

With Sawyer's hand at her back, they made their way to the door, where they shook hands with the preacher and made a comment about how wonderful it was to see the sun shining. Jill couldn't lie and tell him it was an awesome sermon, because she'd caught only snatches of it between keeping Sawyer awake and dozing herself.

She heard someone snort and say, "Oink, oink." Then another one gave a pig snort that wasn't totally unlike Sawyer's snores.

One more oink, and a Brennan said something about a thieving smart-ass. Jill was too short to see who threw the first punch, but the fight was on. The church parking lot, which had been declared sacred, neutral ground, turned into a free-for-all. Fists and profanity flew around like buzzards having it out over a dead possum in the middle of the road.

Those who sat in the middle section of church either quietly circled the brawl to their trucks or else stood on the sidelines. No one, not even the preacher, wadded into the middle of the fracas to try to put an end to it.

Finally, Verdie pushed her way through the speech-less onlookers and right out into the lot. When she reached the middle, she grabbed two ears, a Brennan and a Gallagher, and hauled them off the ground to their feet.

"One of y'all makes a move, I will put a knee in a place that will hurt for the rest of the day," she said loudly. "Stop it right now, or else I'm going out to my van and bringing in some pistol power."

"They started the whole thing by stealing our pigs, and now they're oinking at us and making pig sounds." Quaid Brennan rubbed his ear.

"They're lying about us," Tyrell Gallagher yelled.

"I don't give a shit who stole the pigs or who is lying. If you've got to fight like children, then take it away from the church, the store, and Polly's bar. Those have been neutral places during this whole damned feud, and the next time this happens, I'm not whistling or pulling ears. I'm going to start kicking and asking questions later," Verdie said.

"I want to grow up to be just like her," Jill said.

"Not Polly or Gladys?" Sawyer asked.

"Oh, no. They're mean, but believe me, Verdie is the toughest one of the lot."

Two men had guarded the henhouse at Wild Horse, since Naomi was sure that's where Mavis was going to hit her after the pigs went missing. There was no way those holier-than-thou Brennans were going to get at her big white chickens. Not when it was nearly time to start saving their eggs to incubate for next year's chicken crop.

If they hadn't been standing on the same side of the huge, custom-built coop, they might have seen that the cigarette one of them tossed on the ground and stepped on still had a spark. If they hadn't been hungover from dancing and drinking at Polly's the night before, they might have smelled the smoke before the chickens went crazy, flapping their wings and cackling louder than a rock band.

"What's that smell? You've got to quit smokin', Billy. That damn smoke gets in my nose and, oh my God! The henhouse is on fire. That's why they're throwin' such a fit," one yelled.

"Dammit! Call the house. Call anybody. Get us some help. We'll have to open the doors, or they'll all burn up in there. Those damn Brennans got past us somehow. Naomi is going to fire us for sure," one of the guards yelled at the other one.

He jerked a phone from his pocket with one hand and opened the doors with the other. Mad hens are one thing, but terrified ones are another story. And a mean old rooster damn sure didn't like his harem carrying on like that. Both guards dropped to their knees and covered their faces with their hands when the rooster led the chickens out in flight, squawking and clawing anything in their path.

A sea of Gallaghers swarmed toward the fire. The chickens didn't care if they were masters or servants. They wanted away from the evil fire, so they lit on heads, pecked at ears, fought with people trying to catch them, flew into the trees, and in their fear, dropped a fair amount of chicken crap down on the heads of those trying to coax them down.

Those that had had their wings singed by the fire before they were set loose ran into the mesquite trees and hid in the underbrush. The rooster flogged everyone in his pathway as he made his way toward the nearest barn and flew up to the rafter, where he publicly made known his anger at having his tail feathers plumb burned to a crisp.

"Damn Brennans. Start a fight over in the churchyard, and now this," Tyrell cussed. "They're going to pay."

"You're damn right, and they will pay dearly." Naomi wiped a blob of chicken crap from her forehead. "Even if we can catch them, it'll be weeks before they lay again. I won't have enough eggs to incubate this year, which means we'll have to buy our chickens, and I hate store-bought meat. Damn you, Mavis!" Naomi fished a cell phone from the hip pocket of her jeans and jabbed in the numbers to River Bend Ranch.

"Hello," Mavis said.

"You are a bitch from hell, Mavis Brennan, and you will pay for this," Naomi screamed.

"What in the hell are you talkin' about? Did Orville decide to do right by my granddaughter?"

"Hell, no. He and Ilene are talking about getting married now. But I'm pressing charges against you for burning down my chicken house," Naomi growled.

"Vengeance is mine, saith the Lord," Mavis quoted with laughter. "Since God has taken my side, you'd better watch out, woman."

Naomi raised her fist and yelled, "God didn't do this. Damn it, Mavis, you done messed with the wrong woman because I won't leave revenge in God's hands. I'll take care of it myself."

Jill fluffed up her pillow and pulled a quilt up over her body. She shut her eyes, and immediately that fuzzy feeling that happens before sleep settled in. Then her phone rang.

"Shit! Shit! Shit!" she grumbled as she reached for it.

"Jill, hope you weren't asleep yet, but I had to tell you," Gladys said. "Naomi Gallagher's chicken house has flat-out burned to the ground. They had to turn the chickens free, and they can't catch them. Naomi didn't believe in clipping their wings, so they're in the trees, hiding in the mesquite underbrush, and the rooster won't come down from the rafters in the barn. It's a big mess, and she's blaming the Brennans."

"Did the Brennans do it?"

"Mavis says that God must have avenged her for losing her hogs. She swears that she didn't do it and that she never had any intentions of messing with Naomi's chickens. If she had, she says she would have poisoned them, not set fire to them."

"More fuel for the feud, huh?" Jill said.

She didn't care if the Brennans and Gallaghers burned each other out as long as they didn't let their fires spread to Fiddle Creek.

"You sound groggy. Go on back to sleep," Gladys said.

"Thank you for calling."

"Just thought y'all might want to keep an eye out for either one of the families. They might use Fiddle Creek as crossing ground to get to the other one."

Jill yawned. "So is the pig war now the chicken war?"

"No, this chapter in the feud will always be the pig war, I'm afraid. Doesn't that sound horrible? I'm hanging up now and sleep all day. From now on I'll do the feeding on Sundays. I'll get Polly settled, and I'll only be gone an hour each time. Besides"—she lowered her voice—"I love her, and we get along pretty good, but I'm getting cabin fever, and I can't ask Verdie to babysit all the time so I can get out."

That's when Jill's stomach growled. She'd had a bowl of canned chicken noodle soup for dinner, but she'd been too tired to eat all of it. Now it was either eat something or never get back to sleep.

She pushed back the quilt and padded barefoot across the cold wood floor to the kitchen area. She opened the freezer. Ice cream didn't appeal to her. Nothing in the fridge looked good either, so she went to the cabinets.

"Doughnuts," Sawyer said gruffly.

"You startled me, but that does sound good," she said.

Sawyer reached over her shoulder and picked up the half-empty box of store-bought chocolate doughnuts. "They're not as good as what we got in Gainesville, but they'll make your stomach stop grumblin'. Finn called to tell me that the Gallaghers' henhouse burned. After I eat something, I'm turning off my damn phone."

"Aunt Gladys called me with the same news." She pulled the milk from the refrigerator and carried it to the table, along with two glasses.

"Do you care if they're having roasted chicken for supper next door?" he asked.

She poured milk and slid a glass toward his end of the table. "I do not."

"Then let's both turn off the phones, make the sofa out into a bed, throw our pillows and quilts on it…"

"And," she finished his sentence, "turn on the television to something totally boring for the noise, and sleep all afternoon. But why on the sofa and not in our own beds?"

"Television noise will be louder in the living area.

It'll block out everything. I vote for the sports channel. There's a golf game on this afternoon."

"You don't like golf."

"No, ma'am. I like football, baseball, and basketball, and I like to play those, not watch them on television."

"Me too." She nodded.

"Play or watch?"

"Play, but not today. Pull out the sofa. Do we need to put a pillow in the middle, like they used to do in the old days to discourage hanky-panky?" she asked.

"Honey, my hanky-panky is drooping. If you want that, you'll have to wait until later." He grinned.

They quickly finished their snack, and while she went to get her pillow and quilt, he tossed the sofa cushions on the floor and pulled the bed out. It was covered with a dark-green flannel sheet that looked soft and inviting.

"Hey, where did you get that?" Jill pointed at the fleece-lined soft blanket he carried to the living room.

"Christmas present from my sister," he answered. "Your phone turned off? Mine is."

"Turned off and shoved to the bottom of my purse. And Aunt Gladys said that she's giving us Sunday off from now on. Starting this evening, she'll take care of chores."

She picked up the remote and turned on the television, hit the channel button a couple of times until she found a station showing golf. The sports announcer's tone was a soft monologue—perfect sleeping noise. Before she could lay the remote on the end table, Sawyer was already snoring.

Who needed television? His snores would block out a nuclear attack on Fiddle Creek. She eased down on her side of the sofa and was asleep seconds after her head hit the pillow. At dusk she awoke with Sawyer curled around her back, one arm thrown over her waist and both of them covered with his soft blanket.

—∿∿—

"Was that as good for you as it was for me?" he murmured when she wiggled out of his embrace.

"Sleep, yes. But if you were having some kind of wicked dream, sorry, partner, I didn't share it with you." She yawned.

He sat up, stretched his long legs out in front of him, and pointed at the television. "Wouldn't you love to be there right now?" He blocked out the golf game and pictured a beach with enough roll to the ocean to make it pretty, the wind barely blowing, and Jill in a bikini, lying beside him on the white sand.

She pulled herself up to a sitting position and leaned over to retrieve her quilt that had fallen on the floor. The sports announcer said something about the score in that same whispery-soft voice, and she frowned. "Just how long does it take to play a game, anyway?"

"This is a different one than we started off with earlier," he answered. "This one is in Miami."

"How do you know? You were asleep before I found the station with the first one."

"I woke up when you stole more than your half of my blanket. You didn't answer my question. Already acting like a wife because we've slept together," he said.

"We did not sleep together, and, yes, I'd love to be anywhere away from this feud, even Miami," she argued.

"We did sleep together, and I had to snuggle up to you to even get a corner of my blanket. And why did you say *even Miami*? You don't like it?" He crossed his fingers behind his back like he had when he was a child. Truth was, he'd awakened at four and wanted to be close to her, so he'd snuggled up to her back and draped an arm around her.

"I love the beach, but I don't like that many people."

"Me either. Been there with the rodeo crew a few times, but I like less people too," he said.

She turned over, and their faces were just inches apart. "So you did the rodeo tour?"

"My cousin did, and we followed it when we could. I tried riding bulls and broncs, but I wasn't star quality." He wiggled his dark eyebrows. "My expertise lies in other areas."

"Sawyer O'Donnell!"

"Your mind is in the gutter."

"Yours isn't?" she asked.

"No, it is not. I have several cousins who were rodeo folks, so I know star quality when I see it. I found my niche, though. I usually got a gig as the rodeo clown."

She laughed. "Well, I can sure see that."

"So scratch off Miami for the honeymoon?"

"What honeymoon?" she asked.

"Ours, darlin'. Gladys will make me marry you, since we've slept together."

She put her finger over his lips. "If you don't tell, I won't."

Chapter 12

"SOMETHING ISN'T RIGHT. I CAN FEEL IT IN THE AIR," Sawyer said when they opened the doors into the bar that night.

"I've been enjoying the quiet," Jill said. "Seems like the feud is dying down, even after that chicken house incident."

"It's the quiet that worries me. After the business last Sunday at the church, and Naomi's chickens flying the coop, you can bet your pretty little ass both parties are up to something. They've been layin' low all week."

Jill nodded. "Come to think of it, we haven't seen much of them in the store either. Betsy did come in to buy a couple of whole chickens. Said her grandmother would have to make do until she could build a new hen-house. It was while you were taking a nap on the cot in the storeroom."

Sawyer flipped the top off a Coors longneck and took a long drink from it. "And while you were taking a nap, Quaid came by to pick up two dozen pork chops. Almost wiped out the supply, and I didn't cut up any more for Monday morning."

"It's the Brennans who are fixin' to strike," Jill said. "I wonder what they've got up their sleeves."

"How do you know that?" Sawyer asked.

"Betsy didn't ask about you. I bet there's not a half a dozen of either family in church tomorrow morning.

Looks like this will be a lazy night. We might even get to close up early."

"Or not," Sawyer said when Tyrell shoved his way into the bar. Betsy and a half-dozen Gallaghers followed him and claimed a table in the corner.

"Two pitchers of Coors and seven red cups," Tyrell yelled as he plugged coins into the jukebox.

"I jinxed it when I said that," Jill said.

The door opened again, and Kinsey Brennan, Quaid, and half a dozen Brennans lined up on bar stools. "I want a strawberry daiquiri, and stir it with your finger, Sawyer," Kinsey flirted.

"A Miller Lite and a pitcher of margaritas, and one of Coors for our table," Quaid said.

Jill took their money and watched as they each carried their drink in one hand and a pitcher in the other to a table as far away from the Gallaghers as possible. Even though Jill couldn't hear a word either family said, their body language spoke volumes.

The Gallaghers were loud and boisterous, line dancing to fast songs, swilling beer by the pitcherful, and having a good time. The Brennans nursed their drinks and kept their heads together. Polly was probably right. The Gallaghers should be on Wild Horse Ranch, patrolling every square inch, because the Brennans were likely to strike that very night.

By nine o'clock, the bar was full and noisy, and smoke hovered in the air like fog. Evidently, dancing made folks hungry as well as thirsty, because Sawyer stayed busy at the grill while Jill drew pitcher after pitcher of beer. Thank goodness bar rules said that she didn't carry it to the tables, but that they had to order and pay at the bar. And Polly did not run charge accounts or take checks or credit cards, so it was cash only.

"Looks like a normal Saturday night," Sawyer said during a rare lull in business.

Jill wiped down the bar and nodded. "Maybe they've had enough thieving and burning down henhouses. But frankly, Sawyer, I don't give a damn about the infamous pig war. I want to get through the night and sleep until noon tomorrow. I told Aunt Gladys not to look for me in church. I swear, by this time on Saturday, my butt is draggin' so bad that I don't have the energy to even sing."

"And according to this sexy redhead who kisses like an angel, I snored last week, so I'll be staying home with you," he said.

That cocky little grin of his sent shivers down her back. What was wrong with her? Never before had a few kisses and a shared nap made her throw caution and common sense to the wind.

Then why am I doing it now? she asked herself.

"You are fighting with yourself again," he said.

"Am not."

"Yes, you are," Sawyer said. "Your head cocks over to one side and then the other when you do that. Are you deciding whether to give Quaid or Tyrell another chance? If you want quiet and steady, go with Quaid. If you want a good time and a hell of a dancer, holler at Tyrell. As far as money and fame, you'll get it with either one of them."

She took a step to the side so that she was shoulder to shoulder with him. "For your information, I was thinking about my friend."

"Betsy or Kinsey? I'll put my money on Betsy, since

you and Kinsey have some evil vibes going on between you tonight," he said.

"No, my friend who protects me from the evil feuding family." She grinned.

"Hey, gorgeous, can I get three pitchers of Coors?" Tyrell bellied up to the bar. "And, Sawyer, we'd like seven burger baskets. Load 'em up with everything. Double the grilled onions."

Jill pulled the lever and filled three pitchers and set them on the bar.

Tyrell flipped two bills toward her. "If there's anything left, consider it a tip. If not, let me know what else I owe when the burgers are done. And, darlin', say the word, and I'll wait for you after-hours and we'll go watch the moon from a special spot I know about."

"Sorry, the only thing I'm interested in…" She stopped short of saying that she wanted to fall into bed.

"Is what?" Tyrell grinned.

Too bad his smile wasn't as hot as Sawyer's, or she might have taken him up on a visit to his special spot.

"The only thing I'm interested in is sleep," she said.

"I would love to hold you in my arms all night. I'll be the last one out the door, so if you change your mind, let me know." He picked up two pitchers in one hand, and the last one in the other, and swaggered off to his table.

"Should I tell him that you steal covers?" Sawyer asked.

"What about covers?" Betsy asked from the bar. "I'd be right happy to keep you warm enough that you wouldn't have to worry about covers, Sawyer. Thought I'd wait for the burgers and carry them back to the table as you get them ready. We are starving."

Jill didn't miss the look exchanged between the two women when Kinsey brushed past Betsy on her way outside with a cell phone plastered to her ear.

"I was saying that you can't judge a book by the cover," Sawyer lied. "Get your mind out of the gutter, Betsy."

"Well, hot damn, darlin'! I agree with you on that. Anytime you want to see inside this book, all you have to do is open the cover." She flipped her hand around to sweep from head to toe.

Sawyer ignored her comment. "Three burger baskets right here, and the other four will be ready when you get back."

"Fast thinking there, cowboy." Jill laughed.

"Yes, ma'am."

Kinsey let a welcome blast of fresh air inside when she returned with the phone tucked away somewhere and a smile on her face. She and her cronies, which had grown a table full of people to two tables, put their heads together for another confab and kept glancing toward the bar.

"Either they're about to murder Betsy, which I wouldn't mind, or they're going to try to enlist us into their family for help on the next battle of the pig war," Jill told Sawyer.

"I'm a lover not a fighter," he said.

There was that cocky grin again.

"No sassy comeback. You must be tired," Sawyer said.

"I was thinkin' maybe I'd tell Betsy that you're a lover, or maybe Kinsey," she said.

"They know it already. That's why they're both chasin' me." He laughed.

"Not a bit of ego risin' up from your cowboy boots, is there?"

"Awww, this is Sawyer you're talkin' to, ma'am. Not Quaid or Tyrell. You don't have to stomp on my feelin's because you're mad at them."

"A pitcher of beer and two cheeseburgers, no fries," Kinsey said.

"Four burger baskets for Betsy Gallagher," Sawyer yelled.

Betsy made her way through the crowd and perched on a stool right beside Kinsey. "So how's business? You chargin' more than a dollar to meet some poor old cowboy out behind the bar? I saw you leave a while ago."

"Prices went up," Kinsey said sarcastically. "For prime they have to pay two bucks. When I found out you was chargin' a dollar, I figured I was worth twice that much."

"Don't forget to pay your taxes. I'd hate for the IRS to get you for tax evasion. The righteous Brennan name couldn't stand a mar on it," Betsy said.

"Like the bootleggin' Gallaghers?" Kinsey smarted off.

"Ladies, remember where you are," Jill said.

Betsy leaned forward until she was inches from Kinsey's face. "I see a few wrinkles around your eyes. Won't be long until you'll have to lower your prices or pay the customer."

Then she flipped two dollar bills on the bar in front of the stunned Kinsey and said, "I wouldn't want you to starve to death since your chicken and dumplin's dried up. That should buy you a latte tomorrow morning."

She lined the burger baskets up on her arm like a professional waitress and sashayed her way through the line dancers back to her table. Kinsey swiped all the color from her lips with a paper coaster and smiled at Sawyer.

"I'm experienced, not old," she said.

"I'm not sayin' a word," Sawyer said bluntly.

"I'll take the beer back and return for the burgers," Kinsey said.

The baling on the hip pockets of jeans glimmered as she carefully made her way past the folks two-stepping to Blake Shelton's newest song. Then suddenly she stumbled and fell right into the Gallagher table, dumping one pitcher of beer on the floor and the other on Betsy.

Jill grabbed a mop and headed that way, with Sawyer right behind her. Betsy jumped to her feet, slinging her hands and throwing drops of beer on everyone around her.

Kinsey's eyes went wide in mock shock. "Oh, dear, I'm so sorry," she said coldly. Then she moved closer to Betsy, grabbed her by the shoulders, and licked the beer from her face from jawbone to forehead. The song ended, and the bar went quiet. It was worse than sitting in the eye of a tornado, and more eerie than the music in a horror movie.

"What the hell are you doing?" Betsy quivered like she'd stepped on a mouse in her bare feet.

"A Brennan doesn't waste good beer." Kinsey smiled. "If all you can do is whine and bark, then you don't have a place with the big dogs."

Betsy's hands knotted into fists. "I'll show you a fight, if that's what you want."

"Not in here, you won't. You've both had your fun, now settle down," Jill said.

Sawyer quickly plugged two coins into the jukebox,

and loud noise filled the building again. Jill didn't know if he simply punched in numbers or if he'd chosen the songs, but she couldn't keep from smiling when Gretchen Wilson's voice filled the room with "Redneck Woman."

Jill swabbed up the beer on the floor and put the mop back in the closet. "It says that she's a product of her raisin'. I believe that Kinsey and Betsy should sing along with her," she grumbled when she was back behind the bar.

"What was that? I was afraid the crowd might goad them into a brawl, so I started poking numbers into the jukebox. I'm not sure what I played," Sawyer said. "I was ready to step in if fists started flying, because I was afraid you'd get hurt."

"Hey, I had a mop. I'd have decked them both with the handle." She started to laugh when the song ended and "Romeo," an old one from Dolly Parton and Billy Ray Cyrus, started playing. "Are you sure you didn't handpick these?"

"Hell, no! I'm not interested in being anyone's Romeo, if that's what you are thinking," he answered.

She laughed even harder when the lyrics said that she might not be in love but that she was definitely in heat. "Sounds to me like Dolly Parton knows Kinsey and Betsy both pretty damn good. They're not in love, darlin', they are in heat, like she says in the song."

"It's not funny," Sawyer said.

But it was, because Jill had the same problem. Love and heat were two different things, and she could easily see where Sawyer, with his tall, dark, handsome looks could put any woman in heat. The words said she didn't get as far as his eyes when she was lookin' him over, and

Jill could relate very well. She had trouble listening to that damn song and not letting her eyes stray to the silver belt buckle above Sawyer's zipper.

Good God, when did this happen? A couple of kisses, and I'm wanting to jump his bones? What's the matter with me?

It was a few minutes past eleven when Sawyer finally unplugged the jukebox and announced that the place was now officially closed. The Brennans and Gallaghers had left, and a couple of old worn-out cowboys who'd come close to dancing the leather off their boots shuffled out the door.

Sawyer locked it and picked up the broom. Jill started wiping down tables and chairs. She'd barely gotten past the first table when she heard money clinking down the chute in the jukebox and turned to see Sawyer coming toward her with that grin on his face.

"Will you be my Juliet?" He growled exactly like Billy Ray in the "Romeo" song.

"I'm too damn tired to dance," she said.

He grabbed her hand. "Don't make me waste my money."

He tucked his hands in his belt loops, and good Lord, those jeans did things that gave her hot flashes. It was either dance with him or stand there slack-jawed like a Saturday-night drunk. She tossed the cleaner and the rag on the table, tucked her thumbs in her jean loops, and matched him step for step in the line dance.

When it ended, she was panting so badly that she couldn't even talk. "That sucked every bit of energy out of me."

"You ain't that old yet," he said as Mary Chapin

Carpenter started singing "Down at the Twist and Shout." He swung her out to the Cajun-flavored music and brought her back to his chest for three minutes of swing dancing.

"Please, tell me the third song isn't that fast," she said when it ended.

The whine of the fiddle in an old song softened the lights and the whole atmosphere in the bar. Sawyer pulled her close to his chest, picked up her hands, and put them around his neck. Then he dropped both his hands to rest at the small of her back, and he moved slowly around the floor as George Jones sang "Don't Be Angry."

He softly sang the words in her ear as they danced. He sang about remembering the first time he flirted with her, and asked her not be angry with him when he failed to understand all her little whims and wishes all the time.

When the song ended, he tipped her chin up and kissed her. She heard the whine of the fiddles and a harmonica somewhere in the distance, even though the music had stopped. There wasn't an angry bone left in her body when she rolled up on her toes for the second kiss.

"That, darlin', was the payment on the bet," she said.

He picked up the broom and started sweeping.

"So?" she asked.

"So what?"

"So is my bet debt paid in full?"

"Honey, after that kiss, I will need at least two cold showers to cool my blood so I can sleep."

Chapter 13

CLOUDS SHIFTED BACK AND FORTH OVER THE MOON, and only an occasional star could be found in the sky when Jill and Sawyer locked up for the evening.

Jill inhaled deeply, filling her lungs with clean, cool air. "Thank goodness the bunkhouse and the store are smoke-free, or we'd both drop graveyard dead with lung cancer from secondhand smoke."

"At least the exhaust fan takes most of it out of the bar area, so we don't get what the folks do that are out there around the tables." Sawyer's hand went to the small of her back as he guided her to the truck.

They were inside with seat belts buckled, and he had put the truck in reverse, when both doors opened, startling Jill so badly that she squealed.

"What the hell?" Sawyer said.

Tall men with ski masks, bibbed overalls, and work boots pointed sawed-off shotguns at them. Sawyer's pulse quickened, and adrenaline rushed through his body, but there wasn't a thing he could do. Three guns in his truck, and he couldn't reach a damn one of them.

"Out of the truck right now. You make a move, and I'll shoot this little lady right here in the parking lot. She'd bleed out before you could get an ambulance all the way up here," the one with a gun on Jill said gruffly.

"Hey, slow down. We're not protesting. You can have the truck, if that's what you are after." Sawyer reached for the seat belt and got a tap on the shoulder with the butt of the gun.

"Don't be cute, or you'll never see her again," the man said.

"I'm undoing our seat belts. Don't get trigger-happy. We are stepping out now," Sawyer said.

If only one of them had held a gun, he might have grabbed it and told Jill to run, but not when there were two guns. Jill might get hurt or killed. There wasn't a truck in the world worth harming one hair on her head, but who in the hell would have thought there would be hijackers in Burnt Boot, Texas?

"Hey, Sherlock," the man with the gun on Jill yelled. "It's all yours."

"What are you going to do with it?" Sawyer asked. "Can I get my personal things out of the glove compartment before you take it off to strip it down for parts?"

"Who said we're stripping it down? And, no, you can't get anything out of the inside. You've probably got guns in there. Give me your cell phones, billfold, and your purse, woman," Jill's assailant said.

Sawyer inhaled deeply. Yes, there was a pistol in the glove box, another one in the console, and a third one under the seat. He had a license to carry all three, but it wasn't doing him a bit of good right then.

Sherlock crawled into the driver's seat, backed the truck out, and drove away with it. No skidding tires or slinging gravel—just drove off like it belonged to him.

"Now, you two start walking," Jill's outlaw said.

"To where?" Jill asked.

"Out to the road."

"Are you going to kill us in the middle of the road? Wouldn't it be better to shoot us right here?" Jill asked.

Sawyer could have wrung her pretty little neck himself right then. If they reached the road, there was a possibility that someone might drive by and help them. He reached over and laced her fingers in his. She squeezed his hand gently, and he hoped that didn't mean she was about to try something stupid.

A dark van pulled up and slowed down, and Sawyer thought their problems were solved, until the double doors at the back swung open, and the two hooded men motioned for them to get inside.

"What the hell is this?" Sawyer protested.

The second man shoved the gun into Jill's gut, and Sawyer crawled inside the van. They pushed Jill in right behind him. The doors closed, and the darkness was so thick that he couldn't see his hand in front of his face.

"Jill, where are you?" he whispered.

A hand reached out and touched him on the shoulder. "Right here."

He grabbed it and pulled her into his lap, felt around her face until he found an ear, and pressed his lips close to it. "I imagine this is bugged, so start kicking the side of the van to make noise, and I'll whisper. Who do you know that would kidnap you?"

She kicked and said in a loud whisper, "Nobody. Not even Aunt Gladys or Aunt Polly would do this."

"Gallaghers or Brennans?"

"Both."

"Which way are we going?"

"I don't know. I think we turned around about the time they shoved me in here, but I'm not sure."

The van slowed down as if stopping at a red light or a stop sign. Burnt Boot had only one red light and a handful of stop signs, but Sawyer still couldn't get a bearing on where they were. Or why in the hell either of the feuding families would want to kidnap them.

Tires squealed, and they were thrown against the doors of the van. Whoever was driving cussed loud enough that they could hear him through the metal separating the cab from the cargo area. "Damn tree in the road. You should have checked things out better than this, Dumbo."

"Does that name mean anything to you?" Sawyer asked when they were sitting back up.

"No," she whispered.

"Well, let's get out and move the damn thing. We can't get to where we're going any other way," the one with the deep voice said.

Everything got quiet.

"I'm going to kick these doors open," Sawyer said. "Slide back so you are out of the way."

He raised his foot, his boot landed square on the hinged part, and the doors swung open as if by magic. Trouble was, instead of a midnight sky, there were two more guys in ski masks with guns, pistols this time, motioning for them to be quiet and get out of the van.

"It's the FBI," Jill said. "They're here to save us and then shoot the balls off those bastards for stealing your truck."

One of the men chuckled. "Follow us. Now get in here. Be quiet, and we'll get you out of this."

Sawyer and Jill moved as quietly as possible and crawled into another cargo van. This one was blue with some kind of lettering on the side, and the doors went shut, but not before Sawyer shoved his jacket in between them.

"Why did you do that?" Jill asked.

"I don't think we're being rescued. I think we're changing kidnappers."

"No!" she said.

"Give them time to get around to the front, and then we're getting out. Slide off into that ditch until they drive away, and then we'll start making our way out of this mess. We might have to find a place to hole up until daylight, when we can get our bearings. I think we were driving for about twenty minutes, but I don't have any idea which way…now, Jill, slide out right now. They're starting to move."

He grabbed her hand and opened one door, retrieved his denim jacket, carefully shut the door, and the van pulled away into the night without its passengers. The two men wrestling with the tree finally freed it, and they went in the opposite direction without ever realizing they'd lost their cargo.

Sawyer and Jill exhaled loudly at the same time as they watched from a prone position halfway down a ditch beside the road.

"Now what? We don't know where we are, and our cell phones and money are all gone," Jill said.

"Take a real deep breath," Sawyer said.

"Yuck," she said.

"That, darlin', is pig shit. Where there are pigs, there is a barn or a house or something nearby. We'll follow our noses until we find a barn."

"Why not knock on a door and ask for help?" she asked.

"We might get shot for one thing, and how do we know who we can trust?" He pulled her up, put on his jacket, and wrapped her hand into his. "I'm going to kick some ass when I find out who did this. I'm too damned tired to walk for miles in the cold."

"Get in line, Sawyer O'Donnell. I get first chance at them. I hate to pee in the brush, and I damn sure hate sleeping in a hayloft," she said.

They crawled over two barbed-wire fences, worked their way through a patch of thick mesquite, and outran one rangy old bull before the barn loomed up before them like a silent sentinel in the night.

"I may go back to Corpus Christi and sling hash for a living after this. I'm sick of pig wars and pig shit, and I'm not sure I even like pork chops anymore," she grumbled.

"It's only a quarter mile at the most, and it looks like the pasture has winter wheat growing. It's not tall enough to turn the cows into it, so the going should be good," he said. "Besides, Gladys will call out the Army, the National Guard, and the Texas Rangers when we don't show up for church."

"No, she won't. I told her that we might not be there, and she's not going. She and Aunt Polly are staying home, and Verdie is coming over later to play canasta with them. And, remember, she's doing chores tomorrow, so she won't miss us until Monday, probably when we don't show up at the store."

The barn hadn't been in use for years, but what was left of the tack room still had a couple of well-worn winter horse blankets stored in a drawer. Sawyer carried them to a stall, kicked the straw around to fluff up a bed, and shook out one blanket.

"We've slept spoon style before, and that's the only way we'll be able to stay warm with a bed this small," he said.

"I could sleep standing up in a broom closet. Sawyer, why would the Gallaghers or the Brennans kidnap us? It doesn't make sense."

He eased down on the makeshift bed. "Honey, I don't know what the hell they had in mind, but the one that chuckled was a Gallagher. I don't know his name, but I recognized his voice from one of the guys in the fight at the church. That means they were stealing us from the Brennans."

"But why?" She stretched out beside him.

He wrapped an arm around her. "Anyone who gets into a pig war is bat-shit crazy. Let's find our way home and pretend it never happened, until we can prove it. And then we'll take them out, one at a time."

"No use in wasting time. I'll set fire to both their ranches and burn them to the ground." The last words were mumbled, and then she was sound asleep.

He tucked the blanket tightly around them both and swore that when he found out who'd done this, the pig war would be nothing compared to what he would do.

Chapter 14

JILL DIDN'T WANT TO OPEN HER EYES. SHE KNEW exactly where she was and how she got there and who was snuggled up against her back, but an itchy feeling on the nape of her neck said something was staring at her. If it was a granddaddy long-legs spider, she did not want to see it.

"Hey, are y'all alive?" someone said in a whisper.

Spiders did not talk, so Jill opened her eyes slowly.

"Wow! You *are* alive. I was afraid you was dead, and I ain't touchin' no dead person," the kid said.

A big yellow dog stuck his nose through the wooden slats of the stall and sniffed the air.

"That's Buster, my dog. He's the one who found you first. I come huntin' for him. Can you hear me?"

Jill nodded. "Where are we?"

"In my daddy's barn. We only raise hogs now, so we don't use this barn too much 'cept to store hog feed in and use when a sow has pigs in the real cold wintertime."

"Are we in Burnt Boot?" she asked.

"Are you talkin' in your sleep?" Sawyer asked.

"No, I'm talkin' to a boy and his dog," Jill answered.

Sawyer sat up so quick that the blanket went flying. The end smacked the dog on the nose, and he yelped. "Do you have a cell phone, son?"

"No, I don't, but my mama does. She took it with her over to Miz Ruby's last night though. Miz Ruby is getting another baby, and she needed my mama. Y'all know you ain't supposed to be here, don't you?"

Sawyer rubbed sleep from his eyes. "Where are we?"

"In my daddy's barn. I done told the lady that."

"But where is your daddy's barn?" Sawyer asked.

"In Salt Holler. We're the last house in the holler," he said.

"How do we get out of here?"

"Well, you could go to the bridge if you need to drive across. But if you follow me, I'll show you where you can climb over the fence and then go up to the road and follow it. If you go the wrong way, you'll come to the bridge."

"Do you go to church in Burnt Boot?" Sawyer asked.

"No, sir. I go to church right here in Salt Holler. Mr. Wallace Redding is preaching this mornin'. I like to listen to him."

"Where do you go to school?"

"Burnt Boot."

"Do you know Martin Brewster?"

"You mean Martin O'Donnell. He's done changed his name, you know?"

"Yes, that's the boy I'm talkin' about." Sawyer smiled. "Would you tell him tomorrow morning about finding us here, and tell him that my name is Sawyer O'Donnell?"

The kid nodded. "I'll do it for you if you don't tell my daddy that I let you go. He don't take too kindly to people trespassin'. There's signs up on all the fences."

"I promise I won't tell your daddy," Sawyer said. "If you'll show me which way it is that I need to go to get out of this holler, you can go on home."

"Right back of this barn, you go straight through the corral and past the old outhouse, and you'll see a fence with a red sign that says 'Trespassers will be shot.' Crawl over that fence and go through the 'squite all the way to the road. You can see the top of our barn when you get up on the road. It's pretty steep to get up to the road, but me and my brother have done it, so I reckon y'all ain't too old."

"Which way do we go then?" Jill asked.

"The bus that takes us to school goes…" He looked at his hand and made an L with his left thumb and forefinger. "You go right." He smiled.

"How old are you?" Jill asked.

"I'm eight, but that right and left business gets me all bumfuzzled."

"Okay, but you won't forget to tell Martin in school tomorrow, will you?" Sawyer asked.

He shook his head. "You'd best put them blankets back where Daddy had them. He don't like things left out of place."

"We will, and thank you," Jill said.

"Bye, and y'all ought to get on out of here pretty quick. Daddy is feedin' the hogs, but you never know if he'll need something out of the tack room or not," the boy said, and then he and the dog were gone.

"What I wouldn't give for a cup of coffee," Jill groaned.

Sawyer quickly folded the blanket they had huddled under. "Well, darlin', I'm sure once we hop that barbed-wire fence, beat our way through another mesquite thicket, and climb up out of this holler, there will be a Starbucks sitting right there."

Jill followed his lead, stretching to get the kinks out of her back. "And a hotel right beside it with a soft bed and a big shower." She shook hay from the bottom blanket and handed it to Sawyer. "I'm grateful right now that we had a place with a roof to sleep. We might have been huddled up against a scrub oak tree somewhere."

"Hungry?"

"Yes, but I'll live. You think someone will come along and give us a ride once we're on the road?"

"Could we trust anyone other than Gladys or Polly or Verdie enough to get into the car or truck with them?" he asked.

"Well, shit!" she mumbled as they followed the path through the mesquite thicket.

Bits of hay had woven their way into Sawyer's hair, and his jeans looked like he'd crumpled them up and let a dog or two sleep on them. Jill figured if she looked in a mirror, she'd be in the same bedraggled condition.

"Why would they do it?" she asked.

"If I was a guessin' man, I'd guess that the Brennans got us first and they planned on throwing me out somewhere along the way and then sending Quaid out to rescue you. The way they had it planned is that you'd be so grateful to him for helping you to escape that you would have to repay him."

"But you?"

"I'm collateral damage. They had figured on you taking your own truck, but when we got into my vehicle together, they had to take me with you."

"They would have probably hog-tied you and given you to Kinsey to play with all weekend, instead of throwing you out beside the road." She grinned. "And at the end of the weekend, she'd have you pantin' around her long legs like a male dog after an old bitch in the springtime."

"Maybe that's what she thought, but she would have been in for a big surprise."

They came out of the thicket and there was a wall of mud in front of them. Two little boys might climb that thing like monkeys when there was grass on it, but two grown adults were another story.

"Now what?" she asked.

He crossed his arms over his chest and studied the situation. "If I had a chain saw, I could cut down a tree, and we'd climb up it to the edge. Who'd have thought there would be an embankment like this in these parts? I can see the guard rails up there."

"Me too. I vote that we keep the road in sight and follow it until we come to a better place to climb up," she said.

He nodded and held up his left hand, making an L with his thumb and forefinger. "That way." He grinned as he pointed.

"Yep, at least the sun is coming up and it's not raining or sleeting," she said.

———

Sawyer took her hand in his and trudged on ahead. She looked downright cute with hay stuck in her red hair. And by damn, she was a good sport to boot. She'd found things to be grateful for rather than bitching about her feet aching or no food.

"Are we getting close to the Starbucks?" she asked.

"It's not far. Just keep walkin' and thinkin' about it," he said.

A big bluetick hound bounded out of the brush and fell in behind them. He kept his distance, but when Sawyer looked back, he wagged his tail, so hopefully he wasn't stalking them for his breakfast.

"I smell coffee," she said.

"It's a mirage."

"A mirage is something you see, like a coffee shop or a Dairy Queen up ahead, but an aroma is something different, and I swear I smell coffee and a woodstove," she said.

"If you do, let's hope it's not on Wallace Redding's part of the Holler. From what that kid said, I don't think those folks play well with others."

"He said his daddy's pig farm was the last one in Salt Holler, and when we climbed over the fence, we were out of it," she said.

The hound dog shot out past them and was a blur as he ran ahead. Sawyer cocked his head to one side. "I heard someone whistling. That dog is going home. There's a house up there, and it's not far. Maybe they'll have a phone we can use."

"Or they'd be willing to share their coffee," she said.

Neither of them saw the cabin until they were right up on it. The back half was built into a hillside with only the front showing. That part had a wide porch roof made of split logs and held up by four tree trunks that still had the bark attached. The hound lay on the porch beside an old rocker. When he saw them, his tail beat out a welcome on the wooden floor.

The man who stepped out the door with a sawed-off shotgun in his hands wasn't much over five feet tall and wore bibbed overalls, a red flannel shirt, and worn work boots. The wind blew his wispy white hair in all directions, and his blue eyes had settled into a bed of deep wrinkles.

"State your business. You ain't supposed to be on my

property. Didn't you read the sign that said trespassers would be shot?" he said gruffly.

"I've read a lot of those signs," Jill said. "Are we still in Salt Holler?"

"Not in Wallace Redding's part of the holler. You're at the very end in my part right now," he said.

"Are you kin to the Gallaghers or the Brennans?" Jill asked.

"Hell, no! If I was, I'd shoot myself in the head with this gun."

"We were kidnapped, but we escaped, and now we're trying to get back to Burnt Boot," Sawyer said.

"That damned feud. I heard it had fired up again over a bunch of pigs that got stolen. You give me your word y'all ain't no revenuers from the gov'ment?" He eyed them both carefully.

"I promise. We'd sure like to borrow your phone and call for help, sir," Sawyer said.

"Ain't got no phone, but from the looks of you both, you could use some breakfast. Me and Otis here, we done ate, but there's plenty of flapjacks left over, and coffee is hot."

"We'd appreciate that very much," Jill said.

"Well, don't stand out here in the cold. Come on in here and tell me your story. I like a good tale, and there ain't been nobody to talk to for at least a month. Wallace is supposed to come over next week for a batch of brew, so you can entertain me until then. I'm Tilly, short for Tilman."

"I'm Sawyer O'Donnell, and this Jill Cleary," Sawyer said, glad that Tilly had lowered the shotgun and was holding the door open for them.

"So you are Gladys's new foreman at Fiddle Creek,

and you are her niece who'll wind up with it someday. Now it makes sense why them thievin', feudin' families would want to kidnap you. Crazy sons a bitches ain't got a lick of sense, but they've both been after Fiddle Creek for years. Go on over there and wash up a little bit while I put the breakfast on the table for you." Tilly motioned toward the back side of the cabin, where a pump sat at the end of a makeshift table with a washbasin below it. "Ain't got no hot water heated up, so you'll have to make do with cold, but I expect after a night in the woods, it won't feel too bad. Where'd y'all bed down?"

"In a barn a couple of miles back that way." Sawyer pointed.

"See anybody?"

"Just a kid that gave us some directions out of there. Said that we could climb up to the road, but we haven't found a place that wasn't a muddy mess," Jill answered.

Tilly set his mouth in a firm line. "You'd be some lucky folks. That place belongs to Wallace's nephew, and he's a mean bastard. They ain't friendly in Salt Holler. Ain't but a handful of people is allowed across the bridge. Years ago it was a place where outlaws went. I reckon those that live here are still the offspring of those outrunnin' the law. Me and Otis, we keep our distance from them people."

"But you sell him moonshine?" Sawyer asked.

"Hell, yeah! Got to sell it to someone, and I damn sure don't want people comin' around here. They might bring the gov'ment men with 'em. This way we're both makin' some money, and I ain't got to deal with people. I'm a hermit," Tilly said.

The coffee was so strong that it could melt the enamel

from teeth. The pancakes were rubbery, but the hot, buttered, homemade sugar syrup made them go down right well. Sawyer finished off two stacks before he finally pushed back from the table. "We thank you for your hospitality. Do you have a vehicle that can get us out of this place? We'd be glad to pay you well to take us home to Fiddle Creek."

He rubbed his freshly shaven chin. "Ain't got no car, but I do go to town twice a year. It ain't time yet, but I'm runnin' low on a few things. It's a five-mile stretch up there on the road, and I reckon if you'd be willing to pay me in flour, sugar, and coffee, and if we was to get started pretty soon here, old Bessie would get me home by dark. Way these crazy people drive, I don't like to be out in the wagon after the sun sets."

"Bessie?" Jill asked.

"That would be my mule that pulls my wagon. Y'all'd have to ride in the back, seein' as how the seat in the front only 'commodates me."

"Yes, sir. We'd be obliged, and we'll stock you up on supplies," Sawyer said.

"Then I expect we'd best get goin'. Sun is up, and if we get there by noon, I can load up and get back by sundown," he said. "Days are short this time of year."

"How do you get out of this holler with a mule and wagon? Do you go back to the bridge?" Jill asked.

Tilly chuckled. "I got my ways. Bessie lives across the road on fifty acres I own over there. That's where I keep my wagon. That side is pretty flat."

He pulled a rope and a ladder fell down from the rafters. "Fancy, ain't it? It was made for one of them houses with a ceilin', but I got it fixed up so part of it falls down to here and the other part stays up there to the hatch in the roof. Y'all follow me."

He scrambled up the ladder like an agile little boy. "Y'all comin', or you goin' to stand down there and look stupid?"

Jill started up with Sawyer right behind her. Where in the hell they were going once they reached the top was a mystery, but it was definitely the only way out, other than going back to the bridge. With her fanny practically in his face, Sawyer couldn't control the pictures that flashed through his mind.

Her butt would fit so well in his hands, especially if they were both naked and in his big king-sized bed.

"Okay now, we hit this here button and watch what happens," Tilly said.

A hatch opened up on the roof, letting in sun and cold air. Jill followed him on up the ladder and through the opening to find that the porch roof was level with the road over to the right. And right there was a swinging bridge about twenty yards long, wide enough for one person at a time.

"Cute, ain't it?" Tilly said. "Let me get to the other side before you get on it. Don't know how much weight it would bear. One at a time, and then we'll hitch up Bessie to the wagon and get on our way."

Chapter 15

BESSIE, THE OLD GRAY MULE, HAD TWO SPEEDS: SLOW and stop. A stick of dynamite could not have put any more giddy-up in her pace, but Sawyer wasn't complaining. He could be walking all the way into town and dodging Gallaghers and Brennans on the way.

Jill smiled at the right places when Tilly told the first story, but when he started on the second one, her eyes grew heavy, and she slumped against Sawyer's shoulder. He shifted his weight so that he could hold her steady with one arm.

Tilly looked back over his shoulder and smiled. "She'd be a keeper, son. I can see why the Gallaghers and the Brennans both want her. She'd be a prize even without the water rights on Fiddle Creek. Damn fools ought to know better than to kidnap her, though. They ought to be sweet-talkin' her and bein' nice. But then so should you. She's got that special glow when she looks at you."

Sawyer chuckled. "And what would you know about a glow?"

"Ah, now, there's a lot you don't know about me, son, and I've seen that look in a woman's eyes one time before when she looked at me. I was a young man back then, and I ruined it all. Take my advice and don't let go of the best thing you might ever have. Now where was I? Oh, yeah, I was tellin' you about the day I found my little bit of land and why I bought acres on both sides of the road," he said.

Sawyer listened with one ear and kept an eye open most of the time. Tilly didn't seem to want or need any feedback. He wanted someone to listen, and Sawyer could do that and doze at the same time.

He awoke with a start when the wagon wheel fell into a hole, but Bessie brought them out of it with very little effort. Jill didn't even move. She still had hay in her red hair, and her cheeks were rosy from the cold. Lashes rested on her cheekbones, and the sunlight brightened the few freckles sprinkled across her nose. The curve of her hip coming away from the tiny waist intrigued him. Tilly was right about her being a looker, but he didn't have a damn thing to offer Jill Cleary. He'd saved enough money through the years to put a down payment on a small ranch, but banks were a lot stingier with loans in today's economy than they had been in the past. Still, there was something about her that made him wish he had everything Quaid and Tyrell did, so he could give her what she deserved.

Two trucks passed them on the way into town, and both times they honked and waved, but neither stopped. If it was the feuding families who'd kidnapped them and stolen his truck, they evidently didn't want to tangle with Tilly or his mule, either one.

He groaned. "My truck. I hadn't thought about that. I'll have to call the insurance company and the police as soon as I buy another cell phone."

"What about your truck?" Tilly asked.

Sawyer filled him in on the story, and Tilly shook his head. "Them bastards. Get you a mule and a wagon.

Don't have too many people wantin' to steal old Bessie, and if they did, she'd probably bite the shit out of them. She can be a mean-tempered old bitch when anyone crosses her. Well, would you look at that? You can see Gladys's store. In another five minutes, old Bessie will have us pulled right up to the door."

Jill pulled away from Sawyer and rubbed the sleep from her eyes. "Are we almost there?"

"Just up ahead. Town sure looks dead, even for a Sunday. Ain't seen but a couple of trucks since we left the holler. Did you get a little rest?" Tilly asked.

"I can't believe I slept that long." Jill rolled her head from side to side to get the kinks out. "Thank you for helping us, Tilly. It sure beat walking all morning."

Tilly pulled the wagon up to the front door and hopped down off the wagon seat. "It's dinner time. Reckon we might fix us up a bologna sandwich in the store before I start back?"

"I'll fire up the cookstove and make you a steak, if you want it," Jill said.

Tilly grinned as he held his hand up to help her down. "I got steak and pork at home. But it ain't often I get a big old bologna sandwich."

Jill put her hand in his. "With lettuce, tomatoes, pickles, onions, and mustard."

"Now that's a meal fit for a king," Tilly said.

Sawyer jumped down from the back of the wagon and groaned when his knees protested the treatment they'd been given in the past twenty-four hours.

"Best heed the advice I gave you, son. You ain't gettin' no younger." Tilly laughed.

Jill found the spare key inside a fake rock in the

flowerpot beside the door. She opened the lock and swung the doors open to a warm store. On her way back to the meat department, where she fully intended to slice a couple of pounds of bologna to send home with Tilly, she removed her coat and hung it on the rack.

"What do you want, Sawyer?" she asked.

"Ham and cheese, mayo, and everything you're putting on Tilly's sandwich. I'll get a bag of chips and some pickles, and we can eat at the checkout counter," he answered.

"That's a sissy sandwich," Tilly said.

"Not if you eat more than one to prove you are a man. I'm having two for starters, and then maybe a half a bag of those chocolate doughnuts right there," Sawyer told him.

"You want two?" Jill asked Tilly.

"Yes, ma'am. I reckon that would be right fine," he answered. "And"—he winked at Sawyer—"maybe I'll have some of them doughnuts too."

"What are you drinking?" Sawyer headed for the cold soft-drink case.

"Root beer." Tilly didn't hesitate for a second. "This picnic gets better and better."

Once Tilly started eating, he didn't say another word. He enjoyed his food without conversation. When he finished, he leaned the chair back and propped his boots on the counter. "Well, now, this has been a profitable trip, yes it has. The company has been good, but it is time for me to get on down the road. Bessie will be expecting to get out of that harness come dusk, and she does get bitchy if she doesn't get her way."

"Flour, sugar, and what else?" Jill asked.

"Dinner has paid for the trip, but I will pick up supplies while I'm here," Tilly said. "You ring it up, and I'll pay for my purchases. I'll start out with two pounds of bologna, sliced thick, and one of them big old ham bones for Otis. He'll pout because he didn't get to come along with us."

He filled a cart and Jill conveniently forgot to ring up several of the items. When she totaled his bill, he slapped his leg and laughed out loud. "Young lady, I want you to check me out every time I come in here from now on. Don't be thinkin' that you pulled the wool over an old man's eyes. I had the bill figured, along with the tax, before you ever keyed in the first bag of flour. But thank you, and if you ever need a ride out of the holler again, you come on down to my place. Me and Bessie will take good care of you. Sawyer O'Donnell, you remember what I told you."

"Yes, sir, I will," Sawyer said.

"Y'all want me and Bessie to take you on to wherever you live?"

Sawyer shook his head. "Bessie needs to get on back home. It's not that far for us to walk, and my legs need some stretchin'."

It felt normal when Sawyer tucked her hand inside his as they started toward the bunkhouse. But then they'd gone past the simply friendship stage a while back. She wasn't sure when, because it had kind of snuck up on her. Thinking about it didn't scare her, but felt as right and comfortable as her hand in his.

She stopped so quick that he'd taken two more steps

and dropped her hand before he saw what she was point-ing at. He shook his head. It must be a mirage, because he was so weary, but there sat his truck, not a dent in it, no slashed tires, not even a busted taillight.

"Your truck," she whispered. "Don't touch it. The police will want to check for fingerprints."

"We're not calling the police," he said. "And besides, they were all wearing gloves, so they wouldn't have left fingerprints. This isn't the Hatfields and McCoys. They would have already brought out the rifles and killed each other. That's the way folks fought in those days. This is the Gallaghers and Brennans, and they do things different."

He opened the door, found all three of his guns safely hidden away, his billfold, pickup keys, her purse, and both of their cell phones on the passenger's seat. He was more convinced than ever that the Brennans did the job so they could swoop in and rescue Jill and she'd be indebted to them. Then the Gallaghers found out about it and figured they'd steal the Brennans' thunder with the same plan. Why else would someone drive his truck home? Hell, a car thief wouldn't even know where he lived. And why would they leave all the money, credit cards, and three high-dollar pistols in the truck? Yes, ma'am, it was the workings of the pig war, and if he could prove a single bit of it, they'd all be in jail for what they'd put Jill through.

She had her hands out, reaching for her purse and phone when he turned around with them. "You're right about calling the police. Other than Tilly, who would back us up? And no one would ever believe such a wild story. I'm glad to have my purse and phone back. I need a shower, and then I might feel like a whole woman again. But believe me, Sawyer, they are going to pay for this shit."

"I figured you'd want a long bath," he said.

"That would take too much time. I'll be quiet, I promise."

He opened the bunkhouse door for her. "What's that got to do with anything?"

"You should have the first shower, since it's your bathroom and since you let me snooze almost the whole way home," she said. "So go on, and I'll be quiet while I get cleaned up. I'll even tiptoe when I'm done so I won't wake you."

"You go first. I'll get the sofa ready and find the golf channel." He grinned.

"And lock the door?"

"Little paranoid now, are you? They won't try that tactic again. They'll be holed up in their fortresses, plannin' the next move. But for peace of mind, I will lock the door."

She made a run through her bedroom, shedding her boots and coat and picking up underpants, flannel pajama pants, and an oversized sleep shirt. Then she grabbed her travel pack, a carryall that hung on the back of a door and contained shampoo, deodorant, toothpaste, a hairbrush, and her own shower gel and lotion.

She looked in the mirror before she got in the shower and gasped, "Oh. My. God."

Makeup smeared, hair a total mess with hay still sticking in it, bags under her eyes. She quickly shucked off her jeans, shirt, and underwear, all of which still bore the smell of beer and cigarette smoke, and sighed when the pulsating hot water hit her tired and sore muscles. She tried to be quick, but it took three times of lather, rinse, and repeat before her hair quit shedding hay and the water ran clear. After seeing her reflection, she scrubbed her body down twice with shower gel and hoped the stink of sleeping in a barn that smelled of rat piss and cows was finally gone.

Now you bitch about the sleeping quarters, her inner voice said. *Last night you were glad to have a roof over your head.*

"Oh, hush," she said aloud. "A roof didn't keep it from smelling bad."

She took time to towel dry her hair and run a brush through it, to recheck her reflection and sigh when the bags hadn't disappeared from under her eyes, and get dressed before she left the bathroom.

"I started the fire so you wouldn't freeze. I'll get the sofa bed ready when I get out. My phone is turned off and charging. You might want to do the same with yours," Sawyer said.

She sat down on the edge of Sawyer's bed to wait for him. Together they would make the sofa into a bed when he finished his shower. It wasn't that she couldn't do that job alone, but that she was too damn tired to want to.

The heat was taking its own good time getting from the living area into his bedroom, and the wood floor was cold. She pulled her legs up and wrapped her arms around her knees. Her toes were like icicles, sending shivers all the way up to her hair, still damp from the shower. Maybe she'd get warm if she pulled the fleecy blanket on top of his bed up over her. It would be a means only to get warm. Now, getting under the covers would be a different thing.

The blanket was like warm clouds on a hot summer day when she tucked her toes under it. She eyed the pillows. One still had the imprint of his head, so the right side was his. She was a left-side person. She promised herself that she would lie down on the spare pillow for a few seconds. It looked so inviting, and she was so tired. She'd be long gone before Sawyer finished in the shower. The water stopped running and she could hear his electric shaver going.

———

Sawyer could hardly keep his eyes open long enough to shave, but if he let his heavy dark beard go any longer, the electric razor would bog down trying to get the job done. The room should be semiwarm by now, and the golf channel was already on television. He'd bet dollars to pig shit that Jill had the sofa bed out and was already snoring.

He hurried across the cold floor, only to find the sofa empty. Evidently, she'd given up on him and gone to her room for a nap. Disappointed, he did a quick tiptoe back to his room and stopped in his tracks when he found her sleeping on his bed.

"Got to admit, it's bigger and more comfortable than the sofa, and, darlin', I might share my blanket, but you ain't gettin' all of it," he murmured.

She rolled toward him and threw a leg over his body when he pulled the throw up over them. He slipped an arm under her and buried his face in her still slightly damp hair. It smelled like coconut and ocean breezes. It would be easy to get involved with Jill. They were together twenty-four hours a day, seven days a week, but if it didn't work out in the end, they could wind up ene-mies. And he liked her too well to ruin their friendship.

And yet, his inner voice piped up, *do just-friends sleep all tangled up like a bunch of baby granddaddy long-legged spiders?*

"When they've been through what we have, they do." He inhaled deeply one more time to take the scent of her shampoo with him into his dreams.

Chapter 16

JILL AND SAWYER WALKED HAND IN HAND TOWARD the setting sun. The sand was warm on their bare feet. Sea oats waved in the gentle night breezes on one side, and the ocean's waves gently slapped the sandbar on the other. Sandpipers darted back and forth with the surf, searching for supper, and gulls circled lazily above them. Everything was in its place, doing what it was supposed to do at the end of the day, and Jill's heart was at peace.

She didn't want to wake up, so she refused to open her eyes. It didn't work. The beach was gone, and the only sounds she could pick up were Sawyer's soft snores and the crackle of the stove wood as it burned. He was sleeping on his back with one hand up under his neck and the other arm around her shoulders.

Easing out of his embrace slowly so he wouldn't wake, she propped up on an elbow and studied him without fear of getting caught: dark hair, those thick lashes spread out on his cheekbones, that full mouth that could kiss so damn well, and a broad, muscular chest. But there was more to Sawyer than his quick wit and his outer good looks; he was a hardworking, protective cowboy and had a kind heart.

His eyes fluttered open, and he smiled. "I thought I felt someone or something looking at me. I'm glad it wasn't a man in a ski mask."

"Think Tilly made it home okay?" she asked.

"I'm sure he and Bessie were home a while ago. It's dusk out there," he said.

"Are you my friend?" she asked, bluntly.

"I hope I'm not sleeping with the enemy." He smiled. "What is this all about, Jill?"

"I was involved with a man for two years," she said.

"And it ended badly and you need to talk about it? Why now?"

She sat up and crossed her legs. Indian style, her grandmother called it. "I don't know. It seems like I should, so that the things that are supposed to end will and the sun will finally go down on it all, and…"

Sawyer pulled himself up to a sitting position, adjusted the blanket over their feet, and laid his hand over hers. "Okay, let's talk. You go first, and then I'll tell you about my heartbreak."

She paused. "This is a bad idea."

"How long since you broke up?" he asked.

"More than a year ago."

"Have you talked it out of your system with a girl-friend, your mama, or your aunt Gladys?" he asked. "Don't look at me like that. I have a sister, and I know how females need to talk everything to death."

She giggled like a little girl. "That's why we talk about it so long. We want it to be dead and done with when we finish talking."

"Then talk, and let's get it in the grave. I'm a damn fine listener," he said.

"In the beginning, I thought he was perfect. He was thoughtful and kind, and his daddy had a ranch, so we had lots in common. We'd been dating about three months when he wanted us to move in together, but I didn't want to commit to that. Looking back, I must've realized something wasn't right with the relationship even then."

She kept talking, and Sawyer listened. He didn't nod at the right times and pat her hand, but his eyes said that he was really paying attention. If he'd picked up a little notepad and started to write, she would have sworn he'd been a therapist in another life.

"Evidently, he figured if I was close enough, he could wear me down to do what he wanted. That was probably why his father offered me a job on his ranch. I'd been living with my grandparents and helping out on the ranch, but then they died and we found out that the bank owned the ranch, or at least ninety percent of it. Grandpa had been putting extra mortgages on it for years to keep it running, and it had to be sold at auction to pay the bank. I was out of a job."

"I'm sorry," Sawyer said.

"I had a little tiny trailer out behind the bunkhouse, and my jobs varied from exercising horses to helping haul hay or anything else that needed done. We had this big fight six months ago about him being so spoiled and about an old girlfriend who showed up on the scene, and the whole relationship came unglued. She was in his league, which I definitely was not. She worked in her daddy's oil company but never got out into the real business of drilling."

"He cheated on you?" Sawyer asked.

"I don't know if he did or didn't, but he started dating her a week after I left and went to another job on a ranch a hundred miles away. When that ranch sold a few weeks ago I called Aunt Gladys."

Sawyer squeezed her hand. "You aren't stupid, Jill. You saw it coming and got your heart ready for it."

"I hope that's what it is, and I'm not hard-hearted, hardheaded, and coldhearted to boot," she said.

"Did he ever mention marriage?" Sawyer asked.

She shook her head. "No, and I'm glad he didn't. I might have said yes."

"Regrets?"

"Not a single one. If what we had didn't work, then marriage would have been a big mistake. But I haven't had the nerve to get involved with anyone since him. There are no regrets, not even when I'm right in the middle of this damn feud. Which reminds me, I will get even with them."

"I've got three pistols. I can shoot with two at once if you can handle one and that sawed-off shotgun you seem to be partial to," he said.

Like always, his wit put her in a good mood and made her laugh.

"I'll do some practicing, and I bet we could take out a bunch of those varmints before Sheriff Orville arrived with his doughnuts," she said.

"Which reminds me." He covered a yawn with his hand. "I'm hungry."

"After two sandwiches?"

"That was a long time ago. Taking a nap is hard work. I'll make spaghetti for supper if you'll put a pan of brownies in the oven for dessert."

She cut her eyes up to catch his gaze. "And while we make supper, you will tell me your story, right? Or have you talked it to death with your cousin Finn or your mama?"

"Oh, honey, I pouted and whined worse than a little girl when it happened, nearly two years ago, and it's a wonder either one of my cousins who was with me at the time will even talk to me." He pushed the covers back, pulled on a clean pair of socks, and stomped his feet down into boots.

She felt better immediately. Any tough old cowboy who'd been hurt bad enough to cry wouldn't be ready for a relationship any more than she was.

———⟋⟍⟍⟍⟍⟋———

Sawyer set an iron skillet on the stove and turned on the flame under it. While that heated, he filled a pot with water, added salt and a splash of cooking oil, and set it on another burner to boil. Hamburger sizzled when he tossed a pound into the skillet. Jill whipped up flour and sugar and cocoa together in a big bowl while he pulled out another pan for his special sauce. None of that canned shit for Sawyer; no, sir, he made his own marinara sauce, starting with real tomatoes.

"Okay, role reversal. I'm the therapist. You get to talk now," she said.

"To death?" he asked.

She nodded. "All the way to the grave."

"She and I'd gone to school together since kindergarten. We went to both our junior and senior proms together and dated all the way through college. We got engaged, but she didn't want to rush into marriage. She wanted the big, perfect wedding with all the bells and whistles, and her parents couldn't pay for something that elaborate, so we saved our money. We even had a joint checking account, and when it hit a certain number, we were going to start planning the wedding. We were almost there when an opportunity to go on a cattle drive came up. She told me to take the month and go on. She would be busy checking out venues for the wedding," he said.

"Venues?"

"You know. Places that specialize in that shit. Hell, I didn't care if we got married in the middle of a pasture, but I wanted her to be happy."

"You don't strike me as a man who'd want all that," Jill said.

He grinned. "See there, we've known each other only a couple of weeks, and you can already tell that about me."

"You were gone a whole month?"

He nodded.

"It happened at the end of the drive. We didn't have phones, so she couldn't call me until the end. When I called her, I got the news. She'd met a man at a party from Pennsyl-damned-vania, decided that she was in love with him, and eloped with the fool."

"After making you wait for years for the big foo-rah with all the bells and whistles? Damn, Sawyer. I'd have killed them both and sworn to St. Peter that they committed suicide."

He laughed as he shoved spaghetti into boiling water. "I considered it. Yes, ma'am, I damn sure did. But I wasn't about to let her know that she'd broken my heart, so I went home and pretended to be happy, and I never talked about it again until today. Well, I did mention that she'd come home to Comfort, Texas, divorced and lookin' my way, to Finn when I showed up on his doorstep at Christmas."

"What about the savings account for the big wedding?" she asked.

"It went with her when she eloped."

"Did she apologize for taking it?"

"Hell, no! She said that it was for her wedding, and therefore, it was her money. And, honey, I did not tell anyone that part of the story. Not even my mama or Finn knows that I was that big of a fool," he answered.

"It was her loss, Sawyer. I bet there are days when she wishes she'd made a different choice."

He shook his head. "Maybe. If she does, that's her problem. Trust is what you build any kind of relationship on."

"And you don't do second chances?" Jill asked.

He added the browned meat to the marinara sauce. "Darlin', there ain't enough duct tape in the world to fix a stupid cowboy who'd get mixed up with that again. Besides, I've moved on."

A blast of cold air preceded Gladys into the bunkhouse. When she reached the kitchen, her hands were on her hips and her lips were pursed so thin that they almost disappeared into the wrinkles.

"I've tried to call both of you since early this morning. Don't you have enough sense to pick up your phones?" she fussed.

"Something wrong?" Sawyer asked.

"You hungry? We're having spaghetti, and brownies for dessert," Jill said.

"Yes, I'm hungry, and, no, nothing is wrong on the ranch, but I did go to church this morning, after all. It was too damn cold to go anywhere else, and I've been trying to call both your phones all day."

"I'll put another plate on the table," Jill said, "and we'll explain while we have supper together."

"It's a long story," Sawyer said.

Gladys tossed her coat on the sofa and sat down at the table. "And you'll make a plate for me to take to Polly?"

"There's plenty," Sawyer said.

Gladys pointed at Jill. "You go first. I was scared y'all had both left Fiddle Creek, and I don't want either of you to leave. I like this arrangement."

Sawyer slid half a loaf of Italian bread into the oven. He'd carefully cut it into thick slices and applied garlic butter. All it needed was a little heat and they'd be ready for dinner. "Sweet tea?"

"Yes," Gladys said.

Jill busied herself putting ice into glasses and filling them. "I could tell the Gallaghers and Brennans were up to no good when they got to the bar last night. It wasn't what they said, but the way they kept looking at each other's tables."

Gladys slapped the table with the palm of her hand. Cutlery rattled against plates and tea sloshed against the sides of the tall glasses. "I knew this would have something to do with that pig war. I knew it."

"We can't prove a bit of it." Sawyer set the sauce and the spaghetti on the table. "Bread will be out in a minute."

"Bit of what?" Gladys asked.

"Well, it went like this…" Jill went on to tell the story.

"So I've slept with your niece in a horse stall and in the back of a wagon, Gladys. You going to get out the shotgun?" Sawyer brought out the bread.

"Hell, no! If I had a medal, I'd give it to you for

protecting her," Gladys said. "And the way both families were acting this mornin' in church, I'd say that you've got it right about what happened. But you're also right about not being able to prove it. What did you think of Tilman?"

"You mean Tilly?" Jill asked.

"That's what they call him now, since he's a crazy old moonshiner who lives on the edge of Salt Holler, but that's not what we called him when we were in school with him." Gladys expertly wound spaghetti around a fork. "Damn fine food, Sawyer."

"Thank you, ma'am. Why didn't you call him Tilly?"

"Because he was the smartest kid in school, and in those days, Tilly was a girl's name. It was short for Matilda, and not only was he smart, he was a cocky little fighter who'd black a kid's eye if he got mad at him. He went on to make a lawyer out of himself, and then he ran for the House of Representatives and won twice. In the middle of the second term, he flat-out walked away from his job, bought that land near Salt Holler, and started making moonshine. Nobody really knows what happened. Some folks say it was over the Korean War. Some say it was over a woman. Wallace buys liquor and wine from him, and Tilly, he don't bother nobody," Gladys said.

"He seemed like a nice old guy to me," Jill said.

"The only other person who's ever been on his land is Wallace Redding, and that is to buy shine. No one would ever believe that Tilly befriended you. He don't do that. He comes to the store twice a year for supplies and goes right back home. He talks to me when he's there. I hear he picks up his mail at the post office. They hold it for him for six months at a time, and it's mainly magazines and newspapers. Takes a whole garbage bag for him to haul it out of there."

"Jill could sweet-talk a bear into giving up his honey." Sawyer laughed.

"Oh, hush, I had hay in my hair and looked like the wrath of God had kissed me," she said. "I've never been so glad to see a shower and get a nap in a real bed in my whole life as I was when we got back to the bunkhouse."

"She looked cute." Sawyer grinned. "I thought she did, and evidently Tilly did too. He not only let us into his house, he fed us breakfast and brought us to town."

Gladys stuck her hand into her pocket and brought out a telephone. "Polly, don't you eat any more of those cookies. Sawyer made spaghetti, and I'm bringing you a plate. The kids are fine, but I've got a hell of a story to tell you."

A pause and a couple of nods. "No, it's too juicy to tell over the phone, and, yes, I'll be there in the next fifteen minutes."

She hit a button and shoved the phone back in her pocket. "Reckon I'll wrap up my plate too. She says if I don't get back, she's going to eat the whole bag of cookies, worryin' about what I won't tell her on the phone."

"I'll get it ready," Jill said.

"What should we do now?" Sawyer asked Gladys.

"Go on like nothing happened, and see what comes crawlin' out of the woodpile."

"I'd rather set fire to both ranches," Jill said.

"Nope, Fiddle Creek might suffer, since it's in the middle of them," Gladys said. "Thanks for supper, and I'll see y'all tomorrow."

Chapter 17

JILL COULD NOT PUT HER FINGER ON IT OR FIGURE IT out, but the relationship had risen to a new level between her and Sawyer since they'd bared their souls the day before. Maybe it was what soldiers face in near-death experiences when one saves another's life. But whatever it was, she kind of liked it.

He'd been quieter, had a lot less to say or joke about, and now he was back there in the meat department, cleaning the saw like the health inspectors were due to come look at the store that very day.

The store was empty, and the shelves were dusted, the floor swept, the carts lined up, and the front glass washed on the inside. It was so cold outside that if she sprayed cleaner on that side, it would freeze before it hit the glass. She pulled her tablet out of her purse, hit the right button to bring it up, and went straight to her favorite site for a little retail therapy. She might not actually buy boots or a new bit of bling, but she'd look at it, and maybe that would help her sour mood.

An advertisement for a brand-new spice for chicken wings popped up on the side bar, and that's what gave her the idea. She quickly went to another site that promised overnight shipping if she was willing to pay for it, and she decided it was well worth the cost. She pulled the charge box up from under the counter and wrote the addresses for River Bend and Wild Horse on the edge of a scrap of paper.

The first order was for a case of pork rinds. She carefully checked the box that said it was a gift and not to send any information concerning price or sender to the recipient. On the gift card she wrote "Oink! Oink!" and signed it "Porky Pig." That little prize went to River Bend to the attention of Mavis Brennan.

The second order was for three bags of Chicken Chips doggy treats. The gift card said, "For the Gallagher Bitches" and was signed "Chicken Little." That present went to Naomi Gallagher at Wild Horse Ranch.

Guaranteed delivery by eight o'clock the following evening. She'd entered the pig war, and it put a smile on her face.

"Well, well, it smiles," Sawyer said.

"This from a man who's hardly spoken to me all day," she said.

"Hey, you started off the day real quiet."

"So did you," she shot back.

The bell rang as the door swung open, and there was Quaid Brennan standing there with a shoe box in his hands. He looked downright sheepish, holding a Prada shoe box with the price still written right there on the end. Jill hoped he could take them back, because she damn sure didn't wear a size nine narrow. She wore a six wide. He'd have done much better if he'd brought in a Lucchese box, and he'd have spent a hell of a lot less money to boot, pun intended.

He set the box on the countertop. "I brought you a present. I heard that you had a mouse or two in the bunkhouse over on Fiddle Creek."

"And I'm supposed to catch them in this box? You want to explain the procedure to me?" Jill could feel the ice in her voice, but dammit, he was a Brennan.

"Open it," he said.

She flipped the lid open, and a little gray kitten looked up at her with big green eyes. She picked it up and the purring began immediately.

"Kinsey's mama cat had babies, and this little girl looked like a good mouser to me." Quaid smiled.

"Thank you. I'll take good care of her." Jill cuddled it up against her face and talked baby talk to the critter.

"I'm glad you like her. Maybe I'll give you a call later this week, and we can plan something for Sunday?" Quaid said.

"Sawyer and I had plans for yesterday that got interrupted, so we'll be real busy next Sunday while we make up time. But thank you for the kitten," she said.

Quaid blushed. "Well, then maybe the next week. See you at Polly's sometime."

He was gone before Jill could say another word.

Sawyer reached over and scratched the kitten's ears. "Did you see the expression on his face? We might not be able to prove it, but we were right. That was the face of a kidnapper, right there."

"You want to hold her?" she asked.

"No, you go on and spoil her. It's your cat. What are you going to name her?"

"Ollie," she said quickly.

"I can see you've given this cat idea a lot of thought. Why Ollie?" he asked.

"It's the pig's name on a kid's animated movie called *Home on the Range*."

His dark brows drew down into a single line and then shot straight up. "You are wicked, Jillian Cleary."

"But I'm in a much better mood. A little retail therapy and a new kitten works wonders on me." She grinned up at him.

"So what did you buy? Oh. My. God! Is that a misprint or did whatever come in this box cost that much?" He pointed.

"Oh, yeah. I expect Kinsey wears them to work. And eight hundred dollars for Prada is on the low end of the scale," Jill said.

"Do you…?"

She shook her head before he could finish the sentence. "Not on your life. I could buy two pair of Lucchese boots for that price, and they'd last a hell of a lot longer and never go out of style. You sure you don't want to hold Ollie?"

He reached out, and she put the kitten in his hands. "Here piggy, piggy." He smiled. "Your real name might be Ollie, but I'm going to teach you to come runnin' when I holler piggy, piggy, instead of kitty, kitty."

"And you call me wicked," Jill said.

Sawyer leaned across the counter and brushed a sweet but hot kiss across her lips. "To be so open with each other yesterday, we sure clammed up this morning, didn't we? Aren't people who sleep together supposed to talk more?"

"We aren't sleeping together," she argued.

"Yes, we are. We aren't having sex, but we are sleeping together. Every Sunday so far, and I liked it," he said. "You can sleep with us, little piggy, if you want to." He scratched the kitten's belly, and she rolled over in his arms like a baby and shut her eyes. "Right now, I need to stir a pot of chili I've got going on the stove. You can go with me if your new mommy trusts me."

"I'm not that cat's mommy, and, yes, I trust you. Here, take her box in case you need to put her down while you stir," she said.

She went back to her tablet and was busy plotting her next move in the pig war when the bell rang again, and there was Tyrell. At least he didn't have a shoe box in his hand, or roses either, so that was a good thing.

"Hey, Jill. I missed seeing you in church yesterday," he said.

I'm sure you did. I bet you even looked for me and Sawyer when you got to your destination and the back of that van was empty, she thought.

"Sawyer and I went for a hike," she said.

"Well, I overheard Gladys telling Polly that you had a mouse problem at the bunkhouse, so I went out in our barn and rustled up a kitten for you." He pulled a yellow ball of fur from his pocket and handed it to her by the scruff of the neck. "You'll have to tame her. She's a little wild."

The kitten spit at her and growled, but after a minute of gentle petting, it was as tame as Ollie.

"So do you like her?" Tyrell asked.

"She's cute as a newborn chicken," Jill said.

"She's a cat, not a chicken."

Jill pushed the issue. "But her fur is the same color as a fresh-hatched chicken."

"I guess it is. Well, I've got to go. Hope she's a good mouser," Tyrell said. "You got time for a picnic lunch anytime this week?"

"Looks like a busy week on Fiddle Creek, but thanks for the kitten. I'm sure she'll love the bunkhouse."

"You might want to ask your roommate if he's allergic to cats. If he is, I'll take the kitten back to the barn out on Wild Horse."

Jill smiled up at Tyrell. Was he the one who had been wearing a mask and had taken them from one van to the other? Or had he been one of the first kidnappers? She couldn't tell. It had been dark, and they were all tall men wearing cowboy boots.

"Sawyer loves cats even more than I do. He might even claim this one for his very own," she said.

Tyrell frowned. "I brought it to you."

"And I really do thank you."

"See you at Polly's sometime this week."

"I'll be the one filling pitchers behind the bar," she said.

He shut the door behind him when he left, but a gust of cold air breezed across her face all the same. "Now that's fitting, isn't it, Audrey? Kidnap me and then bring a present to cover it up. Pretty damn cold, if you ask me."

"Did I hear someone talking?" Sawyer asked.

She held up the yellow kitten. "Her name is Audrey because…"

"I watched that movie with Finn's kids. Audrey is the name of a chicken, right?"

She nodded.

"So Quaid brought a playmate for Piggy here?"

"No, Tyrell did."

His laughter echoed off the walls. "Well, come on over here Chick and meet Piggy. We'll see if the Gallaghers and Brennans can get along in feline form."

They set them on the floor behind the counter, and the two sniffed each other. Audrey reached out and swatted Ollie, who promptly swatted back, and then they jumped three inches straight up and landed in a bundle of fur, kicking and biting each other.

"The feuding blood runs deep," Jill said.

"Not necessarily. They're playing, not fighting. They think they are sisters," Sawyer said.

They stopped, flopped down beside each other, and fell asleep with Audrey curled up in the middle of Ollie's stomach.

"Aha," Sawyer said. "And the pig and the chicken shall lie down behind the counter in peace. Think we'll live to see the day the Gallaghers and the Brennans make friends?"

"I wouldn't hold my breath. I don't look good in that shade of blue, and don't be getting too close to me after almost blaspheming the holy word." Jill laughed.

He started around the counter. "Why is that?"

She backed all the way up to the far end, beside the cash register. "Because if lightning shoots out of the sky, I don't want to be the one it gets instead of you."

"Here comes lightning." He pinned her hands behind her back.

She barely had time to moisten her lips before his closed in on hers. He was dead right. It was electrifying, sending jolts of pure desire shooting through her whole body. She wanted Sawyer, plain and simple.

"Ouch," he said when he broke the scorching kiss.

"I didn't bite you."

He pointed to his leg. Audrey was climbing it like it was a tree.

She reached down and picked the yellow kitten from his jeans and held her close. Did fate intervene in the form of a kitten, so they wouldn't take the kissing business to the next level? Was it trying to tell her to pay more attention to the Gallaghers, since it was Audrey who had put a stop to things?

"I had no idea that chicks could claw like that," he said.

"They can't, but cats can," Jill said. "And now it's closing time. We'd best load up enough of that chili for our supper and put the rest in the refrigerator for later. We have to take these critters home before we go to the bar. I won't have them inhaling all that cigarette smoke. I'll get a bag of litter and a couple of cans of food from the shelves if you'll take care of the chili."

"I'll do it," he said. "That was a fine kiss, ma'am. It flat-out weakened my knees."

"Sawyer O'Donnell, you are full of shit."

"No, ma'am, I'm speakin' the absolute guaran-damn-teed truth."

Chapter 18

THE AROMA OF COFFEE WAFTED THROUGH THE BUNK-house that Tuesday morning. Sawyer picked up his cell phone and found that he had no missed calls, that it was six o'clock in the morning, twenty-one degrees outside in Burnt Boot, Texas, and that it was January twentieth, his sister's birthday. He would need to call the florist after he finished the morning chores, or there would be plenty of calls, starting with his mother fussing at him for missing an important day in their family.

He was on his way to get a cup of Jill's strong coffee but stopped to take in the picture before him. Holding a mug, Jill sat on a worn rug in front of the woodstove. Piggy—she had a name, but Sawyer couldn't remember it—danced across the rug sideways, and then Chick grabbed her by the tail, and the fight was on. They made Monday night wrestling look tame, right up until they got tired at the same time. Then they were friends who needed each other to sleep.

Just like you and Jill, his inner voice said.

I slept fine by myself last night, he argued.

Not as well as you did on Sunday.

Sawyer let the voice in his head have the last word. There was no arguing with the truth. He did sleep better when Jill was next to him.

She was gorgeous with the first morning light glim-mering in her hair. Her green eyes sparkled as she watched the kittens play, and suddenly he was jealous as hell that he hadn't been the one who brought them to her. Every time she looked at them, she'd think of Quaid and Tyrell, maybe even going back and reliving what their kisses felt like.

"Hey, you are awake," Jill said. "Coffee is ready. There's a breakfast casserole in the oven, and the girls have been fed."

"You cooked?" he asked.

"Be thankful. Not grouchy."

He poured coffee into a mug and sat down on the sofa. "I'm not a bit grouchy."

"Your words say one thing. Your attitude says another. How can you be grumpy when these two kittens are so entertaining? Even when they are asleep, they make me smile."

"You want honest?"

She nodded. "What's your problem?"

"What do you think about when you look at those kittens?"

She sipped her coffee, a smile covering her face.

His heart grew heavier and heavier. Dammit! He didn't want to be right this time.

"Well, when I look at Piggy Ollie over there, I think of pork rinds. And when I look at Audrey Chick, I think about Chicken Chips. Never knew the latter existed until I found them online yesterday. They are doggy treats, and I guess they taste like chicken. And that makes me smile. No, it does more than that. It makes me giggle like a little girl who found a way to get even with a smart-ass on the playground."

She popped up agilely and sat down beside him on

the sofa. "They also make me think of Quaid and Tyrell, and remind me of the fear I felt in that dark van. I've never been afraid like that before. I've always been able to take care of myself. But I had no gun and not even a hairpin to pick a lock with. I wasn't strong enough to kick down the doors or to get away from the two of them, as big as they were, and they had guns. If you hadn't been there, I'd have been a blubbering, quivering bundle of nerves, but I had faith in you, Sawyer. I knew you'd figure a way to get us out."

He wrapped an arm around her shoulders and drew her close to his side. "Don't underestimate yourself, darlin'. Once you got over the fear, and the anger set in, you'd have kicked ass. How can you love those kittens if they remind you of the fear?"

"It's weird, but they are so cute and funny. Maybe they are the sign that I definitely do not want to get mixed up with either family," she said.

"They won't quit," he said. "And what's this about pork rinds and doggy treats? I love pork rinds, and my sister buys those chips all the time for her spoiled little rat of a dog."

She fit in his arms perfectly. He shouldn't fight the urge to take it past a few kisses to the next step. It wasn't like he'd forgotten how to date. He'd gone out lots of times and even considered a serious relationship once.

The timer on the oven sounded, and for a split second, Sawyer thought his phone was ringing. They both hopped up at the same time.

"Breakfast is ready. I'll get the plates if you'll make the toast," she said.

"Why? Do you burn toast? I'm not surprised that

someone as hot as you can burn bread by touching it," he flirted.

She slapped at his arm, deliberately missing. "That's a pickup line. Not a bad one, either. How many women have heard that?"

"Well, there was Delilah, Gloria, Letitia, Julie, Darcy, should I go on? I'm not sure I can recollect how many women have burned bread for me."

Jill pushed him into the kitchen. "Well, scalding-hot cowboy, get on in there, and let's see if you can burn toast."

He had asked about pork rinds and Chicken Chips, and Jill had managed to dodge that bullet by changing the subject. But now he was probably thinking of all those tall, beautiful blonds and brunettes he'd dated and wishing that he was having breakfast with them instead of a spitfire redhead that had admitted she had been scared shitless.

That's what friends do. They tell each other how they feel, she thought, hoping it might quiet the voice in her head before it ever got started. But the voice had to throw its two cents into the ring. *You went past the friend stage the first time he kissed you. Deal with it. You are attracted to him, and he's definitely been flirting*, she argued. *But Sawyer could have any woman anywhere. Right now he could move to Wild Horse or River Bend, ranch to his heart's content, and have anything he wants. They are both beautiful women, and, dammit, I'm working myself up into a jealous rage.*

The irritating voice didn't have a comeback, which aggravated Jill even more. She pulled the oven omelet out and set it on a hot pad in the middle of the table, put out plates and silverware, and refilled their coffee cups.

Sawyer winked at her when the second round of toast popped up. "I must have lost my power. It's perfectly browned, not burnt. Hey, you mentioned retail therapy yesterday. Have you ever ordered flowers online?"

Dammit to hell and back on a rusty old poker. He'd decided to send flowers to one of those hot women of his past.

"Yes, I have. I send them to my mom in Kentucky all the time," she said. "It's easy peasy. You key in your credit card numbers after you pick out what you want, tell them the date you need it delivered, and hit send."

Suddenly, she wasn't hungry and even the coffee tasted horrible.

"Can they even get flowers to Comfort, Texas?" he asked. "That's pretty far back in the woods."

His old flame was about to get a second chance.

"Don't know the logistics of the whole business, but they get them there when they say they will. I expect they pick out the nearest florist, and believe me, for the price you pay, they can afford to cough up the delivery fee."

He set the plate of toast on the table and hurried to his room, returning with a laptop. "Okay, show me the place you use."

He'd already gotten online, so she went straight for the site, and he picked out the biggest bouquet of red roses offered, typed in all the information, and hit the "send" button. "Wow, that is fantastic. My sister is going to be so surprised when they arrive at her house in a couple of hours."

"Your sister?" Jill spit out.

"Today is her birthday. Let's eat before it gets cold. I'm starving, and there's chores waiting for us to do." He dipped deeply into the egg casserole and picked up two pieces of toast. "It's already buttered, and there's apple butter and grape jam in the fridge if you want it. As for me, I'm planning on a second helping of this scrumptious-lookin' casserole rather than having extra toast with jelly."

Sawyer's sister and Jill were two happy women.

"So is your sister younger than you?"

Sawyer shook his head, swallowed, and sipped his coffee. "Oh, no. She's the oldest of four, and bossed us boys around like she was the Queen of Sheba. She was twelve when I was born, so she thought she had as much power over me as Mama. She still likes to boss me, since I'm the only single one left in the family. And believe me, if I forgot her birthday, the sun would fall from the sky."

"Her name?"

"Martina, and my brothers are Hugh and Kevin. Mama is Latino. Daddy is Irish. They made an agreement that Mama could name the girls with names from her heritage, and Daddy could give the boys Irish names."

"And Sawyer is Irish?"

He grinned. "No, it's English. If Daddy hadn't loved his daughter so much, I would probably be Seamus, or maybe Tomas, but Martina cried when I wasn't a baby sister. Mama had been reading Tom Sawyer to the kids, and if Martina couldn't have a sister, then she wanted a brother named Sawyer. Daddy tried to talk her into Tom, but she'd have no part of it. So he gave in to her tears, and I'm Sawyer."

"It fits better than Seamus or Tom," Jill said.

"Well, thank you for that and for this delicious breakfast. You think we should call a babysitter for Piggy and Chick, or can they stay by themselves until we come back from chores?"

Jill looked at the sleeping kittens. "They'll grow up fast. We'll have to make a medical decision, Sawyer. Do we have them spayed or let them have kittens?"

"We can decide that later. Right now, let them be babies," he answered.

<hr />

It had been a slow afternoon at the store, and both Sawyer and Jill wished for the kittens to entertain them. He propped his feet on the counter, dropped his cowboy hat down over his eyes, and started to snore. She sat on the counter, back to the cash register, and went through emails from her mother and her best friend back in Kentucky. She replied and told them both all about the kittens and what they'd named them. She didn't mention, nor did she intend to tell them, about the kidnapping business.

Her phone rang immediately, and she fished it out of her purse and headed to the back so the conversation wouldn't wake Sawyer.

"Okay, young lady, talk. I can always tell more from your voice than those sterile emails. Two cowboys brought you kittens?" her mother, Barbara, asked.

"It's two of the three that kissed me that day," Jill said.

"The other one did not bring you a kitten. What's the matter with him?"

"He's smarter and does less to irritate me than the other two."

"Please tell me you aren't going to stay in Burnt Boot permanently. Those people in that part of Texas are crazy. Gladys and Polly should act their age and sell all that property to the highest bidder. They are not spring chickens anymore, and it's time for them to retire," Barbara said.

"I think that's what they're trying to do."

Jill got a long martyred sigh for her answer.

"I don't mean retire and put you in charge. Dammit! Jill!"

"It's okay, Mama. I can take care of myself." Jill went on to tell her more about the feud and the way things were happening, leaving out the part about Sawyer's kisses and how they affected her. "And now I have a customer, so I have to go. You should come see me in Burnt Boot."

"No, thank you. You come see me, and we'll go up to Lexington and spend the day in the spa, stay overnight, and shop until we drop."

"We'll talk about it later. Got to go," Jill said.

"Tell your aunts hello for me. I can't believe you're living in that backwater place, but you've always been strong willed and liked boots better than high heels." Barbara's tone was scolding as she ended the call.

"What customer?" Sawyer asked.

"Were you eavesdropping?" Jill asked.

Sawyer shook his head slowly. "But I could hear her all the way over here. I didn't know she was that much against your being here," he said. "Now where's the customer?"

The little bell at the top of the door dinged, and Jill pointed to Verdie. "Right there."

Verdie started talking the second the door shut behind her. "Hey, y'all, looks like it's a slow day. I figured more folks would be in town, what with all the gossip flyin' around. I heard that the pig war tried to do something else over the weekend and failed. Some folks saw Tilly out with two unidentified people in the back of his wagon. It's bein' rumored that a Gallagher was shot, or else that a Brennan and a Gallagher were up to hanky-panky and got caught."

"And what would Tilly have to do with that?" Sawyer asked.

"He'd be bringin' them into town for a price. Gladys done told me the real story, but I ain't breathin' a word of it. Let them think a Brennan shot a Gallagher if they want to." She pushed a cart toward the meat counter. "I need three pounds of shaved ham, a pound of bologna, and a pound of summer sausage. Got that?"

"Yes, ma'am," Jill said.

"What brought you out in the cold this Tuesday afternoon?" Sawyer hung his hat on the rack and headed to the meat market. "I'll take care of your order back here. Jill can help you with the rest of it."

"Lunch makings for the kids. I'm going to pick them up at school while I'm in town. Y'all hear about the new kink in the pig war?" She put three loaves of bread in the cart and added two five-pound bags of apples.

"I think that idea of calling it a pig war is funny, but I bet those two families that think they're better than the rest of us don't think it's a bit humorous," Sawyer said.

"Don't matter what either one of those families like. They shouldn't have started this thing. They act like children, and this new thing is really childish. Pork rinds were delivered to the Brennans this morning, and 'oink, oink' was written on the gift card."

"Oh, really. Pork rinds, huh?" Sawyer chuckled.

"You think that's funny?" Verdie asked.

"Yes, I do. Don't you?"

Verdie nodded. "Laughed my ass off when I heard about it. The Gallaghers thought they were rubbin' in the thievin' of those hogs."

"So you think they really did steal them?" Jill asked.

"Yes, I do, but proving it is another matter, and until there is proof, there won't be no arrests made. Sawyer, put three of those ten-pound bags of potatoes in my cart, please."

"How about I put them on the counter, and then when you're done, I'll take them out to your van?" he said.

"Thank you. Now, I was saying, the Gallaghers got their comeuppance a few minutes later when they got a bunch of some kind of dog treats called Chicken Chips delivered to them." She chuckled and then guffawed.

"And that's funny?" Jill asked.

"Hell, no, but the note was. It said it was for 'the Gallagher bitches.' Dogs. Bitches. Chickens. I think that's funnier than the pork rinds," Verdie said.

"And the Gallaghers?" Jill asked.

"The Gallaghers have been plannin' something for sure. This added fuel to their plans. I'm wonderin' how in the world both of them got things delivered the same day. Oh, well, never a dull minute in Burnt Boot."

"Depends on who you ask," Jill said. "I talked to my mama, and she said this place was boring. She said to tell the aunts hello. I expect that includes you, Verdie."

"I'm not blood kin, but I appreciate being remembered. I always liked your mama when your dad brought her here to visit, but there never was a doubt about her liking this place. She hated every minute she spent here. Now if you'll check out my purchases, Jill, I'll take Sawyer up on loading it for me. Kids will be out of school in fifteen minutes."

Kinsey breezed into the store while Sawyer was outside helping Verdie. She snapped her fingers and pointed toward the meat counter. "Granny needs fourteen pork chops and two pounds of thinly sliced ham."

Jill slowly meandered through the store to the back, taking time to turn a couple of cans of corn around to show the picture better. Be damned if she'd hurry, when the bitch had snapped her fingers at her.

Kinsey tapped her high heel on the wooden floor. "I'm in a hurry. I'm running this errand on my lunch break."

"We've got a sale on pork rinds. You want to pick up a few bags?" Jill asked.

Kinsey's mouth set in such a firm line that it disappeared. Didn't she know that her face could freeze like that? Aunt Polly used to tell Jill that all the time, and she believed it with her whole heart.

"That is not funny. I guess Verdie told you about our delivery?" she said through clenched teeth.

"She might have mentioned it. Fourteen pork chops, or was that fifteen?"

"Fourteen and two pounds of ham," Kinsey said.

"You bitch!" Betsy Gallagher came in like a whirlwind with a tornado pushing it.

"Me? Your damn family is the one who sent the pork rinds."

Betsy got right up in Kinsey's face. "Well, that note you sent to our family with those chicken-flavored dog treats was damn sure rude."

Sawyer hurried inside. "Hey, what's going on in here? I'm tired of telling you that this is neutral territory. I think Jill is taking care of Kinsey. What can I help you with, Betsy?"

"Grandma wants ten pounds of flour and five pounds of sugar, and this is not over, Kinsey Brennan. You think you are so cute. Well, you tell that family of yours to be careful, because you've done pissed off the wrong Gallagher."

Kinsey leaned forward, nose to nose with Betsy. "If you ever send another thing to River Bend, I'll personally burn down Wild Horse and enjoy watching the fire."

"That is enough," Sawyer said. "Betsy, I'll get your flour and sugar and carry them out to the truck for you."

"Will you go home with me for supper?"

"No, I will not. I'm not taking sides or being a pawn in your games either," he said.

Betsy flipped around to follow him to the counter, and Kinsey stuck a foot out. Trouble was that when Betsy was going down, she reached for something to hang on to and got a firm hold on Kinsey's leg, taking her down with her.

The screaming and hair pulling began in earnest, and Sawyer started to wade in to stop it, but Jill put a hand on his shoulder. "Let Piggy and Chick alone. They need to fight and scream. Take this meat order to the front, and I'll bring the flour and sugar. We'll get it all rung up, and if they haven't finished scratchin' and yanking at each other's hair by then, or if one can of food hits the floor, we'll stop them. Can't have the store wrecked, can we?"

"Little retail shopping, huh?" He grinned.

"It sure helped my mood," she said.

They were still throwing punches and screaming obscenities after Sawyer put their orders in the right vehicles and returned to the store. "I don't think they're going to get tired and lie down together to sleep," he said.

"Been at it five whole minutes. I reckon they're tired and waiting on us to stop it so neither one of them will lose face," she said.

"You care if they lose face?" he asked.

She shook her head.

He sat down in the chair, picked up his hat from on top of the cash register, and adjusted it over his eyes. "Call me if they start throwing cans of corn. Don't want the front glass of the meat counter to suffer damage."

Jill picked up her tablet to see if there was anything else of interest concerning chickens or hogs. She stole sideways glances at Sawyer as the fight wore on another two minutes. Sawyer was the man she'd waited for her whole life. The one who eased her fear, made her laugh, and stood beside her. Leaning back in an old metal folding chair, boots crossed at the ankles on the countertop, hat down over his eyes, he didn't fool her one bit. That cocky little grin said he wasn't sleeping or even dozing.

Two very rich men vying for my attention, and I'm interested in a rough old cowboy that I've known less than a month. Am I certifiably crazy?

Kinsey finally broke free from Betsy and ran out the

front door, her hair a mess and one eye already turning color. One heel had popped off those fancy shoes and had scooted up under a shelf. A long rip up one side of that short skirt that barely covered her ass showed the edge of her panties. Scratches ran down the length of her jawline, and she'd best get out a scoop shovel to apply her makeup the next day to cover that and the black eye. The runs and holes in her black panty hose were icing on the cake. Her cute little sports car sped out of the lot, slinging gravel up on the porch.

Betsy didn't look much better when she took off after Kinsey. She swiped away the blood from her lip and nose with the back of her hand, and she also had a black eye. At least her jeans and boots hadn't suffered as much, so she might be the winner of the fight.

"Y'all come on back now, you hear?" Jill called after them.

Chapter 19

KINSEY CHOSE THE STOOL AT THE FAR END OF THE BAR on Saturday night. After the grocery-store brawl, the families had retreated to their corners. Makeup couldn't cover the yellow-looking bruise under Kinsey's eye or the long fingernail scratch up across her face.

"What can I get you?" Sawyer asked.

"Two sticks of dynamite and a hit man," she answered.

Sawyer picked up the bottle from the top shelf. "Double shot of Jameson, it is."

Jill bumped him with her hip. "Here comes trouble."

Betsy shot a few daggers down the length of the bar before she hopped up on a stool at the other end. "Coors, from the tap, and, Sawyer, I want a cheeseburger basket with extra fries."

"Jill." Kinsey crooked her finger. "Tell that hussy at the other end of the bar that we don't need the preacher comin' out to River Bend to talk to us. We know the Brennans have gone to talk to him, but we are not burying hatchets any time soon. We are not having a powwow with the Gallaghers, not even in the church. We'd rather kiss the south end of a northbound brood sow as give them the satisfaction of peace."

"Sawyer," Betsy said, "tell that bitch that he came to Wild Horse without an invitation, and that we told him that we take care of our vengeance. We don't even trust

God with it. And she might as well kiss a pig's ass with those lips. They've kissed worse."

Kinsey sipped her whiskey and looked at Betsy in the mirror behind the bar. "Jill, tell her that I beg to disagree. They've never kissed a Gallagher."

Betsy cackled. "She wouldn't be so lucky. There's not a Gallagher who'd ever bend so low as to kiss her."

Kinsey opened her mouth, and Jill slapped the bar with a wet towel. "Stop it, both of you. Either take your bitchin' outside, or shut up. I'm tired of this constant shit between y'all."

Sawyer flipped the burger on the grill and checked the basket of fries in the deep fryer. Three women within slapping distance of him. Out of the trio, he would have chosen the tall, willowy blond a few months ago. Two of the others were short redheads, and he'd have given neither of them a second look. But he had flat-out fallen for Jill Cleary. She could do better than a cowboy with barely enough money saved to put a down payment on a very small spread. Hell, she could be sitting pretty over on Wild Horse or River Bend, either one. But Sawyer wanted her like he'd never wanted another woman in his entire life. They were soul mates, and looking back, he had known it from the first time he saw her standing in the doorway of the bunkhouse. Even then, in her anger, he'd seen something that had attracted him to her.

"Do you understand me?" Jill asked. "If so, nod."

The two women on the other side of the bar had just tried to kill each other with dirty looks and barbed, hateful remarks, but they both nodded and went back to their drinks.

"Thank you," Jill said.

Sawyer put the burger together and set it in front of Betsy. She picked it up in one hand and her drink in the other and, with a ramrod-straight back, headed to the table the Gallaghers always chose. Leaving food and beer on the table, she went to the jukebox, fished a few coins from her pocket, and plunked them in.

On her return to the table, she tipped an imaginary hat at Kinsey. Loretta Lynn's voice filled the bar with "You Ain't Woman Enough to Take My Man." Betsy made sure she was staring holes in Kinsey when the words said that women like her were a dime a dozen and could be found anywhere.

"So tonight the battleground is in the jukebox. Hope we have enough quarters," Jill whispered to Sawyer.

The next song was another Loretta song called "Fist City." Sawyer could almost see the steam coming out of Kinsey's ears when Betsy held up her beer in a salute. When the words said that if she didn't want to go to fist city she'd better get out of her town, Betsy raised her fist and shook it at Kinsey.

"Would you take some woman to fist city?" Sawyer whispered in Jill's ear.

"Damn straight! I'd tear a woman to pieces to protect what's mine," Jill answered. "I wonder if this is going to go on all night."

"Looks like she's about to have her say one way or the other. Is the shotgun loaded?" Sawyer asked.

"It stays ready."

Several people pushed inside and claimed tables, Gallaghers sitting with Betsy, the Brennans finding their own spot, and the folks who didn't care about the feud taking up the rest of the empty tables. Kinsey tossed back the rest of her whiskey and, without taking her eyes off Betsy, headed toward the jukebox.

Betsy's last choice brought folks out to the dance floor for a line dance, with her leading the pack. Alan Jackson sang "Good Time," which surprised Sawyer. He was ready for another fighting song from Loretta or maybe Tammy Wynette. But Gallaghers, Brennans, and folks that neither Jill nor Sawyer knew filled up the dance floor.

———

"That hussy knew exactly when her backup troops would arrive," Jill said. "Uh-oh!"

"What?"

"Keep an eye on what's about to happen," Jill said.

On one shake of the hip, Betsy bumped Kinsey so hard that she had to grab the jukebox to keep her balance. Betsy mouthed "oops," moved away, and kept on dancing with the crowd.

Kinsey headed for the jukebox and nodded toward the door.

"If Betsy does that again, Kinsey is taking her outside," Jill said.

"Long as they don't dent my truck, I don't care if they kill each other," Sawyer said.

Tyrell left the line dancers and yelled on his way across the floor, "Hey, Sawyer, we need ten cheeseburger baskets, and, Jill darlin', if you could draw us up four pitchers of beer and give us about a dozen cups, we'd be some happy Gallaghers."

Quaid propped a hip on the stool closest to the door. "Double that order, only put poison in theirs."

"No can do," Jill said. "Poison has to be done outside the bar."

"Did you see what Betsy did to Kinsey? Of course you did, and I heard you didn't do a thing to help my sister." Quaid accused as much with his eyes as with his words.

"It was their fight, not mine," Jill said.

Tyrell stopped dancing and swaggered over to the bar. "Betsy didn't need any help. She put that Brennan bitch on the run."

"Like I told the ladies, the fight stops at the door. You want to feud, take it outside," Jill said.

The noise level in the bar went from rock band noisy to eerie quiet when the song stopped. Every eye in the place was on Quaid and Tyrell, and dollar bills started flying out of pockets to land on the tables. Quaid slid off the stool, and Tyrell did the same. They looked at the door, but then set their eyes ahead on the tables where their families were and circled away from each other.

"Like a couple of wiry old tomcats," Jill said as she drew up eight pitchers of beer and evened them out on opposite ends of the bar.

"The fur will fly when they finally howl their last and really get into the fight," Sawyer said with a gleam in his eye. "In this corner we have the pig and in this corner the chicken. One is bigger, but the other has claws of steel. Which one will win, folks?"

"Now that might be a fight worth refereeing." Jill laughed as she wrapped cheeseburgers, stuck a toothpick in the top to hold the paper together, and set the baskets on the bar.

"What would make it different than the one with

Betsy and Kinsey?" Sawyer grabbed her hand and twirled her around to the music, then brought her back to his chest for a little back-of-the-bar two-stepping.

"Hey, we need a pitcher of martinis and one of beer," a tall, lanky cowboy ordered. "And, honey, if you want to dance, I'd be glad to take you out on the floor where there is a hell of a lot more room."

"Rule number one, I have to stay behind the bar. Rule number two, no one but Sawyer can be back here with me." Jill smiled. "Haven't seen you in here before. Gallagher or Brennan?"

"Neither. I jumped over the river from Oklahoma and came to party. Heard there was a damn sexy redhead down here in Burnt Boot, so I came to check things out," he flirted.

"She's sittin' right back there in the corner," Jill said.

"That one looks like she's done been through the wringer. I'd rather have a pretty one like you, darlin'. What are you doing after closin' tonight?"

She set two pitchers on the bar and took his money. "I'm goin' home with this cowboy right here." She pointed at Sawyer. "He's the one I came with, and he's the one I'm leavin' with."

"Just my luck. Day late and a redhead short, and I do like sassy redheaded women," the man said.

Sawyer broke open a bag of frozen fries and dumped them into two baskets, lowered them into the grease, and swayed back and forth to the music. Watching his hips move like that jacked Jill's hormones into overdrive. Who would have ever thought she'd think a man flipping burgers or sweeping up a floor was as sexy as one throwing hay bales or fixing fence? Bulging muscles, a damn fine body, brown eyes, and arms that made her feel oh, so safe—it didn't matter what they were doing.

"I guess Kinsey let Betsy have the last word, because the last three songs have been line dancing ones," she said. Hopefully talking about music would take her mind off the way those Wranglers fit Sawyer's butt.

"Don't speak too early, darlin'," he said as the first single guitar notes started.

"Dear God," Jill gasped.

Kinsey was in front of the jukebox, and when the haunting music of "I Know These Hills" came from the speakers, Jill recognized it immediately.

Every eye in the place darted between the two families, but when nothing happened, folks filled up the floor in a slow country waltz. Kinsey pointed at Betsy and smiled sarcastically. Betsy nodded and pointed back.

"That music haunts my soul every time I hear it," Sawyer said.

"The singer is Sara Beck. Her tone reminds me a little of Alison Krauss," Jill said.

"It does, doesn't it?" Sawyer said. "Changing the subject here. What do you think would happen if a Gallagher fell in love with a Brennan these days? Like if Betsy went after Quaid?"

"God help Burnt Boot if they did." Jill shuddered. "But in all honesty, I can't see Betsy with Quaid. He's way too tame for her. Maybe Declan or Eli, but not Quaid."

The next song that played was "How Deep the Water Runs." Sawyer and Jill both leaned on the bar. His hand covered hers when she shivered.

"It's spooky after last week," she said.

The third song was "Killing Season." Kinsey's eyes

locked with Betsy's, and neither of them blinked. The words said there'd be no rest in the killing season. When the lyrics mentioned the Lord's Prayer and the devil's law, Betsy blew Kinsey a kiss, turned her chair around, and raised her cup in a toast to all the folks at her table.

Sawyer brushed a quick kiss across Jill's cheek. "Don't let it get to you. We're not going out tonight or any other night without taking precautions like we have all week."

The next song was the theme song for the *Hatfields and McCoys* trailer, and the atmosphere in the bar changed immediately. They didn't even listen to the words, but seats were pushed back, and people took the floor for a fast dance. Kinsey Brennan paired up with the lanky cowboy who'd jumped the river from over in Oklahoma, but her eyes strayed to the bar, and she winked at Sawyer several times.

A tall brunette grabbed Quaid's hand, and Jill's eyes came close to popping right out of her skull. That feller had some moves, and when he spun the woman out and brought her back to his chest, she did one of those wiggles that took her to the floor and slowly brought her back up again. Her eyes never left Quaid's for a minute. Quaid flashed Jill a brilliant smile that left no doubt he was telling her that she was missing out on a very good thing.

"There's more ways to kill someone than to shoot them," Sawyer said when the dance ended and several people headed for the bar.

"And which one are we going to take care of first. Kinsey or Quaid?" Jill pulled up a fresh sheath of red cups and put in the dispenser. "I know I keep saying it, but I'm damn glad that we've got each other's backs in this thing, Sawyer. Because tonight has fueled the feud even more than pork rinds and doggie treats."

—⁓—

Like they'd done every night that week, they cleaned up after everyone left, and then Sawyer slipped outside, pistol in his hands. He waited by the truck while Jill locked the bar. Then she settled in and buckled up, and he did the same. Doors locked so there could be no surprises, he tucked the gun away in the console, and they drove home to the bunkhouse.

Jill kicked off her boots at the door and headed straight to the kitchen. "This is crazy, Sawyer. I feel like I'm playing a part in a movie."

"Is it a drama or a comedy?" He sat down in a kitchen chair and removed his boots and socks, wiggling his toes on the cold floor.

"Little bit of both. I can't get those songs out of my head." She headed over to the rug where the kittens were curled up together, asleep in front of the warm stove.

"Me, either." He wanted her to think about a spring pasture full of wildflowers and baby kittens. To get a picture in her head of something other than haunting music about feuding, fires of hell, and bloodletting.

"Mama says to never wake a sleeping baby, but I want to hold them and tell myself that tonight didn't happen. The feeling I had was downright crazy in the bar," she said.

"Mama knows best." He took her hand in his and pulled her back to the sofa. His gaze went to her lips. He'd had her body against his when they'd slept together, but her lips fascinated him. Touching them made him forget everything around him but Jillian Cleary. It put them into a vacuum without stores, bars, ranches, and especially without feuds.

Jill's gaze started at his eyelashes, which totally fascinated her. How could a thick bunch of dark hair be so seductive? Finally she let her eyes travel past his nose and to his lips. The music in her head wasn't haunting, but it wasn't upbeat either. It was like the background music to an old gospel hymn, peaceful with the promise of something eternal.

When she got to his slightly parted lips, the chemistry between them reached a brand-new height. His knuckles moved to trace her jawline, and then his hand splayed out, palm resting on her cheek, pinky teasing her ear, the rest holding her neck steady as his lips closed over hers.

Jill cupped his cheeks in her hands and took the first step to deepen the kiss. Desire fanned the fires of arousal until they were both panting. He moved from her lips to her neck, nuzzling, tasting, driving her crazy.

With one tug, all the snaps of his shirt popped open, and she buried her face in the soft black hair covering his bare chest. He groaned, and she shifted her weight until she was sitting in his lap.

It should not happen, but it was going to. Plain and simple. She wanted Sawyer. She needed him, and not even an act of God was going to stop what they'd started.

His hands circled her small waist and slowly made their way up under her shirt, massaging the tension from her muscles as he traveled upward. "You'd best say stop now if you are going to," he said hoarsely.

"We'd be a hell of a lot more comfortable on your bed, and we wouldn't wake the children," she answered.

Think before you say yes, her inner voice said.

No, she argued. *When you start to dissect something and analyze your findings, it's already dead. And this feels so right.*

He gave her one more chance. "Then you are not saying stop?"

She drew his lips down to hers and answered him with passion.

He picked her up and carried her to the bedroom, and she shut the door so the kittens wouldn't disturb them. She slid down his frame and stood before him, eyes locked with his as she removed his shirt, undid his belt and zipper, and slid his jeans off.

"Commando." She smiled.

He buried his face in her hair and said, "We call it goin' cowboy, not commando. That's for the military guys. Now it's my turn, darlin', and I open presents like I talk—real slow."

His mouth started at her neck and moved down to the tops of her breasts, then suddenly the bra hooks were undone, and he slid both bra and shirt down her arms, covering every inch of her skin with kisses. She pressed her breasts against his chest, and her insides melted into a hot puddle.

Nothing was ever definite, but in that moment, Jill's soul had found a permanent home. And Sawyer was definitely a part of it. He removed her jeans, bikini underwear, and socks, and walked her backwards to the edge of the bed.

"I need you." Sawyer reached for a condom and quickly put it on.

"Not as bad as I want you." She fell onto the bed and pulled him down on top of her. She arched, and he slid inside, his lips never leaving hers. The world disappeared. She and Sawyer were wrapped in a cocoon inside a vacuum. She heard nothing but his hard breath and felt nothing but his body, lips, and hands. She wanted nothing but more and more of what Sawyer delivered.

She tried to hold back, but it wasn't possible. "Sawyer," she moaned, and the cocoon unraveled, the vacuum exploded, and he collapsed.

She reached up and cupped his face. "That was amazing."

His lips found hers once more and he moved to one side, wrapping both arms around her and keeping her near. He pulled the covers over them and whispered, "Stay with me all night, Jill. Don't leave."

"My legs wouldn't let me even if I wanted to," she said.

Chapter 20

JILL STOOD UNDER THE SHOWER, PULSATING WATER rinsing the shampoo from her hair. For the first time since she'd arrived on Burnt Boot, she didn't want to get rid of the barroom smell. The smoke and beer mixed together reminded her of the amazing night she'd spent with Sawyer.

She wrapped a towel around her wet hair and slipped her arms into a thick emerald-green terry cloth robe. Shutting her eyes, she went back to the previous night. Now it was time for the awkward moment when they had to say that it was a one-night stand and start dissecting things. Number one: they had to live together, so it was a bad idea. Number two: they had to work together at three different jobs, so it was a bad idea. Number three: neither of them really trusted in lasting relationships, so it was a bad idea.

A phone rang, and she recognized her aunt Polly's ringtone, so she hurried out of Sawyer's bedroom. Kittens chased her toes peeking out from the bottom of the robe as she almost dived to the sofa toward her phone and answered it on the fourth ring with a giggle.

"What's so funny this morning?" Polly asked.

"Piggy and Chick." Jill sat down on the sofa, and the two kittens climbed the tail of her robe all the way to her shoulder.

"And they are?"

"Kittens," Jill said.

"Well, thank God you don't have pigs and chickens living in the bunkhouse. Where did you get kittens?" Polly asked.

Sawyer put a cup of coffee in her hands and kissed her on the forehead. "Good mornin'," he whispered.

"Do those cats talk?"

"No, that was Sawyer."

"He's a good man—that Sawyer is. You'd do well to wake up and see what's right in front of your nose. Now tell me more about the kittens. Did y'all find that litter in Gladys's hay barn? Old mama cat must've been gone, or you wouldn't have gotten near them. She'll scratch your eyes out if you even look at her babies."

"Quaid brought in Ollie. I named her that after the pig in a kid's movie about a spider and a pig. Then in a little bit, Tyrell brought in a yellow cat, and I named it Audrey after a chicken in another kid's movie. But Sawyer calls them Piggy and Chick," she said.

Polly guffawed. "Don't tell Gladys. I want to tell her. The reason I called is to make sure you didn't get kidnapped again after that craziness last weekend. Are you going to church this morning?"

"Of course. Sawyer is cooking breakfast. How about you?"

"No, not today. We see the doctor this week, and if they say I can start to use crutches, maybe we'll try it next week. I hate this big boot thing on my foot, but Verdie keeps remindin' me that it damn sure beats one of them old plaster casts. She's coming over after church again, and we're going to set up a Yahtzee game. You and Sawyer want to join us?"

"No, ma'am. We're taking naps. Tell Aunt Gladys that we'll be glad to do the evening chores if y'all get into a heated game. Do you still bet on the games?"

"Hell, yeah. It wouldn't be any fun if we didn't put some money on the table. Call us when y'all wake up, and we'll talk about chores. Keep your head low and dodge any bullets in church. I heard the preacher went to both ranches, trying to set up a powwow to make peace, but neither Mavis nor Naomi is havin' a bit of it."

"That's the gist of what I heard at the bar last night," Jill said. "Things got tense, but no fighting."

"Use that shotgun if you have to. That's what it is there for. Most of the time folks don't want to take a chance on whether or not you'll shoot 'em, and they calm right down."

"Waffles are ready," Sawyer yelled from the kitchen.

"Go on and eat. Any man who cooks is a jewel to be treasured. Don't keep him waiting," Polly said.

The table was set for two, as usual, with one exception. Right smack in the middle was an old chipped crock cookie jar. Glazing cracks started at the bottom and wove their way in different directions, some on the sides, with others winding their way around in circles.

"Are we having cookies with our waffles?" Jill asked.

"Look at it closely." Sawyer grinned. "Pay especially close attention to the lid."

"Daisies." She smiled.

"I would have gone out into the pasture and picked some wild ones for you, but it's the wrong time of year. That's all I could find with a daisy on it," Sawyer said.

Rule number one, two, and three disappeared as she rounded the table and looped her arms around his neck.

She rolled up on her toes and moistened her lips seconds before his mouth claimed hers in a scorching hot kiss that fried any remnants of future rules. He tugged at the belt of her robe, and his hands slipped inside to graze her rib cage and come to rest on her waist. Then in a flash, the kiss broke, and he picked her up, tossed her over his shoulder, and headed for the bedroom.

The towel fell off her hair, but she didn't care. For such an up-close view of his cowboy ass underneath those flannel pajama pants, she'd gladly air-dry her hair upside down on the way to the bed, where other delicious things might happen.

Crunching truck tires on gravel brought him to an abrupt stop. She slid off, out of his arms, and her bare feet hit the floor in a hurry when a heavy door slammed. By the time someone was walking across the porch, Jill had picked up the towel and hurried off to her room.

She'd barely shut the door when she heard Sawyer's voice coming from the kitchen. "Good mornin', Gladys. You are just in time for breakfast. I was about to put the waffles on the table. I've got maple syrup and buttered pecan. Name your poison."

"Maple sounds good. I'll get out an extra plate. Where's Jill?"

"She's on her way. I yelled at her a few minutes ago. Did you hear about the tension in the bar last night?"

Jill hurriedly wrapped the towel back around her head, removed the robe, put on underpants and a bra, and then added pajama pants, a sleep shirt, and a pair of socks. "I thought I heard voices out here. Good mornin', Aunt Gladys."

"Good mornin' to you. I'm glad to see that you are both

safe this morning and not wandering around with Tilly, like you were last week. Where'd the cats come from?"

"The clashing cowboys gave them to her. The gray one is Piggy and the yellow one is Chick," Sawyer said.

"I wasn't supposed to tell you, but then I didn't, Sawyer did, so Aunt Polly can't be mad at me," Jill said.

It took Gladys a minute, but when she caught on, she slapped a hand over her mouth and giggled like a schoolgirl. "Piggy Brennan and Chick Gallagher, right?"

"You got it." Jill nodded. "You goin' to church this mornin'?"

"No, I don't want to leave Polly alone that long. Y'all keep your ears and eyes open. Something is brewing. After that stunt with the pork rinds and the dog treats this week, I can feel it in the air. I'll pour the coffee."

Jill glanced over her shoulder toward the end table where she'd left her cup, but it was gone. When she looked back at Sawyer, he winked.

"I'll get the butter and syrup," Jill said.

"Y'all got cookies in that old jar?" Gladys asked.

"No, I found it in the cabinet and put it on the table," Sawyer answered.

Jill touched the lid. "I might make cookies in the store tomorrow to fill it up. Last week when we were making chili in the back room, lots of folks bought chili meat and beans. If they smell cookies, maybe they'll buy chocolate chips and sugar."

Gladys set three cups at the right places and pulled out a chair. "That sounds like a wonderful idea. I bet folks do buy more when the store smells like food. Bring on the waffles, Sawyer. You reckon you could make up another batch, so I could take some to Polly?"

"Got plenty of batter already made up," Sawyer said. "Just before you leave, we'll get them ready for her."

———ᴧᴧᴧ———

The kittens entertained Sawyer that morning as he waited for Jill to get dressed for church. He could hear her mumbling about something through closed doors, but he couldn't understand a word she said. When his phone rang, the kittens shot under the sofa and peeked out cautiously.

"Good mornin', Mama," he said when he'd looked at the Caller ID.

"Are you all settled in and ready for church this morning?" she asked.

"Yes, I am."

"Then why haven't you called?"

He sat up straighter. "Been busy gettin' settled in."

"Oh, is that the story? Well, Finn's mama has called me several times, so don't give me that tall tale. I don't care if you are thirty or forty or ninety. As long as I'm alive, I should not have to hear about you through relatives. And now that I've fussed at you, tell me about Jill Cleary. Callie says she's quite a woman and that she likes her. I trust Callie's judgment."

"Jill is Gladys's great-niece," he started.

His mother cut him off immediately. "I know who she is. I know what she looks like. I want to know what you think of her, and if this is going to be a..." She paused.

"They call it a relationship, Mama." He laughed.

"I couldn't think of the word. Is it?"

"I don't know. We haven't gone on a date. We

hardly have time for anything but working from daylight to midnight."

"That's a crazy job you've taken on, Son."

He shut his eyes and could visualize her sitting in her
rocker, waiting for the time to go to church. Her black
hair had a few gray streaks nowadays, and her round
face was showing signs of raising four kids, but the way
his father looked at her, well, he wanted that kind of
relationship when he did find someone to trust his heart
with forever.

"But the crazy thing, Mama, is I like it. Of course, I
like ranchin' best, but I like all of it," he said.

"Here's your father. You call me more often, or I'll
show up on your doorstep long before spring," she said.

"Maybe I won't call then," he teased.

"Sawyer O'Donnell! It's just that I miss you, Son. I
know you are old enough to make your own decisions,
but a mother is allowed to miss her son."

"Love you, Mama. Tell Daddy I'll talk to him
this week."

Jill's bedroom door opened, and she flat-out took his
breath away. Her hair was twisted up, showing off that
long, slender neck he liked to bury his face in. She wore
a denim skirt slit up the side and pointed-toed black
boots with red stitching that matched the sweater that
hugged her curves.

"Wow. Just plain old simple wow," he said.

"Thank you." She smiled and handed him a long
denim duster with fancy red shiny stones scattered
across the collar.

"You should model for Western-wear catalogs," he
said as he helped her into the coat.

"I'm way too short to be a model, but thank you again. Did Aunt Gladys call? I heard you talking to someone other than the cats."

"It was my mama. She misses me," he said.

"Do you miss her?"

"Sure, I do, and if you are askin' if I'm a mama's boy, the answer is probably yes." He grinned. "Not so much that I have to talk to her every day, but…"

Jill touched him on the shoulder. "Never trust a man who doesn't love his mama. My granny told me that."

"Smart granny." He slipped his arms into his Western-cut sports jacket. "Finn and Callie have been talkin' about us to my folks."

Seating was snug in church that morning. While the Brennans' side and the Gallaghers' side had several empty spaces on their pews, the center section was packed completely full.

With Sawyer's and Jill's sides plastered together all the way from shoulder to knees, Sawyer had a choice: scrunch up his shoulders or drape his arm over the back of the pew. He chose the latter to make a little more room. Quarters so close meant that all he had to do was tip his head slightly to see any part of her, and he liked that very much.

First he studied her profile. Pert little nose, big green eyes with lots of eyelashes, lips made for kissing, and a neck just right to nuzzle. A hint of thigh showing from the slit down to the top of her boots reminded him of the power in those legs the night before, when they were wrapped around his body. A stirring behind his zipper said he'd best be paying attention to the song they were singing from the hymnal they shared, or it was going to be a long, painful church service.

Finn turned slightly in the pew in front of him and whispered, "Y'all should come to Salt Draw for dinner."

Sawyer's head bobbed once. "I'd love to. I'll ask Jill soon as church is over."

"Verdie is going to Polly's right after church, but she left a roast in the oven, and we'd love to have you."

"Thank you," Sawyer mouthed and went back to singing.

He was determined not to look at Jill's lips or her eyes or those cute little freckles that makeup couldn't quite cover, so he let his eyes drift on down. Big mistake!

The red sweater stretched across her chest and hugged her midriff to her waist. With no effort at all, he could visualize what was underneath that soft material. He blinked, but the picture didn't fade, not even when he forced his gaze down farther to the slim denim skirt and boots. It grew more vivid when he thought of her bare feet dangling when she'd been thrown over his shoulder like a bag of chicken feed.

He shut his eyes and let his chin drop enough that Jill would think he was dozing, and replayed the night before in slow motion. Hindsight is twenty-twenty, and looking back, it wasn't probably the best of ideas for them to have sex after knowing each other only a few weeks. But he'd be a complete jerk to tell her that they shouldn't let it happen again because they worked together, because they were such good friends, because they lived in the same bunkhouse. Besides, he didn't want to tell her that, because he wanted it to happen again, and the sooner the better.

In all of his thirty years, no one had ever made Sawyer feel the way Jill did. The chemistry was so hot and so real that it couldn't be genuine. It might be a flash in the pan that would burn itself out quickly, but he didn't want to miss a moment of the heat.

Jill shoved a knee against his, and he sat up straight, eyes wide open.

"Is it over?" he asked.

"No," she whispered. "The preacher isn't even winding down. I didn't want you to start snoring."

"Finn asked us all to dinner. Got a problem with that?"

She shook her head. "I'd love to spend the afternoon with them, long as we can go home in time to catch a nap."

The preacher's gaze started on the Brennan side of the church and moved across the center section to the Gallagher side. "Vengeance is mine, saith the Lord!" He raised his voice as he leaned closer to the microphone.

"Amen," an old-timer yelled from the back of the church.

"There comes a time to let go of the past and move toward a bright new future," he whispered.

Finn's newly adopted son Ricky asked a little too loud, "What's wrong with him, Granny Verdie? Is he yelling to wake us all up and then talking all soft to make us pay attention?"

Verdie nodded. "Something like that."

Jill clamped her teeth shut to stifle the giggle. *Out of the mouths of babes*, she thought. Those kids were so cute all lined up on the pew. Finn sat on the end with Callie next to him, and then the kids, starting with Martin and ending with Sally, who sat right beside Verdie. Looking at them, no one would ever believe they hadn't been a family since the children were born.

Callie and Finn had to have big hearts to take on the raising of four children and to let Verdie move in with them too. Jill examined her own heart and came up short. She wanted kids, but she wanted them to be her own. She glanced up at Sawyer, who was smiling at the comment too. He'd make a wonderful father.

Whoa, woman! One night of wild sex doesn't give you the right to start thinking about babies with him.

She made herself concentrate on the kids sitting in front of her. She'd been to enough church services also to recognize the preacher's tactics, and she wouldn't want to be up there behind that pulpit. No, sir! With a congregation split into three parts, it couldn't be easy to attempt to unify them, not even with scripture. And especially not when the two major factions had refused his offer of help that week.

In an attempt to keep her carnal thoughts at bay, she glanced across the room toward the Gallaghers' side to see Naomi staring straight past her. She followed Naomi's gaze to Mavis, who was firing daggers across the church. Evidently God did not hold the copyright on vengeance.

"When we forgive others, it brings peace to our own lives as much as it gives them peace for their wrongdoings," the preacher said.

Forgiveness was not anywhere in the near future. It would take a lot more than a strong Sunday morning sermon for that to happen.

As long as they didn't mess with her or with Sawyer

anymore, it wasn't her problem, so she wasn't going to worry about it.

<center>~~~</center>

Sawyer's phone made a buzzing noise that said a text was coming through, but he ignored it. It was probably his sister, Martina. She and her family attended a church that started earlier and ended before the customary twelve o'clock.

He loved his family, even his bossy sister and overprotective brothers. He'd really like to take Jill to Comfort to meet them, but to drive that far and back in one day wouldn't work. They had promised to visit Fiddle Creek over Easter, so he could look forward to that. They would bring their RVs and park behind the bunkhouse, and he could show his brothers the ranch while his sister, his mother, and his brothers' wives got to know Jill better.

You take your woman home to meet the mama only if things are getting serious, that smart-ass voice in his head said. *And it might be a good thing to tell Jill that they are planning to visit. That means tell her before the weekend they are arriving.*

Sawyer nodded when everyone around him was shaking their heads. Jill poked him on the thigh. "Are you listening to the preacher?"

He shook his head.

"It looked like you were disagreeing with the Bible, nodding like that," she said.

"I was thinking about something else," he admitted.

She blushed.

"Evidently you were too."

The blush deepened, and his hand dropped from the back of the pew to her shoulder. He squeezed and leaned over to say softly, "After lunch with Finn and Callie, want a repeat of last night?"

She didn't nod, but then she didn't shake her head, but the slight upturn to her full mouth was a yes in his books.

The preacher wound down, making his final plea in veiled words to both families that the feud would consume them if they didn't make peace. Sawyer didn't see either side softening up a bit.

Jill suddenly jerked her cell phone from her purse, which was sitting on the floor right beside her foot. She read the text message, tapped Sawyer on the shoulder, and said, "We've got to go right now."

Sawyer's blood turned to ice. The only reason a person left the church was if a catastrophe had occurred. "Is it Polly?"

"No, but it was Aunt Gladys. She'll meet us at the store. There's a problem on the ranch."

The congregation stopped listening and stared at them as they left the church. When Sawyer opened the squeaky double doors, suddenly a whole sea of Gallaghers hurried outside behind them.

"Damned Brennans," Betsy said. "They've cut the fences between Wild Horse and Fiddle Creek. Our cattle is all mixed up with Fiddle Creek's cows again. We've got to get this sorted out, or we'll have mixed breeds on both ranches if they've let Granny's Blonde d'Aquitaine in with your Angus."

"Shit! I don't want that breed mixed with our stock. They've messed with the wrong woman," Jill declared.

If it was the truth that they'd involved her even more in this crappy pig-shit war, or if they used it as a ruse to try the kidnapping stunt again, she fully intended to join the war and wipe both families off the map. Now they'd spend the whole damned afternoon sorting out cattle, when she could be over on Salt Draw, having dinner with Callie and playing with those kids.

Gladys was fuming by the time they reached the ranch, cussing like a veteran sailor as she showed them the area where more than two hundred head of Wild Horse cattle roamed over a field of sprouting winter wheat. If it hadn't been for the difference in the brands on the hips of the black cows, they wouldn't have been able to tell them apart.

Betsy frowned and yelled at Tyrell. "Someone got it wrong. This isn't our Blonde d'Aquitaine herd. This is just our regular Angus stock."

"What are you doing with that breed?" Sawyer asked.

"It's something Granny wanted to try. But these are our regular Angus cows. Not even a bull amongst them. It won't take long to get them sorted out, and then we'll take all three of you over to Wild Horse for dinner," Betsy said.

Gladys checked the barbed wire. Yes, sir, it had been cut smooth right in the middle between the two metal fence posts. The Brennans had had her sympathies more than the Gallaghers down through the years, but now they'd lost every bit of it.

It took a lot longer than they thought it would. When the job was done and the fence fixed, it was well past two o'clock. Gladys refused to go to Wild Horse but did offer to take Jill and Sawyer down to Gainesville to a little café that made the best chicken-fried steak in North Texas.

"What about Polly?" Jill asked.

"She and Verdie decided to watch movies all afternoon. She'll be fine," Gladys said.

Chapter 21

WHILE THE GALLAGHERS WERE BUSY HERDING CATTLE and fixing fence on the south side of Wild Horse, four Brennan men simply opened the gate on Wild Horse Ranch, down next to the Red River and herded the light-colored, floppy-eared bull and his harem across the shallow stream and up over the bank on the Oklahoma side, where two cattle trucks waited.

The last cantankerous old heifer refused to get into the truck like her cohorts, so they shooed her back across the river and into the pasture before they shut the gate. Careful not to touch anything without gloves, they damn sure hoped the weatherman and the sky weren't lying to them. They needed the driving, hard rain to wash away the hoofprints leading over into Oklahoma.

"Ready?" Russell Brennan asked when his nephew, Quaid, climbed up into the cab.

"Across to the bridge crossing back into Texas, through Gainesville, and to our destination. We should be there in an hour," he answered.

"Maybe they'll think twice before they steal any more of Mama's hogs. The new stock are arriving this week. She's buying Herefords this time." Russell fired up the engine and drove toward the dirt road leading to Highway 32, which would take him to Marietta where he'd catch I-35 south into the outskirts of Gainesville.

"Herefords?"

"Looks just like a Hereford cow. White face, white feet, red body. They're supposed to grow off quick and produce quality meat. But the important thing is no one within a hundred miles of Burnt Boot has them. No one would dare steal them," Russell explained.

They listened to the country music countdown. Russell kept time with his thumb on the steering wheel. It was about time they did some serious damage to the Brennans after the hog-stealing business. He'd told his mother then that they should strike back and strike hard, but she wanted to wait a spell until a time came when they'd least expect it. He had to give it to the old girl, she flat-out knew her way around a feud. When it was his time to rule the family, though, he intended to do things different. He would retaliate immediately, and the Gallaghers would soon learn not to mess with him.

"What would you do, Uncle Russell, say if Leah got it in her head she wanted to get hitched to a Gallagher?" Quaid asked.

"There'd be one dead Gallagher. Do you know something I don't?" Russell's thumbs went still.

"No, sir. It's just that it's been all these years, and it's going to happen someday."

"Not on my watch, it's not. And it damn sure won't be my daughter," Russell said.

An hour later he backed the first of two trucks up to the Salt Holler bridge. Wallace opened the gates, and cattle meandered out at a slow speed, wary of the old wooden bridge under their feet, eyes rolling at the deep ditch beneath them.

Wallace removed his hat and slapped a cow on the flank. She took off, and the rest followed her lead, bawling the whole way to the other side, where they split seven ways to Sunday. Some going to the left, some to the right, some in a hurry, some slowing down to taste what little grass they could find.

When they were all across, Russell pulled his truck forward so the second one could park and do the same thing. Within half an hour, both trucks were on their way to Bonham, Texas, to pick up twenty new brood sows and one boar for River Bend ranch, and the fancy Blonde d'Aquitaine cattle were roaming all over Wallace Redding's property in Salt Holler.

"You know we could have done this with them in church," Quaid said to his driver.

"Yes, but the ones who were not in church were standing guard. When the church goin' ones got the message about the fences, they put out calls for the guards to come help them herd the cattle. Granny had it all figured out, and it worked like a charm. Wonder if they've got the fence fixed and the cattle rounded up yet?"

Quaid chuckled. "I hope that Wallace Redding has a butcherin' day down there in the holler."

—∞—

Lightning zigzagged through the sky, and thunder rolled so close to the top of Sawyer's truck that Jill covered her eyes at one point. Dark clouds boiled up from the southwest, covering the blue sky like black smoke from a wildfire.

The rain hit with gale-force winds after Jill, Sawyer, and Gladys were seated in the small café on the outskirts of Gainesville, going toward Bonham. It completely obliterated any of the traffic on Highway 82 going east or west, but they weren't interested in trucks and cars. They were too hungry to care who was going where that Sunday afternoon.

Gladys picked up the menu the waitress put before her. "We barely dodged gettin' soaked to the skin before we got those cows all sorted out, didn't we?"

"Looks like a toad strangler to me. I'll have sweet tea," Sawyer told the middle-aged waitress.

She looked at Jill, who nodded. "Me too."

"Coffee. Hot and black," Gladys said. "We all agreed on chicken-fried steaks?"

"Comes with mashed potatoes and sawmill gravy, two biscuits, and a side salad, and your choice of okra, black-eyed peas, or corn on the cob," she said.

"Okra," Sawyer said.

"Same," Jill said.

"Peas," Gladys said. "Y'all might want to change your minds. Their peas are like Granny used to make, with plenty of bacon."

"Then bring us an extra side of peas, and we'll share it," Sawyer said.

"Just to get something straight here before we finish and she brings the ticket, this dinner is on me. Y'all are supposed to have Sunday off," Gladys said.

"Make a deal with you." Sawyer grinned. "I'll help take care of feeding this evening if you'll throw dessert in too. I saw pecan pie on the menu."

"Ahh, man!" Jill groaned.

"You don't have to help." Sawyer touched her knee under the table.

She covered his hand with her own and squeezed. Her hand was cold, even through the denim of his jeans. Was she telling him that she wanted to help so that they'd have time to engage in wild, passionate sex? He smiled at that thought and mentally went about undressing her right there in the restaurant.

"Yes, I do have to help," Jill said. "Pecan pie is my favorite dessert ever, and I'll help with chores for a slice of it. It's raining so hard, we won't even be able to see where we are driving when we start home. I hope it's slacked off before it's feeding time."

Another squeeze. Which kind of driving was she talking about? He'd be willing to crawl into the backseat of his truck in the pouring rain and drive in a whole different way than making a truck go forward or backward.

"You'll be able to see just fine in about thirty minutes. Those clouds are on the move. They aren't settling down to stay. They're passing through," Sawyer said. "I should tell you that Finn called before we left and offered to come help if we needed it. He'd heard that the rain was headed our way and didn't want us to get all the cattle sorted out in vain because we couldn't see to fix the fence in the downpour. I told him we'd take a rain check on dinner at Salt Draw."

Jill picked up his hand and moved it into his own lap. When he glanced her way, it was evident that the warmth in the café had little to do with the high color in her cheeks. So her mind had plummeted straight into the gutter, or was it the bedroom in this case too? He grinned and turned his attention to the food the waitress set before him.

"Yes, ma'am, they are some fine peas," he said when he tasted the black-eyed peas.

"Yep, just like Granny made, both of my grannies," Jill agreed.

If every thought hadn't been sexual in the last ten minutes, it might not have felt like they were sharing a hell of a lot more than a bowl of Southern-style black-eyed peas. The feeling they shared over that bowl of peas solidified his thinking—that he was right where he should be at this time in his life and everything was going down the right path.

The rain had slowed to a few sprinkles when they left the café, and the sun was shining brightly when Sawyer parked the truck in front of the bunkhouse. "It's four o'clock. I'll load the feed, and we'll get the evening chores done, and then I need to give my mama a call."

"Too late for a nap, though," Gladys said. "I'm going to help you kids with the chores. If I sleep now, I'll be awake half the night."

"I'm going inside and putting on a pair of jeans and an old shirt. It's a wonder I got any kind of job done in this straight skirt when it came to fixin' fence," Jill said. "And then I'm going to play with Piggy and Chick. I bet they missed us, Sawyer. I won't be long, and I promise to pet them only one time before I come back out to help with chores."

———⁓⁓⁓———

Something Sawyer said about the clouds being on the move and not settling down stuck in Jill's mind as they fed and watered the cattle that evening. Was she like that? Would she tire of the whole Burnt Boot scene and hurry to another place and another job before spring?

Sitting so close to him in church, working side by side with him to get the cattle taken care of and the fence fixed, then pressed up against his side in the café, had put nervous flutters in her gut. She wasn't sure if the message was to fly or plant roots. Maybe feeling right was nothing more than an elusive butterfly.

"Did you call your mama?" she asked as she cut open the last bag of feed.

"I did, but it went to voice mail. She forgets her cell phone most of the time when she leaves the house. I left a message," Sawyer answered.

"Oh. My. Sweet. Jesus." Gladys pointed over the fence into Wild Horse territory.

"What? Is another one cut? Dammit to hell!" Jill said.

"I don't see any dangling barbed wire," Sawyer said.

"Stop the truck. Those big old fancy blondie cattle of Naomi's are all gone. That means they're in with my cows," Gladys said.

Sawyer hopped out of the back of the truck and opened Jill's door. "Why are we stopping here? The cattle are used to being fed closer down to the end of the pasture."

"Naomi's fancy cows are missing from the pen, and Aunt Gladys is checking to see how they got out."

He put his hands on her waist and helped her out like an old-time cowboy would take his woman from a wagon seat. "Well, shit! We'll be out here past dark."

"Y'all two drive on down to the feeding spot, and I'll walk the fence line," Gladys yelled.

Sawyer brushed a quick kiss on Jill's lips and said, "I've been wanting to do that all day." He picked her up and settled her back into the passenger's seat and whistled around the truck.

"So why didn't you?" she asked when he'd buckled into the old work truck.

"Are you getting testy with me?"

"Maybe, if you're too ashamed of me to kiss me in public," she said. "Or hold my hand in church."

"Are you picking a fight because you don't want to continue this relationship?" he asked.

"Why would you ask a fool question like that?"

"Because I've done the same thing more than once the past two years. Start getting close to a commitment and then do some serious backpeddling. You've probably done the same thing since your last breakup, so I understand if you want to slow this wagon down. But let me say something, right now and right here. I'm not ashamed to kiss you, hold your hand, or to stand up in church and tell the whole damn lot of the people in Burnt Boot that we are dating and we are an item," he said. "I'll be damned!"

"What?" she mumbled.

He was out of the truck and pointing before she realized what he was talking about.

"The cattle on this side of the fence all have Fiddle Creek brands. There's not a fancy blondie in the mix," he said. "We might as well feed our herd and tell Gladys to stop walking the fence row. And, Jill, I meant what I said."

Jill inched her phone up out of her hip pocket and called Gladys. "There's nothing down here but Fiddle Creek cows," she said when Gladys finally answered on the fourth ring.

"Looks like their herd, all but for one rangy old heifer, has disappeared like the Brennans' hogs. I wonder if Wallace will be giving us a good price on beef next week." She laughed.

"Aunt Gladys! Have you been buying stolen pork?" Jill asked.

"Wallace told me he bought those pigs fair and square, and he had the receipts to prove it," Gladys said. "I was making a joke. Rain has probably washed away any tracks, and I'll bet you that the fence problem up close to the road this morning was a distraction to bring all the guards to the south for help."

"Smart Brennans," Jill said.

"Oh, honey, Naomi Gallagher is going to shit little green apples when I make the call to tell her that her precious new breed is all gone but one heifer," Gladys said.

"Ain't life a bitch?" Jill hit the "end" button and turned around to find Sawyer so close that she had to put out her hands to keep from crashing into him.

His arms circled her waist, and he gazed down into her eyes. "What's a bitch?"

"Life. Looks like the Brennans created a diversion and stole all those highbred cattle. There's only one lonesome old heifer left over in that pasture."

Sawyer set her up on the tailgate of the truck. "You give a damn about that heifer right now?"

She shook her head.

He lowered his lips to hers, claiming them in a blistering-hot kiss that cold afternoon. When he broke the kiss, his brown eyes still captured hers and held them without blinking. "I mean it, Jill. I like where we are headed, and I don't want to stop, but I will slow down."

She put a gloved hand on each of his cheeks and drew his lips to hers for another searing kiss. When she broke, her eyes bored into his. "I'm not sure what I want, but I know I don't want to stop completely."

"Fair enough," he said. "Let's kick this hay off the truck and go get Gladys. Damned pig war sure has a habit of getting in my way."

Chapter 22

THERE HAD TO BE MORE TO WOOING A WOMAN THAN feeding cattle, minding the store, tending the bar, and sex. That wasn't a bad combination in getting to know a woman, but now that he knew Jill, he wanted to hang the moon for her, make the stars brighter, and force daisies to grow from frozen ground.

"Shit! I forgot," he murmured.

"You talking to me?" she asked.

Kittens scrambled over her lap, chasing each other, rolling around like clumsy wrestlers as they bit each other's tails and ears. In the beginning, Chick was the mean girl, spitting and scaring the bejesus out of Piggy, but these days it was a pretty even match.

"I need to call my mama, or else she'll get in her truck and drive up here," Sawyer answered.

"I probably should call my mama too, but I'm sure that neither wild horses nor the National Guard could force her to drive to Texas, or even to fly here, though."

Sawyer carried two cups of hot chocolate to the living area and handed one to Jill. "So she doesn't like Texas? Do I hear a 'but' in your voice?"

"You do. But there's only one love in a lifetime like what she and my dad had. She still gets misty eyed when she talks about him, and Texas reminds her of him," Jill said.

"You think you'll ever find that love?" Sawyer asked.

Jill thought about the question so long that he didn't think she was going to answer, but finally she said, "Maybe I will. Do you?"

"If I think with my heart and not with my brain." Sawyer scooped her up from the floor, amazed like always that someone with so much power and energy didn't weigh a lot more. He buried his face in her hair and hoped the kittens didn't get underfoot as he carried her toward his bed. "I do not plan on letting my head lead my heart ever again."

"Me, either. Don't forget to shut the door," she said.

Gently, he set her on the bed, and with a few soft, well-placed kisses, he undressed her, then patted the pillow. "Welcome to Sawyer O'Donnell's massage parlor. The hot rocks are out of commission today, but I'm available for a sixty-minute massage if the lady would like one."

"Oh, my God, Sawyer! You didn't tell me there was a lady in the room. Give me my clothes," she joked.

"Then I'll rephrase. Does this sexy, hotter'n hell spit-fire of a redhead want a massage today? I could make a phone call if you'd like the ultimate in hot rocks, scented lotion, and all the fancy words in the sex-to-sexty dictionary. Would you like Tyrell or Quaid?"

She flipped over and glared at him. "Don't you ever do that again."

"What?"

"Bring up those two names in this bedroom when I'm stark naked." Her eyes said that she wasn't teasing or flirting. "Now, here's the deal. I want a massage, and I hear that hunky cowboy named Sawyer is available. But the only way he's going to get paid is if he takes his clothes off to do my massage. Because when I get ready to pay him, I damn sure do not want to take time to undress him."

"Your wish and all that…" He kicked off his boots, and his clothing landed somewhere near the end of the bed, a piece at a time thrown over his shoulder.

"Where did you learn to do that?" Jill moaned when he dug his thumbs into her shoulder muscles. "No, don't tell me. I don't even want to know. Is there anything you can't do?"

"I don't knit." He chuckled. "I'm sorry all I've got for lotion is this cherry-almond stuff from Walmart. I buy it because it's the best I've found for my hands when they get chapped."

"It's my favorite," she said.

His hands moved down her back to the rib area, turning gentle as he worked the kinks out and then harder as he massaged her butt muscles. She could farm him out and make more money than ranching. All she needed was a number machine to nail to the front porch and… suddenly a vision of Betsy lying naked on the bed popped into her mind.

"Hey, you aren't supposed to tense up. You're supposed to relax and let me work magic on those tired, overworked muscles," Sawyer said.

She blinked away the image of Betsy's face and forced herself to unwind. The Gallaghers and the Brennans were not going to spoil her Sunday evening. She didn't give a damn if Wallace did slaughter the pigs and already had those fancy cows packaged up into hamburger meat. She had a naked cowboy giving her the best massage she'd ever had.

When Sawyer finished with her toes, he flipped her over and started back up the front side. Lord, God, almighty! She'd never be able to put lotion on her hands again without thinking of his hands as they discovered every single erogenous zone on her body. That little space between the pad of her foot and her toes, the inside of her knees, halfway up her thighs, and the soft spot where her leg attached to her body— how could they make her hormones hum like a finely tuned fiddle?

By the time he got to her aching breasts, she was fighting to keep her back straight and not arch toward him, to keep from pushing him over on his back and riding him in unabandoned hot sex. But she wanted passionate lovemaking, not a five-minute quickie.

Listening to your heart, are you? the voice in her head asked.

She floated so high above reality that she didn't even argue or answer.

He ended the massage by kissing all her fingers, one by one, and then he settled himself on top of her, his mouth finding hers in a kiss so full of passion that all semblance of gravity escaped. She wrapped her legs around his waist and arched against him. Quickie. Two hours. All night. Five minutes. She couldn't bear another minute without him inside her.

"Now?" he asked.

"I should return the massage, but, holy shit, Sawyer, I can't even think," she panted.

He slid into her body in one fluid movement, and they

rocked together. She clung to him, fingernails pressing into his back, and legs locked around him. His kisses deepened, and her hands moved to his cheeks and then up to grasp his hair. She wanted to touch him, all of him, so her hands roamed from shoulders to his firm butt, down his legs as far as she could reach, and back again.

He took her to the very brink of an exploding climax and then backed off to let her cool down before building up the tempo again. "Open your eyes, Jill, so I can see down to the bottom of your soul," he said between short gasps.

"All you'll see right now is a red-hot desire for you," she answered, then pulled his lips to hers for another searing kiss.

He grinned. "Then keep your eyes open and let me see that."

It was cold in the room, but every inch of her body was on fire. Her toes curled. Her body ached with desire.

"Now?" he asked.

"Three hours ago," she answered.

She imagined a cliff overlooking a deep blue sea. She'd climbed to the top, and when Sawyer said her name in a hoarse Texas drawl, she wrapped both arms around his back and growled his name as they tumbled into the cool water together.

When he could catch his breath, he rolled to one side, but he didn't let go of her. "Hot damn!" he muttered.

"You got that right." She snuggled as close to him as she could get and shut her eyes. She wouldn't sleep. She'd just stay there until her wobbly knees could take her to her own bedroom. But in two minutes she'd drifted off into that wonderful place that consenting adults go when the sex is so damn good they can't move a muscle afterward.

Jill dreamed of a pasture full of bright yellow daisies with half a dozen kids romping around at a picnic. Little red-haired girls dressed in denim shorts and cowboy boots. Dark-haired boys in boots and jeans. And there was Sawyer, a little older with a few shots of gray in his temples, but he still looked at her with the same brown-eyed wonder that she'd seen right before they'd fallen asleep.

She awoke to the sound of running water and whistling. A quick glance toward the clock said that it was five o'clock. That had to be morning, not evening, because the last time she checked, it was past six. Her feet hit the cold floor, and she did a quick tiptoe dance to the bathroom, where she threw back the shower curtain and stepped in front of Sawyer.

"Good mornin'." He grinned. "I was going to let you sleep while I went out to do the chores. There's a cold, blustery wind blowing. Even Piggy and Chick are hugging the woodstove this morning."

"Thank you, but I'm wide awake. We can make breakfast, and then after we eat, we'll do chores. I hate to even think about that day coming when this is in my hands."

"Come summer we'll hire some help for the ranch. Gladys says she gets half a dozen boys to come and help soon as school is out. Polly should be well, and things will let up a little then." Sawyer picked up the shampoo, poured out a healthy amount on her hair, and worked it in from top to bottom. "Now turn around, and I'll rinse it all away before we use the conditioner. Your hair is silky, Jill. With all those curls, you'd think it would be wiry, but it's not."

"Neither is this." She touched the soft dark hair on his chest.

"So you don't want me to shave it all off?"

"Why would you do that? I love it. Little boys have bare chests. Men have hair. Hunky cowboys have just the right amount," she answered.

"Do I get to be in that latter category?"

"Oh, yes, you do." She rolled up on her toes and kissed him. "Holy shit, Sawyer!"

"What?"

"Wet kisses are downright…well, they shoot desire through a body like adrenaline in the flight-or-fight mode."

He chuckled. "You going to fight or run?"

She giggled. "I'm not going anywhere but to the barn for hay, cowboy."

"Not to bed first with that burst of desire?"

She handed him the conditioner. "The cattle would starve plumb to death if we went back to bed, because we wouldn't get out of it all day. Now when summer gets here and they're put out to pasture on green grass and we don't have to feed twice a day, that's another story."

"But then"—he turned her around so the shower could rinse the conditioner from her hair—"we'll have plowing, sowing, clearing land, and all that."

"And then, like you said, we're going to hire some help. Got any relatives hiding down south who might want to move to Burnt Boot?"

"For ranchin', or for the store and bar?"

"Ranchin', and maybe some evenings in the bar," she answered.

"I'll check around. That reminds me, I never did get around to callin' my folks. Did you?"

She smiled up at him. "I'm naked in a shower with you, and you think of your mother? What's wrong with this picture?"

"You mentioned relatives. My mind went to some cousins who might be interested in a job, and then I thought about what their mamas would think of them coming to Burnt Boot. My mother sent me up here to spy on Finn. She didn't expect me to stay."

"Neither did mine when I told her I'd moved here." Jill stepped out of the shower and wrapped a towel around her body. "And, darlin', my mama was the last thing on my mind last night. When we get near a bed, I don't think of anything but you."

He chuckled. "Well, then I will always remember to keep a bed right handy."

—◦◦◦—

On Monday morning, Polly said if she had to stay in the house one more day she was going to climb the walls. So Gladys loaded her up in the truck, took her to the store, and told Sawyer and Jill they didn't have to come in until after lunch.

"Aunt Gladys, why don't we come on in when we finish feeding, and you can take Polly for a ride?" Jill asked.

"Give me that phone," Polly said loudly.

"I could hear what you said, girl. I don't want to go for a ride. I want to talk to people. I want them to come in the store, and hell, I don't even care if they get into a knock-down drag-out fight right here," Polly said. "I don't like this getting-old shit."

Jill grinned. "Well, Auntie, it's not for wimps. Only the strong get to do it."

"You always could out argue a stop sign. But it won't work today. You and that handsome Sawyer spend the day together. After lunch, my ass. I'm staying right here until closing time, whether Gladys likes it or not. I hope everybody in town knows I'm here and comes in to visit."

"Yes, ma'am. I'm not arguing anymore," Jill said.

She visualized a long, lazy afternoon in the bedroom, but it didn't happen. Right after they finished their morning routine, a heifer decided to give birth to a calf that was too big for her. That required an hour of getting her into a barn out of the cold, where the calf would have a better chance of living, and then pulling the bull calf out when he was born butt-first. They'd barely gotten their hands cleaned up and made sure the new little fellow could stand and nurse when the phone rang.

Jill fetched it from her pocket and answered without checking the ID.

"You win," Polly said. "I'm pooped, and if I have to hear another person tell me how their great-aunt or uncle or neighbor's kid broke their leg, I'm going to throw them through the plate glass window. Gladys made me call you. Some friend she is. She wouldn't even do it for me, since I threw such a fit. If you and Sawyer will come on to the store, I'm ready to go home and get a nap."

"We'll be there soon as we go home and get the blood off us," Jill said.

"Shit, girl! Who'd you kill, a Gallagher or a Brennan?"

"Neither one. We just pulled a calf. Tell Aunt Gladys it's a bull, and mama and baby are just fine. We've got them in a stall in the barn for the next few days, though, with this cold weather," Jill answered.

"Take your time but not too much. I'm worn plumb out," Polly said.

Sawyer spent most of the afternoon dozing with his hat over his eyes. Jill got bored with chatting via her tablet with her mother and went to the kitchen to bake cookies. At four, she waved a paper plate with half a dozen chocolate chip cookies under his nose.

"Wake up and smell the goodies," she whispered.

He grabbed her arm. The two front chair legs popped down on the floor, and he pulled her into his lap and tossed his hat on the counter all in one movement. "I'd love fresh-baked cookies, but I'd give them up for a kiss."

"Today is your lucky day, cowboy. You can have both." She set the cookies on the counter beside his hat and plastered herself to his chest.

The temperature in the store jacked up at least ten degrees when their lips touched. He forgot about cookies. She couldn't think of anything but the burning desire for more than kisses.

Finally, he drew back, picked her up, and set her on the floor. "It's after four, darlin', and it's starting to rain. Why don't you let me take care of the ranchin' this afternoon? I don't think there's going to be many people getting out in this weather."

"Sounds good to me…what in the hell is that?" She pointed out the window.

Sawyer followed the angle, but nothing interested him as much as kissing her. She was cute when her lips were all bee-stung with kisses, her hair was tangled, and she had that bedroom look in her eyes.

"Looks like flowers for someone. Maybe Polly shouldn't have left so quick." He picked up a cookie.

"These are scrumptious, but they take a far second to kissing you," he mumbled.

"Mercy, Sawyer. Someone must love Polly a lot to send a bouquet that big."

Two people got out, one lady holding an umbrella over the other one as she carried an enormous vase of red roses into the store. The flowers didn't totally escape the rain, but the few that had been kissed by drops looked even better for it.

"Jill Cleary?" The lady eyed Sawyer up and down as if she'd like to jump over the counter and pounce on him.

"No, that would be Jill over there." He nodded toward the other end of the counter.

"Are you sure they aren't for Polly Cleary?" Jill asked.

"No, ma'am. The card says Jill. Nasty, cold rain out there, isn't it?"

"Yes, ma'am," she said.

Jill tore into the envelope and groaned. "Shit!"

"And I thought you'd like them. My heart is hurt." Sawyer clamped a hand over his chest.

"You know very well you didn't send this shit. You would have sent daisies, not roses. These are from Quaid Brennan."

"Want me to throw them out into the rain?"

"Maybe. Yes. No. I'll think about it. Maybe Aunt Polly would like them after all." She smiled.

Thirty minutes later a different florist van arrived with a long, slim box. Sawyer had no doubts what was inside that one, and he didn't even want to know who they were from. Dammit all to hell on a silver platter! Jill had gotten two dozen roses on the very day he'd asked Finn to pick up a bouquet of those brightly colored daisies he'd seen at the Walmart store. He'd even given him the key to the bunkhouse so he could put them in his bedroom and surprise her with them.

They'd pale in comparison to a vase the size of the Grand Canyon filled with roses, fluffy stuff, and a big red bow, and then a box with long-stemmed ones waiting inside. Not even the corny poem he'd written to go with the daisies would bring them up to the standards of the roses.

"Red?" he asked when Jill pulled the ribbon off and looked inside.

"Oh, yeah. Red, like funeral flowers."

"Where did you get that notion? Red roses mean love, not death."

"Not in my mind," she said. "When we buried my grandpa and my granny, both sets, there were red roses on the top of their caskets. I always think of funerals when I see them, and here are two dozen of the damn things for me to contend with."

"Do we take them home or to Polly?" she asked when they locked up at exactly five o'clock.

"Your flowers, so it's your choice. I take it those in the box are from Tyrell?"

"You got it."

"I don't imagine Polly would want anything from the Gallaghers or the Brennans, even if they came through you," he said.

"Then let's go home."

He drove to the bunkhouse with a vase of roses and a box of the same in the backseat. She ignored them when they reached the bunkhouse, so he carried them in and set them on the kitchen table.

"I'm going to my room to call Aunt Gladys. I'll ask her if she wants these damn things or if I should just toss them out into the yard," she said.

The daisies were lying in the middle of the bed in the green paper. He took the poem he'd labored over for hours that morning and put it on the spare pillow, the one that held her pretty red hair when they spent the night together. Then one by one, he scattered daisies up across the quilt.

"That's about as creative as I can get," he said. "I feel like I'm clashing with money and power."

"Hello! Sawyer, where are you? Aunt Gladys said to do whatever I want with them, but she and Aunt Polly don't want anything from the Gallaghers or the Brennans, just like you said."

"Hungry?" He made his way from bedroom to kitchen table.

"Not really. Mostly angry that they think they can buy me with flowers," she said.

She opened the card on the box again. "From Tyrell, saying thank you for helping take care of the cattle situation." She poked every one of them down into the vase with the ones that Quaid had sent.

"Quaid Gallagher says red roses remind him of me," she said. "I probably should tell them both that they remind me of death and sorrow. And just because I have red hair doesn't mean I like red roses."

"That's a big arrangement to leave on the table. I don't think I can see over them when we sit down to eat," he said.

"Don't intend to leave them here. They are going into my office. Remind me to keep them watered," she said, ripping the bow from around the vase.

"What are you going to do with that?" he asked.

"Watch this. Piggy, Piggy, Piggy," she called out.

The gray kitten perked up her ears and scampered across the floor with the yellow one right on her tail. Jill tossed the bow on the floor, and they attacked it like it was a big red rat, kicking and growling, batting at it and playing tug-of-war with it. She carried the vase into her office and shut the door behind her when she returned.

Sawyer plopped down on the sofa and leaned back, his heart racing and his hands clammy. She slid down beside him, and he drew her close with an arm around her shoulders. "Tired? I'll gladly take care of the bartending alone if you want to stay in for an evening. If I need someone to throw a pitcher of beer on a couple of bitches, I'll call. Hey, I never asked. Why did you come to the bar that night anyway? Seemed like after you doused Betsy and Kinsey, we decided we'd best stick together, but why were you even there?"

"I wanted a cold beer, not in a bottle, but in a frosted mug. I'm not so tired that I can't go to the bar with you, and besides, it wouldn't be fair."

"It's Monday. You know how slow it is on Monday," he said.

"Not this one. Aunt Gladys told me that the Gallaghers' cattle is down in Salt Holler, and even though Naomi is a distant relative of Wallace's, he's going to make her pay for the grass they've eaten and the property they've damaged. So it'll be a busy night with folks comin' around to see what's goin' on next with the feud."

"Property damage?" He made lazy little circles on her arm with his thumb.

"Says they broke through some hog-wire fences, and he had to round up his hogs. Guess the pig war lives on, even when it's really cattle," she said.

"Well, anytime you want to, I'll take a night at the bar alone. But for the record, I sure like it when you are right there with me."

One corner of her cute little mouth turned up. "If Kinsey and Betsy found out you were in there all by yourself, they'd take you away from me. And I don't play well with others."

"Not damn likely." He grinned.

She pointed toward the stove. "Look at the children."

They each had a paw on a section of the frayed and ragged ribbon, as if protecting their interests while they slept.

"Play hard. Sleep hard," Sawyer said.

"Like babies. Too bad the Gallaghers and Brennans haven't learned to play well with others and then plop down and fall asleep," she said. "Got to get changed into my barroom hussy clothes. I left my bra hanging on the doorknob over in your room."

He held his breath when she stood up and headed in that direction.

"Oh my!" Her hand shot up and covered her mouth.

Then there was silence. He waited and waited, started to get up twice, and then sat back down. His hands got all clammy again and his pulse quickened. He waited for laughter at the poem or at least some reaction. But there was nothing for five of the longest minutes he'd ever spent in his life.

———

Jill touched each daisy. They were so bright and beautiful, lying there on the bed as if they'd grown from the stitches that held the quilt together. Then she found the poem and sat down in the rocking chair to read. It was both funny and sweet, tugging at her heartstrings when it talked about how she made every morning as bright as the blue daisy, that the sun was brighter than the yellow ones, and that all he had to do was look across the room at her and she filled his heart with so much color there weren't words to describe it.

Tears ran down her eyes and dripped onto the ink, smearing when she tried to wipe it. When she looked up, Sawyer filled the doorway.

"This is the sweetest thing I've ever had," she said.

"I didn't mean for you to cry."

"I know, but it's so damn sweet. Now help me gather up these daisies before they wilt. There's enough for the kitchen table and the coffee table and for the nightstand beside your bed. I want them everywhere, so I can see them no matter where I am," she said.

Together they picked up the flowers. "I saw some of

those half-pint jars in the cabinet. We'll divide them into three bouquets. They are so bright and pretty, Sawyer. The colors remind me of sunsets. There's nothing more beautiful than a Texas sunset or sunrise. And I'm framing this poem and keeping it forever," she said.

"You won't let anyone else read it, will you? It's kind of corny."

She tiptoed and pressed her lips against his. Their hands were filled with flowers, so they couldn't touch each other, but the kiss was deep and sweet at the same time.

"I wouldn't share this with anyone, Sawyer. It's personal, and it's mine. I'll put it on the nightstand beside my bed. I love it, and I love the flowers."

She stopped short of saying that she loved him. Words were words, and they needed to be heard, but she didn't want to say them until she was absolutely sure that she meant every single one.

She laughed. "You are a prophet."

The parking lot at the Burnt Boot Bar and Grill already had a dozen trucks, and there were people huddled up next to the door, waiting to get inside.

He smiled. "I told you so."

"This isn't even normal for Friday and Saturday." She pulled the keys to the bar from her purse. "Get ready. If they're here this early, it means they'll want food as well as beer and whiskey."

"It's not every day the Gallaghers have to buy back their cattle from Salt Holler. Since they are blaming the Brennans for stealing them, they'll all come in here with chips on their shoulders tonight. And the other folks will come to see the show. Maybe we should charge admission."

"Not a bad idea. Do you ever wish there was another gathering place for the folks, other than Polly's?"

"Never thought of it. Maybe the Gallaghers should build their own bar. I don't think the Brennans would want to own one, with their religious background, but they could continue to visit Polly's," he said.

"Let's get the doors open, but I'll tell you one thing for sure, that shotgun will stay loaded and ready."

"I'll fire up the grill. Keep them eatin', and maybe they won't be so quick to want to fight," he said.

Thirty minutes later, he finally looked up and said, "You are the prophet, Jillian Cleary, not me. That is my fortieth onion burger since I walked in the door. And we've used six bags of frozen fries."

A rush of cold air took her eye to the next customers, and she smiled.

"What's so funny?" Sawyer asked.

"Nothing." She fished in her purse and brought out a bright purple daisy affixed to a hair clip, pulled her hair back on one side with her fingertips, and fastened the daisy right there above her ear. The smile on her face widened when Kinsey and Quaid Brennan claimed a couple of bar stools.

"What can I get you this evening?" Jill asked sweetly.

"Nice touch in the hair there. Looks like you've been to the islands. Hey, Sawyer, you want to fly down to the islands this weekend with me?" Kinsey asked. "We can leave on Saturday night and be home early Monday morning."

"No, thank you. Y'all want something from the grill?"

"No, just a pitcher of margaritas and one of Coors."

"Thank you for the roses, Quaid," Jill said. "That was very thoughtful of you."

"They are beautiful, but not as beautiful as you are. I was hoping you'd see that I'm serious about getting to know you better." His flirting was deliberate and practiced.

"Where'd you get that daisy in your hair anyway?" Kinsey asked.

"Sawyer gave me two dozen today. I picked out the brightest one for my hair." She smiled.

"So you like daisies, Sawyer?" Kinsey asked.

He set two pitchers in front of her. "I like Jill."

She put a bill in his hand. "As in you are dating, or as in you are friends?"

He laid her change on the bar. "As in what I said. The rest is our private business."

"Well, you don't have to get pissy about it," Kinsey said and flounced off to claim a table not far from the jukebox.

As luck would have it, Betsy and Tyrell were the next two to let a little fresh air into the bar. Betsy raised an eyebrow at the daisy in Jill's hair. "Is it beach night at Polly's or what?"

"Nope, it's nothing but a normal Monday night. Y'all get those cows back yet?" Jill asked.

"We're negotiating a deal," Tyrell answered quickly.

"Oh, thank you for the roses," Jill said.

"Just a little thank-you for all the help. They weren't as pretty as you, but then nothing is that gorgeous." He winked.

"So what's with the flower? Sawyer, darlin', would you fix us up six cheeseburger baskets and a couple of pitchers of beer?"

"Comin' right up," he said.

Betsy's eyes had trouble staying above his belt buckle, and the expression on her face told the whole story about what she'd like to do if she ever got past the buckle and zipper.

Jill drew up two pitchers of beer and set them on the bar. Tyrell put a couple of bills in her hand, and she made change. He grabbed her hand and bent over the bar to kiss her fingertips.

"Darlin', I'll put red roses on every flat surface in my house if you'll agree to let me cook supper for you. You choose the menu, and there's no strings attached," he whispered.

The very picture in her mind made her feel like she was smothering. That many red roses in one place. She'd feel like they were coming after her, like zombies in the apocalypse.

Betsy picked up the beer and started back to the table. She stopped after a few feet and looked over her shoulder. "Tyrell, bring the cups, please. And why do you have that flower in your hair, Jill?"

"Sawyer gave me daisies today, and they were so bright and pretty that I brought one to work with me."

Tyrell's face went dark. All the flirting turned to anger, and the determination into rage. He dropped her hand, and his strong jaw worked like he was chewing gum. "So are you two together now? Why aren't you wearing one of my roses?"

"Because you and Quaid both sent red roses, and besides, I like daisies better," she said.

"So that's the way it is."

"I've never led you on."

"But you never completely shot me down, either."

"Yes, Tyrell, I have. You just didn't know it. We'll holler right loud when the cheeseburger baskets are done," she said softly.

He nodded curtly and joined Betsy at a table in the corner.

"We might have entered the war as a third country," Sawyer said.

"They'd better hope not. When I fight, I go in with intentions of winning. Bless their hearts, there might not be anything left of them when the dust settles if they continue to pull us into this war, not even a beefsteak from one of their blondie steers."

Chapter 23

Something had happened. Something big.

Jill wasn't sure what it was, but Sawyer didn't like it. He'd been distant most of the evening. After the sweet daisies and the note that had brought tears to her eyes, she'd thought they'd climbed up on a higher level in their relationship. But something had sure enough ticked him off royally. Had Kinsey or Betsy finally convinced him to go out with them?

A stab of jealousy shot through her faster than any speeding bullet or two-edged hunting knife. A picture of either of them lying naked on his bed, getting a full body massage, played through her mind. She could almost feel the smoke coming out of her ears as the image sharpened and grew brighter. Would he scatter daisies on the bed for them? Would he write poetry about them?

The jukebox was unplugged. The flashing lights around the outside had gone dark, and it was tired of singing for the people. Smoke still hung above the tables, but a lot of it had escaped as the packed house fanned in and out of the door.

Sawyer's expression was blank, set in stone. If he smiled, cracked a joke, flirted, or even looked her way, it would most likely shatter like broken glass. Whatever his problem was, if he didn't want to talk about it, then he could damn well fix it without her help. She was tired, cranky, and ready for bed—as in sleep.

And you thought he could walk on water. Men are men, and they are all rascals, the mean voice in her head taunted.

He finished sweeping and started getting the bar ready for the next day—checking everything at least twice, like he always did. The grill and fryers were turned off, the red cup dispensers were filled to the top so she wouldn't have to stop for supplies, and the last of the beer and margarita pitchers were in the dishwasher.

She made sure toilet paper, paper towels, and soap were in both bathrooms, and sprayed a healthy dose of disinfectant spray into the air before she shut the doors.

"Ready?" He waited beside the door, the bulge of a handgun not far from his belt buckle.

She breezed past him, crossed the cold gravel lot to his truck, and had her hand on the handle when the beeping noise told her he'd opened the door remotely. A norther hit with a blast of colder air, sending dead leaves, cigarette butts, gravel, and dirt into a swirl. It would be fifteen degrees colder by the time they reached the bunkhouse. She'd love to curl up in his warm arms under the fluffy blanket, but that wasn't happening.

They drove home in complete and uncomfortable silence. She glanced his way a couple of times, but his neck was stiff and his eyes set on the road ahead. Before he could be the cowboy gentleman and open doors for her, she bailed out of the truck, stormed the short distance to the porch, used her own key to get inside, and went straight to her bedroom, without even stopping to talk to the kittens.

A loud slam told her that he had done the same thing. Bathwater started, she stripped down to nothing but socks and caught her reflection in the mirror. The daisy had wilted, some petals twisting toward the middle, others hanging limp. She removed it carefully, ran an inch of water in the bathroom sink, and floated it. Maybe it could be saved with a little rehydration.

Tears welled up and ran down her cheeks. She shouldn't have wasted even one of her daisies. All the others would last for a week if she changed their water daily, except for that one she'd popped the stem off and wrecked to show the feuding cowboys that their roses didn't impress her.

She sunk into the tub, her spirits sinking even lower. She didn't like this feeling of distance between her and Sawyer. They might have started off that first day on shaky ground, but he had become her best friend, her partner in three different jobs. Maybe even her soul mate.

"Whoa!" She brushed away the tears and slid down into the water, getting her hair wet so she could wash the stink of smoke from it. "I'm not going there tonight, not when he's being such a jackass."

<hr/>

Pulsating hot water kneaded at the sore muscles in Sawyer's back, but he couldn't be still long enough to let it work all the anger knots from his shoulders and neck. He turned the knob, threw back the curtain, and picked up a towel.

The jar of daisies sitting beside the bed caught his eye. He didn't want to look at them, but he couldn't force his eyes to look at anything else. When he did finally glance away, his eyes came to rest on the indentation in the pillow where he'd left the poem. He quickly dressed in pajama pants and a thermal-knit, long-sleeved shirt, but all he could think about was Jill with tears in her eyes and the poem in her hand.

"Dammit!" He threw himself on the bed, wiping out the hollow place with his head and getting a whiff of her perfume at the same time.

It was light and airy like Jill, not heavy or musky. Just sweet and sassy at the same time, drawing his thoughts to that first evening when she'd barreled into the bunkhouse with a shotgun. They'd come a long way since then, but tonight had sure enough put the skids to another step forward.

The kittens chased through the crack in the door, deftly climbed the bedcovers, and jumped around like windup toys from one side of the bed to the other. Piggy stopped short of falling off the edge and discovered a purple daisy petal hung up in the stitching on the quilt. One little gray paw flew out, and she swatted it, growling down deep in her throat. Chick arched her back and tiptoed from one side of the bed to the other. When she saw the evil purple alien, she fluffed up her tail, and the two of them fought over who'd kill the wicked thing first.

"You two are crazy, fighting over a daisy petal." He almost smiled. "Maybe you can't forget where you came from after all."

They grew tired of the petal after they'd killed it half a dozen times, fell down on the blanket at the same time, and went to sleep with Piggy's leg thrown over Chick's ears. It didn't take long until the voice in Sawyer's head sounded off loud and clear. He put a pillow over his eyes, but it didn't go away.

"Shut the hell up!" he demanded, but it kept right on.

Of all the dumb-ass, stupid things to fight about. A damn daisy, and one that you sent her at that. It wasn't like she put a rose in her hair. Hell no! She put them all in her office behind a closed door, so she didn't even have to look at them. Granny told you that settling differences before sleeping was the secret to a happy relationship...okay, so she said marriage...but a relationship should work the same.

He sat up in bed and grabbed a pair of socks from the bottom drawer of the dresser, pulled them on his feet, and headed for her room. They might argue until dawn, but the air had to be cleared.

The sight of her sitting on the sofa, lit only by the moonlight flowing through a window, stopped him at the door. She held a ragtag daisy in her hand and carefully laid it in a bowl of water on the coffee table. Shiny tears dripped from her chin and ribboned down to her jawbone. She looked so fragile, with her chin quivering and her shoulders hunched over the cereal bowl, that his heart ached. He swallowed hard, but the lump didn't disappear. He wanted to take her in his arms and make the pain go away, but his feet were glued to the floor.

"I ruined it, Sawyer. Just to show off to those fools who don't matter, I ruined one of my precious daisies. It looks pitiful," she said. "And you are mad at me. A part of me wants to tell you to go to hell, but the other part wants to kiss you, because my heart is hurting, and I'm still mad at you, so don't try to talk me out of it. You are clamming up and being all holier-than-thou, like you are better than me."

He switched on the light and joined her on the sofa, leaving a foot of space between them. "Evidently, I'm the dumb old cowboy who gives you daisies so you can flaunt them before the rich cowboys to make them jealous. Or maybe you were showing me that all I had was daisies when you could have been wearing an expensive rose in your hair."

Her shoulders squared up, and the tears dried. She glared at him with flashing green eyes. "I'm not guilty of such shit! Dammit, Sawyer. I wore the flower in my hair because of what you said."

"What I said?" he asked through clenched teeth.

"Yes, you said something about us not being together in public for the whole world to see. I can't quote it word for word, but the idea is there. I was so damned proud of those daisies, I wanted to take a jar full of them to the bar and tell everyone that finally a cowboy gave me what I wanted. But I decided to wear one. I thought you'd be tickled that I was telling the world that we were together, but instead you got all pissy and mad and won't even talk to me."

"Miscommunication," he said.

"What's that supposed to mean?" she asked.

"I let my past get in the way, and you did the same."

The kittens bounded out of the bedroom, two energized bundles of fur after their romp with the purple petal, now ready to dive into their food bowl. Piggy growled at Chick, but the yellow kitten was a scrapper, pulling a portion of the dry kitten nuggets her way with her claws.

"You have to talk to me, Sawyer. From now on, you have to tell me outright if something upsets you," Jill said. "It's not miscommunication. It's flat-out no communication. If I'd known the flower in my hair was going to set you off, I wouldn't have worn it."

"I do not have the right to tell you to take a flower out of your hair, Jill."

"Well, I damn sure can't read your mind, Sawyer, so you are going to have to use words."

"Would you have taken it out of your hair if I'd asked?"

"We'll never know now, will we?" Piggy finished eating and scampered over to Jill's foot. "Do you think we are worth trying again?" Jill reached down with one hand and drew the kitten up to her lap.

"We've come a long way to start from scratch," he said.

"This isn't a trust issue. It's a communication problem. We don't start from the beginning. We start from about"—she looked at the clock on the wall above the stove—"six hours ago. Are we worth six hours?"

"Hell, yes," he said. "I'll make an effort to talk more."

"I'll try to speak before I act on impulse," she said.

He offered his hand. "Shake on it?"

She put hers inside his. "Now can we please go to bed? I'm so sleepy and worn out emotionally that I can't even think straight," she said.

He picked up Piggy and laid her on the rug in front of the stove with Chick, then he returned to the sofa, picked Jill up like a bride, and carried her to the bedroom. He gently laid her on her side of the bed and pulled the covers up over her body.

"Hold me, Sawyer. I need your arms around me to reassure me that everything is fine between us," she said.

He realized he'd forgotten to switch off the light, but it didn't matter right then. He needed to feel Jill's body next to his, to smell her hair and to kiss that soft spot below her ear. Tonight he didn't need wild kisses, makeup sex, or even any more words. That things were settled between them before he shut his eyes was enough.

She slipped her hand into his. "Are we good, Sawyer?"

"Yes, Jill, we definitely are."

Chapter 24

VERDIE TURNED AROUND IN THE CHURCH PEW AND winked at Sawyer. "I didn't think Gladys would miss another Sunday or let y'all stay home, either," she said.

Gladys smiled. "That would set the rumor wheel on fire."

"Why?" Jill asked.

"They'd say that y'all were laid up in bed together," Gladys whispered so the children sitting beside Verdie couldn't hear.

Jill's face burned, but she took several deep breaths and hoped to hell that her aunt didn't notice.

"You. Are. Blushing," Sawyer whispered softly in her ear. "Would you go to dinner with me after church?"

"As in a date?"

He nodded. "As in a normal, plain old date."

"Are we telling Finn and Callie that we have a date and can't take them up on another invitation to their place?" she asked.

"We will if they ask. Is that a yes?"

"It is a definite yes," she said.

The preacher took the podium, and the whole congregation settled in for a sermon. Jill could almost hear the old men behind her getting comfortable for their Sunday morning nap.

"Good morning. It is less than two weeks until Valentine's Day, a day of love and romance. I've been asked"—the preacher shuffled his notes—"to announce that there will be a Valentine's party right here at the church on Friday, the thirteenth."

A few people chuckled.

The preacher held up a palm. "I know it's considered an unlucky day, but we're going to put that wives' tale to the side for our party and think of it as a wonderful day of romance. There will be a dinner, and Kinsey Brennan has said that she and Quaid are having a speed-dating evening for the young single folks, so get ready for lots of fun."

He went on to announce that the nursing-home visitation had been postponed that week due to a conflict of schedule and that there would be a baby shower on Wednesday. Jill hadn't heard the names of the prospective new parents before, but they weren't Gallaghers or Brennans, so they were most likely sitting in the middle section of pews.

"I'll expect everyone to respect the church and be civil to each other during our Valentine's party," he said seriously.

The tension level rose from a solid five all the way to a ten in seconds. The Brennans shot dirty looks across the heads of those folks in the middle section, looks which no doubt meant to tell the folks on the other side that, by golly, they would be civil only if they wanted to and not because the preacher told them to.

"And now I'd like to introduce you to Ruth and her mother-in-law, beginning with the Book of Ruth in the Old Testament," the preacher said.

Evidently, he was going to preach on love that morning, which was a wonderful topic for the first of February in any other church at any other time. But he'd already lost his crowd when he made that statement about being nice. Still, he plowed on, raising his voice to wake up the dozing folks at the right time, lowering it to get the attention of those who were drifting away to think of something else.

Jill blocked all of it out of her mind and let herself get giddy thinking about a real date with Sawyer. It was crazy, but she couldn't help it. They'd been through so much together, including some damn fine hot sex, but this was a date. It wasn't friends with benefits; it was the real thing.

She glanced over at the Brennan side and locked gazes with Quaid. There were no daggers, but he was not smiling. His jaw was set firmly, and the look in his pretty eyes said that he still had a lot of fight in him. A cold chill chased down her spine. Surely the two families wouldn't do anything to take Sawyer out of the picture.

Sawyer's hand covered hers in the narrow space between them and squeezed gently. Could he read her mind? Was he assuring her that he could take care of whatever the Brennans threw at them?

She tried to listen to the sermon, but starting in the middle didn't work so well, so she looked at the Gallagher side of the church. Be damned if Betsy wasn't eyeballing Sawyer like she had something pornographic in mind. Before Jill could blink, Betsy caught her eye and smiled. She made a pistol with her thumb and forefinger, aimed it at Jill, and snapped it as if she'd pulled the trigger. Then her eyes shifted to Sawyer, and she blew him a kiss off the tips of her fingers.

Holy freakin' shit! The Gallaghers are going to shoot me, and the Brennans are going to do away with Sawyer.

Gladys poked her on the arm. "What's goin' on?"

Jill shrugged. "Just my overactive imagination, I'm sure."

She kept her eyes straight ahead until the preacher finally asked them to stand for the benediction that Quaid Brennan would deliver. Sawyer did not drop her hand when they were on their feet but held it firmly for the whole congregation to see.

Immediately Finn and Callie turned toward them, and Callie asked, "Hey, y'all want to try again for dinner at Salt Draw with us today? And while I'm thinking about it, you want to go to the antique show in Gainesville next Sunday?"

Sawyer held up her hand. "We have a date, so we'll have to take another rain check."

"And, yes, for next Sunday," Jill told Callie.

"Maybe we can invite these cowboys and make it a double date next Sunday," Callie suggested.

"Shopping?" Finn raked his hands through his dark hair. "The only way I'll agree is if Sawyer does. Otherwise, it's going to be a long Sunday afternoon nap for me."

"I'll go," Sawyer said quickly.

Gladys raised an eyebrow. "Two dates in as many weeks?"

"It would be three," Jill said, "but we'll have to work the bar on Friday night. If we didn't, I might ask Sawyer to go with me to the Valentine's party."

"And I'd refuse," Sawyer said seriously.

Jill cocked her head to one side. "Why?"

"Because I don't want none of that speed-dating shit that Quaid and Kinsey have come up with. I don't trust them. I'd rather sling burgers behind the bar with you all evening as do that stuff. Let's have a Valentine's party of our own at the bar on Saturday night. We'll talk to Polly about it."

"You're going on a real date?" Callie's daughter, Olivia, asked.

"Yes, we are." Sawyer grinned.

"Is Jill going to wear a fancy dress like Mama did when she went on a real date with Daddy?" Olivia's eyes glittered at the memory.

"How fancy was it?" Jill asked.

"It was the Christmas parties at Wild Horse and at River Bend," Callie explained.

"I don't think I'll get that dressed up for a dinner date," Jill said.

"When you do go to a party like that, will you come over to Salt Draw and let me see you? Mama looked like a princess," Olivia said.

"I will, and I bet your mama did look beautiful," Jill said.

"She was the queen, not just a princess," Adam said shyly.

"Yes, she was." Finn grinned.

It was the smile that said Finn and Sawyer were related. Jill wondered as they moved along with the congregation to the front of the church if maybe it hadn't been the smile that had captured Callie's heart in the very beginning. It certainly had been that quality that she first noticed.

No, it wasn't. It was the way he filled out those jeans, and those dark eyes that bored right into your soul, her inner voice argued.

She let the sassy voice have the last word, because she couldn't very well do battle with the truth. Besides, today was going to be perfect. No Gallaghers. No Brennans. No feud. Not even the faintest whiff of a pig war. It was the first date with Sawyer, and first dates were always exciting.

Even when you've already had sex?

She smiled and thought, *So, I got things backwards. Maybe that's what it takes to make something work. God only knows, I did it all the right way before, and it didn't last.*

She refused to listen to any more doubts and fears. "So where are we going for dinner?"

"You like Tex-Mex, American, or barbecue better?" he asked.

"Tex-Mex sounds really good," she said.

"Then Chili's it is." He grinned. "Need anything from the bunkhouse before we go?"

"Not a single thing." She smiled up at him.

"I thought we might catch a matinee afterwards. You've got a choice of six. I'll even promise to stay awake in a chick flick if that's what you choose." He guided her toward the pickup with a hand on her back.

She wore a chocolate-brown corduroy skirt that morning with a matching jacket. She'd chosen it because it reminded her of the color of Sawyer's eyes. The pointed-toed, heavily detailed cowboy boots were stitched in turquoise that matched the turtleneck sweater she wore under a jacket.

"Have I told you today that you look mighty fetchin' in that outfit?" he said as he opened the door for her.

"Only three times," she answered.

"Well, then make it four."

After he shut the door, he rounded the front of the truck, climbed inside, and started the engine. "So what is it that you like in the Mexican line of food?"

"All of it, from enchiladas to tacos and everything in between. I don't think I told you before, but my mama is half Latino. My grandmother was a Torres from just over the border in Mexico."

"Does she make good tamales?" he asked.

"Oh, yes, she did, but she passed away. Haven't had decent ones since."

"My mama makes all the Mexican food, but I'm real fond of her tamales. I don't eat them in restaurants, because they can't begin to compare to hers," he said. "They're coming up here in the spring to see Fiddle Creek, so maybe we'll talk her into making tamales for us while she is here."

Jill's gut clenched up in a knot. "This is our first date, Sawyer. It's too early to talk about taking me home to meet Mama."

"I'm not. She's not coming to Burnt Boot to meet you, Jill. She's coming to see me." He grinned. "We are too busy with all that's on our plate, so the family is coming to Burnt Boot for Easter weekend. We might even have an Easter egg hunt out in the pasture behind the bunkhouse. Depends on whether Finn's folks all make the trip too."

"Where are they all going to stay? We don't have a single two-bit motel in Burnt Boot," she asked.

"They have RVs. Remember, we're a rodeo family, so we have trailers and RVs. All they'll need is an electricity outlet, and they're set to go," he answered. "Don't get your little Irish knickers in a wad, darlin'. They'll love you. Now tell me something more about this double date you and Callie have cooked up for next Sunday."

"The antique stores and a lot of the little downtown places have a romance weekend planned, with sales and sidewalk sales if the weather permits," she said.

"So you like antiques?"

"Old things, like old people, have such personality. Someday when I have a home, I want to furnish all of it in either handmade furniture or those with stories behind them. Imagine telling your child that the chair in the corner was the one that your grandma sat in when she read her Bible in the evenings by a kerosene lamp."

He nosed into a parking spot in the crowded lot beside Chili's and turned to face her. "I like that idea, Jill. Mama has an old buffet in the dining room that her grandpa made. It's pretty rustic, but there's something settling and homey about the old thing. But what I like even better is that we're going out today as a couple."

He cupped her face in his hands and kissed her, sweetly at first and adding more passion with the second and third kisses. "And I really like the way that makes me feel."

"Well, shit!" she said.

"What?" He drew back to his side of the console.

She pointed. "Sure you want to go here?"

He followed her finger to see Betsy, Tyrell, and three other Gallaghers going inside the restaurant. "What in the devil are they doing here?"

"We could go somewhere else," she said.

"They're not going to run us off or ruin our day," he said. "It does look like there is a rat in the henhouse, though. Someone is spreading news faster than we can even make it."

Betsy looked up with an evil little grin on her face when Sawyer and Jill came in out of the cold. "Looks like we all decided to eat out today. Sawyer, have you met my cousins? Of course you know Tyrell. This is Eli, Hart, and Randy." She pointed as she made introductions.

Hart stretched out a hand. "I've seen you in church and at Polly's."

Sawyer shook it and smiled. "Nice to meet y'all. Now if you'll excuse us, we've got reservations."

"How'd you do that?" Jill asked when the waitress took them to a private corner table.

"Made them just before church, soon as I knew the place was opened. If you'd have turned me down for a date, then I'd have called and canceled," he said.

"And if I'd wanted to go somewhere else?"

"I had it all covered. Finn canceled for me at the other two places."

The waitress handed them menus and took their drink orders before she disappeared. Sawyer leaned across the table and captured Jill's hands in his. "I'm just going to say this, and then we aren't giving the feud any more attention today. I recognized Hart Gallagher's voice as one of the men who stole us from the Brennans. I knew I'd heard that voice in the bar before, but I wasn't sure until right now. It's not proof that we can take to the sheriff, but it's enough proof for me."

"This isn't a coincidence about them being here too. Someone ratted us out," Jill said. "But I refuse to let it ruin my date. Now tell me, Sawyer O'Donnell, are you more Irish or Hispanic?"

"Half and half. Love the Mexican food but also love a good Irish whiskey on occasion. They're both really good lovers, you know. Hot-blooded and stand by their women." His eyes met hers and twinkled in the dimly lit restaurant.

As luck would have it, the hostess sat Betsy and her four cousins at the next table. Tyrell was so damn close to her, that Jill caught a whiff of his expensive cologne every time she inhaled.

"If they follow us to the movies, I'm going to get the pistols out of the truck and start shooting," Jill whispered.

"We can leave if you want."

"Not on your life, darlin'. Now we were talkin' about you. So how did your mama and daddy meet anyway?" she asked.

"Mama's daddy was a horse trainer for my daddy's parents up in Ringgold, Oklahoma. When her daddy took her up there to visit, my daddy met her, and they fell in love."

"How old were they?"

"Mama says fifth grade, but Daddy swears he saw her first when she was in the third grade and knew he was going to marry her even then. They were young when they married. Daddy had just finished his first rodeo tour, and she was right out of high school. They bought a trailer and moved it on his folks' ranch, and he went to work for them."

"That was what, thirty years ago?"

"Try forty-five. They had my sister and two brothers pretty quick, and I came along as a complete surprise."

Jill laughed. "That's why your sister bosses you around. You were her real, live baby doll."

The waitress came back with their sweet tea and took their orders. Sawyer leaned over and kissed Jill on the tip of the nose. "Now tell me about your parents."

The Gallaghers were right there, but they weren't important, not anymore, not when Sawyer's eyes were locked with hers and his hands were on hers on top of the table.

"They went to school together their whole lives. Daddy's folks lived out on the ranch, and her folks lived on the outskirts of town. She was determined not to marry a cowboy, and Daddy was determined that his future was in the military, so Mama says they were suited for each other. They were going to travel the world, but after basic training, Daddy got stationed in Wichita Falls for the first two years, then he was deployed to the Gulf War, and he never came home. I was just a baby, so Mama went back to southern Texas with me. She met my stepdad a few years later. He'd come to town to set up a new bank for his company, and they met at a party. They fell in love, married, and we moved to Harlan, Kentucky, but I came back to Texas to visit my grandparents every summer."

"Kind of got in your blood, did it?"

"Grandpa said the ranchin' bug skipped my daddy and landed on me." She smiled.

He raised her hand to his lips and kissed each of her knuckles, slowly, one by one. When his lips touched the last one, there could have been Angus bulls roaming around in the restaurant and she wouldn't have seen them. The Gallaghers, as well as all the other customers, vanished. She and Sawyer were the only two people in the whole building—hell, maybe in the whole state.

The waitress brought an appetizer of salsa and crispy tortilla chips. Sawyer picked up a chip and dipped heavily into the salsa. "Open up, darlin'."

He slipped it inside her mouth and then did the same for himself while she chewed. When they'd both swallowed and sipped at their tea, he leaned across the table again and kissed her on the mouth. "A hot kiss with a cold tea back, can't beat it." He grinned.

"It's amazing all right," she said softly.

Their food arrived, and Jill filled a fork with her chicken enchiladas for Sawyer to taste before he got the taste of his beef tacos in his mouth. "See, the sour cream sauce is great."

"Not bad." He kept his hand on her forearm an extra few seconds. "But Mama's are better."

"I'm starting to wish we'd driven to Comfort, Texas, for dinner," she said.

"It can be arranged any Sunday you want to go. Of course, we'll be on the road about ten hours. Five down there, five back, but we'd have a wonderful two-hour dinner with the folks, and just think of all that time we'd have, just the two of us in the cab of a truck without any distractions," he said.

"Well, thank you. It might be a nice date later on in the month. We could leave early on Sunday morning and not have to be back until Monday at noon if Aunt Gladys would do the Monday morning feeding for us," Jill said.

When they were ready to leave, Jill glanced over at the Gallagher table to see the whole bunch of them staring at her. She smiled and hung her thumb in Sawyer's belt loops, letting the rest of her hand fall onto the upper part of his firm butt. The heat coming from Betsy's glares was even hotter than her fingertips on Sawyer's butt. It didn't take a degree in advanced psychology to know that whatever plans the Gallaghers had made to ruin her day had backfired and that there would be consequences.

—◈—

Sawyer didn't hesitate when he bought tickets to the movies that afternoon. They were seeing the newest romance film, and in that very moment, Jill knew she'd found the cowboy of her dreams.

"I can't believe you like love stories," she said.

He threw an arm around her shoulders and stopped inside the lobby at the concession stand. "Popcorn?"

"I couldn't put another bite of food in my mouth right now, and I never drink at a movie, because if I have to go to the restroom, I'm afraid I'll miss something important," she said.

"Then we'll have ice cream afterward. And about love stories? Have you ever watched *NCIS* on television?" He found seats for them at about the halfway mark in the theater.

She moved all the way to the center of the row to get the best view possible. "*NCIS* is on the top of my favorites list, but what's that got to do with romantic movies?"

"Tony?"

"What about Tony? I think Michael Weatherly does a fantastic job of playing that character."

"I'm Tony when it comes to movies," Sawyer said.

"Ohhh," she said. Tony was always spouting off a reference to a movie, old ones particularly.

"So you like them that much, huh?"

"When Mama visits in the spring, she's bringing my collection. I'll have to build shelves or else run you out of your office for all of them."

"I'm not using the wall space. You can cover all of them with shelves if you want," she said. "Oh, my!"

"What?" he asked.

"Those roses are still in there. I bet the water is soured and they're dried up and stinking."

"Time to throw them over the pasture fence." He grinned. "Where's the daisies? I noticed that you'd finally taken the bowls out of the bunkhouse."

She was glad he couldn't see her scarlet cheeks. "I couldn't throw them away. They are getting pressed between layers of wax paper in the pages of several books."

"All of them?"

"Yes, every one of them."

"Excuse me." A lady flipped down the seat next to Sawyer and settled in for the show.

"So sorry." A man with a half-gallon-sized container of popcorn sat down next to Jill.

The seats behind them and those in front of them quickly filled up, and the smell of buttered popcorn filled the air. It was an expected aroma in a movie theater, but something wasn't right. She could feel it down deep in her gut. The feeling was verified when Sawyer squeezed her shoulder and leaned over to kiss her gently on the ear.

"Don't look now, but we've got Gallaghers behind us and Brennans in front of us. Kinsey is sitting by me, and her knee is pressing against mine."

"What in the hell is going on?" she asked. "We're not

part of their pig war. And why are both families here? Did they band together against us?"

"Shhh, the movie is starting," Quaid said beside her. "Well, imagine this. You are going to the movies with me after all." He offered her popcorn.

Jill ignored him and cupped her hand over Sawyer's ear. "There really is a rat in the woodpile. I can understand the restaurant. We talked about it in church, and someone could have easily overheard, but they had to be stalking us to show up here."

Sawyer pulled her to her feet. "Excuse us. Got to make a popcorn run. Oh, hello, Kinsey. Didn't recognize you in the dark."

"We'll gladly share." Kinsey smiled.

"Wouldn't want all the Gallaghers behind you to think we were takin' sides," Jill said.

"So what do you want to do now? See another movie or what?" Sawyer asked when they were finally out of the theater and in the lobby.

"Let's get out of here and go to the antique stores. Callie said they're open on Sunday afternoons. We could just browse for a little while and then go home and take a nap." She shivered and said, "Quaid beside me. Tyrell right behind me. I may never like popcorn again."

Sawyer chuckled.

"What's so funny?"

"Do you think that they are like Tony and love to watch all movies or that this is going to be a real chore for all those guys?"

A smile played at the corners of her mouth. "I'm not sure there'll be a theater still standing in a few hours, with both of the feuding families in the place. I hate that you've lost your money on a movie we won't even see."

"Money is just dirty paper with dead presidents' pictures on it." He chuckled again. "Now let's go pick out the furniture for your dream house."

—◦◦◦—

"Well, isn't that the cutest thing? I can see it sitting on a chest of drawers in a nursery." Jill picked up a teddy bear made from an old quilt. The primary colors were yellows and browns, and the piece making the fat little bear belly was a yellow daisy on a brown background. He had chocolate-colored buttons for his eyes, and someone had painstakingly embroidered his nose and mouth.

Sawyer knew handiwork when he saw it. His maternal grandmother always had a hoop and a needle lying close by, and he'd watched her embroider from the time he could pull up to her rocking chair.

"It's a cute little bear." A few weeks ago, any talk of a nursery would have sent him spinning and running toward the woods. Now it didn't seem like such a big deal.

"Oh, look at this, Sawyer. Both of my grandmothers had these and used them right up until they passed away." She held up a metal ice tray with a lever in the middle that released the thick cubes.

"Mine still do. Let's buy it and display it to remember our first date," he said.

She held it in her hand, working the lever up and back several times. "Where would we put it?"

"How about in the freezer with water in it to make ice?" he said.

"I love it. Then every time we fill up a sweet tea glass, we will remember how much fun we had today."

She was absolutely amazing. Most women would have whined for days about how the Gallaghers and the Brennans had destroyed their entire day. But Jill brushed it away like a fly on her shoulder.

She was looking at a display of gravy boats when he carried the ice tray to the front counter. He hoped that she couldn't see the bulge in the side of his jean jacket made by the patchwork bear. He might not be ready for a nursery, but he had other ideas in mind for the daisy bear.

"Please put these in a big bag that you can't see through," he told the cashier.

"A little surprise for someone?" Her mouth curved upward in a shy smile.

"Yes, ma'am. Hopefully, a big surprise later on down the road."

Chapter 25

GLADYS, POLLY, AND VERDIE WERE SITTING AROUND A table at the back of the bar when Jill and Sawyer unlocked the place and went inside, out of the blustery cold February wind.

"Guess the groundhog wasn't lyin' last week when he predicted six more weeks of winter, was he?" Verdie said.

"What are all y'all doin' here?" Jill asked.

"We're having a beer and trying to decide what in the hell we can do to end the pig war," Verdie answered. "And we had to convince Polly that her bar was still in one piece."

Polly lifted her bottle of beer. "Y'all have done a fine job of keeping it running for me. Thank you."

"You are welcome, Aunt Polly, but why would you think you could end the feud?" Sawyer asked. "If it's not this, it'll be something else. It's been here for a century, and it'll take something major to end it for good. You might end the pig war, but the feud will keep coming back to life over and over again."

"You got a point there, but it really got hot today," Gladys said. "Tyrell Gallagher sent Leah Brennan a lovely box of long-stemmed roses. Tyrell is denying it to Naomi, who is threatening to have him drawn and quartered in the church parking lot. Mavis wouldn't even let Leah bring them in the house. She said that they were probably poisoned with arsenic."

"Not arsenic, that other stuff. What's it called?" Verdie tapped her chin.

"That shit that's worse than bubonic plaque," Polly said.

"Anthrax?" Sawyer asked.

They all three pointed at him. "That's it!"

Jill tied an apron around her waist. "She really thought the Gallaghers would send over anthrax?"

"Before she'd let Tyrell and Leah start dating, or any other Gallagher and Leah for that matter, Mavis would give them a bath in it," Verdie answered.

"We all knew the day would come eventually when one of them fell for the other side, and we knew it would be a big battle. It's just hard to picture Tyrell interested in Leah. If anyone would have a torch for her, it would be Tanner." Polly sighed.

Jill's eyes opened so wide she couldn't force them to close. She knew in her gut what had happened, because she'd done the exact same thing with the doggie treats and the pork rinds.

She slapped the bar. "Sawyer?"

"What'd I do?" He chuckled.

"This is a come-to-Jesus moment, which means it's confession time," she said.

"Forgive me, darlin', for I have sinned, but they tried to ruin our date, and they shouldn't have brought us into their shitty old pig war to begin with. And I'm not really sorry for a bit of it." He bowed his head and looked up at her with a broad grin and mischievous eyes.

"What are you two talking about?" Gladys asked.

"We're talkin' about roses, Chicken Chips, and pork rinds," he said.

"And you did all of that, didn't you?" Verdie asked.

"Guilty. But we didn't ask to be kidnapped, have to sleep in a barn, or ride home in a wagon. We didn't ask to be surrounded by them at the movies or for them to try to ruin our dinner. They deserve payback," Jill said.

Gladys clucked like a hen gathering in her chicks before a storm. She pulled her phone from the pocket of her bibbed overalls and hit two buttons. "Mavis, honey, I don't think you need to send Leah to a convent just yet. I'm not at liberty to say who sent the flowers, but they are not from Tyrell or any other Gallagher. They were sent to stir you up. No, I don't care what you say. I won't tell you how I found out or who they are from."

A pause while she stared at the ceiling.

"No, they aren't from Tanner, either. I believe you done stirred in the wrong shit pile and upset some folks. Now that's all I'm saying. Why don't y'all call a truce? The church party is Friday night. Be nice if the feud was over by then, wouldn't it?"

No one had to strain to hear Mavis's answer. "Call a truce? Are you bat-shit crazy, Gladys Cleary? The Gallaghers stole my hogs, and there will be no truces. And you tell those smart-ass informants of yours that if I find out who they are, they are dead."

"Guess we'd better dig the foxhole a little deeper," Sawyer said.

"Their bark is a lot worse than their bite, but I don't reckon there's going to be a truce before Valentine's Day," Verdie said. "I'm going home now unless y'all want to have a dominoes game at Polly's house."

"Give me a bottle of that Jack Daniel's," Polly told Sawyer. "And, Jill, it don't matter how many people are in here tonight. You turn off the jukebox and the lights at eleven o'clock."

"I'll do it," Jill said.

"And just for the record, that was funny as hell." Verdie chuckled. "That'll teach them to keep their feudin' at home and not involve other folks in their battles."

"Shit, Verdie! Whole town has been connected one way or the other since the damn thing started. Let's go play dominoes and drink Jack Daniel's. It'll get even funnier in an hour or two," Polly said.

They hadn't been gone more than a few seconds when Jill's phone rang. She whipped it out of her hip pocket and said, "Hello, Callie."

"I just heard what happened yesterday. Need some help tonight at the bar? I'll leave the kids with Finn and bring my six-guns," she said.

"I might take you up on that if it gets too rowdy. Keep your phone on and your boots ready. Don't have to tell you to keep your guns loaded," Jill said.

"You do not. If they want to bitch and bite, they can do it, but they'd best leave the O'Donnells alone."

"I'm a Cleary," Jill said.

"Hopefully not for long. I'll be ready if you need me."

The call ended, and Jill held it out, staring at it until Sawyer's arms wrapped around her from behind and he kissed her on the neck. "Bad news?"

"I don't think so. I reckon it could have even been good news. We'll just have to see what Callie meant. She did offer to bring her six-guns to the fight if things got out of hand here in the bar tonight." Jill eased around and rolled up on her toes for a real kiss.

His tongue teased her mouth open, and his hands

dropped to cup her rounded butt. His belt buckle pressed into her stomach, but she didn't care. Her hand tangled itself into his thick dark hair, holding his head steady so she could deepen the kiss even more. His hands circled her waist, and her feet left the floor as he sat her on the workstation behind the bar. Her legs automatically wrapped around his waist and held him tight.

They both heard the truck doors slamming outside at the same time, and she dropped her hands and her legs, slid off the bar, and set about refilling the red-cup dispenser. Sawyer threw two meat patties on the grill, along with a double handful of chopped onions.

Everything but their speeding heartbeats was normal when the door flew open and more than a dozen folks from Wild Horse Ranch claimed either bar stools or tables.

"Man, I miss the days when all I did was ranch and worry about new baby calves or whether the hay crop would be good," Jill said.

"Me too," Sawyer said. "Come spring, I vote we hire help for the bar."

"Got anyone in mind?"

"I do. My cousin Rhett is lookin' to get away from Comfort. He's a damn fine rancher, but he's single, and I don't think he'd mind workin' the bar. We'll have to talk to Gladys and Polly though."

"Does he look like you?" Jill asked as she filled pitchers with beer and took money.

"You can tell we're cousins, but he's a wild cowboy, not a tame one. He's got a ponytail, rides a motorcycle, and has a longhorn tat across his shoulders."

"You think you're a tame one?"

"Compared to Rhett, I am."

"Hey, Sawyer, I disagree with that," Betsy said from the end bar stool.

"With what?" Jill asked.

"I think with the right cowgirl, Sawyer could be one wild ride," she said.

Jill ignored the remark. "What are you drinking?"

"We need two pitchers of beer and six cups over at our table. Sawyer, we'll take six cheeseburger baskets with extra fries," Betsy said. "And, darlin', anytime you want to quit all this extra-duty shit and just ranch to your little old cowboy heart's delight, you jump the fence over onto Wild Horse, and I promise you can ranch all you want to."

Jill set the pitchers on the bar and made change for the bills Betsy handed her. It would have been so easy to accidentally knock the beer over in her lap, but Jill figured between her and Sawyer, they'd meddled enough. Let the chips fall where they would; she was done with the whole lot of the pig war. What was it Granny used to tell her?

Oh, yes. She shuddered as she remembered the quote. *Those who stir in the shit pot should have to lick the spoon.*

"Poor old Rhett," Sawyer mumbled.

"What about Rhett?"

"I just feel sorry for him if he does come to Burnt Boot. He won't have a pretty little redhead to watch his back. He'll be on his own with these women swooping down on him like buzzards after roadkill," Sawyer said.

"Maybe Betsy will be his pretty little redhead."

Sawyer shook his head emphatically. "They're too much alike. They'd kill each other in an afternoon."

The bar was surprisingly Brennan-free all evening. There were plenty of Gallaghers and other folks to keep it busy for a Monday night, enough that Jill was dragging when she got back to the bunkhouse that night. Sawyer sank down on the sofa, and she joined him. Piggy and Chick came out from under the kitchen table where they'd been putting the fear of two kittens into a rolled-up ball of socks. She picked them both up and handed the yellow one to Sawyer.

"They need some attention before we fall asleep," she said.

Sawyer scratched the kitten's ears. "Let's put up a sign that says the Gallaghers can come in the bar on Mondays, Wednesdays, and Fridays. The Brennans can do business with us on Tuesdays, Thursdays, and Saturdays. Same with the store."

"For that, we do hereby, being sane of mind and too tired to screw each other's brains out tonight, shall promise that we will stay away from Wild Horse and River Bend. If they shall, being almost sane of mind, do hereby promise to never kidnap or flirt with us again, we will give our solemn word before God and both these kittens to never delve into retail therapy in retaliation again, heretofore and all that bullshit. Signed Jillian Cleary and Sawyer O'Donnell."

Sawyer chuckled down deep in his chest. "Who says I'm that tired?"

"You might not be, but I am. I'm taking a shower and going to bed," she said.

"Whose bed?"

"Mine. It's supposed to be raining in the morning, and it'll take us twice as long to do our ranchin' chores. I don't want to have to get up after two hours of sleep and kick hay bales or work with fifty-pound bags of feed."

"Wow, girlfriend, you sure put a lot of faith in my ability. It's midnight. You think I could last for three or four hours?"

She put the gray kitten in his lap, kissed him on the cheek, and headed for the shower. "I don't have a doubt in my mind."

Sawyer leaned his head back on the sofa. Try as hard as he might, he could not keep the grin from his face.

Chapter 26

THAT SUNDAY MORNING WAS AS COLD AS A MOTHER-IN-law's kiss, but there was no wind rattling through the mesquite. With layers of warm clothing and warm sunshine, it didn't seem as cold as the thermometer on the side of the bunkhouse said it was.

They'd run out of small bales of hay and were down to their last row of big bales. Sawyer drove the tractor with an enormous bale on the front fork. He set it down in the middle of the pasture and put the tractor in reverse. The double prongs left it lying right there, with cows gathered around like it was a big, round dinner table.

Jill shimmied down out of the passenger's seat, pulled clippers from the pocket of her overalls, and cut away the mesh wrapping so the herd could really get at the hay. "At least with the big bales, we don't have to do this but once a day. I'm going to talk to Aunt Gladys about making all big bales next year. There's a little more waste, but in dollars and cents, it makes more sense…"

"She's old school, so I doubt that she'll go for that idea, darlin'," Sawyer said. "The old ranchers don't feel like they can face winter without a couple of barns full of the old-fashioned hay bales. The round ones don't compute to them."

"She and Aunt Polly are both too old to be doing work this hard. They should be retired and enjoying life, maybe taking one of those senior citizens' cruises. They could take Verdie with them and have a big time."

"Good luck with that," he said. "See that mesquite thicket over there? That's the one I want to clear off and plant more grass for grazing or for baling. If we make it another six weeks until spring without buying hay, we'll be lucky. The barn is empty."

"I know, Sawyer. I vote we put in more acres of alfalfa for baling and wait another year to increase the herd. There's at least a quarter of the ranch we could reclaim, and then we'd be ready for more cattle." She slapped a heifer on the flank, and the cow shifted a couple of feet to the left so Jill could make her way back to the tractor.

"I talked to Gladys, and she said for me to go ahead and see if Rhett was interested in a job right now. At first, he's going to help clear land."

Jill's heart fell into her boots. Another man in the bunkhouse would mean a lot of changes, and she liked the way things were. She had free run of the whole place, including Sawyer's bathroom and bed. His cousin might be wild with his tat and ponytail, and he might not even blink at her coming out of Sawyer's room in the morning, but just thinking about it put high color in her cheeks.

"We can clean out the room I was going to make into an office for him."

"I thought that was going to be my movie storage room," Sawyer said.

"We can't throw him out in the yard with a blanket and a pillow."

"Why? He's tough." Sawyer chuckled.

"So when are you going to talk to him?"

"Maybe this evening when we get back from our second date," he said. "Hey, do I get a kiss or maybe even get lucky on the second date?" He put his hands on her waist and lifted her from ground to tractor seat in one fluid movement.

"Lucky doesn't arrive until the fourth or fifth date, in my books," she teased.

He kicked at the cold dirt like a little boy. "Well, shucks."

"But we can find another antique to remember our second date by," she said. "I really like that old ice tray. It's amazing how much easier the cubes pop out of it than they do when I twist one of the plastic ones. Never know about the lucky issue though. If that cute little bear with the daisy on her belly is still there and you buy her for me, I might rewrite the rules in my book, and you could get lucky on the second date."

The smile on his face rivaled the sun when he looked up. "Then we'll definitely look for the bear. What makes you think it's a girl bear?"

He jogged around the back end of the tractor and climbed inside the cab.

"It's a girl bear because no self-respecting boy bear would have a daisy on his belly," she answered.

Sawyer started up the engine and turned the tractor around. "Maybe he's not afraid of his feminine side. Maybe he even watches old movies."

"Nope, it's still a girl bear, and her name is Daisy."

"And if we buy Daisy today and bring her home, I might get lucky?"

"Maybe you won't, but I might," she teased.

He stopped the tractor in front of the barn and pulled

her across the bench seat to his side. "Lucky takes on a whole new meaning with you, Jill. I'm lucky for every single moment I get to spend with you." He tipped up her chin, and she got lost all over again in his dark eyes. When his lips covered hers, the kiss was so sweet and so passionate that she had to keep the tears at bay.

"I thought the preacher was going to talk forever. I've looked forward to this all week. It's our first date since we got married," Callie said as the waiter seated them in the little café at the back of one of the antique shops.

"Blue plate special today is your choice of chicken-fried steak or meatloaf, served with mashed potatoes; your choice of okra, pinto beans, or green beans; and a basket of hot rolls," the waiter said. "Or you can choose from the grill menu. You should try our onion blossom or jalapeño poppers for an appetizer. They're really good. I'll take your drink orders now and be back when you've decided."

"Sweet tea," Jill and Sawyer said at the same time.

Callie and Finn nodded.

"And bring us a double order of the poppers and an onion blossom," Finn said.

"You hungry, darlin'?" Callie asked. "Or do you think we are?"

"Starving. My stomach was growling so loud, folks around me thought I was snoring in church," Finn answered. "Hey, I thought Mavis and Naomi might lock it up right there in the church house after church. Anyone else see what happened?"

Jill shook her head.

"They came up to shake the preacher's hand at the same time. That meant one had to step aside," Callie explained. "Even Verdie held her breath."

"Why?" Sawyer asked.

"Because it would be like losing a battle in the war to whoever took second place, right?" Jill asked. "Which one lost?"

"Neither," Callie said. "Verdie stepped between them and started talking. She steered them out of the church without stopping to visit with the preacher at all. She rambled on and on about Salt Draw and the kids, and neither of them said a word to her or to each other. When they were outside, they went straight to their own trucks."

"Damnedest thing I ever saw. Verdie said that she did it because she didn't want our date ruined." Finn laughed. "I love that woman."

Callie touched his arm and looked up into his eyes. "As much as you do me?"

"Oh, honey, I don't love anyone that much." He kissed her on the tip of the nose.

"How would two old women rolling around and tearing up their panty hose ruin our date?" Sawyer asked.

"I didn't ask. I just figured Verdie knew what she was talking about," Finn answered.

"Sweet tea for everyone," the waiter said at Finn's elbow. "The appetizers will be here in about three minutes. Have you decided on dinner?"

"Chicken-fried," Jill said. "Steak fries, pinto beans, and ranch dressing on my salad."

"Sawmill gravy or brown gravy?" he asked.

"Sawmill," Jill said.

"Same for me," Callie said.

Finn handed him the menu and said, "Make it three."

"Meatloaf and mashed potatoes, corn, and ranch dressing," Sawyer said.

"It won't be as good as Granny O'Donnell's," Finn whispered when the waiter was out of earshot.

"Neither will the chicken-fried steak." Sawyer grinned. "Did I tell you that they're all coming for Easter?"

"Mama says my side is coming to Salt Draw. I thought we'd have the egg hunt at Salt Draw, since we're the ones who already have kids," Finn said.

Already have kids? The line ran around in Jill's head in a continuous loop. Jill felt the color leave her face.

"Are you okay?" Sawyer asked.

Her head bobbed twice. "How many family members are you talking about?"

"Couldn't begin to get a head count," Finn said. "My family is coming to Salt Draw, and then there's Uncle Cash's crew from over in Ringgold. They usually have Easter at their ranch, but Granny says since I'm the newest one married, everyone is coming to Burnt Boot."

Callie laid a hand on Jill's shoulder. "Most of them came to see us a few weeks ago. Couple of the cousins were standoffish until they figured out that I wasn't some kind of crazy, pistol-toting woman. By the time they all left, I think they'd accepted the fact that Finn and I were married and adopting four kids fairly well."

"If we have Rhett hired on at Fiddle Creek, his family might load up and come too. So that would be even more O'Donnells," Sawyer said.

"Rhett is lookin' for a job? Why didn't you tell me? I would have put him to work weeks ago," Finn said.

"Gladys said I can hire him, so don't you go tryin' to

steal him from me. I need the help more than you do," Sawyer said.

Callie moved her chair closer to Jill. "Let them argue like cousins. Tell me, how are things going? Any more trouble with the feud? It has kind of died down this week."

"I think it's just simmering," Jill whispered. "They've figured out they aren't getting Fiddle Creek through me and probably think that since Sawyer and I are going out on dates that he's angling to get it. But he's not that kind of man, Callie."

"Don't know an O'Donnell that thinks like that. They are all the salt of the earth, which reminds me, don't be scared of them. I saw the fear in your eyes. They'll love you because you love Sawyer," she said. "Now tell me more about this ice-tray thing. Finn told me y'all bought an ice tray on your first date."

Jill had a moment of mixed emotions. First, she wondered if Sawyer told Finn everything they did, and it brought heat to her cheeks. On the other hand, she was glad that he was as excited about the ice tray as she'd been. And then her cheeks burned like fire when she realized that Callie had said that she loved Sawyer, right out loud in public.

Jill cleared her throat and tried to get control of the blush by talking. "We found the old metal ice tray and the cute little handmade bear on the same shelf. We bought the ice tray to remind us of our first date and how much fun we had."

"And this week we're buying the bear," Sawyer said.

"Is it in this antique store? The one we are having lunch in?" Finn asked.

"When did you two stop arguing and start listening to us?" Jill asked.

"When he convinced me that he needed Rhett more than I did, and besides, I think Rhett would be damn good at keeping peace in the bar." Finn covered Callie's hand with his. "What are we buying to celebrate our date today?"

"I'll find something," she said.

He brought her hand to his lips and kissed her fingers. "It can't cost any more than their ice tray."

"We'll just see about that." She smiled.

The waiter set an enormous onion blossom and a platter of jalapeño poppers in the middle of the table and refilled all their tea glasses. "Your food will be ready in about fifteen minutes. We've been really busy today. I apologize for the wait."

"No problem. We're not in a hurry," Callie said.

The waiter flashed a brilliant smile and headed off to another table.

"Is it?" Finn reached for a popper and dipped it in the sauce.

"Is what?" Sawyer followed his lead.

"Is the bear in this store?" Finn asked.

"No, it's in the one next door, but I want to look in this one when we get finished eating. This is really cool, having a café adjoined to the store, isn't it?" Jill answered.

She felt like she'd known Finn and Callie her whole life instead of a few short weeks. They felt like family, and she couldn't wait for the opportunity to spend time with their four kids.

Finn was probably right. The dinner was good, but it wasn't like Granny made. After they'd finished, they shopped in the store, and Callie bought one of those cute little jewelry boxes with a tiny ballerina that twirled when it was opened. Then she found a couple of old baseball cards for each of the boys.

The bear was gone when they reached the next store on the block. The man behind the counter that day told them that his wife had sold it the week before to a young couple who planned to use it in their nursery.

"Great minds think alike," Jill said.

Sawyer planted a kiss on the top of her head. "We should have bought it last week."

"At least it will make some little baby laugh." Jill sighed.

Finn and Callie had just wandered off to the back of the store. Jill and Sawyer were near the middle, looking at cream pitchers, when she felt someone staring at her.

Kinsey Brennan wasn't six feet from her when she looked up. "Well, hello, Sawyer. I'd like you to meet my date, and my boss at the firm where I work part-time. Gage, this is Sawyer; Sawyer, Gage. And this is Jill Cleary. Her aunt has a little spread next to River Bend."

Sawyer extended his hand. "Pleased to meet you. Y'all finding anything interesting?"

Kinsey looped her arm through Gage's, and he patted her hand. "Oh, yes, we found a lovely little side table for my office. I'm moving from part time to full time."

A tall man, but not quite as tall as Kinsey, he wore a three-piece suit and loafers. His thick blond hair was styled in a perfect, feathered cut, and judging by the crow's-feet around his eyes, Jill would guess him to be ten years older than Kinsey.

"Y'all have fun now. See you later," Kinsey said.

Sawyer waved and went back to the cream pitchers. "One down. One to go."

Jill slipped her hand in his. "Don't count on it."

He raised an eyebrow.

"Did you ever hear of the turd theory?" she asked.

He shook his head.

"It goes like this. You think if a certain obnoxious person wasn't in your life, then everything would be just peachy. Then that person is miraculously out of your life, and behold, another turd floats to the top," Jill said.

"Well, hello, Sawyer," Betsy said. "I'm surprised to see you here. Jill, not so much, but a guy?"

"I rest my case," Jill said. "Are you buying something special, like Kinsey is? We just met her new boyfriend and heard she's going to work full time."

Betsy leaned a shoulder over toward Sawyer. "What wonderful news. Now she's out of my way with you, Sawyer. Got to run. Grandma is next door having ice cream with some of my cousins. I just snuck away to say hello when I saw y'all coming in here."

Sawyer didn't even acknowledge that the woman was talking. He squeezed Jill's hand and whispered, "We won't ever be able to get away from them, darlin'. They are part of Burnt Boot, but we don't have to let them control our lives. How about this one for our second-date present?" He picked up a carnival glass pitcher and held it out to her.

"I vote we get something more practical. Like this." She held up a cast-iron pan that made muffins in the shape of corn on the cob. "Grandma Cleary had one like this, and I loved the muffins when I was a little girl."

"Granny O'Donnell still uses one like that. Let's buy it," he said.

Dusk had begun to settle when they got home that evening. Jill called Gladys before they left town, and she wanted them to pick up fried chicken for her and Polly. When they went by the house, she met them at the door.

"We'll come in for only a minute. It's cold out here, and we're doing the chores tonight. You and Aunt Polly just stay warm and have chicken for supper."

"Thanks, darlin'," Gladys said. "I was dreading getting out in this."

Jill bent and hugged Polly and gave her a kiss on the forehead. "Stay warm, and we'll see y'all tomorrow."

"Thanks, sweetheart. Maybe I'll feel like a couple of hours in the store tomorrow morning," Polly said.

"Too late for a nap." Jill removed her denim duster and tossed it toward the sofa. The cats jumped on it, clawing and attacking the stones with their hind feet. She had to scramble to get it away from them before they left it in shreds.

Sawyer hung his jacket on the rack inside the door and scooped her up in his arms. "I don't want to sleep, but I want you," he said softly as he headed for the bedroom. He kicked the door shut with his boot heel. "And I don't want to share you with the children."

"Confession time. I couldn't wait to get home for this," she mumbled.

He set her on the edge of the bed and removed her boots and shoes. He ran a hand up the inside of her thigh and inhaled sharply when he found no underpants.

"Surprise! Surprise!" She grinned impishly.

"My God, Jill."

"If you hadn't been so busy arguing with Finn at the dinner table, you might have discovered it earlier." She brushed his hand out of the way and stood up, removing her sweater and bra as she did.

"If I had, the shopping trip would have never happened and we would have had sex in the bathroom at the antique store." His lips settled on hers as he removed her skirt and let it fall to the floor.

She pushed him back on the bed, straddled his body, and removed his boots.

He cupped the cheeks of her butt in his hands and massaged gently as she removed his socks, then she flipped around, and his hands went to her breasts, his eyes never leaving hers as she finished undressing him.

She took advantage of him being ready and guided him into her in a firm thrust. Putting her hands on his chest for leverage, she began a steady rhythm. She'd had a full day of foreplay. Every time he threw an arm around her shoulders, it turned her on. When their hands brushed against each other at the antique stores, she burned for him. When his fingertips tucked an errant strand of hair back behind her ear, she'd wanted to haul him to the nearest motel.

"I want to kiss you," he said as he flipped her over on her back. "And this isn't going to last five minutes if we don't slow down."

"Quality beats out quantity every time," she mumbled just before his lips landed on hers.

In a wild blast of sparks, it was over. Her head felt as if it would explode, and he said something that sounded faintly like, "I love you," but she couldn't be sure if that's what she heard with her ears buzzing the way they were. She might have answered with the same thing, but her breath was coming in such short gasps that she couldn't utter a single word, not even his name.

Chapter 27

THE ADVERTISEMENTS CAME OUT IN THE GAINESVILLE newspaper on Wednesday. As luck would have it, the quarter-page ads for the two celebrations were side by side. The one for the church advertised romance, good Christian fun for the whole family, refreshments, and a potluck dinner at the Burnt Boot church, beginning at six o'clock on Friday night, February 13. The admission fee was a covered dish, and there would be speed dating for the single folks.

The Burnt Boot Bar and Grill ad was right there beside it, with a pretty heart border and martini glasses clinking together. It advertised no cover fee, a sweetheart deal of two-for-one all night on pitchers of beer and burger baskets, and promised that the jukebox would be playing love songs from six to midnight on February 14 at no charge to the patrons. Down at the bottom of the ad in small print was a paragraph that advised folks not to drink too much and/or to bring a designated driver.

"It's official. Our butts will be dragging so bad by closin' time tomorrow night, we won't need to sweep the barroom floor." Jill tossed the newspaper on the tractor seat between her and Sawyer.

"Polly says she only does this when Valentine's Day falls on Saturday, so it just happens every seven years. She wanted to come help us. Said she could hobble around behind the bar and at least do some grilling," Sawyer said.

"She and Aunt Gladys are going to man the store all afternoon for us to decorate. Neither of those old gals realize they aren't twenty anymore, so that will tax them both." Jill shook her head. "I'm glad we've started using big hay bales, so she'll stay in most of the afternoons and let us take care of things."

"We need to convince Gladys to let us make more big bales." He started up the engine and drove the tractor to the line of round bales at the edge of the pasture. Driving the fork on the front into the middle of the four-foot, firmly packed bale, he raised it up and carefully backed up.

"We've got the equipment for small ones, and as long as Aunt Gladys is alive and the hay barn is standing, I reckon we'll be making both sizes," Jill said.

Sawyer wiggled his eyebrows. "Time to do other things."

"Speaking of which, did you talk to your cousin Rhett?" she asked.

"I did, and he didn't even hesitate. He'll be here Tuesday morning, so after this party is done on Saturday, we should clean out the office for him," Sawyer said. "His first job is clearing land, so we can start planting. I don't want to get this low on hay another year."

"Hey, look here," she said.

Sawyer whipped around, and she snapped a picture of him with her phone. "Mama wants to know what you look like. I'm sending this to them right now."

"What brought that on?" Sawyer asked. "We were talking about Rhett."

"I'm going to be occupying a bunkhouse with two cowboys. Mama is not going to be happy about that. I'm sending her a picture of you now, so she can get used to the idea of what you look like, before I send her one of Rhett with a tat and a ponytail." Jill poked the right buttons to shoot the photograph through cyberspace.

Sawyer parked the tractor and helped Jill down to the ground, drawing her closely to his side with one arm, kissing her cold lips, and taking a selfie picture with the other hand.

"Why did you do that?" she asked.

"My family has seen pictures of you, darlin'. I'm sendin' this one to Rhett, so he knows before he gets here that you belong to me," Sawyer said.

"Your family," she gasped. "When did you take pictures to send them?"

"Which time?"

"You sent more than one?"

He chuckled. "Well, there was one day I only sent one."

"Sawyer, are you joking?"

He shook his head and took her hand in his, pulling her toward the bunkhouse. "I promise I did not take any of you in my bed or in any other compromising situation. But you were so darn cute in that outfit you wore when we bought the cast-iron pan that I took several in the antique store. And there's some of you taking the roses to the office room and playing with the kittens."

"How...?"

"You thought I was texting." He grinned.

"And?"

"Mama says that she can't believe I've fallen for a redhead. Daddy thinks you are cute, and Rhett, well, he needs to know that he hasn't got a chance." Sawyer removed his coat and hat and helped Jill with hers.

"How about hot chocolate while we spend some quality time with Miss Piggy and Miss Chickadee? Then we'll go to the store a couple of hours early and make Gladys take Polly home. She'll be tired by then."

"The cats' names have evolved. They sound like hookers in an animated movie." She laughed. "Is it the truth? Have you fallen for me, Sawyer O'Donnell?"

"Yes, Jill Cleary, head over boots, I've fallen for you." He brushed another kiss across her lips and headed to the kitchen.

She snapped half a dozen pictures of him, one of nothing more than that tight butt as it walked away from her. "Paybacks," she said when he looked over his shoulder and she took another one.

"Just remember that I can do the same thing." He turned around quickly, ran toward her like a football tackle, and without slowing down, picked her up and carried her into the bedroom. "Forget the chocolate. We'll get warm another way."

"Hmmm. Chocolate or sex? Which one?" She cupped his face in her hands.

"You decide." His dark eyes fluttered shut, and she barely had time to moisten her dry, still-cold lips before he found them.

No contest. Chocolate took a backseat.

———※———

The bar was so slow on Friday night that time practically stood still. They opened at six, and the first customer arrived at seven. He was a middle-aged fellow from across the river, who just wanted to sit in the corner, nurse a couple of double shots, and listen to a dollar's worth of old Hank

Williams tunes before he called it a night at eight thirty. The next customer that wandered in was Hart Gallagher, who'd gotten tired of the church party. He bought a pitcher of beer and plunked quarters into the jukebox.

"Bet you he's playin' beer-drinkin' songs because he's got the hots for a Brennan woman and he can't have her," Sawyer whispered to Jill.

"It's pretty plain that something has his mind in a twist," Jill agreed.

Sawyer was right. For the next hour, the jukebox spit out sad songs while Hart finished off his beer.

Gladys called at ten to tell them the party was winding down but that it had been a success. "Everyone had a wonderful time, and the potluck was great."

"Mavis and Naomi?" Jill asked.

"Sat on different sides of the fellowship hall all evening, surrounded by their grandchildren and children. They didn't kiss and make up, but they didn't start a food fight, so I guess it was a draw where the pig war is concerned. I really don't know what else they could do anyway," Gladys answered.

"Aunt Polly worn out?"

"Yes, but she won't admit it," Gladys said. "She wants to know how things are going there."

"Two customers all evening. Couple of double shots of Jim Beam and a pitcher of beer is all we've sold. Won't even have to sweep the floors. If Aunt Polly had brought the decorations down here from her house, we could have the place ready for tomorrow."

"Polly says for y'all to shut it down and go home. Tomorrow is going to make up for tonight, and you need your rest."

"Yes, ma'am. You don't have to beg me to shut the doors tonight," Jill said.

"Mama, please tell me I didn't wake you." Jill shut her eyes and could picture her mother. Tall, thin, and blond. Big doe-colored eyes and a smile that was a dental record.

"Did that feud and scalding-hot cowboy suck all the memory out of your brain? Remember, I'm a night owl," her mother said. "If I'd known he looked like that when you told me you were going to Burnt Boot, I'd have kidnapped you myself."

"I think I'm in love," Jill said.

"Either you are or you aren't. Which is it?"

"I am, but I need you to talk me out of it," Jill said. "Oh my God, I'm fanning myself with my hand, and I'm telling you this because you can't see me, and you are my mother, but I don't know who else to call."

"You've slept with him?"

"He brought me daisies," Jill answered.

"You didn't answer my question. Have you slept with him?"

"And we bought an ice tray and a cast-iron pan together, and we have two kittens, Miss Piggy and Miss Chickadee."

"Are you in love with him, Jillian?"

"Yes, just like you were with my daddy."

"You both like ranchin'. He bought you freakin' daisies, and you bought an ice tray and cast-iron pan together. What in the hell are you waiting for, girl? Propose to him," her mother said.

"But, Mama, I've only known him six weeks."

"I proposed to your father in three weeks. When it's right, you know it. You still didn't answer my question."

Jill laughed. "I'm in the bathtub, and the water has gone cold. I'm going to end this call and get out. And, Mama, I'm not going to answer that question."

"Where are you sleeping tonight?"

"That is need to know, and you don't."

"Hey, now, we've been sharing some pretty big secrets."

"Good night, Mama," Jill said and hit the "end" button.

Sitting in the rocking chair, towel drying her hair, and thinking about the conversation, she didn't hear her bedroom door crack open. She was so deep in her thoughts that she didn't even see Miss Piggy chasing a bit of ribbon across the floor.

"You take my breath away," Sawyer said. "No wonder I fell in love with you."

As if in slow motion, her head raised. The hinges squeaked when he pushed the door wide open. The thought that ran through her mind was that she'd have to put some oil on them or she'd get caught sneaking across to Sawyer's room after Rhett arrived. Then she wondered if she'd heard what she wanted to hear, not what he'd actually said.

"Say that again," she whispered.

"I said I've fallen in love with you, Jillian Cleary. My heart has known it for a while. It just took my mind a while to catch up," he said.

"One more time, just so I'm sure there's no water in my ears."

He took the towel from her hands, picked her up, and sat down in the rocker with her in his lap. "I love you, Jill."

"I love you, Sawyer," she whispered.

"That makes me the happiest cowboy in all of Texas," he drawled. "I'd planned all these beautiful scenarios to say those three words, but they just slipped out tonight. I guess we aren't destined for roses and romance."

"Roses? No, darlin', we are not. Romance? It goes much deeper than just saying words, although they are beautiful and I want to hear them every single day. FYI, right here in our bunkhouse at the end of a workday is the best place ever to say it for the first time. Romance is wonderful, Sawyer, but it needs actions to back them up. Your bed is bigger than mine, and I'm not sleeping alone anymore, so…" She hesitated.

"Yes, ma'am, I'm right good at showing instead of telling." He stopped any further talk with a searing-hot kiss.

Decorating the next day involved stringing up some crepe paper, putting a glittery heart garland around the mirror behind the bar, using red paper liners in the plastic burger baskets instead of the customary white ones, and hanging a big red foldout heart above the jukebox. It took all of thirty minutes to do that and take the chairs down from the tables.

"Now what? I was expecting an all-afternoon job," Sawyer said. They could go back to the bunkhouse and spend the afternoon in bed or maybe drive around the ranch and talk about the changes they'd like to make.

He looked around the pitifully decorated bar. He'd been out to dance and drink on Valentine's Day, and this place sure didn't scream romance.

"If we had a pool table, I might suggest a nap on it until opening time," she said.

"How about a trip into town? If we hung a paper heart over where the Gallaghers sit and one above the Brennans, it might put an end to the pig war," Sawyer said.

"It'll take more than a paper heart to create that miracle. But I do think we need more than this after that big ad in the paper," she agreed. "Let's make a run into Walmart— no wait, isn't there a party store in that outlet mall?"

"I wouldn't know. Guess we could check on it first, and if there isn't, we could go on into Walmart." Sawyer was already getting their coats from the backs of two bar stools. "Last time I was in a bar on Valentine's, they had put little fancy things on the tables. Folks fought over who got to take them home."

"I know what you are talking about. They have a weighted bottom with something that looks like red heart fireworks shooting out of the top. Lord help us if Betsy gets drunk and takes one to Kinsey's head." She slung her purse over her shoulder.

"Hey, Jill," he said as he took her hand in his.

"Hey, what?"

"I love you," he said.

"Hey, Sawyer, I love you back," she told him. "Red plastic tablecloths?"

"You sure are romantic this afternoon," he teased.

"What's not romantic about red plastic tablecloths?" she shot right back.

"For starters, they'd be real easy for Betsy or Kinsey to accidentally-on-purpose grab if they were fake falling. Can you imagine Betsy if a whole table full of burger baskets landed in her lap?"

Jill laughed as he opened the door and helped her inside his truck. "It might end the pig war and begin the burger war."

"Where they throw food rather than steal pigs."

When he was inside the truck, she said, "Or where they poison food instead of stealing livestock, so scratch that idea. We just need some cutesy things that remind the folks that it's a fall-in-love day, not a war day."

"How about a couple of bags of those heart-shaped red hots and some of those conversation hearts to go on the bar instead of pretzels and peanuts?"

She pulled her wallet from her purse, ripped off a check, and fished around until she found a pen. "I'm going to make a list. Candy for bar. Keep thinking, and I'll write it all down as we travel."

By the time they reached the outlet mall, the back side of her check was filled with ideas. He parked, and hand in hand, they started toward the party store. It was two stores up from the jewelry store and just past the leather-goods place where they sold boots, saddles, and all kinds of hand-tooled jewelry and luggage.

"Want to dash inside the leather store for a few minutes?" he asked.

"No, darlin', I want to get this list taken care of and then get an apple dumplin' over at that Cracker Barrel place," she answered. "But it doesn't take two of us to buy party goods. You go to the leather store if you want to."

He gave her a quick peck on the cheek. "I'll only be a few minutes."

He darted into the leather store for about thirty seconds and then went straight to the jewelry store. He wanted a necklace with a heart pendant to give her for

Valentine's Day. The one he'd seen online had a banner across it with *I Love You* written in tiny, sparkling diamonds. If he couldn't find that, then a bracelet with interlocking hearts, but it had to be yellow gold.

"Help you, sir?" an older woman said from behind the counter. "I bet you are doing late Valentine shopping."

"Yes, ma'am. I was thinking a heart necklace," he said.

"Sold the last one a few minutes ago. This year, folks are going in for infinity symbols more than hearts, so we didn't order many of those. Want to see what we've got left?"

"Yes, thank you. Yellow gold."

"That limits it. White gold is still the rage with the young girls. Yellow gold hasn't been in vogue in years. In my opinion, it's far classier. We have one double infinity bracelet in yellow gold. It's all the way to the end of the display case beside the collection of antique rings we just got from an estate sale." She motioned for him to follow her.

She brought out the bracelet, and he nodded.

"I like that better than hearts. I'll take it."

"Wrapped? We have some lovely red-rose wrapping paper."

"Yes, but nothing with roses," he said.

"Pink hearts?" she asked.

"Or yellow daisies," he answered.

"For Valentine's? We do have some yellow daisy paper that we got for Easter, but…" She paused.

"That's what I'd like."

"Be right back then," she said.

He leaned on the counter and looked inside at display

after display of diamond rings. It was way too early to think about that, but he wondered what Jill would choose. Then his eye settled on the small black velvet ring case with the antique rings. Six in all, and every one of them yellow gold.

The last one in the case was Jill. No doubt about it. That was what she'd choose, and it wouldn't be just an engagement ring. It would be her wedding band as well. One emerald, half the size of a dime, graced the middle. Diamonds were scattered in the open scrollwork around it. The stone was the color of her eyes; the diamonds the twinkle in them when she was happy.

"Gorgeous, isn't it?" The clerk set his wrapped present in front of him. "Cash or credit card?"

"Can I look at that ring?" he asked.

"The diamond one in the middle?"

"No, the emerald," he said.

"It has a story behind it," she said.

Remembering what Jill had said about liking things with a story behind them brought a smile to his face. "Written down?"

"No, just what the folks told my boss when he bought the rings. That one was the only one they knew much about. It was given to a lady in 1880 as a betrothal ring. She and her husband were married fifty years before he died, and although she was elderly, she was still healthy. Three days after he died, she joined him. They said it was from a broken heart. Her son inherited the jewelry and gave that particular ring to his grown son to give to his fiancée. They were married sixty years when she died, and he lived only a few days afterward. It was put in a lockbox and sold last week at a jewelry auction."

"Third's the charm." He held the ring up to catch the light.

"I could hold it for you if you'd like to buy it," she said.

"Thank you, but not now," he said.

She put the ring back in the case and rang up the price of the bracelet. He handed her his credit card and started out of the store, but he couldn't push the glass door open. His feet were glued to the welcome mat, and he couldn't get the ring out of his mind or the voice that kept reminding him that he'd never find another one like it.

"Have you changed your mind about the bracelet?" the clerk asked.

"No, about the ring. I'll take it. If you'll put it in a box, I'd appreciate it, but I don't need it wrapped," he said.

———

At five minutes to opening, they finished getting the bar ready for a proper Valentine's Day party. No one who brought their sweetheart out for the evening to the Burnt Boot Bar and Grill would be disappointed in the setting now. Heart-shaped paper coasters circled jar candles burning brightly in the middle of each table. The jukebox sported a huge foldout heart taped securely to the front and had already been filled with enough money to play all night.

Standing behind the bar and taking one more look, Jill nodded at Sawyer. "Turn off the lights except the ones behind the bar. I'm opening the chute. And look at who's first."

"I asked Callie where she wanted to go, and she said here," Finn said. "We'll need two cheeseburger baskets, two pitchers of beer, two red cups, and we're going to claim a table. The parking lot is full. We're lucky we got in first."

In ten minutes there wasn't a table to be begged, borrowed, or stolen. The bar stools were full, and folks milled about in tight little groups, waiting for their names to be called to pick up their beer and food.

Sawyer only had time to look up from the grill when he put baskets of food on the worktable. Cheeseburgers had red toothpicks. Hamburgers had pink ones. Jill yelled out names and filled pitchers as fast as she could.

Betsy showed up at seven thirty, with Tyrell right behind her. "Wow, Sawyer, you did this up really neat. I never thought this old run-down bar could look like a New York City nightclub."

"Just needs a strobe light," Tyrell said.

"It wasn't all my doin'. Jill and I worked together on it," Sawyer said.

Jill and Sawyer were swamped behind the bar until Callie and Finn took pity on them and pushed their way back behind the bar to help.

"Give me that list of folks waiting for food. I'll call out names and take care of getting the money to the cash register," Callie said.

"This is your night out," Sawyer argued.

"And y'all are family. We'll have fun," Callie said.

"You two are lifesavers. We were about to drown," Jill said.

"This is a huge crowd." Callie went to work, drawing beer and putting empty pitchers into the dishwasher.

Finn pulled a white apron over his neck, wrapped the ties around his waist, and tied them in front. "I'll help with cookin', if you ladies can man the bar."

"We can do that." Callie was already busy pulling beer handles two at a time.

"No trouble with the feud this evening, I take it," Finn said.

"There's not room for them to feud. The dance floor is full, people are sitting in each other's laps, and some folks are eating standing up," Sawyer said.

"Romantic, ain't it?" Jill laughed.

They thought things had slowed down fifteen minutes before midnight, but Betsy Gallagher yelled that she wanted ten burger baskets to go. "We're takin' the party to the river. You want to join us, Sawyer?"

"No, thank you."

Tyrell pulled two cases of beer out from the refrigerated section at the end of the bar where Polly kept milk, beer, and juice. "Put this on Betsy's bill. Is it buy one of these, get the other one free, Callie?"

"Not in your wildest dreams," Callie said.

"Add a bottle of Jack Daniel's to that bill." Betsy handed Callie two bills. "I need to drown my sorrows over that long, tall cowboy. Seems I can't entice him with anything, so I'll have to move on and find another one. He'll never know what he missed."

"Truth is," Callie said above the noise, "I think maybe he hasn't missed anything at all. Good luck findin' another one."

"Poor old Rhett. Betsy is liable to set her cap for him next." Jill laughed softly.

"We'll have to warn him." Sawyer finished the

burgers at two minutes until the hour and turned off the grill.

"We're not cleaning up tonight," Jill said. "I'll call Aunt Polly's cleaning lady, and she can take care of all this Monday morning. I'll put all the money and the register log in the bank bag. We'll shove it in the safe and count it later too."

Sawyer nodded. "Sounds good to me. And, Finn, you really saved my ass tonight. I couldn't have kept up without you."

Finn laid a hand on Sawyer's shoulder. "It was fun, but don't call me to do this every February. This bar stuff is hard work."

Callie removed her apron and hugged Jill. "Women who work together on Valentine's will be related by the next Valentine's."

"Who said that?" Jill asked.

"I did." She laughed. "Come on, handsome cowboy. Take me home and to bed."

Jill raised an eyebrow.

"I'm not that tired." Callie winked.

Jill reached up to the top shelf and handed her a bottle of Jack Daniel's. "Happy Valentine's Day, and thank you."

Chapter 28

THE BUNKHOUSE LOOKED WONDERFUL, SMELLED WON-derful, and felt even better when they got home that Saturday night. The peace and quiet when Jill walked inside surrounded her like Sawyer's arms. She dragged a chair from the table to the woodstove. Both kittens scampered away to safety at the noise coming across the wood floor, and Sawyer raised an eyebrow.

"What are you doing?"

"Making it still Valentine's Day."

"I can reach the clock. I'll do it. How much of Valentine's Day do you want left?" he asked.

"Thirty minutes."

He wound the clock back to eleven thirty. "Now what?"

She went into her bedroom and returned with a box of maple doughnuts and a long, thin box. "Happy Valentine's Day, darlin'. Open it. I can't wait to see what you think of it."

He sat down on the sofa, and she joined him. She'd found the romantic coupon book at the store where she finished buying party supplies. It had a coupon for a romantic breakfast in bed, one for a picnic to the place of his choice, and several that made her blush when she read them.

He chuckled when he picked it up from the box, laughed at the first coupon, roared at the ones that made her blush. He hugged her so tight she thought her ribs would break and kissed her a dozen times. "Thank you, darlin'. It's a present that will last all year if we use one a week. And doughnuts too. Wait." He peeled off the one for breakfast in bed, anything he wanted, and handed it to her. "I want doughnuts, your strong black coffee, and you for breakfast in the morning."

"I think that could be arranged," she said.

"Happy Valentine's Day." He pulled a long, slim box from the coat he'd draped over the back of the sofa.

"Did you buy me the same thing? If so, we'll have to use two a week," she said.

"Open it and see," he said.

"Oh, Sawyer," she gasped when she opened the box and saw the bracelet. "It's beautiful." She threw her arms around his neck and kissed him so passionately that her knees went weak. She recognized the infinity symbol and hoped that it wasn't just a trinket he'd bought but that it really told the story of their lives together.

"Double infinity. No end in sight for my life with you."

"And none in sight for mine with yours," she said.

Tears filled her eyes as she handed the bracelet to him and held out her wrist. "Put it on me. I love that it's yellow gold."

He fastened the bracelet around her arm, and she shifted her position until she was sitting in his lap, arm held out so she could look at the bracelet. "Did you have it special made?"

"No, it came right out of the counter, but I knew it was you when I saw it."

"I'm going to wear it all night so I can see it first thing when I wake up in the morning. Infinity means never having to say good-bye, doesn't it?"

—⁓—

"Yes, it does. I could never bear the thought of telling you good-bye. There was a ring in the store that had a story." He hadn't meant to tell her about the ring until the right moment. He'd already planned the perfect proposal, right before his parents came at Easter. Then he could introduce her as his fiancée if she said yes.

She touched the bracelet with her other hand. "A better story than this?"

"You be the judge when you hear it," he said.

When he finished, tears were rolling down her cheeks and leaving drops on the front of her hot-pink Western-cut shirt. "I love that story. The ring would carry wonderful blessings with it. Did I tell you that I don't believe in luck? I believe in blessings, though, and coming to Burnt Boot was the best blessing I've ever been given."

The moment was perfect right then, but Sawyer couldn't make himself reach into the other coat pocket and bring out the little white box with the ring inside. It was too soon. They needed more time.

"I feel the same, even if we did get off to a rocky start there at first." He hugged her tighter, wanting never to face a morning without her. If she passed away the next morning, he was sure that in three days he would join her, just like the people in the story about the ring.

Miss Piggy and Miss Chickadee made a running leap for the sofa, climbed up the arm, and chased each other across the back. On one trip from end to end, they got tangled up in his coat and the ring box fell out.

Jill was so intrigued with her bracelet that she didn't see it, but Sawyer saw it as a sign. She could say no, and he'd ask again every Saturday night until she said yes, but he was about to give her the chance to refuse or say yes.

He set her to one side, dropped down on one knee, and held out the box. "Jillian Cleary, I love you with my whole heart. Will you marry me?"

He popped the box open, and a fresh batch of tears started. "It's the ring, isn't it?" she whispered.

"I figure we might have seventy years together with it," he said. "We can have it sized later. Please say yes."

"Yes, yes, yes." She threw her arms around his neck.

He removed the ring and slipped it on her finger. "Fits perfectly. Was meant to be. Your eyes are the same color as the emerald."

"I love it. It can be my wedding band too. I don't need another one, Sawyer."

"Long engagement or a short one?"

"Thirty-six hours. We'll be at the courthouse Monday morning as soon as it opens."

He gathered her into his arms and carried her to their bedroom. "I was hoping for Easter. I didn't dream you'd say yes and want a simple wedding at the courthouse."

"Why wait? I'm sure that I want to be with you the rest of my life. And besides, you can have the office for your movies now. Rhett can have my room, and I'll never have to sneak across the cold floor to sleep with you," she said. "And you'll always remember our anniversary, because it will be right after Valentine's Day.

"I was going to propose in a romantic setting," he said.

"Nothing is more romantic than this night. I love you so much, Sawyer. I never thought I'd be blessed to find my soul mate."

"Oh!" she gasped when she saw the little bear from the antique store on her pillow.

"That is to remember our first Valentine's Day together," he said.

"I love you, Sawyer." She brought his lips down to hers.

He kicked the door shut with his boot heel and gently laid her on the bed. "Infinity, darlin', starts right now, and it has no end."

Dear Readers,

A few months ago, four cowboys showed up in my virtual world with a story to tell. I'd met three of them—Sawyer, Rhett, and Finn—in *Cowboy Seeks Bride*, but the fourth one, Declan Brennan, was altogether new to me. But the other three cowboys said they wanted their own series and that Declan was an integral part of it, since he's a Brennan. Seems the Brennans and the Gallaghers have been in a feud for more than a hundred years in Burnt Boot, Texas, and who better to tell me all about it than Declan Brennan?

After writing the first two books in this series, I'm not totally sure the Burnt Boot gossip vine could survive without the feud. There's a possibility it would be listed on the top of the endangered species list. But the pig war in this book leaves us all with the idea that the feud will never be settled.

Summer is beginning here in southern Oklahoma as I finish this book. Winter finally left us about two days ago. We had forty-eight hours of gorgeous spring weather, and then boom, it was tornado weather and heat. But you will be reading this book when it's winter, and that's when Sawyer and Jill first met, in the bitter-cold wind in Burnt Boot. So bundle up, pour a glass of wine or a cup of hot chocolate, and settle in for another adventure in Burnt Boot.

Special thanks my Sourcebooks family for all the hard work and dedication they put into my books, from editing to proofreading to the absolutely awesome covers. All you folks who work behind the scenes do a fantastically (I'd say fantabulous here, but it might not get past my proofreader) great job, and I appreciate every one of you. A big hug and special thanks to my editor, Deb Werksman, and the staff in the Sourcebooks office on the east coast. A bow to my publisher, Dominique Raccah, who continues to publish my books and encourages me with her smiles. Again, thank you to my husband, Charles Brown, who for many years has supported this wild dream of mine of being an author. To my family, friends, fans, and readers…y'all are all loved and appreciated.

Keep your boots on. There are more cowboys on the horizon.

All my best,
Carolyn Brown

How to Marry a Cowboy

Cowboys & Brides series

by Carolyn Brown

New York Times and *USA Today* Bestselling Author

—⁓—

She's running from her past

Mason Harper's daughters want a new mama in the worst way, and when a beautiful woman in a tattered wedding gown appears on their doorstep, the two little girls adopt her—no ifs, ands, or buts about it. Mason isn't sure about taking in a complete stranger, but Lord knows he needs a nanny, and Annie Rose Boudreau stirs his heart in long-forgotten ways…

And he's the perfect escape

Annie Rose is desperate, and when a tall, sexy cowboy offers her a place to stay, she can't refuse. After all, it's just for a little while. As she settles in deeper, her heart tells her both Mason and her role as makeshift mama suit her just fine. But will Mason feel the same way once her nightmare past catches up with her?

—⁓—

"Brown continues her streak of satisfying contemporary Western romances…" —*Booklist*

For more Carolyn Brown, visit:

www.sourcebooks.com

The Cowboy's Mail Order Bride

by Carolyn Brown

New York Times Bestselling Author

She's got sass...

Emily Cooper promised her dying grandfather that she'd deliver a long-lost letter to a woman he once planned to wed. Little does adventurous Emily know that this simple task will propel her to places she never could have imagined...with a cowboy who's straight out of her dreams...

He's got mail...

When sexy rancher Greg Adams discovers his grandmother Clarice has installed Emily on their ranch as her assistant, he decides to humor the two ladies. He figures Emily will move on soon enough. In the meantime, he intends to keep a close eye on her—he doesn't quite buy her story of his grandmother as a mail-order bride.

A lost letter meant a lost love for Clarice, but two generations later, maybe it's not too late for that letter to work its magic.

"While the romance is hot, there is an old-world feel
to it that will bring out the romantic in every reader,
leaving them swooning and wishing they had their
very own cowboy."—*RT Book Reviews*, 4 Stars

"Carolyn Brown's characters become my friends and
I find myself laughing with them, crying with them,
and loving with them."—*Bitten by Love Reviews*

For more Carolyn Brown, visit:

www.sourcebooks.com

How to Kiss a Cowboy

Cowboys of Decker Ranch series

by Joanne Kennedy

—◦◦◦—

This cowboy is living a charmed life

Winning comes naturally to bronc rider Brady Caine. Ruggedly handsome, careless, and charismatic, the rodeo fans adore him and the buckle bunnies are his for the taking. He's riding high when he lands an endorsement deal with Lariat Western Wear that pairs him up with champion barrel racer Suze Carlyle.

Until one wrong move changes everything

A stupid move on Brady's part lands Suze in the hospital, her career in tatters. Now it's a whole new game for both of them. Brady is desperate to help Suze rebuild her life, but he's the last person she wants around now. Suze's got plenty of grit and determination—learning to trust Brady again is a very different matter.

—◦◦◦—

Praise for Joanne Kennedy:

"Joanne Kennedy's heroes are strong, honest, down-to-earth, and sexy as all get out." —*New York Journal of Books*

For more Joanne Kennedy, visit:

www.sourcebooks.com

How to Handle a Cowboy

Cowboys of Decker Ranch series

by Joanne Kennedy

—⁓—

His rodeo days may be over...

Sidelined by a career-ending injury, rodeo cowboy Ridge Cooper is desperate to find an outlet for the passion he used to put into competing. So he takes on the challenge of teaching roping skills to troubled ten-year-olds in a last-chance home for foster kids, and finds it's their feisty supervisor who takes the most energy to wrangle.

But he'll still wrangle her heart

When social worker Sierra Dunn seeks an activity for the rebellious kids at Phoenix House, she soon learns she's not in Denver anymore. Sierra is eager to get back to her inner-city work, and the plan doesn't include forming an attachment in Wyoming—especially not to a ruggedly handsome and surprisingly gentle local rodeo hero.

—⁓—

"Realistic and romantic... Kennedy's forte is in making relationships genuine and heartfelt as she exposes vulnerabilities with tenderness and good humor."—*Booklist* Starred Review

"The sex scenes are juicy...and the plot moves seamlessly."—*RT Book Reviews*, 4 Stars

For more Joanne Kennedy, visit:

www.sourcebooks.com

Rough Rider

Hot Cowboy Nights Series

by Victoria Vane

———————

Old flames burn the hottest…

Janice Combes has adored Dirk Knowlton from the rodeo sidelines for years. She knows she'll never be able to compete with the dazzling all-American rodeo queen who's set her sights on Dirk. Playful banter is all Janice and Dirk will ever have…

Until the stormy night when he shows up at her door, injured and alone. Dirk's dripping wet, needs a place to stay, and Janice remembers why she could never settle for any other cowboy…

———————

Praise for Victoria Vane:

"Erotic and sexy…absolutely marvelous." —
Library Journal on the Devil DeVere series

"The Mistress of Sensuality does it
again!" —*Swept Away by Romance*

For more Victoria Vane, visit:

www.sourcebooks.com

Slow Hand

Hot Cowboy Nights Series

by Victoria Vane

In rural Montana...

Wade Knowlton is a hardworking lawyer who's torn between his small-town Montana law practice and a struggling family ranch. He's on the brink of exhaustion from trying to save everybody and everything, when gorgeous Nicole Powell walks into his office. She's a damsel in distress and the breath of fresh air he needs.

Even the lawyers wear boots...

Nicole Powell is a sassy Southern girl who has officially sworn off cowboys after a spate of bad seeds—until her father's death sends her to Montana and into the arms of a man who seems too good to be true. Her instincts tell her to hightail it out of Montana, but she can't resist a cowboy with a slow hand.

"A red-hot cowboy tale... Their sexual chemistry crackles." —*Publishers Weekly*

"Delightful, funny, page-turning steamy sexy, and the romance makes you wish you could pull Victoria's characters straight off the page." —*Unwrapping Romance*

For more Victoria Vane, visit:

www.sourcebooks.com

Desperate Hearts

by Rosanne Bittner

USA Today bestselling author

❧

She's a woman with a secret

Elizabeth Wainright is on the run. Accused of a murder she didn't commit, she has no choice but to cut ties with her old life and flee west. The last thing she wants is attention, but when her stagecoach is attacked, she suddenly finds herself under the fierce protection of one of Montana's famed vigilantes... whether she likes it or not.

He's a man with a code

Lawman Mitch Brady is sworn to uphold justice in the wild lands of 1860s Montana. He's never met a man he's feared, and he's never met a woman more desperately in need of his help. Something's shaken the secretive Elizabeth, but as he gets to know the beautiful city belle, he finds the only thing he wants more than her safety...is her trust.

❧

Praise for Rosanne Bittner:

One of the most powerful voices in Western romance." —*RT Book Reviews*

For more Rosanne Bittner, visit:

www.sourcebooks.com

Texas Mail Order Bride

Bachelors of Battle Creek

by Linda Broday

New York Times bestselling author

———————— ❧ ————————

Rancher Cooper Thorne thinks his life is finally on an even keel—until Delta Dandridge steps off the stagecoach and claims she's his mail-order bride. Brash and quick-witted, the meddling Southern belle is everything Cooper thought he never wanted...and everything his heart is telling him he needs.

But Cooper swore long ago that he'd never marry, and he aims to keep his word...especially now that the demons from his past have returned to threaten everything—and everyone—he holds dear.

———————— ❧ ————————

Praise for Linda Broday:

"Takes me back to a West that feels true. A delightful read." —Jodi Thomas, *New York Times* bestselling author

For more Linda Broday, visit:

www.sourcebooks.com

To Love and to Cherish

A Cactus Creek Cowboys Novel

by Leigh Greenwood

USA Today bestselling author

❦

Torn between a desire to be free...

When Laurie Spencer said "I do," she just traded one pair of shackles for another—until her husband's death leaves her with an opportunity to escape her controlling family. Determined to be independent, Laurie approaches sexy rancher Jared Smith with an offer she hopes he can't refuse...

Jared's determined to make it in Texas, but with the local banker turned against him, his dream may be slipping through his fingers. When Laurie offers a partnership, it looks like his luck may be changing...but when she throws herself in the deal, Jared's not sure he'll be able to respect the terms of their agreement and keep his hands to himself.

There's something about Laurie that awakens every protective instinct Jared has...and when all hell breaks loose, there's nothing and no one who'll be able to keep this cowboy from her side.

❦

"Greenwood is a master at Westerns!" —*RT Book Reviews*

For more Leigh Greenwood, visit:

www.sourcebooks.com

About the Author

Carolyn Brown is a *New York Times* and *USA Today* best-selling author. *The Trouble with Texas Cowboys* is her seventy-second published book. She credits her eclectic family for her humor and writing ideas. Her books include the Lucky trilogy: *Lucky in Love*, *One Lucky Cowboy*, and *Getting Lucky*; the Honky Tonk series: *I Love This Bar*, *Hell, Yeah*, *Honky Tonk Christmas*, and *My Give a Damn's Busted*; the Spikes & Spurs series: *Love Drunk Cowboy*, *Red's Hot Cowboy*, *Darn Good Cowboy Christmas*, *One Hot Cowboy Wedding*, *Mistletoe Cowboy*, *Just a Cowboy and His Baby*, and *Cowboy Seeks Bride*; and her bestselling Cowboys & Brides series: *Billion Dollar Cowboy*, *The Cowboy's Christmas Baby*, *The Cowboy's Mail Order Bride*, and *How to Marry a Cowboy*. Carolyn has launched into women's fiction with *The Blue-Ribbon Jalapeño Society Jubilee* and *The Red-Hot Chili Cook-Off*. Now she's having fun with her new Burnt Boot series, beginning with *Cowboy Boots for Christmas*. She was born in Texas but grew up in southern Oklahoma where she and her husband, Charles, a retired English teacher, make their home. They have three grown children and enough grandchildren to keep them young.